Moonlight

Moon Trilogy – Book 3

GUITTA KARUBIAN

CONTENTS

DEDICATION
Women, Life, Freedom

I dedicate this book to Freedom — the ability to breath air on your terms. Everyone deserves the right to be free to express their truth.

Yet today, over three thousand years after Cyrus the Great created the world's first charter of human rights that freed slaves and guaranteed equal freedoms to all, the people of Iran — led by w0men — are leading the fight for the most basic of freedoms.

They are putting your lives on the line for the right to protect their dignity and freely express what they believe in; for the right to explore options in relationships, fashion, music, art and literature, all of which are born of freedom.

The lives of those incredibly bold woman and men who gave their lives for the cause of freedom should not be forgotten nor wasted; let us hear them calling from their graves, urging us to build on what they've done.

It's time.

To life!

ACKNOWLEDGMENTS

I thank the many people who have supported me in writing this book, both by encouraging me in the pursuit and by helping along the way. And thanks to you, the reader about to begin *Moon Child*, Jolie's story.

"There is a field beyond all notions of right and wrong. Come, meet me there."

Rumi, poet and mystic

PROLOGUE

Tehran, Iran 1961 – Six years ago

$\mathscr{A}$s soon as the words were out of my mouth, I'd have done anything to take them back.

Anything.

My mother dropped her cookie, and her cup shook and rattled, spilling *chai* as it fell onto the saucer. Her eyes fixed on me for a moment as though she was surprised to see me standing by our refrigerator. Then she suddenly sprung up and rushed towards me, her arm raised high, and swung a blow to the side of my face.

"You think a woman seen having tea with a strange man in pubic is nothing?" she screamed.

My face stung. My heart jumped. *This was bad!* The kitchen spun around me. I trembled with fear.

"You went to America to drink *chai* with men?"

In seconds, my mother, Zahra Khanom, the Queen of Control, had turned into a madwoman.

1

Her sister, my aunt Bahia, rushed to us, trying to protect me from another blow. But before she reached us, Maman hit me again with the back of her hand, this time smacking me on the other side of my head by my ear. That side of my head felt hot and pressured. Everything turned red.

I was scared! My heart felt as though it would break through my chest. I'd never been so afraid. I'd fallen into a deep dark hole because of what I'd said.

I cowered, afraid that Maman's raised arm was about to strike me yet again, but it froze in mid-air. And then, God help me, she started slapping her own two cheeks and swaying from side to side.

"Allah," she cried. "What have you done to me? My daughter is ruined! I've lost my child! The daughter I raised is spoiled! Poor me! Poor, poor unfortunate me!"

Though I was frightened for Maman's well-being as well as my own, I was too stunned by her blows and her vehemence to move or utter a sound.

Then, to my horror, she began to beat herself, hammering her chest with both fists. I'd never before seen my mother out of control. She is *always* calm and composed with the air of a queen. Yet there she was. Her eyes were rolled up to the ceiling, and she had grabbed the bottom of her silk blouse and was pulling it down and apart, ripping it. a

"*Ayondeh-moono seeya kardee!* You've ruined our future!" she wailed. I was mortified to see her like that, howling like a wounded animal. "No man will want my daughter now." Another button came loose. I yearned to reach out to her, but my fear and shock had paralyzed me. I couldn't believe what was happening.

She began shaking her finger at my absent father. She was furious, yelling at him as though he was standing right there, alongside me. In all my eighteen years I had never heard my parents raise their voices in anger. But there she stood, screaming at my phantom Babajon.

"You, foolish man! You, *stupid* man! I told you not to send our daughter to that hellhole of sinful dogs and cats. I *begged* you!"

As the unbelievable unfolded, I could only stare at this version of Maman. It didn't occur to me that she was having a total breakdown.

She clutched her sister, sobbing into her chest. "I begged him not to send her to Amreeka!" she said. "I swear by everything holy, I did! I told him not to let her go!" I heard her gasps amid the sobs. "He promised me she'd be fine. 'She's different than other girls,' he said." Still holding onto her sister, she looked up again, as if appealing to the heavens. "Now what do I do?"

She shook my aunt. "She has met with strange American men alone! My daughter! With no chaperone!" My aunt looked as helpless as I felt. "What will I do with my corrupted daughter?"

When she turned back to me, I saw confusion in her eyes, but there was also hatred there.

"Amreeka!" She spat out the word, barely missing my face. "Let it rot in hell!" She spat again. *"Khok bar sarrash,* dirt on its head! *Ensha Allah,* Allah willing, *berreh bemeereh,* may it go and die!" Her fists were clenched at her sides, her arms rigid, veins like blue snakes crawling up towards her pink silk sleeves.

She took a few steps away from me and I thought she might begin to calm down. *But no!* She pivoted on her thin high heels and came back to grab my shoulders. Her sister watched helplessly as her freshly manicured nails dug into my skin.

I thought she was about to hit me again. Instead, she shook me violently, as if trying to shake all things American out of my system. "You will not go back to that immoral hellhole! Do you hear? Oh, no, you will never go back to your Amreeka! You will not return to that disgusting place. UCLA? Los Angeles? Your California? May it all be bombed!"

My Jasmine! "Maman –"

"*Khafeh shoh! Kooft!* Shut up! Choke on your words and die!"

She let go of me only to point a commanding finger so close to my face, I instinctively pull my head back. "You will tell your father you are *not* going back," she screamed. "Do you hear me?" I nodded.

I have to get back to my baby!

She folded her arms and stormed away then turned back to look at me, her neck craned, her eyes, large and fiery. "You will tell my Hadi nothing of this," she shrieked. "Do you understand?" I nodded again. I would do anything to end her tirade.

I turned away from her, but she took a firm hold of my chin and yanked my face back to face hers. "Did you hear me? Say, yes! Not one word!" she continued. "You will tell your father *you* do not *want* to go back." With hands on her hips she nodded. "There is no point in telling your deluded father what you have become. Allah knows what it might do to him. It could kill him in his condition."

His condition? My beloved Babajon?

"Maman, what –"

"*Khafeh shoh,* shut up, *Jendeh Khanom!* Whore Lady! *Bemeer,* die! Don't *Maman* me. I am not the mother of a girl like you who thinks nothing of spending time alone with men. I cannot stand to look at you. Get out of my sight. Go!"

I couldn't move. My feet were lead, my knees, cotton.

Her sister, my Aunt Bahia, took hold of my arm, pulling me away and supporting me as I made my way to my room and away from my mother's wrath to a life forever changed.

PART ONE: BEFORE

My life is gone, but breathing I still fake.

— ~ HAFEZ, POET

1

THE INVITATION

August, 1967 - Six years later

*I*t is two months before Coronation Day.

Everywhere I look, the capital city, like every other city and village in Iran, is preparing for the week of royal celebrations scheduled to take place the last seven days in October. These days will be remembered and cherished by most Iranians long after the grandeur, glitter, and opulence that mark the era end.

Though autumn's chill will soon be felt, the temperature is still warm as preparations for the Coronation, begun over a year ago, continue. Hundreds of statues of Shah Pahlavi are being readied for unveiling. Almost seven thousand schools, hospitals and other projects are being rushed to completion in time for the royal event. Carnivals, concerts, parties, and celebrations have been taking place in every village and town in the country this entire week.

Nights, the skies are ablaze with one million dollars' worth of fireworks. Days, planes drop seventeen thousand, five hundred thirty-two roses over Tehran, one for every day of the His Majesty's life. The palace has taken out life insurance policies for every baby born on Coronation Day in the province of Gilan, the Empress' birthplace. Tens of thousands of convicted criminals are being granted amnesty. Charges against thousands more awaiting trial, are dropped

I do not share in my countrymen's excitement. Though six years have passed since the day my words imprisoned me here, I will not be among those liberated in honor of the celebrations.

I have no love for the country whose laws bind me against my will to a husband I loathe.

Rostam comes home this evening, obviously excited.

His large, tall frame moves fast, and he's strutting like a peacock with feathers spread open. He holds an oversized envelope in one hand, the ever-present cigarette in the other, and gloats as he holds the white envelope out for me to see. His name is imprinted on it; it bears the royal seal.

"Rostam has been invited to two royal events! *Two!* Rostam is going to the royal concert *and* to the dinner party afterwards!" Beads of perspiration glisten on his forehead. He is too flustered to inhale the cigarette he holds. I watch as the long ash falls onto a flower on the red silk carpet. "This was hand-delivered to my office. Rostam has been called for by Aalaa Hazrat, his Superior Excellency. What do you say?"

I nod. "Good for you."

He eats his dinner hastily, throws his dinner napkin down and leaves the table without a word. I listen as he makes several phone calls sharing the news of his royal invitation.

In bed, he taunts me. "You don't deserve me," he says smugly.

"With this invitation, Rostam can go out right now and can have his pick of young girls. Rostam can be out with any woman … any number of women – even two, or three. You are lucky."

I only wish he had gone out. I'd taken to wearing unflattering pajamas to bed until he ordered a wardrobe of French lingerie and commanded me to wear only those to bed. The shameful thing is, that despite my loathing him, my body continues to respond to his.

Early this morning, Rostam is again on the telephone, spreading news of his royal invitations.

He first calls the person he most despises, followed by his government contacts, the most powerful and influential first, and finally his business associates and family, the wealthiest among them at the top of his list.

I overhear him. "Yes, yes, of course they have invited her – she is Rostam's wife. I must see to her. She absolutely will not embarrass Rostam," and I learn I am to accompany him at the events.

Since then, our lives have been consumed with preparations for the royal events. Rostam has carefully studied photos of the shah and has instructed his tailor to make him a suit for the evening similar in cut to that favored by His Majesty. He has also turned his attention to dressing me, making a series of appointments with my dressmaker to discuss the design of the gown I shall wear. I am silent as together they decide it will be made of heavy satin in a sunlit yellow, in the empire style. He has commissioned Van Clef and Arpel, the jewelers who have designed Farah Diba's crown for the historic event, to design the choker I am to wear. It mimics the colors of Iran's flag, three stands, one of emeralds, one of diamonds (not yellow), and one of rubies.

As the date approaches, the Iranian media increases news of the upcoming coronation until there is almost nothing else but talk of the slated festivities surrounding the historical ritual and the international dignitaries arriving from all corners of the world to attend. Newspapers list the gifts presented to the royal family by world leaders. Though all are generous, the two most extravagant seem to be Kuwait's gift of two black Arabian stallions and Tunisia's gift of a solid gold olive tree.

During a televised interview with His Majesty, the famed broadcast journalist asks why the coronation is taking place some twenty-six years after His Majesty ascended to the throne.

Shah's demeanor is, as always, dignified and regal. He sits straight, his legs crossed as is his custom, one arm draped along the arm of his chair, the other in his lap as he responds with the royal 'we'. "There is no honor in being the king of a poor country," His Majesty answers. "We refused to hold this important event until we had brought Iran out of the poverty it was in when we inherited the Peacock Throne."

The reporter runs off some statistics showing there has been a significant increase in our country's per capita income through the last years. "Your Majesty, with the success of the White Revolution you introduced four years earlier, indications are that Iranians today are, in fact, in a far better position economically, academically, and socially."

His Majesty nods. He speaks solemnly. "Yes. That is correct. I felt it was also important that there be a male heir."

Shah Reza Pahlavi divorced his second wife in 1958 because she proved infertile. Less than two years later he married Farah Diba and now has a son who is approaching his seventh birthday, almost concurrently with Shah's own forty-eighth.

"And so," His Excellency continues, "We feel it is a propitious time to hold the coronation, and We believe the Iranian people – who have historically shared their shah's personal challenges– deserve to share in the celebration of this happy event as well."

This morning Rostam chuckles as he reads the front page of the newspaper over breakfast. "Your American President, that Mr. Johnson, has come to attend Shah's coronation," he says. His tone is amused, as if this entire production is being staged for his entertainment. "They've all come. The French one, de Gaulle, and the Russian one is here. Gandhi is here. Queen Elizabeth is here, and she and your shitty president should be kissing our feet for all the oil we've given them!"

He laughs again, eggs sputtering out of his mouth. "Let them see what we have, who we are!"

And then he booms, "Let them see Rostam!"

I say nothing.

2

MY MISERABLE HUSBAND

*M*arrying Rostam was the last thing I did born of my own free will.

God help me! It was 1961. I was eighteen and completely desperate, held hostage by my mother who had hidden my passport and exit papers, making my return to UCLA otherwise impossible.

I had no other way to get back to my secret child in Los Angeles.

Of all my regrets, becoming Rostam's wife is at the top of the list.

When Maman spread word that I had decided not return to Los Angeles and would stay in Tehran, I was accosted by *kostegars*, suitors who came to our home to offer proposals of marriage, often two in one day, one visiting us for afternoon tea and another after dinner.

Rostam was one of these *khostegar*.

The evening he came to our home I discovered that as the exclusive distributor of American music in Iran, he travels to Los Angeles from time to time. That was all I needed to know. When he proposed to me the very next day, I, who had refused all previous *kostegars*, consented to marry him after we agreed to spend our honeymoon in Los Angeles.

It sounds ridiculous. I know. But as I said, I was desperate, with no other way to get back to Jasmine. I saw Rostam as my only way out of Iran and my ticket back to the baby daughter I'd left behind.

In truth, I thought I was being smart. I thought I would outwit both my mother and my new husband.

My plan was fly to Los Angeles with Rostam only to lose him and run to Jasmine. He would never find me. *How could he?* He didn't know I had a baby and had no knowledge of any of my friends there. So, I married this incredibly arrogant man, so egotistical that he often speaks of himself in third person, as though royalty.

On the morning of my first day as Rostam's wife, while my new husband was tying up some ends at his office, I picked up our plane tickets, laying on his desk. Rostam had lied to me. We would not be going to Los Angeles. The tickets were for *Rome!*

Enraged, I grabbed a small bag, threw in a change of clothes, the two round trip tickets to Italy, and my all-important passport and exit visa as well, which were on the desk alongside the tickets. I was jubilant. The documents Maman had confiscated from me, making my exit out of Iran impossible, were in my hand. I hurriedly added a few pieces of the jewelry I'd received as wedding gifts the night before, ran out of the house and hailed a taxi. I made a run for Mehrabod airport and once there, I rushed to exchange the two round-trip tickets to Rome for a one-way ticket to Los Angeles.

With the plane boarding in just minutes, I dashed through passport control. I was thrilled, knowing I was returning to Los

Angeles where Linda and Adam would tell me which adoption agency they had taken Jasmine to, and I would cancel the adoption, bring my daughter back to me and make a life there for the two of us.

Incredibly, just steps away from the boarding gate, the unbelievable happened: I heard my name being called over the loudspeaker.

"Layla Shamshiri, please report to Security." I was stunned. I was being paged! *How could anyone have known where I was?*

I turned and saw six policemen walking in three pairs in different directions, apparently searching for me. Two were at passport control, showing something what turned out to be a photo of me to the official there.

One spotted me and nudged the other, then called out, "Khanom Shamshiri!"

I quickened my pace.

By then they had passed the control desk and were quickly advancing in my direction. It seemed impossible that they could have known I was at the airport, and yet, they shouted out my name.

"Stop, Layla Saleh Shamshiri!" My knees weakened, but I kept moving.

"Khanom Shamshiri, stop! You are ordered to stop!"

By then I was so close to freedom that the flight attendant had his hand out to take my boarding pass. As I extended it out to him, I was grabbed by the two policemen who'd been chasing me. I tried to pull away. I could see the photo they held, a picture of Rostam and me, taken minutes before our wedding ceremony.

They held me fast. One said, "Please. May we see your passport?"

Apparently, my escape had been doomed at its inception.

Apparently, no sooner had I'd hurried out the front door, that Hassan — Rostam's valet, driver, and all-around man — had telephoned his master who in turn contacted his poker friend, Tehran's Chief of Police. The Chief immediately alerted Tehran's police, including those stationed at the airport.

Following my foiled escape, Rostam took all the jewelry I'd thrown in my suitcase and put it in his safe. Then he left me under house arrest to be guarded by the watchful eye of Hassan while he left to vacation alone for ten days in Italy, days that were to have been part of our honeymoon.

I call Hassan The Rat. Not because he snitched on me when I made that run to the airport, but because he so resembles a rodent, short and stout, with beady eyes, and a jawline that seems to reach up to meet his nose, the way a rodent's does. His voice is gruff, and he is, like his master, a chain-smoker. He is forever scurrying around the house, hovering underfoot, like the rat he resembles.

On his return home, Rostam initiated regular payments to me of a meager allowance and decreed that I was always to leave the house during the day with Hassan as my escort.

In addition to his unattractive looks and his snitching, the man makes me uncomfortable whenever we are alone.

He is everywhere I turn, making me feel as if he is watching to make sure I don't steal anything from his master's house.

<hr />

Since my failed attempt to escape Rostam, I have become the victim of his abuse.

During those ten days locked in his house under house arrest, it was most crucial that I explain my delay in returning to Los Angeles to Adam and Linda Dunn, the brother and sister, two friends I'd left my baby with, but it was impossible. Before leaving for Italy, Rostam had made sure I had no way of contacting anyone.

When my friends didn't hear from me, I lost my child.

Convinced that I would never return to her, they had taken my baby girl to an adoption agency.

The plan I'd hatched, meant to deceive everyone, not only failed, it backfired. I thought Rostam would be my ticket out of Iran. As it turned out, he was my ticket to hell. I deserve every tear I shed.

So, in the end, all I'd managed to do was to change my warden from my mother to my husband.

I'd been a complete fool and I am filled with remorse for having married the son of a bitch.

Yes, there is no doubt that Rostam lied to me with his promise of honeymooning in Los Angeles.

Yet, in fairness, I had deceived him as well. He married a fraud.

Some part of me wants to recount my lies to him and admit that I had not been the virgin he believed he'd married. Oh, the hundreds of times I've yearned to tell him of the trick my mother had played on him by having surgically recreated my virginity with that hymenoplasty.

Most of all, I want to scream out that I'd married him only to secure a seat on an airplane to Los Angeles.

I want to see him explode when he learns I'd secretly given birth to a baby there.

3

THE SHADOW OF GOD

Coronation Day, October 26, 1967

*C*heering crowds have lined the streets for hours to watch the storybook carriage drawn by white horses make its way to Golestan Palace where the Coronation ceremony is to take place.

No doubt, Maman is watching it from her bedroom balcony. Rostam and I are watching it all on television.

Inside the Grand Hall of the palace, His Majesty, Mohammad Reza Shah Pahlavi, Shah of Iran, places the crown said to be the most opulent crown in the history of monarchs on his own head, announcing that the people of Iran are crowning him through his hands.

Afterwards, His Majesty will make history again, crowning his third wife and Queen Consort Farah Diba as the first Empress in Iran's history. This will be her reward for birthing a male heir, thereby ensuring the continuation of the Pahlavi line.

Kneeling before her husband, she will receive the crown laden with precious stones, including one thousand four hundred sixty-nine diamonds and thirty-eight emeralds, the largest of which weighs over ninety-one carats at its center.

Should Shah precede her in death, she will be the first woman in Iran ever to reign as Regent until her son, Crown Prince Reza Cyrus Pahlavi, takes the throne.

The ceremony at the palace was two days ago, yet the celebrations continue.

Tonight, wearing the yellow gown and the choker that_my husband_designed for this occasion, with my hair mimicking Farah Diba's trademark up-do, I join Rostam to attend the events he has so looked forward to.

We first attend a concert in Shah's honor, seated far from the royal box. The concert is not very exciting. It is like any other moderately enjoyable concert. As expected, there is a lot of pomp and adulation for the royal couple and we listen to selections composed in their honor.

One piece is quite lovely. The words speak of His Majesty as "the shadow of God." Rostam likes that selection. Afterwards, he will continually repeat the chorus.

Dinner follows at the Golestan Palace.

When I won first prize at the national science contest in high school, I was one of a handful of students invited to a luncheon at the Palace, followed by a short speech by His Imperial Majesty about the importance of education. But for Rostam, this is a first.

We are seated at one of three long tables. Shah Pahlavi and Empress Diba are seated at the middle table. We sit at the table to His Majesty's right, which Rostam assures me is the more important of the two side tables.

When His Majesty rises from his seat to address his guests, he is as charismatic as I remember from my high school days. He says the evening is a tribute to the people he has called together this evening, leaders in every sector of Iranian business. He says that the future of Iran is tied to our ability to go into that future with new technologies, new ideas, strong leadership and a clear vision.

I suppose that explains why Rostam, whose company is far and away the largest Iranian distributor of Western music — so very popular in our country — has been invited. But I don't understand why my father has been excluded.

I am seated between Iran's most successful automaker and the owner of Tehran's largest land developer. Rostam sits across from me, between their wives. It is obvious from their name that the land developer and his wife, Khanom Javidi, are Jewish. Rostam does not hide his bigotry.

"How interesting that your husband would be in land," he says to Khanom Javidi. "Of course, you Jews have always done well with land." He is blowing smoke in the woman's direction. His statement catches not only my attention, but also her husband's.

Khanom Javidi smiles, and says graciously, "Yes, fortunately." Her husband looks at her across the table and smiles.

Rostam takes another drag off his cigarette. He pats the absent dust off his pants and speaks casually, his smile, a poorly disguised sneer. "Yes, even when you steal it." Everyone who hears him understands he is referring to the young State of Israel.

Khanom Javidi turns crimson. She turns her entire body away from him without another word. The gentleman on her other side has also heard Rostam. He immediately gives Khanom Javidi a warm smile and engages her in chit-chat. Her husband looks up again, eyeing Rostam curiously and sees that his wife is ignoring the fiend.

Rostam dares to reach out and pat her thigh. He is totally out of line. "I'm joking," he says. It is obvious he was not.

How dare he?

I want to smash the bastard's ugly head! I try to offer a whispered apology to her husband. He brushes off my attempt. "There is always a shark in the ocean," he says.

The lamb is being served. Incredibly, Rostam again elbows Khanom Javidi and mutters, "I doubt this is kosher."

I look down. I am wringing my hands. I can't eat. I don't want to be here. I want to crawl under the table. I can see Khanom Javidi staring glass-eyed across the table at her husband. He looks at Rostam and chuckles, making me startle; that is the last thing I expect him to do. As he cuts into his dinner, he turns to me without pausing and says, "How do you live with this man?"

All the way home, Rostam rants about how foolish His Imperial Excellency was to include Jews at a dinner meant to gather the most elite members of the Iranian business world.

"Seat Rostam next to Jews?" He takes a puff of his cigarette and shakes his head and exhales. "They're rich, but that doesn't make them important."

I can only wonder at Rostam's connections. The palace invited my oaf of a husband while my own father, owner of Iran's largest pharmaceutical company, was ignored. For now, it is a mystery.

In time I will understand why.

4

THE CROWN PRINCE

1968

Since the Coronation, Rostam's_rancor toward me has increased.

He has begun to compare himself with His Majesty and inevitably, me with the Empress.

"Why haven't you given Rostam a son?" he yells. "Why can't you do the one thing you can do? For God's sake, you're a woman!"

Each time he screams at me, I shrug and shake my head in mock shame.

He has no idea that he did once impregnate me.

From the time I married, the thought of bringing Rostam's child into this world has repulsed me.

I had done everything I could to protect myself from that very thing. Without prophylactics available, I had taken to douching with vinegar and various herbs. Yet, within the first months of our marriage, I found I was pregnant. I had no need of a doctor to confirm it; I was certain I was with child.

When I had discovered I was pregnant in Los Angeles, I'd been horrified to learn that, unlike Iran, abortions were not then legal in the United States. Although legal here, an abortion required my husband's written consent. So, aborting the pregnancy had been out of the question.

Panicked, I swallowed a book of matches, a huge amount of baking soda and gave myself innumerable douches for the next three days. I spent hours in a steam bath. I lifted and moved heavy objects around the house. On the fourth day, I called on Maman for tea and staged a serious fall down her staircase. The searing pain of stomach cramps was immediate.

Maman, who had no idea I was pregnant, begged me to lie down, but I insisted on getting home as soon as possible, reassuring her that I would call the doctor if needed. The Rat was waiting outside with the car and, though I longed to lie down on the back seat in fetal position and clutch my lower abdomen, I was determined to cause a miscarriage, so, I continued to walk upright a good part of the way home with The Rat following me closely. By the time I arrived home, I was bleeding heavily.

My guilt prevented me from looking into the toilet bowl before flushing.

I cried for my lost baby. But my remorse was outweighed by the knowledge that the pig would never know he had fathered a child.

In truth, it wasn't only that I so loathed Rostam, it was also that I felt a fierce loyalty to Jasmine. My abandonment of her had convinced me that I was undeserving of another child.

Soon after birth control pills became available, I met a female gynecologist at a gala dinner held to raise funds for the new hospital she is affiliated with, and as Rostam walked the room looking for men to ingratiate himself with, we two talked.

Dr. Nina Jaffar is a lovely woman who has gone to medical school in England and cares very much about the plight of Iranian women. I discovered that she is unhappily tied to an alcoholic in an arranged marriage and has three children. I noted her phone number. Two days later, I called her office for an appointment.

Her compassion – and trust – motivated her to risk supplying me with monthly birth control pills without my husband's knowledge or consent. Since then, I have secretly been taking birth control pills religiously for 21 days every month.

If couldn't raise David's child, I will rot in hell before I willingly bear Rostam's!

We are in Rostam's richly furnished grand salon where the gilded gold is blinding.

We are standing on the champagne-colored silk Isfahani rug. Rather, I am standing. Rostam is pacing.

"Damn you!" he says. "Our Empress has borne Reza Cyrus for Shah." He turns to look at me. "You? You have given Rostam nothing!"

I see a cold meanness in his eyes. His condescending attitude is barely tolerable, his bellowing voice flows like poison into my ears. When he sneers like this, his beige suit emphasizes the yellow of his nicotine-stained teeth.

I yearn to leave him!

I had hoped that passage of The Family Protection Act would make it possible for me to initiate a divorce. Now that it has become law, I see it is of no help at all to me. It goes no further than to compel a Muslim man to obtain the consent of his wife before taking a second wife. Without that, the first wife can petition the court for a divorce.

Though I pray Rostam will take a second wife so I can advise the court that I have not consented, I know he never will. He will never divorce me, though I don't know why. And he has made it abundantly clear that should I try to leave him again, with or without my parents' help, he will drag my name and my family's name through the mud. Thanks to his powerful contacts, I have little doubt that he can and would do exactly that.

He will never let me go. This will be my life.

Yet I dare. "Why don't you divorce me? Marry a woman who can give you a son."

Rostam rushes to me with a raised arm, ready to slap me, yet, by the grace of Allah, this time he does not. Perhaps I think, he is expecting a guest soon and is afraid his imprint on my cheek will be obvious.

He grunts. "You really are a donkey. When will you get it through your donkey head? I will never divorce you."

He is scrutinizing my face as if daring me to react to what he just said. I do nothing, say nothing. He resumes pacing around the room, his shoulders rounded inward, his arms crossed. He is like a giant monster.

"Did you see the way the Crown Prince walked down the red carpet?" He's waving his arms stiffly, this way and that, as if making way for the young boy's walk down the red carpet. Saliva is sputtering. "Seven years old and leading the way for the king! You would think he is already a king himself!"

He brings out his handkerchief and wipes his mouth. There is that untamed danger lurking just under the surface of his words. "And you! After seven years of fucking you, you still aren't pregnant."

He paces a bit more, then he turns to me. "What am I supposed to tell people when they ask if I'm a father yet? What do I tell my friends? My parents? People I do business with?"

I long to tell him what to say, but I remain silent. His desperation makes him too dangerous to chance it. He takes a step closer. "What is the matter with you?" he says. "You and the Empress both studied abroad. Why are *you* so *stupid*?"

I am silent, my gaze cast down, feeling a thrill at seeing him so frustrated.

"Enough! It's time for you to be seen by a doctor."

At the fertility doctor's office, I speak very little, only answering questions regarding my moons and their regularity. Rostam takes over, doing most of the talking.

As the doctor is conducting the physical exam, probing, and taking images, blood, and urine samples, I'm recalling the day at the UCLA student medical center eight years ago, when my test results indicated I was pregnant. How ironic that now I am now being examined because Rostam believes me to be infertile! I only pray that the birth control pills do not show up in these tests.

In the end, of course, I am pronounced perfectly normal and healthy. "Your wife just needs to relax," the doctor reports. "Perhaps the problem lies with you? We can run tests, count your sperm–"

Rostam turns an ugly shade of burgundy. "Stupid man!" he says to the doctor. "Are you crazy? You must be! Do you know how many girls I have impregnated?"

Impregnating me has become his obsession and month after month his frustration mounts.

5

POMP AND CIRCUMSTANCE

Oct 12, 1971 – Oct 16, 1971

*T*oday marks the start of a five-day event celebrating two thousand five hundred years of Iranian monarchy founded by Cyrus the Great.

I imagine Cyrus' ego was as big as Rostam's. But then, then Cyrus was a King. The charter of human rights, which he created begins,

I am Cyrus, king of the world, great king, mighty king of Babylon, king of the land of Sumer and Akkad, king of the four quarters, son of Cambyses, great king, king of Anshan, grandson of Cyrus, great king, king of Anshan, descendant of Tease's, great king, king of Anshan, progeny of an unending royal line..."

The man definitely had a sizable ego.

Arrangements for the ultra-extravagant event began a year ago, and still, there is work in progress everywhere. Professional craftsmen and artisans of all kinds have been tapped to work on the awesome preparations for the occasion. Engineers, architects, logistic specialists, publicists, writers, photographers, interior and landscape designers, horticulturists, chefs, carpenters and so forth, have come from around the world to prepare for the extravaganza. Iran has seen nothing like this since the Coronation six years ago.

His Majesty's motive for putting together this massive five-day production is his desire to impress the world with Iran's grandness, while also increasing Iranians' nationalistic pride and inflating our love for the monarch.

Politically, Shah's goal is to create an alliance with Ethiopia, Turkey, and Israel that will prevent the rise of Arab power in the Middle East and to this end, Hailie Selassie, the emperor of Ethiopia, is to be the guest of honor.

This morning, a week before the start of the celebrations, Maman phones me. *"Cheghadr Khodah doostesh darreh!* How God loves her!"

"Loves who?"

"She's coming to Iran with her husband for a visit during the celebrations, thanks to her son-in-law."

"Maman, *who?*"

"Your Khaleh Elahe."

"Oh, that's so nice!"

Aunt Elahe is Babajon's sister and her only sibling. She left Iran for America in the 1950s with her husband and their only child, Jila. My cousin had been my roommate during my first year at UCLA until she left school to marry Majid, one of my childhood friends. They moved to Oklahoma and Aunt Elahe and her husband — recently laid off — joined them with a new job awaiting him there. I'm looking forward to seeing Jila and Majid. I haven't seen them since I attended their wedding in Oklahoma.

Jila knew David. She had been with me when I first met him,

and we'd three had spent time together. She knew how I felt about him. But she doesn't know that he proposed to me or that he went to Israel, and she certainly doesn't know I bore his child. Yet, I am certain she has never uttered his name to her parents and would never say anything about him to my parents or to Rostam.

I think her parents are sweet. They were always kind and hospitable to me while I was in Los Angeles. True, Elahe Khanom talks incessantly. She is the chattiest person I've ever met, but I find her entertaining.

My mother has always thought the worst of Jila's parents, believing them too far below her social status to bother with. She also mocks them because she is convinced that Jila somehow tricked Majid into marrying her, which is not true and difficult to justify when Maman herself conspired to trick Rostam into marrying her own daughter.

"*Che dun-yaee!* What a world!" she continues. "That cow couldn't afford to take the bus to the bazaar in a rainstorm and now she flies around the world, all because her daughter snagged a rich man, a meal ticket for her and her worthless husband!"

"Maman, Jila didn't 'snag' Majid." This is not the first time I'm telling her. "I was there. He fell madly in love with her the first time they met."

It's true. He was immediately smitten, and Jila was soon crazy about him. But Maman isn't listening. Once my mother has made up her mind, she is like an onion that cannot — will not — change. Though Maman has always thought little of my father's sister and her husband, I know Babajon will be happy to see them, so, I'm glad they're all coming.

"*Che dun-yaee!*" she repeats. She sighs one more time. Then her tone changes, the resentment gone, and she says, "Bahman is coming, too."

"When?" I am eager to reunite with Shireen's brother and meet his new wife, Mahnaz, the Iranian girl he met and married while studying architecture in London. Shireen and Taymoor met Mahnaz during one of their trips to Europe, but my Uncle Mansoor, nor his wife, Haideh Khanom, have yet to meet their daughter-in-law.

It was Bahman's friends I regularly played with as a child. I came into my moon while playing with the pack of boys. I panicked, seeing blood on my shorts; I had no idea what was happening to me and couldn't imagine where the blood was coming. The boys, all of whom were older, understood that I'd come into my moon, but their upbringing made it impossible for them to tell me. That day was the last I spent time with a boy without a chaperone – until America.

"What did you say, Layla? I didn't hear you. My head has been pounding since I heard the cow is coming."

"I asked when they're all coming."

"Soon," she says as if reporting an on-coming calamity. "Next week."

"Will Aunt Elaha stay with you?" I ask.

Shoo-khee mee-kon-ee? Are you kidding? Our house won't do for Her Royal Majesty, Elahe Khanom. Now that Jila has married a man with money? Nonsense! They will all stay at that new hotel. To all the prophets, I don't know anyone luckier than her."

That is an amazing remark coming from my mother, undoubtedly one of the luckiest women in Tehran — if not all of Iran. She has everything she could ever want and spends her days doing little other than pampering herself. She has the most wonderful husband in the world. Blind to her many faults, Babajon adores her beyond measure.

"Layla, why don't you throw a party to celebrate their visit? Let them see your home and know the wealth that surrounds you is greater than their daughter's."

I cannot listen to this. She sounds too much like my shallow, arrogant husband. I need to hang up.

"I'll discuss it with Rostam," I say before ending the conversation.

When my mother brings it up again, two days later, I tell her that Rostam nixed the idea because there is a good chance he'll be out of town.

I never bring up the subject with him.

The major events of the celebration take place at the ruins of Persepolis, the city that had been the capital of the Persian Empire until it was destroyed by Alexander the Great.

Teams of workers have toiled to rid the desert area of thousands of poisonous snakes and scorpions. The airplanes delivering guests will land in Shiraz, and as a result, the entire city is being cleaned up, teams of bulldozers demolishing old village houses. Almost every house and shop facade is being repainted.

An entire city is being created in the deserts of Persepolis.

Individual private air-conditioned tents with walls of velvet created in France have been readied for the guests with every comfort and convenience available to them. Baccarat crystal, Limoges china, Porth Ault linens, stacks and stacks of exclusive Robert Haviland cup-and-saucer service, as well as five thousand bottles of wine have been brought in. Elizabeth Arden has created a new line of cosmetics and named it after Queen Farah. The world-famous Maxim's of Paris will lead the team of chefs and caterers. Except for Iranian caviar served in quail eggs, all the food and wine will be flown in from Paris. Foreign dancers have been hired to perform.

Simultaneous celebrations will be held in the capital city. There are reports that the Palace has spent one hundred million dollars preparing for the anniversary celebrations in Tehran alone. The amount being spent at the Persepolis site to create those tents and bring in all the food, wine, linens, chefs and all else is far more staggering.

This will be the last of the opulent events His Majesty will produce. Many believe this celebration is the beginning of his end. Some say that the event at Persepolis, meant to nurture Iranians love for the monarchy was instead the turning point that marked the downward spiral and final death of Iran's monarchy.

Those opposed to Shah complain about the unnecessary extravagance, the huge expense of such a major event, and ask why so few Iranians have been invited. They complain about the huge amounts of wine, food, and other things, including labor, that have been imported, arguing that Iran could have supplied everything. It is said that His Majesty stole from his own starving people to pay for the festivities. Khomeini, living in exile, has called it the "evil celebration."

Why does all this make me anxious?

Because I am crazy with worry about Ferri.

As the anniversary bash begins, students are arrested for writing anti-crown graffiti. The liberal Iranian press openly criticize Shah. Headlines read, "Lavish at the Expense of Starving People," and "An Insult to Our Culture to Serve French Food." Banks are attacked. Cinemas are bombed. Police are assassinated. There are promises of a blood bath at the site. SAVAK has detained almost two thousand people.

Meanwhile, Ferri has become increasingly anti-monarch and now leans towards communism. I fear my angel is among the demonstrators, and I am terrified by the thought that something may happen to her.

I pray she won't be arrested.

6

NEITHER HERE NOR THERE

*T*hroughout my life, bias has left no room for the truth of who I am.

My life has been defined by a clash of cultures, a clash that has created a morass of challenges for me.

While attending UCLA in California, I had imagined that upon graduation, I would return to Iran and continue my life where I'd left off. I realize now how impossible that was, how naïve I'd been to think I would live a new country with a culture so different from what I'd known and remain unaffected – never mind the allure of one that allowed a girl of seventeen such sweet freedom for the first time in her sheltered life.

I left Tehran with suitcases filled with myths I'd been told about men, virginity, love … and these myths had formed my values.

Then America instilled new beliefs in me. I discovered that much of what I'd been taught was pure bogus. By the end of my first year in Los Angeles, I'd become a different person. I had lost my compulsion to abide by the principles I'd been raised to follow.

The first time I was not under my parents' watchful eyes, I

ripped off everything I'd been taught as I would a woolen dress in a steam room.

You could say I became a traitor to my own heritage.

Conveniently, there were only a handful of Iranians in Los Angeles in the time I was there, making the chance that my parents would hear of my activities extremely slim. That knowledge inflated my courage. I felt I had the freedom to conduct myself as I wanted and choose how to live. My behavior while in LA reflected my changed values.

I hadn't interacted with boys without a chaperone since I'd come into my moon at the age of twelve, yet there I was, surrounded by them.

They were everywhere – in the streets, on campus and in classes. Something in me yearned to experience them. Eventually, I began to interact with them, then to experiment with my sexuality.

I drew the line at sleeping with any … until David.

When I returned to Iran I was no longer the young, naïve girl I'd been when I left Iran.

I had refused David's proposal of marriage and had secretly given birth to Jasmine. I was a woman and a mother, sophisticated in the ways of love, joy, sex, heartbreak and pain.

I'd come to view Iranians and their way of life through the eyes of a Westerner. I made a connection between the systematic oppression of women in my country and the result of what was too often, female shallowness.

By the end of my second week in Tehran, having seen friends and family, I was looking forward to my return to Los Angeles at the end of that month. (Of course, that was not to be.)

Despite the freedom I had in America to act in disregard of the values I'd been taught, I was still not totally liberated.

True, I'd followed my heart when I'd decided to lose my virginity to David. I loved him completely. Yet, the vestiges of the Persian girl within me mandated that I refuse his proposal of marriage, and so, I lost the love of my life.

Why?

Because Zahra Khanom's daughter could never marry an American, a man raised in California, a Jewish man who would want to live on an Israeli kibbutz.

～

The clash of culture followed me home.

If I had imagined that I could deceive my mother and hide my changed attitudes from her, I was wrong. With only those few words that fateful day in the kitchen, when I dared ask if our neighbor had been thrown out of her home and banned from ever again seeing her children simply because she'd sat down to have a cup of tea alone with an unrelated man, Maman recognized I had changed, and had likely come to reject the standards she had raised me to respect. The possibility that others would discover I had changed threatened to embarrass her beyond anything she could endure.

So, on the heels of her discovery that I'd lost my virginity, came surgery to reconstruct that virginity through a hymenoplasty and my marriage to Rostam, born of desperation.

～

I am keenly aware that I threw away every chance I had for happiness.

My choices have boxed me in.

I am lost in feelings of fear and despair, of untold grief and loneliness, self-disgust, helplessness, even hopelessness. The time

34

my mind is at peace is when I dwell on memories of my time in America and the only hopeI I have left for my future is reuniting with my child.

I have deceived so many and made so many bad decisions. Yet I have never for one moment regretted my time in America. I am not sorry for one minute of my time with David nor for the night our bodies joined in such bliss and created Jasmine.

How astounding to think that I let the man I love walk away and lost our child in exchange for obedience to Maman and marriage to Rostam! I have no one to blame but myself.

I am paying a heavy price for the terrible decisions I made.

The truth is that I deserve the life I made for myself.

I am a spineless fool.

7
HAPPY BIRTHDAY, JASMINE

May 16, 1968

*J*t is Jasmine's seventh birthday.

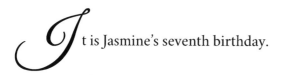

The moon was a white blur in last night's storm.

I lay in bed listening as the downpour of rain slammed against our bedroom windows and Rostam's snores, and thinking about my daughter.

There had been a similarly heavy storm the night Jasmine was born. I had been alone and so afraid.

David had taken his broken heart and left for Israel only days after I'd refused his marriage proposal. He'd yearned to contribute to the young country's survival by becoming an army medic and, whether because I'd convinced him there was no future for us, or out of anger and frustration, he left no forwarding address.

Two months later, I discovered I was pregnant from our one night together.

Having committed what I had been raised to regard as the heinous sin of relinquishing my virginity before marriage, I was about to give birth to a bastard.

I had no choice but to keep my shameful pregnancy, and then my child, a secret. I was initially convinced that I had no option but to give my secret child up for adoption. I'd thought my religion, my culture, my lineage and my mother left me no choice but to abandon my newborn baby. After all, Jasmine was the living proof of my shameful sin, the result of a relationship that was itself taboo. Had she been discovered, I would be labeled a *jendeh*, a whore, and my life in Iran even would have been … well, even worse than it is.

As I'd lain in the hospital writhing and moaning, my bedsheets wet with sweat awaiting the birth of my fatherless child, I had only the elderly nurse and the raging storm, those sudden claps of thunder, to keep me company.

As miserable as I was, I clung to the knowledge that my shameful pregnancy was coming to an end.

Rostam has already left for the office, but I linger in bed.

This morning the rain is gentle. The white fog has lifted, stretching upwards to the sky, making way for sunshine. Raindrops glisten like so many crystals.

A bird lands on my bedroom windowsill.

I have seen similar birds with these fawn-colored wings and that distinctive black and white design in the Bakhtiari Provinces of the deserts. Somehow, this one has made its way to the city. Its long beak taps against my windowpane. It peers inside and cocks its head. After a moment, it ruffles its feathers, shaking the remaining rain from its wings, dances a two-step on the sill and takes flight. I wonder if it will find its way home. Locked in my gilded cage, I wish it luck.

I sigh as I recall how I had kept in the shadows through those long months of pregnancy, hibernating in Adam and Linda Dunn's apartment.

Months earlier, I had treated Adam terribly, all because he had kissed me when I still – incredibly! – thought a kiss marked me as a *jendeh*, a whore. Still, though I had treated him so unfairly, the day I learned I was pregnant, he happened to see me crying outside the Medical Center and insisted on rescuing me.

I will never be able to repay Adam, and his sister Linda, They were my emotional rocks and my sole support during those furtive seven months. Their kindness was immense. Sister and brother were both amazingly generous with their time, their care and concern, thoughtful beyond limit, and I will forever be grateful to them.

I named my little baby Jasmine after the sweet-scented, nocturnal white flower that grows on the vine, thriving wherever it's planted. Determined to ensure that she was placed with loving parents, I'd anticipated participating in placing her.

But my immediate priority was my mandated stay in Tehran for a summer month, to begin only two weeks after my delivery. I was anxious as I prepared for what would be a command performance at home, hiding my recent pregnancy and delivery from my parents.

Resolved to meet with an adoption agency on my return to Los Angeles no more than four weeks later, I left my little girl behind in the care of Linda and Adam. They agreed to communicate to me through Ferri, my best friend in Tehran.

I spent several weeks at home and it seemed I'd performed well. No one guessed my secret.

Then, only three days away from returning to Los Angeles, I opened my mouth and spoke those few words that peeled away the layers of Maman's charming exterior and showed her to be the monster she truly is. Seven years ago, those few words – "That's all? Just tea?" – chained me to Tehran and changed my life.

Ironically, it was Maman's cruelty that made me realize how passionately I wanted to raise Jasmine. How I longed to give my little girl the love, the honesty, the respect and understanding my mother had never given me! To think even for a minute that the child I created with David could be raised by strangers, now seemed ridiculous.

I must have been insane to think that anyone would love her more or care for her better than me. I would have given the world to have my daughter at my side. But it was too late. Jasmine was lost to me and the ache in my heart will never heal.

All my attempts to return to her failed: My plan to marry Rostam and ditch him in LA failed; my attempt to escape, flee to the airport and fly to LA failed; my efforts to contact Linda and Adam and make it clear to them that I'd changed my mind and wanted to raise Jasmine failed when Rostam made communication with the outside world impossible.

Meanwhile, my projected absence of four weeks extended to more than three months, and even then, I could not supply a clear return date. Without the ability to explain my prolonged absence, Adam and Linda believed I'd never return.

Oh, I can't blame them. "The last straw," as the American's say, was when they heard that I was marrying an Iranian man who knew nothing of my daughter, and logically assumed that I had decided to stay in Iran and begin a new life that did not include Jasmine.

I can envision Linda at the adoption agency sharing the sad story that Jasmine had been born out of wedlock to a young college student, a visiting foreigner, who that had left the newborn with her and her brother to return to her country, then kept delaying her return before suddenly marrying back home.

The infant's father?

Oh, he never knew of the pregnancy and is now presumed dead or is simply lost somewhere in Israel.

In any event, Linda brought the little girl in need of a mother and father to the agency. I can just see the agency person – a woman, no doubt – nodding in sympathetic understanding while eyeing Jasmine, quietly sizing her up, determining how adoptable she was.

I only hope that my baby's chances of being placed in a good home were heightened by the fact that she was still an infant and pretty.

⟿

Realizing I'd lost my child, filled me with a deep feeling of desolation.

I'd visited a mosque for the first time in years, hoping to find solace there. Instead, I met Setareh, a mystic who gave me a prayer to recite daily, foretelling that if I saw Jasmine in my dreams I would one day find her. I did dream of her three times. I try to keep that thought alive.

That frayed piece of paper is with me always and I dutifully recite the prayer I have memorized several times a day. I await the day the mystic had promised would come.

I pray my child is healthy and that she has been enjoying a good life these seven years. Having forever lost the chance to raise – or, likely, even see – my daughter again, all I have left to give her are my prayers. That's how horribly I failed as a mother and that has been my most unforgivable failure.

Still, I remind myself that I am still a young woman and no longer naïve. I am just waiting. Waiting for a miracle.

Anyone paying attention will notice that every year on this day, I order a cake with flowers on pink icing. I will be serving it tonight with *chai*.

It is time to get up and face the day.

8

AT MY COUSIN'S HOUSE

1969

I welcome the cramps that herald the start of my moon.

Wearing my robe, I slip into my slippers, wash up, and join Rostam in the dining room table, set for breakfast. "Good morning," I whisper. Still standing, I am looking down in mock shame. As usual, he neither looks at me nor responds.

After a moment, he lifts his eyes from the newspaper, having realized I have not yet sat at the table, and looks at me. He barks, "*Harf bezan!* Speak!"

With my eyes still downcast, I shake my head. "I'm in my moon," I murmur. "I'm sorry."

He lets go of the newspaper, throws his fork down, picks up the lit cigarette in the ashtray, and starts to storm out. At the door, he turns to glare at me. "Be ready to leave at five."

I sit at the table and enjoy my breakfast of *chai* and barbarri with feta cheese and sour cherry jam in peaceful solitude, then dress. Afterwards, I curl up on a chair overlooking the back garden and finish reading "I Know Why the Caged Bird Sings," a wonderful book that describes the loneliness and longing of children assaulted by rape and racism. These feelings resonate with me. I have been raped by my husband and have an up-front view of a racist.

The day goes by and before I know it, I must leave for Shireen's house. Not wanting to keep Rostam waiting past five o'clock, I hurriedly see to my makeup, throw on my fur, collect my scarf and handbag and leave the house.

As I open the front door and step outside, it begins to rain in earnest once more.

With no time to find an umbrella, I hold my handbag over my head and hurry to join Rostam in the back seat of the car.

He hasn't spoken to me since his return home from the office, and he is silent in the car. His anger at my failure to have conceived yet another month is evident in the way he holds his cigarette and the set of his face as he stares outside his window or straight ahead.

As we drive through the neighborhood, I see a woman stepping out of her shiny chauffeur-driven car, her driver making sure to carefully cover his lady with a large black umbrella.

This rain, this change of seasons, the change in temperature … none of it makes much of a difference in the lives of Tehran's women of leisure. Their daily routine doesn't change. They continue to fill their weekly calendars with hair and manicure appointments, spa facials, massages, exfoliation treatments, waxing and threading unwanted hair, meetings with their dressmakers and, of course those luncheons, which make all the other appointments so necessary.

As the weather turns colder, they simply wear thicker, warmer furs on the walk to and from their chauffeur driven cars. They hardly feel a drop of rain.

Today's outing to Shireen and Taymoor's house has been arranged by Rostam. No doubt he needs something from Taymoor, possibly another prestigious contact or some advice about how to deal with someone, likely someone he's met through him.

Rostam feeds his relationship with my cousin's husband for the benefits it reaps, introductions to the people Taymoor knows, due mainly to the man's pleasing disposition and his abundant wealth, a wealth that comes from his birthright and not worldly achievements.

I take advantage of his silence to offer a reason other than my returning moon to explain his foul mood. "Is something the matter?" I ask.

"I need to talk to Taymoor," he mouths, staring ahead.

Shireen and Taymoor can't wait for us to fully enter their marble palace.

They stand ready to greet us as soon as their servant opens the door. Taymoor is not wearing a suit, but rather, navy pants and a burgundy sweater, a sign that there will only be the four of us today. He shakes his head enthusiastically, before kissing me on both cheeks and embracing my husband.

"His Majesty has gone too far," Taymoor says, launching into his favorite subject as I'm handing my chinchilla coat, along with my hat and scarf, to his servant.

Afsoneh takes them and smiles at me. She takes Rostam's coat and hat.

Shireen grabs my cold hand. Her hand is soft and warm. "Come on, Layla. Who cares about men's grumbling? Let's go talk. I have exciting news."

"Are you all right, my darling?" Taymoor asks. She nods and shakes her bangled wrist then whisks me away, our heels tapping on the white marble floor and step down into the grand salon, a cold cavern of white and mirrors.

Though Rostam approves of my time spent with Shireen, nothing has changed between us; I barely tolerate her.

We two are not only cousins. Growing up, we were also class-mates and neighbors. In fact, despite outward appearances – both of us are now married to wealthy Iranian men – I have less in common with her than ever before.

I resent my life, but Shireen lives her privileged life with gusto as a pampered wife and mother. She is living the life she has always dreamed of. Taymoor, over a decade older than her, gives her the freedom to spend his enormous wealth as she likes.

I grew up to the soundtrack of Shireen's endless complaints. Unsurprisingly, my cousin's complaints are now fewer. But she is still Shireen, still idolizes Hollywood stars, adores material excess, and continues to believe "it's not fair" where I'm concerned. She has forever believed I am luckier because I'm thin. I am luckier because I have not had to endure the misery of pregnancy and childbirth. And I am luckier because I'm not hampered by young children.

As we step into the grand salon, she lifts her head and thrusts her chest out. "Look what Taymoor surprised me with yesterday." She pulls on the collar on her suit jacket, baring a necklace. It is laden with large stones in Shireen's favorite color – emerald. I cannot help but marvel at the ostentatiousness of the piece.

"And look!" she said excitedly, pulling her short hair back behind her ears to unveil earrings of the same color with stones that cover her earlobes.

"Shireen, they're really something!"

She is unable to contain her joy. "Aren't they beautiful?" she asks, exposing her new necklace a second time. "Taymoor is so happy

"Oh, Shireen, that's wonderful! How many months?"

We are seated on the long white couch. She helps herself to a plate of dried fruits and Belgium chocolates set out on the table in front of us. As I reach for a piece of chocolate, she launches, on cue, into her longtime chant.

"It's just not fair, Layla! You never gain any weight!"

For some godforsaken reason, this woman who is loved and pampered by her husband, about to have another baby born into a happy, secure home, living her dream, with everything money can buy ... This woman who knows nothing about the child I've lost, the great love I've lost, the brute that Rostam is, or the jail I live in ... This woman truly envies me as she has her whole life for being thinner, smarter — and, she believes, childless.

I listen to her complain about her the difficulties of another pregnancy she is not looking forward to, of motherhood and of her weight, which she has always battled. Her love of sweets may be due to her name which translates to "sweet." And, though her voluptuous figure has softened with pregnancy, she still has those lovely violet eyes set in a pretty face, like her idol, Elizabeth Taylor, whom she has always called, "Liz."

Afsoneh serves us tea, smiles again at me, and whispers a hello. I take a sip from my cup while Shireen puts down her empty plate and takes two dates and two pieces of baklava to enjoy with her tea.

"It will be three months next week," she answers.

She rests her hand on my thigh. "I'm sorry for not telling you sooner, Layla, but I've only told my mother. No one else knows yet." She will be happy to tell her friends that she is giving her husband another child. She takes a sip of her *chai* and finishes the first piece of baklava.

She fingers her earrings. "He's given me a matching ring, but I'm already so bloated that I can't get the damn thing on! I need to have it resized."

Jasmine was born in May!

"Congratulations! That means you'll deliver in May?"

"Well," she says, biting into a piece of baklava, "I'm hoping the baby is early. The doctor says it could be late April." She drinks more *chai* and bites into a date.

"Really, Layla, you can't imagine how what it's like to walk around with a baby kicking in your belly." I remain silent. "Oh, Layla, why don't you get pregnant? I wish you were. We could complain to one another."

"That would be nice," I say, keeping my expression blank while I feel my heart pulsating in my throat.

"Just think. Our mothers were pregnant together with us, and our children would be as close as we are. I mean, really. We grew up together, we played together, went to school together … It's only right."

"Maybe next time." I pause, then add, "I'm happy for you."

I realize I'm pulling at my wedding ring. It doesn't budge.

Shireen sighs. She puts down her empty plate and teacup. "I don't know if there will be a next time," she says, lowering her voice, though from where we sit, the men cannot hear us. "I hate being pregnant. I gain so much weight." She cups her breasts. "Breastfeeding makes me feel like a cow."

She chuckles and sways. "I bet you won't gain weight when you're pregnant." I smile in the face of her ignorance.

"Why *aren't* you pregnant, Layla? Doesn't Rostam want children?"

I nod. "He does."

"Well, have you been to a doctor?"

"Yes." I shrug and shake my head, acting innocent and stupid. "He says it just hasn't happened yet. It will. It's just taking time."

It's time to change the subject. I ask her about her recent trip to Europe. "How was Italy?"

"Oh, we spent hours shopping in Florence. The gold we bought! If you ever want to buy gold jewelry, you must go to Florence."

"Did you like Rome?"

"Taymoor did. He loved the sights. I fell in love with their leather." She chuckles. "I swear, I must have bought out all the leather goods they had. It's all so soft." She puts her empty plate on the coffee table. "I'll show you what I bought; you might want one of the handbags."

With that she stands up and arranges her hair, making sure her ears show.

"Well, let's go eat. I'm starving."

Afsoneh serves the four of us supper.

Taymoor brings up the subject of the next elections, and the two men passionately discuss the pros and cons of the Parliamentary candidates.

Shireen interrupts, waving her hand to get their attention. "Why not ask Layla who to vote for?" she says. "Iran would improve by leaps if people were as smart as Layla. A woman like her is smarter than any ten men you can show me." She sounds belligerent.

Rostam's mouth falls open. No words came out, but his eyes ... oh, his eyes. They linger on our hostess.

Shireen's ever-present gold charm bracelet has caught on her jacket, and she shakes her arm to free it, so, oblivious to his reaction, she continues on in a matter-of-fact tone. "And her friend, Ferri – I'm not crazy about that girl, but she's really super smart, too – I bet she knows oceans about all this stuff." Her eyes land on me. "Right, Layla?"

Rostam's spoonful of food freezes inches from his mouth. He follows Shireen's eyes as they land on me, his own reflecting a mix of curiosity and daring.

He is ready to dissect my reaction to what Shireen has just said about my best friend. It is ironic that my bigoted husband hates Ferri simply because she was born to Jewish parents when Ferri doesn't like organized religion for the very reason that she believes it serves to separate people.

I must make sure to sound natural and calm when I react to Shireen's statement about Ferri. I have plans to see my best friend on Thursday, our first meeting since my marriage.

I look Shireen straight in the eyes and shrug. "She was smart. But I haven't kept in touch with her for years." I pray my voice sounds even.

I watch Rostam from the corner of my eye. He looks relieved to hear my newest lie and resumes his conversation with Taymoor, tearing into proposed national legislation that further limits the amount of money one can take abroad. Many wealthy Iranians have sent money to Europe, Israel, or the States as a precaution against the possibility that our monarchy could topple at any moment and cause a financial collapse. Any further limits on taking money out of Iran is not good news.

"Rostam *jon*," Taymoor says, "now what will become of us all?"

"I wish that was his only crazy idea!" Rostam says. "*Shah devoneh shodeh!* Shah has gone mad!" He slams the table for emphasis.

The two of them bemoan the new mandatory profit-sharing plan for employees, and I feel a swell of pride recalling that Babajon instigated a profit-sharing plan in his company when I was eleven years old. It has apparently worked out well. His company, Saleh Pharmaceuticals, continues to thrive, despite the onslaught of western medications introduced daily into the Iranian market.

Lighting his third cigarette at the table, Rostam says, "What the hell is Pahlavi thinking? He says he's against communism. Well, isn't it communism to give these people a share of money from my personally owned business? Why should I? Let him give them his money and his sister's – if she can cut down on her drugs."

"Well, be careful who you complain to about that," Taymoor says, giving Rostam a pointed look.

When the U.S. and Britain arrested Mossadegh and propped His Majesty back on the throne in 1953, the American CIA created SAVAK, allowing our shah to monitor and control anti-government activity in the country. Anyone could be an agent of SAVAK. The agency spreads its net wide and doesn't distinguish between the working class and the elite or the intellectuals. Brutal tactics are used against anyone deemed to be Shah's enemy. The many SAVAK agents are unidentified, which gives the impression that the agency is omnipotent and omnipresent. Complain too loudly to an undercover agent about His Majesty or his programs, or speak too harshly about the lifestyle of his twin sister, Ashraf, and you might by snatched from your office one day or from your home in the middle of the night, arrested without notice or warrant, and taken to a prison, perhaps to Evin, the most feared prison in Iran.

"I'm complaining to you!" Rostam booms "In your home!"

I suddenly know how to rid myself of Rostam!

I will simply go to the authorities and snitch on my husband, tell them he is spouting anti-shah sentiments.

In the next minute, I immediately realize my plan is far too combustible. My attempted escape at Tehran's airport the morning after our wedding was thwarted because of Rostam's close friendship with Tehran's Chief of Police, a member of Rostam's *doreh*, the group of five regular poker playing chums who alternate hosting the game. When it is Rostam's turn to host the game, I greet the men, then excuse myself and retire. I have glimpsed the bond of male camaraderie that exists between them. God only knows what other powerful friends Rostam has.

What if I end up in Evin prison?

"And Shah is devaluing the *toman*," Taymoor continues, referring to our country's reduced buying power. Yet I am certain our host will not have to sell Shireen's jewels anytime soon.

Again, I wonder what Taymoor thinks of Rostam and can only conclude he thinks him boorish and crude and has most probably allowed Rostam to cling to his coattails out of respect for the fact that I am his wife's cousin.

With supper finished, Rostam requests that he and Taymoor be served *chai* in Taymoor's study, and the two men leave the room.

I linger at the table, while my cousin runs to get something she wants me to see.

Shireen returns, holding a copy of Silver Screen magazine.

My cousin began reading American movie magazines when we were still in school and has never stopped. She turns to a dogeared page, unfurls the magazine and jabs a photo of the beautiful Iranian ex-Queen, Shah's second wife, just inches from my face. "Layla! You have to see this! Look! Look at this picture of Soraya!"

I read the caption accompanying her photo. *"The ever-beautiful Soraya."* Apparently, Soraya is now hob-knobbing with actors and has become a member of the international jet set.

"She looks so sad," I say. "Her eyes look dead."

In fact, her eyes have looked devoid of any life in every photo I've seen of the her since she left our king.

Shireen sighs. She sits back down and puts the magazine on the table between us. "They still call her, *Soraya, once the beautiful*

Queen of Iran," she says, "and they still point out that she couldn't conceive during her eight years of marriage." She shakes her head. "It's so unfair to her." It is rare for my cousin to show a sentimental side.

Then she surprises me with the most insightful comment she has ever made. "I'll bet she became infertile because of that typhoid fever."

I wonder if that could be possible. It sounds plausible. After all, Soraya's wedding to the His Excellency was postponed for two months due to her very serious illness, and still, she had been so weak, cold, and frail at the wedding ceremony that at the last minute, her fluffy wedding dress had to be thinned out, the under layers cut away and a mink coat draped over her shoulders by the shah before she could walk down the aisle.

In photos taken during their seven-year marriage, they looked like two people who were very much in love. When Soraya proved to be infertile, and His Majesty was pressured to produce a son to assure the continuance of the Pahlavi dynasty, he had begged Soraya to allow him to take a second wife, exclusively for the purpose of conceiving an heir. She refused, and seven years later, in 1958, His Majesty was forced to divorce her.

We Iranians listened to the broadcast of our weeping shah announce the news of their divorce. It was a sad time for all of us. The beautiful, young Soraya had found her way into our hearts, as well as his.

"Remember when we saw them taking her pictures down at the movie theater?" I ask. "They were doing the same thing at the post Shireen nods.

Shireen has had enough of Soraya.

She's eager to bring the subject back to herself. "Don't you love this dress? Isn't it divine?" In the photo, Soraya wears a green sheath. "I took this picture to my dressmaker so she could copy the dress. I know I can't wear it now, but if she makes it large enough,

I can wear it after the baby is born, right?" She stands up and poses, holding the photograph up to her torso. She's so happy. So excited. I nod.

"And it will look wonderful with my new emeralds." She exposes her new necklace again and then she starts jumping up and down in her heels, like she did as a child whenever she was excited. I nod again.

My cousin has so much to look forward to.

Though it hurts my pride, I must admit that Shireen has always been stronger, more determined, and more focused than me.

She's always known what she wants, and she's aimed to have it all without apology. She's living the life she's craved.

To Shireen, marrying a man more than a decade older was fine provided he had enough money and a generous heart. Money, oodles of it, was what she'd always wanted, and she has more of it than she had dreamed of. As for love, it was never high on her list of requirements for marriage, and I had once pitied her for having married a man she didn't love. Yet, I would bet she loves Taymoor now. He obviously adores her.

My cousin has historically openly shared news of her life with me while I've never been able to share anything significant about mine with her, always too afraid it would somehow get back to my parents or Rostam.

Of course, she knows nothing of my baby, a beautiful daughter lost somewhere in America, fathered by a man I truly loved but had turned my back on.

I've made all the wrong choices.

And she thinks I'm smart?

9

MAMAN

I had left for UCLA believing my mother wanted only the best for me.

On my return home, I came to realize Maman wanted what was best for her.

She had no desire to know me, my aspirations, my fears, or anything else about me. In her world, I am to fulfill her dreams, bolster her reputation, and enhance her prestige. Period.

My interest in microbiology always repulsed her. She believes an educated girl repels the right husband.

In her view, girls are best off marrying soon after high school, and had always assumed that immediately upon graduation, I would marry a suitably wealthy Iranian man and supply her with grandchildren.

The idea of her daughter attending college was absurd. Living in America was totally unacceptable to her, and certainly leaving home — for four years! — to live in Los Angeles, "the hellhole of Hollywood," where "immoral people have sex in the streets like cats and dogs" was her worst nightmare and completely out of the question. In short, my enrollment at UCLA went against everything she had planned for me, and she had been solidly against it. She was certain it could only have been the result of having been given the evil eye.

A year and a half later, when I'd blurted out those few words in our kitchen during my summer visit home and she confiscated my passport and exit papers, she was immensely relieved; she was finally able to prevent my return to L.A. Most unfortunately, it also made it impossible for me to return to the baby whose existence she knew nothing about.

I've wondered if my mother would have acted any differently if she'd known of the baby I'd left behind and have decided that it would not. She only cared that I was home and finally able to fulfill the dreams she had for me – albeit, by handcuffing me to a country I no longer wanted to live in.

Hearing those few words I thoughtlessly blurted out in the kitchen that day signaled to Maman that her daughter's values had changed while in America.

Afraid that I'd lost my virginity as well as my values there, she immediately delivered me to a doctor to be examined. Following her instructions, he gave me a shot that knocked me out before examining me. Then, while I was still unconscious, he apparently shared the news that I was no longer a virgin so Maman had him perform a hymenoplasty, the barbaric procedure based on false assumptions. It involves the surgical removal of a thin layer of the internal vagina and sewing it across the vaginal opening, recreating a hymen. Our culture's praise of virginity is that entrenched in our culture.

Because I'd recently given birth, the procedure was more involved, and the aftermath, extremely painful. I lay in bed, bleeding, with pain pills for a few days.

Nonetheless, I owe the doctor my thanks, for although he unquestionably had deduced from his examination that I had delivered a baby barely a month earlier, he had kept that information from my mother. So, while his handiwork was barbaric, I suppose I should be grateful. If I knew how to find him, I might thank him for his discretion.

In any event, my fate had been sealed. I wasn't going anywhere – except to my husband's home – as a virgin bride.

At my wedding, Maman was delirious with equal parts of joy and relief.

By preventing me from returning to America, she believed she had saved me from a life of sin. Because of her, I married a wealthy Iranian man who shared our religion, and, thanks to her handiwork, I passed the test of virginity on our wedding night. She has kept possession of the bloodied virginity napkin as proof.

And though I have given her no reason to think that Rostam is the brute and bigoted bully that he is, I don't believe she would care if she knew that either. Her only concern has always been how I am seen by others. After all, as her daughter, what I am reflects on her.

Yes, Maman was delighted that the hymenoplasty had hit its mark. But as the months and then the years have gone by and I haven't conceived, her relief has ebbed. She has become increasingly nervous about my childlessness.

Though I have shared the findings of the fertility doctor, confirming that there is nothing wrong with me, she must be frustrated at her inability to do anything about my childlessness.

My marriage has bought her the tree of respectability and she desperately wants the fruit of that tree.

She would demand a grandchild if she could.

1 0

ANY NEWS?

1970

atherings like tonight are hosted by the women in the family, each of us endlessly repaying the kindness of the others.

This evening, our hostess is Shireen's mother, my Aunt Haideh Khanom. I've always liked her and thought she and Mansour Khan, Maman's brother, are a loving couple.

Rostam and I enter the house where I'd spent so many hours in my early years dancing with Shireen in her bedroom and laughing at her parrot.

Aunt Haideh greets us at the door with that easy smile, filled with warmth. She looks wonderful tonight in a burgundy suit that compliments her chestnut hair and olive complexion.

After greeting Rostam, she embraces me. "Layla, you look lovely!"

I am wearing a new fur coat, this one, a full-length sable,

Rostam's latest attempt to draw attention to his wealth. When I take it off, she adds, "And what a pretty dress!" My dress is short, woolen, black and covered with large red, orange, and yellow flowers. I thank her.

She winks confidentially. "Any news?" She is asking if I've discovered I'm pregnant since the last time I saw her. That was two weeks ago. I shake my head.

"Nothing," I say with a smile.

"Rostam *jon*, the men are in the game room smoking and solving the problems of the world. Layla, you come with me."

She leads me into the large salon where Maman is seated on one of two long couches set facing one another. I bend over and kiss her, then sit beside her.

I watch as Aunt Haideh, who was trailing me, stops to hug her granddaughter, Talah Elizabeth, now about seven years old. The girl has been fidgeting with the dish of pistachio nuts in a bowl set on the coffee table, and as soon as her grandmother lets go of her, she goes back to trying to break a particularly tight shell.

"She's lovely," I say.

In fact, Talah is on her way to growing into an attractive young woman with Shireen's violet eyes and her father's full lips. Yet I find it so tiring to always comment on a female's looks –– as I feel I must —while ignoring her intelligence, her kindness, her talents and all else.

"*Meemeeram barrash!* I die for her!" Haideh Khanom tells us with eyes that shine with love. She sits down on Maman's other side.

"May it be your turn soon, Layla *jon. Ensha Allah*, Allah willing. Wouldn't it be wonderful for you and Shireen to raise your children together?" She reaches across Maman to take hold of my hand. "They'll have each other like you and Shireen do. Wouldn't that be wonderful?" My mother turns from Haideh Khanom to me, then and back to my aunt and again at me.

What can I say?

I want to scream out, *I have a daughter! A beautiful daughter ... and her name is Jasmine!"*

I only sigh. "Yes."

Perhaps that sigh was louder than I'd meant it to be, or perhaps I look sad for my dear aunt has apparently changed her mind. "*Khob,* okay, don't upset yourself. It shall be whatever Allah wants." She sits back in her seat, having decided that was that.

Just then, Mamanjon Tallat– as my mother-in-law insists that I call her – approaches. "Layla *jon,*" she says.

I stand to greet her with a kiss on each cheek. When I offer her my place on the couch, she continues to stand. She stares at my belly. "*Khabareh khosh?* Good news?" I shake my head in answer. She asked me the same question when I last saw her two weeks ago as well. Her face falls.

Rostam's parents are worried. *What is the problem with the girl? Does she repel her husband in the bedroom? Is she infertile?*

She takes my place on the couch and the others move to make room for me. I sit on the other side of my mother.

Mamanjon Tallat speaks airily. "Rumi says, if you want to conceive you should have sex in the sunlight." We look at her blankly. "*Beh Koran,* on the Koran, he has written that the same sun that makes the flower grow and ripens fruit makes a woman more fertile." We three look at one another. "And saffron and rye are wonderful aphrodisiacs," she continues. Throwing a sidelong look at Maman, she adds, "But I am sure that mother and daughter have shared these secrets."

"*Albatteh,* of course!" Maman says.

My mother has never shared *any* secret with me.

My dear Haideh Khanom rises to my defense. "Layla doesn't need rye," she says, smiling radiantly. "Leave her alone." My loyal aunt has defended me from my mother-in-law while my own mother remains silent. She goes on. "The lovebirds don't need a baby yet. When Allah wants them to have a baby, they'll have one."

"Well," my mother-in-law says, busy with her sleeves, "Forgive me. I guess I'm just too anxious to see my only son's baby."

The subject of my pregnancy is always the subject of the day.

Wherever I go, whether to family or friends, the question comes up. "*Cheh tazeh?* What's new? Are you pregnant?" And wherever there is a baby or a pregnant woman, I hear, "May it soon be your turn." Translation: *Hurry up and get pregnant!*

I excuse myself and leave the ladies. I spot my grandmother, Naneh Joon, my father's mother, sitting by the entrance to the dining room. In her sixties, and almost twenty-five years younger than her husband, stoop backed, frail and arthritic, she could easily be mistaken for a woman twenty years older.

She is alone now that Agha Doctor passed. Two bouts of pneumonia while I was away in California had weakened my grandfather terribly and, though he lingered on for over a year after his last return home from the hospital, he never fully recovered his strength and passed away soon after my return to Tehran.

I bend to kiss her. "Oh, my lovely Layla *jon. Gorbonet berram!* May I be sacrificed for you."

Babajon approaches from the direction of the kitchen holding a glass of water for his mother.

Nana Joon takes out two blue and white capsule and one small white pill and downs both with the water.

My father looks as handsome as always.

This evening he's wearing a dark navy suit with a white shirt and a tie of navy and red. His cufflinks shine in the light from the crystal chandelier above us.

"Look at my daughter!" he's beaming with pride as always

when he sees me. I feel the warmth of his love as we exchange cheek kisses. Then he puts his lips to my forehead, giving me his special kiss. "How is my golden girl?"

My father's health has come to be of paramount importance to me.

When Maman made my return to Los Angeles impossible, she forbade me from saying anything of the truth to him because of his health. He couldn't know I'd lost my virginity in Los Angeles; so, he couldn't know about the hymenoplasty.

I couldn't tell him that Maman had made it impossible for me to return to Los Angeles and UCLA. I had to tell him that the decision to remain in Tehran had been mine.

Why these lies?

I had longed to tell my father everything as it unfolded. But, as I said, Maman's threat, telling me his health might not endure the shock, had stopped me. According to her, he couldn't take the stress of knowing the truth. But she would not tell me what ailed him. Since then, I've watched my beloved Babajon like a hawk. His energy level seems good and he works as hard as ever.

Soon after his father passed away, Baabajon suffered a heart attack while on his way home from work. Fortunately, he was already back in the city and Abbos, his driver at the time and the man to whom I will always be grateful, had the presence of mind to rush my father to Tehran Metropolitan Hospital. During Babajon's stay there, I discovered that this was not his first attack.

I learned he'd suffered a minor heart attack while I was in Los Angeles, just three months before I'd given birth to Jasmine. He had sworn both Maman and his doctors to secrecy. Not even his own mother had known.

It hurts me to know he'd kept the truth from me ... but there was so much I had kept from him.

After that second attack, Babajon had gone to Israel where they ran further tests and performed a state-of-the-art procedure rendering him an excellent prognosis.

Returning home, he'd reported that so long as he took care of himself, he would be fine for many years to come. His regiment includes daily exercise, daily medication, a diet low in fats, and stress control. Since that attack, my own heart was never quite the same. I am concerned for my beloved father.

"Have you taken a walk today?" I ask now.

He drops his head in chagrin. "I'm guilty. I have not."

"But you must! The doctors said you must take a walk every day."

"Well, shall we take a short together?" he asks.

"That's an excellent idea," I say. "We can leave now and be back in time for dinner."

He asks, "Perhaps it's too cold for you?"

"No, it's fine. I'll get our coats."

11

THE WALK

*W*rapped in our coats with shawls at our necks, we leave Aunt Haideh's house.

Outside, the strong wind pushes the clouds around and assaults us mercilessly. Fallen leaves whirl around us as we start down the street. We are initially silent, tightening our shawls, acclimating ourselves to the cold.

I'm happy to be with Babajon.

I adore my father. He has always been there for me. He's a truly good man. A self-made success who has never been anything but kind. He's loved by all his many employees, his success neither questioned nor resented.

Growing up, I spent many of my happiest days in the laboratories of Saleh Pharmaceuticals. It was because of Babajon and the time I spent at his laboratories that I developed my love of microbiology. Early on, Babajon understood my passion for the science in a way my mother never did.

I was certain that upon graduation from high school I would have to put an end to my education and marry. Much to Maman's disgust, Babajon had other plans for me.

At my graduation party, he surprised me with the gift of four years at UCLA in their budding microbiology program. He choreographed my stay in Los Angeles, arranging for my cousin Jila, his sister's daughter, already a student there, to share an apartment with me.

He'd sent me on my way to live my dream.

⁓

Soon enough, Babajon surprises me with his probing.

"Layla, I've wanted to talk to you alone for some time. I can't lie. I am concerned about you. You've been married several years, and I'm still not sure you're happy." Hearing this, my breath freezes. "You know I was surprised when you said you wanted to marry Rostam but you convinced me. Still, I worry that you made a mistake, that you're unhappy."

Of course he can tell. My father knows me well. I put my arm through his and try to sound convincing. "I'm happy," I say simply, not trusting myself to say more.

Babajon stops walking and turns to me. The wind blows his dark brown hair so that it seems to stand up straight. "Layla, you are my beloved daughter. I know when you have dark clouds in your eyes no matter how wide your smile."

What can I say?

There is no way in the world I would break my father's heart. I will never let on what a horrible man his son-in-law is. It would only hurt him, and that's the last thing in the world I want to do. And Allah help us all if he tries to help me leave Rostam.

"Sometimes I miss my studies. That's all. I don't think I was meant to grow up and become a wife. Something in me just wants to stay in school and play with my schoolbooks and microscopes forever." I chuckle. "It's just unrealistic."

It hurts me to keep so many truths from my father. Now, when it is obvious to him that I am unhappy, I lie to the end, insisting I'm happy. I will never allow him to know what a son of a bitch he has for a son-in-law, or the huge part Maman had in securing my misery.

I only wonder how well he knows the woman he married.

Even now, I am afraid that were he to know the truth, his love for me would force him to try to separate me from Rostam and the bastard has promised that if my parents try to interfere, he will drag my family's name through the mud. With his vengeful heart and his powerful contacts, I don't doubt his word. So less is more and I volunteer nothing.

With his hands deep inside his pockets, he stops and studies my eyes. I pray he cannot see them clearly in the dark. "I know you love to learn and you were excited to go to UCLA. You were happy whenever we spoke on the phone and you seemed so happy when you came first home, even saying you needed to return for exams. Then suddenly, you decided not to go back. I don't understand why you didn't return to UCLA. Why *did* you decide to stay in Tehran?" he asks.

I lie again."I missed Iran," I say and shrug, looking past him. "I missed my home and you and Maman."

Babajon shakes his head as though frustrated at his inability to erase whatever clouds he has seen in my eyes and get to the truth. We continue our walk, the crackling sound of leaves crunching underfoot. The strong wind seems intent to tear off what leaves remain on the trees and carry them away.

We resume our walk.

"You were never very close to Shireen," he says, changing gears. "It was Ferri that was your best friend. She was smart, too. Whatever became of her? What is she doing?"

My stomach knots.

I have to be extremely careful not to tell him anything that might one day find its way back to my husband. "I don't really know," I say. "I haven't seen very much of her. We drifted apart when I got married."

Another lie! I will be seeing her on Thursday.

"That's a shame," my father says. "I thought you would be friends for life. I liked her." I hate myself.

I am more than anxious to change the subject. "Babajon, what do you think of Bahman's decision to stay in England?"

Having graduated from the London Academy of Architecture a few months ago, Shireen's older brother has sent word home that he is engaged to an Iranian girl who had also attended school in London. Bahman's family is distraught at his decision to take up residency there.

The shoulders of Babajon's coat slump. "It's difficult for Mansoor and Haideh. They're unable to understand their son's desire to stay away from the country of his upbringing, his home and his family." He chuckles. "But I can see why he'd want to stay where he is. Can't you?"

"You can?" I ask in surprise. I ignore the question.

"*Albatteh!* Of course! I understand the attraction," Babajon says. "Things are very different in the west." He continues, "When a young man like your cousin is exposed to those differences, it's understandable that he might want to remain there." I hear him sigh. "Particularly when the woman he loves is there." He nods and pushes his hands further inside his coat pockets. "Truth be told, there were many things about the American way of life that I admired while in college there," he says.

"Really?"

He nods, then chuckles again and smiles. "Of course. But there were things in Iran that I couldn't deny were more to my liking."

"Like what?" I ask.

"Like your mother," he says. "I wanted very much to marry Zahra and there was no way she would live in the U.S. I never forgot her exact words. *I cannot live in that country that still wets its diapers!"* He laughs as if he may or may not agree with her description of America, but in any event, he finds her comment to be at the very least, charming. Adorable. Delightful.

I never believed Maman's view of the United States to be insightful. I know how she detests America, how she looks down on the younger culture and how she despises the morality – or immorality, as she insists – of the West.

Maman has never liked what she doesn't understand, and can't control.

But now, hearing my father say that he was once so open to living in the U.S. jolts me. How many thousands of times have I wondered what my life would have been like if I'd been raised in America? *Would I have married my David and gone to live with him in Israel?*

"I was willing to make a comfortable life for us here," Babajon continues. "Fortunately, I have been able to do that. I am thankful to Allah that my efforts have been rewarded far more than I'd hoped."

This time, I stop. I turn to him. "But Babajon, you can't keep working as hard as you have. You must take care of yourself and not strain or overexert yourself."

"Layla *jon,* you know Saleh Pharmaceuticals is not just for you, your mother, and me. It is responsible for the lives of all the families of the people who work for Saleh. I can't let them down. And our products help so many."

I am about to object when he puts his arm in mine and we continue walking. "Don't worry, Layla. With the ingredients that we've added to our products from Israel, our medicines will all surpass the effectiveness of our old ones threefold and more. It's remarkable! And I have secured long-term contracts for supply from Israeli vendors, so, Saleh's future is secure." He turns to me, and I see the smile on his face, the enjoyment that comes from knowing he is making products that help so many people.

The irony is not lost on me that the future of Saleh Pharmaceuticals and my family's future are both tied to Israel.

Somehow, it seems just.

If I cannot be with David, our bond to Israel connects us. Though our country has not established formal relations with Israel, Iran has maintained a strong and solid relationship with the small country.

I yearn to fall into my father's arms, tell him everything about David, tell him of our daughter, and tell him that I could have been living in Israel with them both. I want to cry in his arms. I want to pray with him that, contrary to unofficial reports of years earlier, David is still alive as I believe he is.

Instead, I ask, "Will you be going to Israel often? There's so much violence. Will you be safe?"

"Don't worry, Layla. Nothing will happen to me."

When we go back inside the house, I am in a melancholy mood.

12

THE BOOKSTORE

Tehran, 1971

I will soon see my angel for the first time in all these
years.

Ferreshteh Kohan has been my best friend since the day she
saved me from my high school teacher's wrath.

She's smart, sassy, daring and loyal. She's also the only person
in Iran who knows everything I've gone through, and she's
supported me through it all. When I'd first returned to Tehran
after giving birth, it was Ferri who received mail sent for me from
Linda and Adam.

Early on, Ferri recognized Maman as the monster she is. She'd
encouraged me to sleep with David and later, had begged me not
to marry Rostam. Then he forbade me to communicate with her
because she is Jewish. It's ironic as Ferri always hated organized
religion for the very fact that it separates people.

Though I have always been in awe of her strength, her fearless-

69

ness, and her ability to stay calm in all situations, I have been equally chilled by the way Ferri historically courts danger. The girl likes to play with fire.

In high school, she was secretly meeting with Hamid, her young, unmarried Muslim teacher, despite the knowledge that her life would have been ruined had the truth found its way to a whispered rumor.

Pursuing a relationship with him was the equivalent of playing with a four-alarm fire. Yet, their clandestine meetings continued after high school. Then, during my first summer home from UCLA, she shared the news that her relationship with Hamid was no longer platonic. They had become intimate.

Her anti-shah politics give me an additional reason to fear for her safety.

When recent student demonstration at Tehran University were quelled by the government, I was appalled by the brutality of the seemingly unprovoked attack against unarmed students. Certain that Ferri, whom I believe now teaches at the University and has been most sympathetic to the cause of the students, was likely among the demonstrators. I have been in fear that her anti-government activities will send her to prison.

I have longed to see my angel and know she is alive and well and will finally be seeing her for the first time since I married.

True, Hassan shadows me everywhere I go. Yet, there are places The Rat's macho attitude will not allow him to be caught dead in – my gynecologist's office, my hairdresser's, manicurist's and dressmaker's shops. When I visit there, he will either run a short errand, sit chain smoking in his car, or lean against a storefront wall, leering at passing women.

One afternoon, I made a quick, surreptitious phone call to Ferri's house–behind the closed doors of my manicurist's shop, careful not to let anyone know who I was on the phone with. I am not a fool. I know that Rostam and his money can make people talk.

I wasn't sure the. Number I had was still working and it was wonderful to hear her voice. "I know where we can meet!" Ferri said. "Does your bodyguard like to read?"

"Hah!" I said, "No. I don't think he knows how."

"Good!" Ferri said, "Let's meet inside Crown Bookstore on Pahlavi."

"Yes. That's perfect," I said. "I'll say I want to buy some books. I'm sure The Rat will stay outside and smoke."

I'd missed the sound of Ferri's laughter. "That's hysterical! You call that little man, 'The Rat?' Fits perfectly! Let's hope he doesn't rat on you!"

I was anxious to end the call. "I can meet you Thursday at four o'clock." And then I thought to add, "If I'm not there, it's because something went wrong, and I'll see you there at the same time the following Thursday." I hung up, amazed to realize how easy that was. I could have called her long before this.

Knowing I would be seeing my angel in a matter of days, each one seemed to take forever.

Thursday is finally here.

When we arrive at the bookstore, The Rat opts to stay in the car, his pack of Winstons already in hand.

As I exit the car, I am afraid that Hassan will spot Ferri and recognize her as the girl he did not let into our house. It was on that fateful day that Ferri had come to deliver that final letter in which Linda had written, *enough is enough*, and had set the absolute last date by which I could reunite with my child before she would take her to an adoption agency.

Rostam had put me under house arrest and had deputized The

Rat as my warden before leaving to honeymoon alone for ten days in Italy. So, when Ferri announced her name at the door, The Rat, as blatantly anti-Semitic as his master, had blocked her way.

I enter the bookstore and spot my angel standing in the back. I hurry to her, and we fall in each other's arms. She is dressed, as always, in a pleated skirt and a simple black top. Her dark eyes shine. My face nestles inside her long, dark hair, taking in the faint scent of cigarette smoke mixed with the scent of shampoo in those thick curls. I am at once excited and relieved to see her.

Oh, how I've missed my angel!

We are flanked by books on both sides. The section on our right is marked, "History," and on our left, "Biographies." We speak in hushed voices.

Ferri speaks first. *"Joonie!"* Hearing that special term of endearment is food for my hungry soul. "Let me look at you."

Though I am concerned about Ferri, she is examining me, looking for a black eye or some other sign of Rostam's mutilation on my exposed body parts and relieved to find nothing. *"Joonie,* I've worry about you all this time. I know Rostam is a miserable brute."

"I'm all right," I say.

"Is it terrible?" she asks.

"No, things are not too bad as long as I do what he wants."

Ferri is not fooled. "Living with him must be like living on a barbed wire fence," she says.

I change the subject. "Tell me about you."

"There's not much to say," she says. "I'm teaching at the University, and I love it." I ask about her family. "Well, my little sister is engaged."

"Well, congratulations to little Rachel."

She asks about my parents, and I tell her they're both well.

"Is your mother still a monster?"

I chuckle. "Maman is nervous about her lack of grandchild. I'm not running on her schedule."

"Well," Ferri says, "isn't that just too bad for the monster."

I sigh. "I should have married David."

"But *Joonie* –" she starts.

I cut her off before she makes excuses for me. "Ferri, please don't justify my stupidity. I made foolish decisions. Period. You told me I should follow my heart. I didn't. David tried to tell me, too." I shake my head. "I should have listened to you."

Ferri takes me in her arms and holds me. "It's okay, *Joonie.*"

I pull away. "It's not." I shake my head. I didn't marry David because I thought my lineage, my culture, our different backgrounds and religions prevented our marriage. I know that was absurd. I thought I owed it to my parents, to Maman. And when I realized my mistake, it was too late. With everything she's done, I can't forgive her for forcing me to abandon my child ... for making me lie to my father. All because I didn't think it was a sin for a married woman to have tea with some man." I shake my head and laugh. "So ridiculous!"

"Not to her," Ferri says somberly. "After all, she did take you to some doctor who did what he did."

I shrug. "Ah! That's old news. Tell me more about you," I say. "I want to know everything. Are you living at home?"

"Thank heavens, no. I was visiting when you called, but I'm living in the University's housing for professors."

I immediately wonder if that makes it easier for her to see her old teacher. "Are you still seeing Hamid?"

She smiles. "Yes. He's so wonderful! He's talking about marriage, which *isn't* going to happen!" she says.

I know her reluctance to marry is not based on their different religions nor even on their age gap. Ferri is simply dead set against the institution of marriage. She believes it's unfair to women, oppressing them, chaining them to a house and their duties as a housekeeper and depriving them of a satisfying sexual life.

Her tone is cautious as she next asks if I want another child.

"With Rostam?" I shake my head and echo her comment. "It *isn't* going to happen." We put our hands to our mouths to muffle our laughter.

I start to get a little nervous, afraid that at any minute Hassan might wander in. I glance at the entrance. All is clear. "When is your sister's wedding?" I ask.

She sighs, shrugging. "My poor little sister. They're throwing *kostegars,* suitors, at me and forcing her to delay it hoping the older daughter will marry first – but," she repeats, "that *isn't* going to happen!" We laugh again.

Maman had scheduled up to two and even three daily visits by *kastegars* after my hymenoplasty, hoping to marry me off to any one of them; but Ferri is a lot smarter than I am.

Still, I worry about her and her anti-shah protests, and tell her so. She brushes away my concern. "You've always worried about me, *Joonie.* And I keep telling you, you really have nothing to worry about."

"But what if you get hurt at one of these demonstrations? Or worse, you get arrested and thrown in jail? What would I do? Ferri, you have to appreciate the risk you're taking."

She scoffs. With exaggerated clarity, she says, "*Joonie,* please-do-not-worry-about-me! I'll be fine. I won't get hurt and I won't get arrested. I promise you." I so want to believe her. "*I* worry about *you* and that ass you're married to. I know he's hurt you. He should be shot. You deserve better. Please, tell me the truth. Does the bastard still hit you?"

I shake my head. "I told you, not if I do as he says."

"You were always so happy," she says wistfully.

I look down and notice a piece of yellow paper laying on the tile floor with a partial drawing in thick black ink of a woman's face and her up-stretched arm. It is likely torn off a flyer advertising a book new. Women wanting, demanding more power. *Hah! A joke.*

"I wonder," I say.

"What is there to wonder about?" she asks. "You were happy before your monster mother had her way."

I shrug. "I don't know anymore. Maybe I've just needed to think of my past as having been happy; maybe time coaxes our memories into something sweeter than what really was. I mean, we're only seeing what we've passed through from the back and backs can be deceiving."

"Layla, I think you're just questioning your past because you're unhappy in the present." She pats my arm. "Trust me. I was there. You were happy and you deserve to be."

"I really don't know, Ferri. I remember spending hours and hours playing alongside the boys when I was a young girl, filling up jars with insects. The boys all thought I'd be afraid of the creeping things because I was a girl. But I loved watching the jars fill up until they were brown with all those crawling bodies, hundreds of crawling legs. I watched as they hit one another, climbing up, trying to escape."

"And?"

"Well, now that I'm trapped inside Rostam's world, I feel like one of those bugs." I shrug. "I've decided that freedom is a basic desire, an instinct."

Ferri takes my hand in hers and looks into my eyes. Her's are two pools of compassion. "Freedom *is* sweet *Joonie*," she says, smiling at me. "That's why I demonstrate."

I so love this woman!

I hug her. I don't want to let her go.

"I envy you, Ferri. I always have. You've always been your own person. You've done as you pleased. Followed your beliefs. I envy your courage." I sigh. Ferri is the only person I can be honest with.

"I want more than anything to leave Rostam, but I can't. I don't have that kind of courage anymore. I tried and failed, and I won't

75

try again." I shake my head. It's futile. "I can't even leave my house without a spy."

She's silent.

"I just can't forgive myself. I know this life is the result of choices *I* made. I *chose* to give up the freedom to do what I want and live my life as I want. I *chose* to abandon Jasmine. Now, I can only wonder how my child is, where she is, pray that I'll see her one day, and pray that David is still alive."

With no one around whom I could speak candidly to, I haven't had the opportunity to take a moment to hear my own thoughts. I am surprised at how depressed I sound.

We're both quiet until Ferri surprises me. "I checked with the post office for a while." She is speaking hesitatingly, as though unsure how I'll react to what she has to say. "I … I used to check the post office from time to time … for the first two or three years. You know, just to see if there was any mail for you from Los Angeles." I stare at her. She is too good a person, too good of a friend. I'd never have guessed she would do that. "I … I didn't want to miss the chance that Linda or Adam may have written to you, sent you a photo … In any event, there's never been anything."

I'm overcome with love for her. Even though we two hadn't spoken, she'd done this.

"Thank you."

Books fall and the thud reminds me it is time to leave.

"Ferri, I should go. I'm afraid he'll come in to look for me if I stay too long. Let's meet again. This is a perfect place. You can't call me. You know that. Let's just agree to meet here two Thursdays from today. Okay? If I'm not here, it's because I couldn't come, and we'll meet the following week."

"*Joonie*, I'd love that. But I have schoolwork and exam time is coming. Let's make it the first Thursday next month at four. Okay?"

I agree. We hug. I leave the bookstore holding the two books I grabbed and paid for.

Seated back in the car, I say to Hassan, "That's a wonderful bookstore."

He looks at me through the rearview mirror, surprise registered on his face. It isn't often that I volunteer to speak to him.

I sit with a wry smile on my face. *I have done it!* I've outsmarted the bastard, and I've seen my angel! And I will see her again!

The paradox isn't lost on either of us that our secret haven is a bookstore – our favorite place as schoolgirls.

13

DAVID!

1973

$\mathcal{I}$ dreamed of him last night.

He took me in his arms and danced with me. He reached out to hold me, and my universe took the form of his face, its light from his eyes, my life source from his floating breaths.

He drew me close, and I bathed in the fragrance of his skin, so intoxicatingly sweet. As the heat of his body burned slowly through to me, I was caught in the web of his arms, so strong, and his breath, so gentle. His full lips, as vulnerable as my heart, were mine.

Then he took that final step that pivoted my being and rendered me his. We were part of one another and moved together, held together without effort or thought, dancing to a soft ballad of bittersweet love. And when desire pushed us even closer and I pressed against his male warmth, we celebrated the love between us.

I awoke twice during the night, my heartbeat irregular from sheer bliss, and when I fell back asleep, he was still there with me.

"I will love you for as long as I live and forever after that," he said.

He pulled away and I awoke with a start.

I linger in bed, not wanting to separate from him. My heart is still quivering. I still see him holding me, loving me.

Yet beyond our love there is fear. I don't understand why he's visited me now ... or ... I do. I am frightened because we were meant to be together, but we are not.

My great regret is losing David.

David Kline was the shining star of my life.

He was surely the hallmark of my American adventure.

I knew I could never marry him. I simply could not present an American Jewish husband to my parents. I was expected to marry an Iranian man when I returned to Iran. I knew that. Nonetheless, the moment I met David I dove headfirst into an ocean of love with no idea how strong the tides of love were or how helpless they would render me when I finally lost him.

I was to save my virginity for my husband. That was an Iranian girl's First Commandment, Second Commandment and so on.

Because of that, I steadfastly refused to sleep with him despite hundreds of mutual proclamations of love – until I thought I'd lost him to another girl. My reluctance flew out the window then. I could not let him go. I was certain he had met a Jewish girl while in Israel who had slept with him. That was her allure. I would not let her have him.

I decided that I would never love another man as much as I loved David. The decision was made. I decided I would give my virginity to him. He could not leave me, knowing that I'd given him my most cherished possession.

And so, I seduced him.

I had never guessed that physical love could be so extraordinary, so totally magical. I was his completely and we made love as we'd been born to meld together in ecstasy. There was a liquidity of movement that allowed me to luxuriate in wanton abandon, a wondrous joy. Submerged in love, I experienced complete freedom. No decision. No indecision. No margin for thought. Only blissful submission.

At breakfast in the coffee shop the morning, I discovered there had never been another girl. David had become enamored of Israel after his trip there, while was in Tehran for my first summer home.

Amid the enemies surrounding its borders, the young, desert country was determined to blossom, and my David was determined to be a part of that. As there was no stopping Israel, determined to survive and flourish, so there was no stopping David, intent on contributing what he could to the country. As a doctor, he would be a medic in the Israeli army.

Over toast and eggs, he proposed to me. He begged me to join my life to his, to go to Israel with him and be at his side.

"You know how much I love you," he said, "you're everything to me. Marry me, Princess. We'll go together."

I cried. I pleaded with him to stay. I sobbed. I begged him not to go. I yearned to keep him in my life a little longer. His proposal and my refusal signaled the death of our relationship. He wiped my flowing tears with those strong, soft, warm hands I so loved.

He couldn't understand my hesitation when the night before had proven my love for him. I remember the words I spoke, words that strangled a future together.

"I can't call my parents and say, 'Hi, Babajon, Maman. I'm calling to say I'm in love with an American named David. You've never met him. You see, I gave him my virginity last night and we're getting married because I love him. Oh, did I tell you he's Jewish? And by the way, I'm not going to be coming home. I won't be finishing UCLA either – which was why I came here in the first place. No, you see, David has decided that we will live in Israel on a lovely *kibbutz* in poverty under the constant threat of war because, you must understand, they need doctors like David, my Jewish doctor."

Stupid me! I actually believed I had to let him go.

"I can't just get up and marry you, leave everything, my heritage and who I am, my family, my studies, marry you and go off to Israel," I said. "There are people around us who love us. We have obligations to them."

Stupid, stupid me!

He tried to tell me that nothing mattered but our being together. He tried to tell me I was wrong to put our religions, my parents' judgment, or anything else ahead of our love, a love that few people find in their lifetime. I have only myself to blame.

Stupid, stupid, stupid me!

Months after he left for Israel, I learned I was pregnant. He would never have left me if he'd known I was carrying his child and would have returned if he knew, but I had no way to contact him. At some point, I went to his parents' house to ask his address and was told David was missing and unofficially presumed dead, but I would have known if he had died. I would have felt it.

I was certain the man I loved was alive and, through the years, I have prayed that the man whose memories have fueled me through my darkest times still lives.

And then that dream …

I eagerly anticipate every meeting with my angel.

As usual, we meet at the bookstore on a Thursday. And, as usual, I am worried about my friend, evermore the activist.

The last time we'd met, Ferri was understandably upset. She told me she had gotten a call from a fellow professor at the University of Tehran who had been visiting West Germany. She had spoken with such passion, as though she was sharing a most exciting secret, and, I suppose in a sense it was a secret as none of the Iranian media had covered the story.

"Shah and his wife had an embarrassing time in West Germany," she had said. I asked why. "Over 5,000 Iranian students demonstrated against them a few days ago and a riot broke out. Over forty people were hurt, half of them policemen, and there were almost fifty arrests. One student was shot in the head by a policeman and died."

As I enter the bookstore today, I am eager to know if she has calmed down. As usual, she is already in the rear of the store. I run to her and throw my arms around her. Hers wrap around me and won't let go.

"Look at you!" I say. "You're wearing fishnets!" In place of her usual black knee-highs or black pants, Ferri is wearing the latest craze in stockings. It is the first time I've seen her succumb to fashion in all the years I've known her.

When Ferri does not respond to my outburst, I realize she hasn't met me with her usual bright smile. Her expression is somber. I'm alarmed.

"What's wrong, Ferri?" I ask. Her eyes are so very sad. "What is it?"

I know something has happened, something bad. My mind jumps to the worst and I guess that her secret liaisons with Hamid have finally been discovered. No, perhaps Hamid has been arrested, or a family member has met with some calamity.

"What's happened?"

She simply stares at me, seemingly at a loss for words. Then slowly, her eyes on mine, she holds out a folded a copy of The International Herald Tribune. The banner headline reads, *War Erupts in Israel!*

With shaking hands, I take the paper from her. The lead article reads, "Planes and Tanks in Action!" I glance back up at her sad face and I know. My legs go weak.

Somewhere in the article, she has underlined a sentence in blue ink. *With the patrol and also killed in the attack was Dr. David Kline, a medical field officer in the Israeli army.*

Ferri is ready to catch me as I fall.

I can't begin to imagine how difficult it must have been for her to break the news. Ferri has always known what David was to me. When I realized I had lost my child, our tears had joined. Now, to be the one to tell me this ….

On October 6 this year, Egypt and Syria attacked Israel on Yom Kippur, the holiest day of the Jewish calendar, in the hope of regaining territory in the Golan Heights, lost to Israel six years earlier during the 1967 war.

In their attempt to oust Israeli troops from the area, Egyptian troops found their way into the Sinai Peninsula and attacked the Israeli Defense Forces by surprise. Israel's counterattack recaptured the area, and a cease-fire went into effect nineteen days later. The war ended.

But wars cost lives. Men died.

Ferri has the presence of mind to stop me from taking the marked copy of the article home. I manage to compose myself as I make it to the car. Sitting in the backseat, I find enough voice to instruct Hassan to stop and purchase a copy of that day's International Herald Tribune. He mutters under his breath as he hands me the paper. "Iranian papers are no longer worthy of Khanom?"

It is not until I am in the solitude of my bathroom behind the locked door with the paper on my lap that I break down. I read the article carefully from top to bottom. There it is, David's name among the six Israelis killed in the attack.

I mourn David's death in private.

That wonderful, man, those gentle hands, that warm, caring heart, that intelligence, that incredible voice and gorgeous face, Jasmine's father ... the love of my life is dead! Killed in the land he went to heal, the country I lost him to.

He gave his life for what? War? Israel? Judaism? Damn religion! *Was it worth David's life?* I immediately answer myself. He believed it was.

～

Knowing how much he loved Israel, its people, and what it stood for, I pray his parents will deem it appropriate to bury him there.

He had loved Israel. In the end, he gave his life up believing it was worth the cause, while I have given up mine for an empty life in a country I can't leave.

I want desperately to go to the old synagogue on the outskirts of the city to ask the rabbi to say a prayer for him and light a candle in his memory. Perhaps David will feel my presence there. But I have no doubt The Rat would accompany me, and it is impossible to think of an excuse I could present to Rostam that would justify my desire to travel to the Jewish quarters in the city, let alone to enter a synagogue. Ferri, my Jewish angel, promises me she will see to it that the rabbi recites the appropriate prayers for him.

With David gone, I am completely devoid of any hope that I will ever again love or be loved. I realize I'd harbored the fantasy that I might miraculously find myself together with David in the future. That fantasy has been destroyed. I must accept the fact that this loveless life is all there will ever be for me.

I have no choice but to be stoic. I will discipline myself, thicken

84

my skin even more, and give up any dream of happiness and all hope of escape. I will humble myself and be thankful for what I have.

And there is still Jasmine.

If I have learned nothing else, I have learned that life can change drastically with the next wind. So, I continue to cling to the hope that a miracle will one day unite me with our child.

I mourn my David and turn my attention to living my daily life, albeit as a ghost.

14

AT THE RESTAURANT

1974

*I*t's another oven-hot summer.

Day after day the sky is blue. The air is as dry as an oven and has that stillness that comes when the season of storms has passed. The full trees show off their greens, and fragrant flowers proudly display a variety of colors.

I have kept to myself throughout these summer days, spending time in our gardens. The hues and scents of the various flowers soothe me some. I hear the buzzing of insects as I sit comfortably in the shade and read my books, sipping cold water imbued with the attar of roses or cucumbers.

At the height of summer, with The Rat creeping around, I don't dare wear anything more revealing than a summer dress, so only my s and legs turn berry brown.

This evening, we meet Shireen and Taymoor for dinner at a favored restaurant.

As the four of us make our way to the outside table we'd reserved, we pass a very pregnant woman, with two toddlers at her skirt. Shireen watches her until the three turn the corner and we take our seats, then she speaks.

"It's just not fair! Men don't appreciate what we women go through to have children." Taymoor strokes her . She looks at him accusingly. "Did you see that woman? She has two little children and is pregnant again!" She shakes her head. "Well, I'm done with pregnancy and babies!"

"What do you mean?" Rostam parts his dark lips, the color of a bruise, and bears his yellow teeth in a cross between a smile and a sneer. He means to put the little lady in her place. "You won't open your legs for your husband anymore?" His tone is at once daring and patronizing.

"Oh, I'll open my legs," Shireen says boldly, "but no more pregnancies. I've joined the rush on birth control pills." She looks pleased with herself.

I watch as Rostam starts to smile, then hesitates for a millisecond and turns away from her. His raised hand pauses in the air for the slightest moment before connecting his cigarette to his lips.

I can see the light in his eyes switch on, and in that moment, I know that he knows. He says nothing. He simply inhales his cigarette and passes a palm over his thigh. He is unusually quiet – even solemn – the rest of the night, watching me from the corner of his eye as understanding takes him over.

He remains silent on the drive home. I sit in the back seat alongside him, looking at his profile hyphenated in the light cast by street lamps, feeling very uncomfortable. No, this is fear I'm feeling.

Finally, I must break the silence. "Shireen looked well," I say. His response is a torrent of smoke exhaled out his open car window.

When we enter the house, he storms into our bedroom. He is a cyclone of silent action.

Had we met Shireen and her husband for dinner *last* night like we were supposed to, there would be no pills for him to find. They would be already at the bottom of the big blue Kotex box in the back of the bathroom cabinet along with the few pieces of jewelry that I've kept from him. I always hide them there every month.

But Shireen had begged off last night, saying she had a bad headache. As a result, we pushed our dinner date forward one night. Now, there is nothing I can do but watch as he opens my dresser drawers and dumps their contents on the floor. I watch and wait. It is inevitable. He will soon find the packet of pills I've brought home this very afternoon. It is just a matter of minutes – no seconds – until he opens the right drawer ... or the wrong drawer.

I want to run. I want to hide.

"Here!" Rostam is holding the crushed packet of pills in one hand and turns, swinging at me with his other. His fist hits me on the side of my head with the full momentum of his turn. I am knocked to the floor. As my butt hits the ground, the room spins around me.

"You pig! *Jendeh!* You whore! Your husband fucks you and you take pills because you don't want a child?" He raises the fist holding the crushed pills above his head. I am sure he is about to hit me again. "All this time, you've taken these in secret? You don't want to be a mother? What kind of a person are you? What kind of a *woman* are you?"

I want to ask him what kind of an idiot he is if he still can't see the obvious: I am the kind of woman who does not want his child. But he doesn't seem to care about what I want just then.

"How *dare* you? How *dare* you? You will not make a fool of me any longer!" he booms. "You will never make a fool of Rostam again!" He goes for my hair and grabs it, pulling it and me up. "Do you hear me? Never! And you *will* bear me a son."

And then he rapes me.

15

SURPRISE!

August, 1974

This is not my first pregnancy.

Yes, it's early, but I know the signs. The night Rostam confiscated my monthly packet of birth control pills and raped me, he impregnated me. The doctor says it can happen. She's right. It happened. I am with child.

I panic. This pregnancy is the result of rape. It is not the first time the brute has raped me. The bastard will go unpunished again. No one will know how violent he is and how he abuses me. He does not have to answer to anyone, and that injustice adds to my raw pain. My hatred of him and his barbarism, his feeling of entitlement, is monumental. Once again, I am his victim.

I am thinking of how I can end this pregnancy.

My thoughts are starting to shift away from Rostam and his violence to the new life forming inside my belly.

I know I can find a way to end this pregnancy. I've done it before.

But do I want to?

What do I want?

Sitting quietly, undisturbed, I think about who I am today and what I want now. Not what Rostam, or Maman, or Tallat Khanom, or anyone else wants. What Layla Saleh wants.

What do I want?

I want to turn each of my past mistakes into a rung on a ladder I can climb to experience some happiness in my life, making up for all the hardships I have endured.

How do I do that?

I begin to imagine what it would be like to have this child.

My immediate thought is how different these months of pregnancy would be from the nine months I carried Jasmine.

This pregnancy – this child – wouldn't be a secret that could destroy my life. No, in place of the shame and desolation I'd experienced when I was pregnant while at UCLA, the announcement of this pregnancy would be celebrated. This baby would be more than welcomed into the world by everyone. In fact, they might shout out the news from the mosque's minaret along with the daily calls to prayer.

This pregnancy could be also be a chance for me to atone for having abandoned Jasmine. I'd never leave this baby. No matter what happens, I would *never* abandon this baby.

I would make sure my daughter is protected. I would never allow her to be abused by Rostam or anyone else. Nor would I force her to marry or tell her who to wed. We would talk about men, marriage, sex, and love. I might share the life lessons I've learned, but I'd let her make her own mistakes as well. In short, I would do the opposite of everything Maman did with me.

I see this pregnancy as a chance to mother honorably.

Perhaps this could be the start of a new life for me.

I am not the same woman I was when I began taking those pills. My youth has passed. I am in my thirties – thirty-two to be exact – and feelings of isolation, loneliness, and the pointlessness of it all, are exhausting. Every day is like every other day, with nothing to look forward to. This child can change my life.

Mothering can only enhance my life with a fresh start, new experiences, a chance to feel fulfillment, and perhaps know some happiness. Raising a child will give meaning to my days. It will be the perfect answer to this apathy that protects me from my pain.

And I have longed for love to return to my life. I yearn to love unconditionally again. I am anxious to nurture someone, care for someone, put someone first in my heart and give of myself, completely. My child will take all the affection I have bottled away.

The flood of positive thoughts and feelings I have about this pregnancy surprises me, and soon, I'm thanking God for this chance to redeem myself. I even silently thank Rostam for giving me this child, though I don't begin to forgive his abuse.

I will have something to live for at last.

This daughter will give me a new start. I will name my daughter Bahar, which means spring, for she will herald the new start of my life.

Not surprisingly, when I announce my condition, my long-awaited pregnancy is welcomed by many. When my belly pops out almost immediately, the women say it is my pride sticking out. No one has guessed it is because this is not my first pregnancy. Only Ferri knows that.

Rostam is certain it's a boy. After all, he is as deserving as His Majesty. If Rostam is right, I will do everything I can to ensure that my son is nothing at all like his father, neither egotistical nor cruel. He will grow to be a blend of David and Babajon. He will be kind, charitable, compassionate, appreciative, and joyful.

I am committed.

It is December, my sixth month of pregnancy, and I am preparing to attend a gathering at Shireen and Taymoor's home celebrating Yalda, the winter solstice, the longest night of the year.

I have just bathed, and I'm drying myself when Rostam enters without knocking and sees me naked. Looking up, I see a look of disgust on his face.

"You look hideous!" he says with that sneer I know so well. "I don't know how anyone could ever think pregnancy is beautiful. A pregnant woman should never be seen naked. You truly look disgusting!"

The audacity to call me hideous!

I want to strangle the insensitive bastard! The man disgusts me.

With three months left to go, I tire easily and have begun suffering from an aching back and legs. I'm pregnant as the result of his rape, pregnant with the child he so wanted. Yet not once has he touched my swollen belly or evinced any desire to feel his baby kick.

I remember how Adam and Linda had loved to put their hands on my belly and feel the waves of Jasmine's movements. I've seen Taymoor put his lips to Shireen's huge belly to plant kisses there and heard him speak to his unborn child. I can only imagine how David would have behaved had he been with me when I was pregnant with Jasmine. I wonder if Shah thought his pregnant wife looked disgusting.

And if he did, did he tell her?

I didn't think it possible to resent Rostam's belligerent thoughtlessness any more than I already have, but this episode is a new low. There is simply nothing about him, not a morsel of anything that I can respect.

Yes, this will be Rostam's child. But it will be mine as well, and I will guard my child from his malice.

By my calculations, my due date is sometime in March.

I take my morning sickness as reassurance.

I will have this child.

16

RITE OF THE RING

March, 1975

Spring has returned, and the gardens begins to flourish as I approach my due date.

My favorite flowers, narcissus, and hyacinths, begin to blossom and bloom. The temperature in the city is rising by degrees and I welcome the warmth and each passing day that brings me closer to meeting my child.

Shireen and Taymoor have included us in their gathering tonight, the last we will attend before Norooz, the Persian new year.

As always, when we drive up their circular driveway it is impossible to miss the giant statue of Shireen that stands on the vast front lawn. I remember my reaction the first time I saw the giant statue. I was amazed at my cousin's massive ego and baffled at the lengths her husband had taken to cater to it. The first time Rostam saw it, his reaction was very different. He said he'd make certain his statue would look more like him and that the marble would have no veins. Surprisingly, he has not yet commissioned a sculptor to do the job.

We enter the huge box of marble and mirrors and I begin to circle the guests seated along the perimeter of the huge salon. Chairs line the walls and spill into the adjacent room, lining those walls as well.

Making my way past the large Venetian mirrors, the life-sized bronze statues, the huge urns, the gilded clocks, and the French furniture, my low heels click on the white marble floor as I pay my respects and issue greetings to the seated guests. They all merge into a sort of never ending, hand-holding, cheek-kissing monster and I wish we had arrived earlier, so I could sit and be greeted, rather than having to make these interminable rounds. It is exhausting.

I catch sight of Maman sitting in her usual spot on the couch about midway through this circle. Smiling, and bowing slightly several times in the general direction of those whom I have not yet greeted, I head her way. She is wearing her formal party smile. No doubt, she is happy to show off my huge belly and the jewels Rostam has chosen to take out of his safe for me wear tonight.

As I make my way to her, I am hailed by Shohreh and Marlie, two high school classmates. At Shireen's reunion tea that first summer I'd spent home from UCLA, they had both encouraged me to forget my "meecro-whatever" studies at UCLA, stay in Tehran, and marry a rich man. Both women are already mothers, and Marlie is visibly pregnant again. But other than their thicker waistlines, they haven't changed at all. They are still impeccably made up and manicured, with perfectly coiffured hairstyles, wearing the latest designer-silk pantsuits, expensive jewelry, and made-to-last smiles mastered years ago. Tonight, as they welcome me with open arms, I feel the sharp pang of self-loathing. I was a holdout who betrayed my own principles. Their lives have gone on as they had. I am the one who has changed. Before, I had pitied these women. Now, as I listen to their prattle, I envy their apparent lack of bitterness. I tolerate their advice about nannies and the jabs they make at their husbands for barely a minute before taking my leave.

As I continue on my way to Maman, I catch sight of Rostam's back. He is standing in the middle of the second salon, holding a drink in one hand and a cigarette in the other, apparently engaged in conversation. His large frame makes it impossible for me to see who he's speaking to. Then he leans toward an ashtray on the coffee table to his left and the man who stands before him comes into my view. When my eyes fall on the stranger, our eyes lock and I feel flushed. His chocolate brown eyes seem to pierce through to my soul. In the next second, Rostam is back, covering the man like a wide curtain. I want to meet this mystery man, and I'm about to join the two of them when I hear my mother, whom I have momentarily forgotten, call my name. I turn and continue towards her, still feeling strangely connected to the phantom man. His face, those eyes … he is etched somewhere in my heart.

Just as I am to reach Maman, she leaves the couch and makes her way to the dining room. I follow. Babajon is in the dining room as well.

On the wall above them looms a blowup of the autographed photo of Elizabeth Taylor signed, "To my friend, Shireen." With all her trappings of wealth, this photo of her idol I'd mailed her from California is easily one of my cousin's most cherished possessions. I love it too, for it reminds me of happier times spent in Los Angeles … another lifetime.

Long tables are set along each wall of the dining room, all set elaborately and overstocked with food. Multiple servants are present. Everything looks perfect – except for a lone piece of *zolubia*, a sweet, fried pastry that has fallen on the floor by the dessert table and has, as yet been undetected by the servants. I fight the momentary urge to pick it up when Babajon greets me warmly, as usual.

"Look at my Golden Girl," he announces as though I were royalty. People nearby turn to look at me. "Does she not look wonderful?" He chuckles. "She looks even more beautiful pregnant."

My lips curl.

How I love my father! What a difference between him and the father of the baby I carry! And again, it strikes me just how very lucky my mother is.

"How are you, Babajon?"

"Far too excited about becoming a grandfather. You know, too much excitement isn't good for me." He sits down, feigning exhaustion. "Can't you hurry this up?" he asks.

"I'll see what I can do," I answer.

"No, you won't!" Maman's tone is stern. "You'll do nothing of the kind! This is one time you will *not* listen to your father!"

She catches herself and quickly scans the room until she's satisfied no one has witnessed her spontaneous outburst.

"Layla *jon*, sit. Rest," she says, calmly.

Babajon offers me his seat. "With your permission, ladies," he says, "I am going to say hello to some friends. Zahra *jon*, I will be back soon. And I will see you, my Golden Girl." He kisses me on the forehead and walks away.

My Aunt Haideh appears. "Ah, you're here, Layla *joon*! We've been looking for you." She takes hold of my hand. "Let's go see what's in there," she says, pointing to my belly.

Maman and I follow her out of the dining room. She calls for Shireen and Tallat Khanom to join us. Nana Joon and Aunt Bahia have also joined the procession.

On our way, we pass Rostam. He has left the phantom man and is watching Taymoor and another guest play chess. "If I could play this game," he muses, "I would be superb. I'm sure I'd beat you both."

I look away.

We enter a bedroom.

I am told to lay down on the bed and remove my wedding band. Aunt Haideh takes it and ties it to a thin piece of string she holds over my belly. I've seen this done with other pregnant women. It is a custom meant to determine the baby's sex. If the ring moves in a circle, the test predicts a boy. If the hair swung back and forth, it signals a girl.

When they first hold the string above me, it goes back and forth for a few seconds, then slowly starts to circle. It's signaling I'm carrying a boy. Maman clasps her hands to her chest and glows. But the women hem and haw, unsure of the result.

"Give it to me," Naneh Joon says.

There is silence among the women as my grandmother takes the dangling ring from Aunt Haideh and holds it over my belly. This time the string moves in a clean circle from the outset.

Khaleh Bahia shouts, "I knew it! it's a boy!"

Maman has her hand at her heart. Her mouth hangs open. My jubilant mother-in-law nudges her. "I have been saying it's a boy. She's carrying high."

The women clap their hands and shout, *"Mobarrak, Shozdeh daree!* Congratulations, you have a prince!"

And then comes their high-pitched wailing of *lee-lee-lee-lee*, the sound of rejoicing.

17
MY SON

1975

$\mathcal{M}$y child, you have been preparing to be born for many months.

Today is March 15 and you are due at any moment. I look for signs that you are ready to start your journey into this world. I clock your slightest signal, your lightest move.

And I await.

My water breaks as I stand over the sink this morning, brushing my teeth.

Hassan drives us to the hospital, Rostam urging him to go faster and faster, screaming at him every few seconds to be more careful where he is going. I concentrate on my breathing.

My son is born on March 17, 1975, four days before Norooz.

Labor is nothing like the arduous day I had spent at the UCLA hospital awaiting Jasmine's birth. With no one to greet her and nothing to look forward to, Jasmine had no reason to hurry into this world. In contrast, my son springs out of my loins, and within two hours of arriving at the hospital, I am the mother of a seven-pound, six-ounce son.

I am immediately enamored of the baby the nurse puts in my s. The start of this new year will be the start of a new life for me.

Rostam insists that only a name good enough for the Crown Prince will do for his son and names him Ali Reza, then almost always addresses him as Shozdeh, which means Prince.

He insists that we bury his foreskin in an "illustrious" place. "Stupid woman!" he says. "Don't you know anything? Listen and learn. If Rostam wants Shozdeh, my little prince, to be a judge, his foreskin shall be buried under the courthouse. If Rostam wants him to be a banker, it shall be buried under Iran's largest bank and so on."

I listen to this stupidity. Instead of arising my rancor, it only amuses me.

"Professor?" he continues. "No." Of course not. "What does Rostam want Shozdeh to be?" He actually believes I care and pauses before answering to heighten the suspense. "Rostam wants his son to be great! He is destined for greatness, no doubt. Destined to be a great leader, the greatest our country has ever known. That will make Rostam proud. So, my stupid little wife, his foreskin shall be buried under … hmm, let me think. The Palace or Parliament?" He paces as he mulls this over, his hand at his chin, scratching. Finally, he says, "I think Parliament. Yes, Parliament. Then, once he is our country's leader, Shozdeh can decide if he wants to be King."

I simply nod and say, "Fine."Rostam can do as he likes with Reza's foreskin. I only want the rest of him.

I hold my infant to my breast. He is perfect, so innocent. I vow for the hundredth time that I will be the very best mother to him.

As the days pass, his father has little to do with his son, and I pray his lack of participation will continue forever.

I want to bond with my child, to come to know everything about him and cater to his needs. I refuse to pass his care over to a nanny other than when necessary. As a result, my days are busy.

I am at peace with the world.

The two of us enjoying a cup of *chai,* sitting in one of the gardens.

Maman is understandably delighted that she finally has a grandchild. She had endured anxiety, and unkind remarks veiled as sympathy – in particular, from Rostam's mother – far too long and had blamed my lack of fertility on the evil eye. *"Sheshm zadan,"* she would say, "they have given us the evil eye."

Now, with the arrival of the long-awaited baby and the fact that it is a boy, so treasured in our culture, Maman is ever on close alert for the evil eye. When someone comments that I look well, or, that my baby is beautiful, Maman's immediate response is, *"Begoo mush'allah!* Say, 'well done; Allah's wish has come true." She believes those words effectively repel the evil eye of jealousy that lurks behind compliments.

"Just let them try to call you a *jendeh,* whore, now," Maman says out of the blue. She bears a self-satisfied smile. She gazes down at the sleeping infant in her arms. She looks as pleased as I've ever seen her.

"Has someone called me that?" I ask.

"No. But when a woman doesn't conceive, things can get ugly. Your husband and his parents could have made it an excuse for him to leave a perfectly good wife. They could have used it — or searched for some other alibi — and righteously divorce you and remarry so he could have a child. He could have said you've always been a *jendeh,* a whore."

If she only knew!

"But Maman, you have the virginity napkin from our wedding night to show them. It has my blood on it."

Maman looks at me from the corner of her eye. "They are not stupid villagers, Layla. Blood is blood."

Her statement amazes me! Ferri had said those exact words to me: *If you love David, sleep with him and marry an Iranian later,* she'd said. *Don't worry. There are ways of cheating your husband with the virginity napkin. After all, blood is blood.* The truth is, that when I lost my virginity to David, hardly a drop of blood had shown on the sheets.

Life is a circus!

"So, now I am a mother," I say to Maman. "You can relax."

"Yes. I have a grandson! A *shozdeh,* a prince! You are secure at last! They will never dare say one bad word against the mother of their first-born grandson and their heir. Nor would Rostam allow it."

I do not tell Maman that Rostam is the master of sham, the master of illusion. If he does not allow a bad word against me, it is only because, at that moment, it does not suit his purposes. I know, without a doubt, that if I ever again try to leave Rostam, he will tell his parents, my parents, and the world, whatever lies are needed to keep them from even wanting to help me. I rub my temples.

"Are you alright, Layla? Do you need to lay down?" This kindness is new.

"No, I'm fine."

Tonight in bed, I think about how absurd my life has been, the times I stood at the threshold of a fork in the road and I wonder how different my life would have been if, each time, I had chosen the path other than the one I followed.

What if I hadn't decided to leave Iran so unexpectedly and travel to America for college? What if I had not slept with David? Not gotten pregnant? What if I had accepted his marriage proposal and had gone to Israel with him? What if I hadn't decided to separate from Jasmine? What if I hadn't married Rostam? What if I hadn't caused that miscarriage? What if … a million things.

The list goes on and on. With my mind swimming, I leave my bed and go to my son's room where I stand, gazing at him in his crib. I lift him and hold him in my arms. He doesn't stir. I feel his tiny body, so fragile. I smell his beautiful round head, so warm in my arms. The scent is like nothing else is the world. My heart expands and I know nothing but my love for this child.

I walk around the house for a bit with Reza in my s before returning him to his crib with a last kiss until morning and return to bed. Whatever other bad decision I may have made, the decision to have this baby was the right one.

I am struck with a pang of guilt — no, a feeling of great remorse. I never allowed myself to face my true feelings about Jasmine; I held myself back from accepting my love for her, David's child, the baby I had nurtured and bore. Still laying on the delivery table, I had turned my head away and had refused to hold her; I'd felt nothing but shame. Now it is the recollection of that feeling of shame, my total failure to acknowledge my beautiful daughter that shames me.

Falling asleep, I recall a lecture given by my favorite professor at UCLA. It was intriguing ideas like his that had made me increasingly fascinated with my chosen field.

Rene Dubos believed the study of microbiology improves the quality of human life. Professor Dubos' studies had concluded that those who live a longer, healthier life were not those who had experienced the least amount of struggle, danger, or illness.

Rather, it was those who had shown the most *resilience* in the face of their challenges.

I look back at the events of my life so far. Although I have had my fair share of challenges, losses, and unexpected changes in my life, I have survived them all. Surely, that shows resilience!

Added to that, I am finally doing something that really matters to me, namely, caring for my son. If Dubos' theory is right, I can look forward to a long, healthy life. Hopefully, from here on, my days will be happier. *Resilience* is the key.

I must remain resilient.

18

ZAHRA KHANOM GLOATS

1977

I am tired this morning.

Well, I suppose I'm not as young as I used to be. After all, I turned fifty last month, though both my bearing and my face is that of a woman no more than forty. I look at photos of myself from a decade ago and can honestly say, I haven't changed. Unlike other women, I haven't gained weight with the years, haven't taken on a matronly figure, that widening through my middle. I could wear the same clothes I wore when I was in my thirties – though, of course, I never would.

Still, the years leave their mark. There was a time I could entertain night after night, never feeling a thing. But after last night's celebration, I'm feeling lazy this morning. I don't want to leave my bed. Granted, it was a special night that required special preparations, It's not every night a woman throws a party on her grandson's second birthday.

And what a grandson *Gorbonnesh beram!* May I be sacrificed for him. *Meemeeram barrash!* I would die for him! He's adorable and so smart! And he's so good natured! He made me so proud in front of everyone.

He is the boy I would have had if Allah had blessed me with the son Hadi so deserved. Allah did not heed my prayers. I know I've failed him in that single area. Though I have done so well in every area, I have never hidden the truth from myself that despite my background, my high class and no matter how fine a home I've kept, without a son I have not been as good a wife as those who have presented their husband with a son. That is my one failing. Now at last, Hadi can feel the joy of watching a small boy grow into a man — *ensha Allah,* God willing, if my husband's heart allows.

I had hoped and prayed that Layla's husband might be like a son to my dear husband, but it has turned out that they are not close. I am not complaining. No, *shokreh Khodah!* thank God! Rostam provides well for my daughter. The man could never dream of the life she'd led in America or of how he was duped. I thank myself for my artful ploy.

Yet there is something strange about the man.

Why does he speak of himself as 'Rostam' instead of saying 'me?' It's as if he's speaking of someone else!

And his constant smoking! How can Layla stand to be near him? I enjoy the occasional cigarette, but this man is unable to breath longer than a minute without lighting up! His teeth are dark yellow. He's like a cigarette-smoking factory.

In all these years, I have not heard Rostam speak intelligently about poetry, politics, science — even sports – or any topic other men are interested in. I assume he knows the music business well; after all, he's extremely successful. Still, it is a shame that he is nothing at all like a son to Hadi. In fact, he doesn't even seem to be close to his own father. But I cannot complain. The man accepted my corrupted daughter as a virgin and is none the wiser.

Without a doubt, Layla has finally done well for us after all. My daughter is beautiful, smart, married to a very wealthy man, and the mother of a brilliant boy, a *shozdeh*, a prince!

Still, my heart did yearn for a son-in-law that Hadi would have been closer to. The two share nothing in common and have little to say to one another. Rostam is wealthy, yes, but he is uneducated. He knows nothing of Rumi or Hafez, can't recite a single poem and doesn't appreciate the poetry Hadi recites so beautifully.

Hadi has often asked me if I believe our daughter to be truly happy with Rostam. I have continually reassure him; no man would have been good enough for his "golden girl." He should not worry or stress. I tell him that if she were unhappy, she would tell us. As long as she doesn't complain, she is happy.

Why wouldn't she be? She's married to a very wealthy man and anyone can see he treats her like a queen. She has anything and everything she could want. Why, some of her jewelry even rivals Shireen's! And now the girl is the mother of a fine boy.

Her husband could never dream of what her life was life before him or how he was duped. I thank myself for that artful ploy. Allah was with me the day I had the doctor restore her virginity. I gave Layla her life back, though she didn't know it then. Hadi will never know how close we came to complete disaster! In three days Layla would have gone back to that hellhole they call Amreeka. God knows that would have become of her and our good name then!

Vye, vye! I shudder to think of it even now. Because of me she has this wonderful life. I am so proud of that.

And Rostam's mother, that bitch, has been dancing for my daughter ever since she gave birth to her only grandson. How long did I tolerate her instructions on what my daughter had to do to become pregnant? Now Layla can do no wrong in her eyes.

And Haideh? How much longer could I watch as my brother's

wife welcomed one grandchild after the other while I had none? Of course, theyre all girls. I don't mention it to her, of course. I say nothing. Still, she must envy me my grandson.

How long I waited and prayed for a grandson!

Last night's affair was another huge success. The food was diving. The musicians were excellent and people danced all night. And Ali Reza's birthday cake! No one could get over it. The exact replica of the child himself. I can still hear the gasps when the cake was rolled in. And delicious! I will have a slice with my breakfast this morning.

Motherhood has changed Layla. She seems far more content. She is *sangeen* now, more dignified, as well she should be. She's happily married and doesn't speak a word of germs and her miserable *meecrobio*-whatever anymore. That is a sign of how happy she is.

And she's still so lovely. We share that lack of self-consciousness, but I see how women eye her with envy and men watch her when she enters a room even now. Her coloring, reminiscent of early dusk, is unlike either mine or Hadi's. And her wide, hazel eyes with those think black lashes that curl so luxuriously upward to her perfectly arched brows and her long, elegant neck … that thick chestnut hair — that, unlike Shireen and the others, she's had the good sense not to cut short — and her full lips, the high cheek bones she inherited from me … it's no wonder Rostam adores her so.

I have the good fortune I deserve. It is not luck. I am responsible for Layla's happiness, for my grandson, and for my choice of husband. And what a wonderful husband I have! Hadi is a very good man and has given me the life I deserve and the home I am proud of.

I must take care that no one gives us the evil eye again. The jealous ones are dangerous. But I say nothing of this to Hadi. I try not to unduly stress him.

I think women like Haideh are jealous of me. They always have been and I suppose they always will be. They look at Hadi and see how wonderful he is compared to their own husbands – including her husband who is my own brother! – and can't help but be jealous of me.

They see how poised I am in all situations, the elegance of my home and my personal style. There is nothing the least bit nouveau riche about me. My dinner parties are not to be compared for their good taste. It is no surprise they envy me!

Life is good.

19

THE BALL

I have deduced that my husband's business is blessed by the Palace.

His music business presents an ideal situation for His Royal Majesty. It is both extremely lucrative, and, more than that, it brings Rostam into close contact with Americans of some importance, a fact that is attractive to our western-bent leader.

I now understand that Rostam had been invited to the Coronation because of his business dealings with the Palace.

It is not uncommon for private business to go into partnership with the Palace, enhancing their opportunity for success. The royal family has interests in shipping, hotels, factories, construction projects, publishing, banking and almost every other facet of life. I wonder how Saleh Phacueticals has stayed clear of His Majesty's participation — or vice versa.

My husband also seems to have access to some Iranian government officials and diplomats around the world, in part because of Taymoor's contacts and likely due to Shah's influence as well. As a result, he is from time to time invited to social events hosted by, or honoring, dignitaries.

Today, he is to leave for Los Angeles to meet with record labels regarding ongoing distribution contracts. He instructs me at breakfast, between sips of his coffee and drags of his ever-present Marlboro.

"Tomorrow night you will go to the Ambassador Bakhti's party as my representative. You will explain that I have been called away. You will wear the diamond jewelry I will leave with Hassan and that new bright red gown with the sable coat." He squints, takes a drag from his cigarette, exhales to the ceiling, and says, "You will *charm* the ambassador."

I am feeding Reza and don't look up. I simply nod in acknowledgement. From the corner of my eye, I see him loading jam on a piece of barbarri as he says, "Unless, of course, you would rather come to Los Angeles with me. Would you like that?"

I feel his eyes on me, testing me, watching me carefully to note my reaction. I have none. "I would rather not leave Reza," I say. In truth, I have no desire to go to Los Angeles. My son needs me at home.

Hearing my response, Rostam immediately becomes animated again. "Very well, then. You will attend the Ambassador's event as I said."

I have no idea which ambassador Rostam is talking about, but I will set out to charm the pants off him.

The night of the ambassador's party, I wear the silk fire-engine red dress as instructed.

It is almost completely backless and shirred at the bust line, accentuating it. My heels are high and match the red in peau de soie. The diamond earrings he has selected for this evening, are terribly gauche, so I wear my hair down and loose, somewhat covering them. I wear the ring, a large solitaire marquise and the necklace, which would not have been my choice. But I don't care. This is not my party.

Dressed, I leave the house.

The Rat is at the crest of a bad cold, sneezing, coughing up phlegm, and looking – to my secret delight – completely miserable. My guess is that he has a fever as well. Sick as a dog, he nevertheless drives me to the prestigious address. He will rest in the car with his tissues, nasal spray, and Babajon's Saleh Galoo Cure until I am ready to return home.

I leave the car and approach the heavy door of what looks like a cross between a mansion and a fortress.

~ EHSAN ~

She passes through the oak doors, and when my man takes her wrap, every eye is on her.

She has entered a world of people dressed only in black and white. Yves Saint Laurent is everywhere. Women are wearing the frilliest of white blouses, some with French cuffs, under black tuxedos, or gowns of black or white. None match her beauty. I am wearing black trousers with a white dinner jacket and a black and white bow tie. Apparently, she hadn't known the theme of the night's gathering.

Seeing her in that red dress, her bare skin the color of early dusk, thick waves of chestnut hair cascading down, and the look of surprise in those lovely eyes, I want her as I have not wanted a woman in many years.

Fortunately, I am standing by the entrance when she arrives, chatting with guests. I swoop up two glasses of champagne from a server's tray and welcome her. As I approach, I have the feeling that I have met her before, likely sometime in the distant past. But then, if I had, I would not have let her go.

I will always remember every word we speak, every move of her lovely head, every expression on her beautiful face from that very first moment.

"*Salam, khosh amadeed,* hello and welcome." I extend my hand. "Ehsan, your host."

Her eyes are hazel and framed in long lashes. Her silken skin glows.

"Thank you." She looks at me somewhat questioningly, her chin tilted as she asks, "I'm sorry, haven't we met?"

So she senses a past meeting as well. "I doubt it. I would have remembered you."

She smiles. Her smile is warm and radiant. Her full lips match the color of her dress perfectly. Behind their sparkle, her eyes hold secrets.

"I'm Layla Saleh, Rostam Shamshiri's wife. Unfortunately, my husband has been called out of the country on business and couldn't make it this evening. I am here in his place." She scans the room then points to her dress. "And I am terribly sorry for this."

I shake my head. "Nothing to be sorry for." Her lovely shoulders relax. "I'm sorry I won't see him here. However, he has sent you and so I can't complain." I hold a glass out to her. "Would you like some champagne? Or would you prefer a glass of wine?"

"Champagne please," she says, taking the flute from my hand and thanking me. Before taking a sip, she says, "Agha Bakhti, I truly apologize for being dressed so inappropriately."

I scoff, waving away her apology. She is dressed perfectly. "Ah, please don't bother yourself. My staff thought it would be a nice touch to give the evening a theme. I thought it was a good idea, a way to kill the boredom of the seeing the same people over and over again, but I find it is still a bore. How refreshing to see a new face." I lift my glass. "Please, enjoy the champagne."

After she takes a quick, tiny sip, she says, "But this is terrible! I'm so sorry! I didn't see the invitation and Rostam forgot to tell me." She tries to hand me her drink and repeats, "Please, allow me to go home and change." She holds her drink out to me.

I don't accept it and take hold of her arm. I am being forward, I know, but I don't want her to leave. "Oh, no, you mustn't do that. You look wonderful. Too wonderful to change." She shakes her head. "Khanom Shamshiri, since your husband was not able join us, please allow me to be your escort this evening. I'm the host, so no one can question what my escort is wearing.

"You are very kind. But I won't embarrass you."

I laugh. "I would not be embarrassed. I would be honored."

Another smile. "Then, thank you."

Something about this woman entrances me. I offer her my arm. She takes it and we make our way across the foyer. We reach the long salon.

Amid the trays of hors d'oeuvres, champagne and wine floating throughout the room, I stop at a vase filled with crimson roses. "Ahh. Just what we need." I snap off a red bud and place it on my lapel. "Now, we are a match." I am rewarded with her lovely nod.

I continue leading her through the room, nodding to guests we pass and introducing her to some. These affairs are generally swarming with Tehran's power brokers. I survey the room, seeing moons of power, invited out of necessity, holding court.

There are men representing every aspect of Iran's bourgeoning place in the world, bankers, oil brokers from the West, officials of the Iran's National Oil Company, and importers of various industrial wares, as well as several dignitaries, a few other Iranian ambassadors and deputy ambassadors from various countries. A photographer is on hand, as always, memorializing the event.

The women are clustered in groups, laughing now and then as

they chit-chat. A few couples are engaged in seemingly light conversation with one another. The men are mostly grouped together, smoking pipes, cigars or cigarettes, many with a drink in hand. Some are having serious conversations, using this gathering as an opportunity to either persuade or dissuade.

"Oh, there's Ali Hussein," she says, recognizing His Majesty's top aide, standing across the room.

"You know him?" I am ready to guide us to him.

She shakes her lovely head. "He lived on my parents' street, but I don't know him." When I ask if she'd like me to introduce her to him, she declines. After a few moments, she frowns. "I truly am sorry, Aghayeh Bakhti. Your female guests are still staring at me. I don't think they're happy to see my red dress."

"Women can be unforgiving of a woman in a red dress," I say. "Especially when both the dress and the woman wearing it happen to be very beautiful. Please don't let their shallowness bother you. And I insist you call me Ehsan. Please. We are friends, and I am not an old man."

We are approaching the long banquet table set alongside the wall at the end of the room. "Ehsan Khan," she says, "tell me, do I sense that your general view of women is a bit dim?"

"No, not at all. Or more truthfully, not my view of *all* women. Certainly not you, of course, Khanomeh Shamshiri. But –" my eyes sweep the rooms – "but in truth, unfortunately, I suppose I do not hold most of the women here in high esteem."

"My name is Layla," she says. "I hope I am not so old that you would address me as Khanom." She smiles.

I bow in acknowledgment. I am caught off guard when she asks, "Khanomeh Bakhti was not able to be here tonight?"

"Actually, I am a widower." I answer. I suddenly feel awkward. I'm not sure why.

"Oh, I'm sorry," she says. Her eyes convey compassion.

"Thank you." There is a sudden silence, as if neither of us knows quite what to do with that fact.

I take the initiative and in my desire to end the silence I almost blurt out, "Elise was badly injured in car accident five years ago. Unfortunately, her injuries were very serious. She suffered several broken bones and a bad head injury that, changed her ability to … well, changed her. She'd was also injured internally. A kidney was removed. She spent months in the hospital. When she came home, she was weak and in pain. She was no longer the same person. She had changed, due to that injury to her head that caused problems in her brain." I stop and take a breath. I haven't spoken of this for a long time and it's still difficult to recall the memory. The story is almost done. "She was mostly bedridden at home for the last year with nurses round the clock. She passed two years ago."

"How sad. That must have been very hard."

I nod. I put my empty champagne glass down. "Yes. But I have found it helps to focus on the present. And I have my work and my daughter. It has been most difficult for her."

"Yes, of course. How old is she?"

"Lisette is sixteen."

"So, she was fourteen when she lost her mother? I can only imagine how difficult it's been for her."

I nod. "Fortunately, Lisette is very wise. My daughter is sixteen going on forty-five."

Her lovely giggle sounds like a babbling brook. "Does Lisette like Iran?"

It is my turn to laugh. "My daughter is very opinionated." As I'm speaking, I nod acknowledgement to a passing guest then turn my back to him just a bit, hoping he will pass us rather than stop and chat. I want no distraction. "She likes the country. But she objects to the Iranians views on some things. I can't say I blame her. After all, she was raised in France. There's a universe of difference between the French or European woman's view of life and the Iranian's view."

She changes the subject again, curious to know the nature of my relationship with her husband. I sigh, then chuckle. "Ahh! Rostam *jon*. He is unforgettable. I was introduced to him by a mutual acquaintance, Aghayeh Moloyed."

"Taymoor Moloyed?"

"Yes. You know him?"

"Taymoor is married to my cousin, Shireen."

I smile at the mention of her cousin's name. "Ahh, Shireen is quite a woman. They make a marvelous pair."

"How nice that you and my husband have become friends," she says, bringing the conversation back to where she wants it.

I think I'm detecting a note of sarcasm in her tone, born of insincerity, as though she is more upset than pleased that I have any relationship with her husband. Or perhaps I am reading into things. I am certainly not happy to call Rostam Shamshiri a friend. In fact, her use of the term sends a slight stab of repulsion through me, and I want to make it clear to her that there is no friendship between us.

"Your husband is quite a businessman. He has approached me because he is interested in doing some business with France."

"Oh!" She looks genuinely surprised.

I cock my chin towards her. "Layla Khanom, do you happen to speak English?"

She nods, then in perfect English, says, "Please! Not Layla Khanom. My name is Layla. I studied at UCLA for two years."

UCLA! I'm delighted. This gorgeous woman is certainly not anything like this roomful of cookie-cutter women. She is not afraid to use her brain.

"Excellent! Then we shall speak only English."

"As our ambassador to France, shouldn't you be speaking French?" she asks slyly.

"Naturellement. But I also studied in the States, and I prefer to speak English when possible."

"College?"

"Yes."

"Where?"

"I received a Master of Political Science from Harvard." Later, I will wonder when she was at UCLA. I know we could not have been in the States at the same time; she is much younger.

She nods approvingly. "Very nice. I'm impressed."

I feel my chest inflate. "Ah, then it was worth it." She smiles coyly, as though my compliment has embarrassed her. Speaking English enhances the feeling that we are in our private world.

We are standing at the buffet table. I see the ice carving of three fish, dancing around a mermaid set in the center of the table, and I'm annoyed. It stands more than three feet tall. Things like this seem ridiculously unnecessary to me, but I understand they are expected.

The Beluga caviar – roe of the sturgeon found in the Caspian, by far the most expensive caviar in the world and one of my most favorite indulgences – is set out in a large rectangular bucket-like dish. I'm about to prepare some caviar on toast for her. As I reach for a plate, my hand grazes her forearm. Her skin feels as soft and as smooth as it appears. "Do you care for some caviar?" I ask. She nods enthusiastically. With my hand over the lazy Susan, stocked with anything one could want to top the caviar with, I ask, "And how do you prefer it?"

"Naked," she says.

I give her a wicked smile. "Layla Khanom, excuse me, but do you mean without any clothes on?" Her laugh is delightful, full yet feminine.

"No. I mean I like it without any topping. No eggs, no onions … nothing. In fact, I'd rather no toast."

"Ah, I see. You mean just caviar."

"That's right. Just caviar. Like a villager." Her smile is like sunshine on a cloudy day. "Naked," she repeats.

"I doubt the villagers of Iran are enjoying caviar," I reply.

I want the time to look at her, undisturbed, to study her features and discover why her beauty is so unique.

She takes the serving spoon from my hand. "Like so." And again, my hand brushes against hers.

She puts several heaping spoons of the black roe onto her plate then deposits a huge amount into her waiting mouth. "Delicious," she declares. "Too delicious to be ruined with anything."

"So, you are a purist." I say.

"I suppose I am."

After another spoonful, she asks, "Tell me, what business does my husband intend to have with France?"

The question surprises me. I wonder if she keeps abreast of her husband's business or if she is simply curious.

"He is a very enterprising man," I say.

I don't like her husband. I didn't like his style. He seems extremely arrogant. And now that I have met his wife, I like him less. I wonder at the unaccountable match. It is hard to believe this woman is married to that man. He is not worthy of a woman like Layla. She is educated, beautiful, charming, and not at all like him. In fact, I find nothing disagreeable about her.

"Well, I know he is the largest distributor of American music in Iran," I continue. "He has his eye on French music. He's told me he believes that after the English wave, a wave of French music will rock the world and he very much wants to be the distributor of that music in Iran. He's asked me to set up appointments for him in that regard. You know, put in a good word for him here and there."

"I see." She is thinking. She nods her head a bit.

"As I said, your husband is a very enterprising man. I am not sure why he would believe I have contacts in that area. He would also like me to assist him obtain certain trade benefits." I want her to know how aggressively pushy he has been with me.

"Trade benefits?" I have her total attention.

"Yes. He is under the impression that, due to my diplomatic status, I can help him bypass tariffs, customs costs and the like." Her expression reflects what I take to be embarrassment. Perhaps, she is even aghast.

"I don't know what to say," she says. "My husband is …" She puts her plate down on the table. She is obviously uncomfortable.

I put my plate down as well. "Please, Layla Khanom, don't upset yourself. We are not responsible for what our spouses do. Please. I understand your position." She nods and takes in a deep breath. I surmise she's heard that before. "Wait here," I say. I leave her and rush back with two more glasses of champagne and give her one. "Please, drink this."

"Thank you." She takes a sip. "I don't know what to say."

"There is nothing to say." I mean it. Her reaction has told me what I want to know about her feelings for Rostam. "Have some more caviar," I say and pile as much caviar as I can on a fresh plate.

She laughs that delicious laugh again. "What are you doing?"

I laugh as well. "I am making you naked." We stand together in comfortable silence for some moments, she is enjoying the caviar and we're both drinking champagne.

"Tell me," she asks. Her embarrassment has apparently passed. "Do you enjoy being an ambassador?"

I shrug. "It's a difficult job. But, it must be done. I would rather do the job than to have an Iranian, who does not understand the French as well as I do."

"And you feel you understand the French well?"

I don't take offense. I know she is asking out of genuine curiosity. "My dear madam, I was married to a French woman for over seventeen years, and I have a French daughter. Having lived with these two women and navigated successfully, I can take on the entire country of Frenchmen."

"Are French women so different from Persian women?"

'To underrate the differences would be a mistake," I say.

"And what exactly are these differences?" She asks. There is a new light in her eyes. She is playfully goading me, and I'm enjoying it. After a sip of her champagne, she continues. "Are French women more alluring?" she asks. "I suppose you'll say they're coquette, whereas Persian woman try to be *sangeen*, poised and more sedate?"

Her curiosity makes for an excellent conversation. After another sip of my drink, I say, "I will tell you this. I have found that when a French woman is sexually unfaithful to her spouse, she will share the details of her affair with her best friend."

"I see," she says. "And Iranian women are not unfaithful?"

I laugh at the idea. "No, no, I'm afraid you miss my point. Iranian women are as sexually unfaithful as the French women. The difference is that the Iranian woman will never dare tell her best friend about her affair."

"Ah," she lifts her glass up. "And that's because the Iranian woman is expected to be faithful, a good little girl who would never jeopardize her reputation by telling even her best friend," she guesses.

"Again, I must correct you," I say, shaking my head and waving my arms as I tend to do when making a point. "No, not at all. You see, I'm afraid it's because she would suspect her husband to be having an affair with her best friend."

She chuckles. "And would she be wrong?"

I shrug. "I refuse to answer on the ground that it may incriminate the entire male population of my homeland," I say.

She scoffs. "Well, you certainly are a diplomat. And tell me, what about American women? Do you have an opinion about them as well?"

Just then the band began to play and a roar of appreciation is heard around the room.

"American women are more difficult to generalize about," I answer, without hesitation. "They are neither this way nor that when it comes to sexuality, neither fish nor fowl, but rather a melting pot of everything that follows from their mixture of backgrounds and beliefs. But I will say this: They are not as progressive in their sexual ideas as they would have you believe."

The time flies by. I arrange to have her to sit by me at dinner. I do not leave her side for a moment except to go outside to the waiting cars as soon the meal is over to find her driver. He is asleep in the driver's seat with tissues strewn all around the front seat. I knock on his window, and when he awakens, startled, I instruct him to go home, assuring him that my personal staff will see Khanom Shamshiri safely home. He has little choice but to do nod and as I instruct.

Thanks to Layla, it is a memorable night. It is certainly the most fun I'd had in years. She is intelligent, witty, an excellent conversationalist, and very easy on the eyes. Quite aside from all of that, I cannot not deny that I am attracted to this woman as I've been attracted to none other in a very long time. I think she enjoys my company as well. Our chemistry is palpable.

Most of the guests have left, and we both realize how late it is. "I'm afraid I've overstayed," she says. "May I ask that your driver take me home?"

"Nonsense!" I say, "I will take you. Come."

"But you can't! You still have some guests."

"Trust me," I console her. "They will not even know I've gone. As long as they have access to the bar, they will be happy until I return."

"Truly, it's not necessary for you to bother yourself."

"Bother? I insist." With that, I call for her coat and we go out through a side door.

We arrive at her house, and I open her car door, extending my hand to help her out. It is the limit of our physical contact. It feels wonderful to hold her arm for a fleeting moment. The house is dark. I escort her to the front door. "Thank you for a lovely evening, Layla Khanom," I say.

"Yes, thank you. I had a lovely time as well." I hate the darkness that masks her lovely smiling face.

Neither of us are in a rush to separate.

"You must come to the house for dinner when Rostam returns."

I nod. "I hope to see more of you and Rostam." It is half true.

With a last grasp of her lovely hand, followed by a salute, I bid her goodnight.

20

THE DINNER

1977

This morning, I have a spring in my step and a wiggle in my walk.

As I watch Ali Reza play on the soft blanket I've laid down, I relive last night. I will do so many times. I smile when I think of all the attention Ehsan lavished on me. I recall bits of our conversation, his perfect English, and I chuckle, recalling his response to my question about Iranian women. He has etched a permanent place in my heart. And when he voiced his preference for the western way of thinking, it warmed my heart to know that our views are compatible. From the minute he met me at the door, I felt our meeting had been inevitable, as though we'd already met or were meant to meet.

I should thank my husband for the most enjoyable night I've had since our marriage. Sending me there in a red dress was a mean trick and terribly underhanded. But on some level, it was pure genius. Rostam must have known the theme of the night was black and white and guessed that my red dress would draw attention to me. He will never know how grateful I am.

When he returns home from his trip, the first thing he says is, "How was the ambassador's party?"

It was glorious. Of course I don't say that. I answer in an offhand way. "It wasn't bad. The Ambassador was sorry you couldn't attend." In fact, he was delighted Rostam hadn't been there, and so was I. Last night I reconnected with a part of me I thought was gone forever. Ehsan made me feel alive as a woman again.

Rostam's eyes tighten almost imperceptibly. "And was he pleased to see you there?" He spent every minute of the night with me. I shrug. He persists. "Did you charm him?"

I shrug again. The fool sent me there only to further a one-sided business relationship. "He was hospitable," I finally say, stone-faced. "He tried to make me feel comfortable, seeing how uncomfortable I was as the only person not wearing black or white." I thought it best not to mention that I had been seated on Ehsan's right at dinner. Rostam smiles. He is a treacherous fox. And yet, I think smugly, last night his treachery backfired.

I have concluded that Ehsan is marvelous: intelligent, charismatic, entertaining, and exceedingly appealing. He is tall and walks with a stately grace, like someone of importance used to being watched. His chocolate eyes dance. They light up when he smiles that warm and easy smile. He exudes so much positive energy, and his laugh is so filled of mirth that I am still infected with happiness. And, though there was barely any physical contact between us, the warmth of his skin and his wonderful masculine scent drew me to him.

He has moved something in me that I thought had died. The truth is, I was so intensely attracted to him that when he walked me to my door, I found I was completely open to whatever direction our relationship might have taken at that moment. But if

Ehsan had any ideas, he didn't follow through. He simply said goodnight, leaving the thought of what might have been to tease my passion.

I long to see him again. I told him I wanted to invite him to our home for dinner, but I can't suggest that to Rostam. I know he won't be in Tehran forever; he will have to return to France. I will have to watch myself, careful not to show any interest in the man.

I am bathing Reza and startle, suddenly realizing where I had seen those chocolate eyes before. Ehsan was the phantom man I had glimpsed talking to Rostam in Shireen's living room years ago. Even then, with just a glance, I had been drawn to him like a a spot to a leopard. I'd looked for him again same that night, but he was gone. Then last night I was virtually thrown at him by Rostam!

To my delight, when Rostam returns home from his office, he says he will call Ehsan "and see what he has to say."

I am curious to know what he will tell Rostam and more curious to confirm that he, too felt the strong immediate attraction between us.

I put my son to bed and go to the kitchen for a last cup of tea. Rostam is there, directing Jaleh, our cook, who in turn instructs Hassan. "Make sure the butcher sells you only the finest," she says. "*Ba-varresh na-kon*. Don't believe him. You must look for yourself."

"And this one time," Rostam adds, "don't chisel him about the price. Just make certain it's the best."

Hassan bows, retreating out of the room with a handkerchief at his nose and his fist at his heart. No doubt, he has told his master that he didn't drive me home last night, but doesn't know that Ehsan had insisted he drive me home himself.

Rostam turns to me and smiles like an oily snake. "Ambassador Bakhti will join us for dinner tomorrow."

My heart leaps at the news. I'll be seeing Ehsan soon again. "*Borak'Allah,* bravo! You did your job well," he says. This is the second time in our marriage that Rostam has been proud of me. The first was the day I'd delivered him a son.

"Will anyone else join us?" I ask.

"Taymoor will come after dinner, for tea. Without Shireen."

I nod. Of course. Rostam will want Ehsan's attention all to himself during dinner with me there as bait. Then Taymoor, the man who introduced him to Ehsan, will join us, without Shireen there to distract, to assure Ehsan that it will be a good thing to help the big ape in his business aspirations.

I will bet my life that if his business in France is successful, Rostam will offer Taymoor nothing for his trouble, not even a delivery of flowers with a "Thank You" note.

The day goes by like a dream in slow motion, and finally it is evening. I cannot wait to see Ehsan walk through the door.

I dress, looking as good as I dare, and, as I finish, the doorbell rings.

I am careful not to show my delight when I see Ehsan.

I want Rostam to disappear so the two of us are alone with Reza. He refuses Rostam's offer of a drink and actually focusses on my son, fascinating him with comical facial expressions, holding him up high in the air like Babajon does, and putting him on his lap to trace his finger on the child's tiny palm playing *'guillow, guil-low,'* the Persian version of "this little piggy." He is giving my son far more attention than his own father does.

At the dinner table, Ehsan allows his host to play the big shot, nodding and agreeing with him at regular intervals. Rostam is talking about how important his work is and how the music of the West – and particularly rock'n roll, the music of the young – liber-ates youth from the yoke of whatever oppression they believed they suffer. He makes sure not to limit the magic of the music he imports to Iranian youth.

I cringe. *What a bunch of poppycock!* As if the oaf cares about liberating anyone from anything! It is disgusting to hear him ramble on about something he cares nothing about. He would sell handguns to a child bent on killing his own mother if it paid well.

The difference between the man I've married and this elegant, kind, and educated man seated before me is beyond measure. Twice, Ehsan dares to give me a look, but only twice. They are looks that say, "I know he's speaking *mozakhraf,* nonsense, and you know he's speaking *mozakhraf.* Doesn't he know that we know? Those looks are more meaningful than all of Rostam's pontificating.

When Rostam is curt with our servant, berating her for not having the salad at the table the moment we were through with our main course, I am afraid Ehsan thinks I actually have feelings for the bully, or that money is more important to me than living with a man I can respect. I pray not.

Dinner ends and Taymoor arrives. Between making drinks for himself, Taymoor and now Ehsan, snapping at our servants and pandering for Ehsan's attention, Rostam manages to kiss his little prince good night. I excuse myself as well, knowing that is what Rostam expects.

Taymoor bids me goodnight with an embrace, but Ehsan only extends his hand. Our grasp lingers longer than necessary, and the warmth of his hand shoots through me again.

I take my leave knowing we will meet again.

2 1

THE MUSIC OF PARTING

1977

I am happy.

A week has passed since Ehsan was at our house for dinner and I have been missing him terribly, but I have just learned that he has invited us to the opening of a concert "by invitation only" held at the gardens of Bagh Ferdose tonight.

We meet him at the pavilion. When we find seats, any hopes I have that I will sit between Rostam and Ehsan are squashed when Rostam signals me to enter the aisle first. He follows me in, leaving Ehsan to sit on his other side. I am sitting beside a matronly woman.

The entire night I listen to the tonbak, santur, nay, and kmancheh, playing classical Persian music, feeling tortured, knowing Ehsan is just on the other side of Rostam. I would give anything to be sitting next to him; for one grazing of our bare hands.

I console myself with the thought that we will have dinner afterwards. But when we arrive at our table at the restaurant on Pahlavi Avenue, we are met by two couples already seated and waving at Ehsan, calling for him to sit between them. I discover that this gathering is his farewell dinner. He is scheduled to leave for France tomorrow. Rostam makes the grand gesture of paying the bill for all seven of us.

At evening's end, Ehsan invites us to his home. "When you come to Paris, I would be honored to take you and Khanom Shamshiri to dinner." I assume that Ehsan has agreed to assist Rostam move ahead with exploring his business interests in France.

With a huge grin, Rostam slaps his benefactor's back and nods. "*Albatteh!* Of course!"

There is no way in Hell that Rostam would allow me to accompany him to France. I will never be included at that dinner table.

And so, the man who turned me back into a woman has left Tehran today, and that is that.

Though he is gone, meeting him has changed me in some primal way. Knowing that he will eventually come back, buoys my spirits. I now have two things to look forward to every day: another day with Reza and the chance that on that day Ehsan might return to me.

The man has a home in my heart. I can so easily imagine having an affair with him. In fact, I want it badly and would gladly enter into some arrangement. The truth is that, had he stayed in Tehran, I would have encouraged it. There was a time I would not have dreamed of being unfaithful, but that time is gone.

It is late morning during the second week he is gone. While the Rat is driving Rostam to his office, a letter is delivered to the house. The address is written in a strong, masculine hand and bears Ehsan Bakhti's return address.

Though the envelope is addressed to Rostam, I feel certain Ehsan has meant for me to see it. That is the only reason for mailing it to the house rather than to Rostam's office. I am also certain that it is not the consulate's address penned in the top left corner of the envelope. It Ehsan's home address.

I ache to open it and read what he's written, but, of course, I have to wait for Rostam to come home, open it, and pray he hints at its contents. I carry the letter into Rostam's home office and place it gingerly on his desk, then find myself pulled back by the envelope. I return to the room and hurriedly scribble the return address onto a small tear sheet from Rostam's notepad and stuff it into my pocket. I hide it with my most valuable possessions. I will most likely never to use it. Surely, I will never write or visit Ehsan. Still, having possession of that piece of paper is like having his photo.

But I don't need a photo to remind me of his visage.

PART TWO: AFTER

The eye goes blind when it only wants to see why.

— *~RUMI, POET AND MYSTIC*

22

IT HAPPENED

1977-1979

The year I meet Ehsan marks the end of the Iran I know.

In one generation, my country changed from a rural society to an industrial, modern and urban country. In retrospect, many Iranians believe the change was too rapid and too radical and that a corrupt and incompetent government has not met its promises.

In November of 1977, Shah Reza Pahlavi visits the White House only to be met with protesting Iranian students. The protest is ultimately quashed with the use of tear gas. A month later, President Carter visits Iran and describes our country as "an island of stability in one of the most troubled areas of the world."

His Majesty's decision not to renew the twenty-five year contract set to expire in 1978 by which Great Britain and the United States receive a large share of Iran's oil strips away a major reason for the two countries to back His Majesty when civil unrest rocks Iran. Their goal is no longer to protect him, but rather, to prevent Iran from falling into communist hands. To that end, they will tacitly support Khomeini, bolstering his leadership, perhaps viewing the elderly, and apparently harmless, religiously anointed ayatollah as only an interim head of government that- *oops!* surprises them by becoming permanent.

In 1964, His Majesty had resisted his advisors' counsel encouraging him to execute the rabble-rousing Ruhollah Khomeini for committing many acts of violence, including burning and looting the countryside in protest against the shah. But His Majesty had deemed it sufficient to exile him to France. Now the ayatollah is a powerful threat to the monarchy.

There are those who say Khomeini is not a true ayatollah and is, in fact, an agent of the West. But would an agent of the West have demonstrated against the monarch so violently that Shah exiled him in 1964, a time when the West supported Shah?

Shah's most ardent opponent has historically been the cleric, unhappy since Shah's father began westernizing the country upon taking the throne. The mullahs want to take the country back to the way it functioned before the Pahlavis westernized it.

They are aghast at the loss of the *chador* that covers a woman from her hair to her toes, leaving only her hands and face showing. They believe its absence robs women of their modesty, provocatively leaving too much of their body in plain view.

They also abhor the measures that give women greater rights, including the right to vote and to prosecute rapists.

As our country's largest landowner, the Muslim cleric is also incensed at Shah's land reforms, which they believe has robbed them of much of their land.

Their time to rule is close at hand.

The people's resentment and outrage directed towards the Pahlavi family begin to explode.

Conversations criticizing His Majesty have been private in the past out of fear of arrest and possible torture by a member of SAVAK, Shah's secret police. Now they are brazenly public. Newspapers carry open letters criticizing the monarch and the accumulation of power and wealth his family holds amid widespread poverty.

The first truly massive clash between the people and the shah takes place in the religious city of Qom on January 7, 1978. His Majesty is called "the puppet of American imperialism." As Iran has been the first Muslim country to recognize the State of Israel and establish close ties with that country, the clerics also accuse our shah of being "the agent of Israel."

That same month, the major Iranian newspaper carries an editorial on the front-page written by the Palace that vilifies Ayatollah Ruhollah Khomeini. In response, tens of thousands gather to demonstrate their opposition to the contents of that letter. The main bazaar in the city of Qom, the city known for its many religious conservatives, closes in a protest to the article as well.

That protest results in the death of at least five people. In response, ceremonies are held in cities across Iran mourning deaths of the Qom protestors. During these protests of solidarity, a student protestor is killed in the city of Tabriz. That causes further rioting and more violence, creating the repetitive sequence of protests and violence in a majority of larger Iranian cities.

September 8, 1978, is declared Black Friday. Depending on the source, shootings in Tehran leave between as few as eighty-four and as many as fifteen thousand people killed and up to eight thousand people injured.

Hoping to quell the discord, His Majesty names a new head of SAVAK. His first act is to release hundreds of detained clerics.

Nonetheless, another cleric has been arrested and riots again flare up in cities throughout the country. Martial law is declared in the large city of Isfahan.

Intellectuals, Iranians who have studied abroad in democratic countries and returned home, journalists and political activists, writers and other artists begin to openly attack the monarch and his government. They want to replace the monarchy with democratic elections.

The several communist organizations, including the Mohajedin, and Tudeh, to which Ferri has pledged allegiance, join in the nationwide strike believe ousting Shah Pahlavi will liberate Iranians from the "evils of Western imperialism."

These various communist groups are passionately opposed to Khomeini and compete with the cleric for power. However, while these groups are forced underground by the shah, the extensive network of mosques affords the clergy the use of a powerful, existing, organized structure beyond the monarch's reach and this fact ultimately enables the Muslim cleric, and in particular, Khomeini, to push towards the lead in the revolution.

The cleric's protest against the westernization of Iran is made clear in August of 1978 when they set fire to Cinema Rex in the southwestern city of Abadan, killing four hundred eighty people.

Demonstrations against the monarch are now a daily occurrence, with crowds shouting, "Down with Shah." The killing of demonstrators in cities both large and small, results in ever greater anti-shah protests.

In the last half of 1978, my country is virtually paralyzed by strikes and demonstrations. In response to these continuing and growing demonstrations, His Majesty imposes martial law throughout the country.

The revolution is under way. The monarchy is in crisis.

Meanwhile, His Majesty who was initially kept in the dark about his cancer diagnosis two years earlier, is now prescribed Predno, a debilitating drug. It is later said that the drug affected many of his decisions at these crucial times.

On January 16, 1979, the defeated shah and his family leave Iran for a life in exile, and on Feb 11, 1979, the revolution is declared successful.

Initially, the revolution does not have an Islamic theme and is not propelled by religion, so, when Khomeini returns to Iran from his fifteen-year exile in France and is cheered by the crowds, I, along with most Iranians, expect that he will become some sort of Muslim Pope. But the Shi'ite clergy, numbering in the tens of thousands, has something very different in mind.

Promising an Islamic government that will guarantee "the freedom and justice that Shah did not provide," Ayatollah Khomeini has become the face of the revolution.

In the midst of the demonstrations, my heart thumps with worry for my angel. I know her passion for what she believed in can easily put her in mortal danger.

When Shah's overthrow became imminent, my Ferri was jubilant. Then, when it becomes apparent that the communists had lost control of the revolution and the Shi'ites had taken over the government, she is inconsolable. She is again filled with hope when political parties are free to organize and campaign for the national election that will be held. She is certain the communists will win any election.

"Joonie," she says to me when we meet at the bookstore one Thursday, "we Tudehs want to keep the spirit of the revolution alive. We are ready to join with the other communist organizations and parties to create a coalition where we all work to

contribute in creating of a new government based on a new constitution."

Then the election offers only us only two choices: the monarch or the religious mullahs — Shah or Ayatollah; other groups are not included in the proposed new government. The mullahs win. They also win a majority of seats in Parliament, albeit through perhaps questionable means.

Ferri, along with many Iranians, is despondent, hopes deflated.

In December of 1979, Khomeini becomes Iran's Supreme Leader.

Excluded from the new government despite promises that they would be included, these various factions rise up against Khomeini's government but are summarily squashed, their members often executed. My anxiety level for Ferri's safety has shot up.

Meanwhile, Khomeini calls for the people of Iran "to endure hardships and pressures," so that our leaders might fulfill their main obligation, which "*is not to the people of Iran, but to spread Islam across the world.*"

The United States allows the former shah, now in exile, to enter the country for medical attention. In retaliation, a group of Iranian students storm the American Embassy in Tehran in November of 1979, and fifty-two American diplomats are held hostage for four hundred forty-four days. With that siege, the ayatollah shows he is prepared to go to any length in service of his mission.

In December of 1979, Shah leaves the U.S. for Egypt where his family is granted asylum and in 1980 at the age of sixty, he dies there of cancer, while back here in Iran, in his black turban and robes, the Ayatollah Khomeini hastily begins to un-westernize Iran and take my country back to what it had been before Shah's reign sought to westernize it.

Meanwhile, there are those who swear Khomeini is neither Iranian nor an ayatollah. Some say he is — or was — an American agent. But those who speak out, questioning his background and credentials are the very people he immediately silences with death.

In record time, Iran has become a haven for ardently religious Muslims. For the rest of us, it has become a mix of Hell and insanity.

Iran is now the Islamic Republic of Iran.

My country has become a stranger to me.

23

PORTABLE PRISON

Tehran, 1979

*A*t first I'd dared to hope the humongous changes around me were temporary, as if the whole thing was a horrid prank.

It wasn't.

Khomeini's first act as Supreme Leader, after changing the name of our country from Iran to The Islamic Republic of Iran, has been to mandate women to cover themselves with the *chador* when in public or anytime they are in the company of an unrelated male. Overnight, the streets of Tehran are filled with seas of women covered from head to toe with black *chadors*.

I am haunted by a recollection of myself as a young girl seeing our pious neighbor, Parveen Shirazi, wearing a *chador* whenever she left her home and when we visited her home, as Babajon was not a blood relative. No one else in our neighborhood or social standing wore a *chador*. It had been decades since the shah's father had discouraged Iranian women from wearing it.

As a child, seeing our neighbor walk down the street with her head down and covered by the black *chador*, I thought she looked like a large crow.

The word *chador* translates as *tent*.

Seeing Parvin Khanom in her *chador*, I'd think how absurd it would be for my mother, so finicky about her looks, her fine clothes hidden under a sheet. Imagining my cousin Shireen, with her excessive jewelry, her designer suits and dresses, completely covered with a long, unattractive sheet had made me laugh. Nor could I imagine Ferri, my radically independent friend, wear one, even in jest.

But it is no longer funny. The *chador* is not optional, and black crows are suddenly everywhere. Along with Maman, Shireen, Ferri, and thousands of Iran's women, whether Muslim or not, I am now compelled to cover myself with the *chador* when in public or in the presence of an unrelated male.

The *chador* changed my life long before Khomeini's mandate.

I was at UCLA when Parvin Khanom's husband forbade her to wear the *chador* in the company of his western business associates. Saying she could not be a 'part-time *chadoree*,' she had apparently put the black sheet away forever.

Later, she had been seen seated at a table with a man inside a hotel restaurant, her husband banned her from their house and forbade her to ever see her two young sons again — in short, her life was ruined. My life was dramatically changed as well when I forbidden to leave Iran and return to Jasmine.

It was my second annual summer month home. When I heard what misery had befallen our neighbor and then heard *why* it had happened, what she'd done — sharing a cup of tea with a man in plain sight, I blurted out, *"That's all?"*

That's the day, I became victim to my mother's narcissistic act of barbarism and lost all contact with my daughter.

⁓

Khomeini has created The Revolutionary Guards, a group of armed men, meant to protect the populace. It seems they are everywhere.

The Islamic Revoution Committees — later to be named The Morality Police or Guidance Patrol — roam the streets, checking to make sure we women are well hidden under our *chadors,* with no more than a wrist and our face showing, not an ankle, arm or a strand of hair visible. Makeup has become forbidden – no nail polish, no mascara, no lip gloss, no blush – nothing that might ignite a man's sexual nature. Apparently, Iranian men have nothing but sex on their mind day and night.

If picked up for failure to abide by these mandates, one's face might be cleansed with sandpaper. If the crime involves nail polish, nails might be pulled out. The poor woman caught showing too much hair might be lashed with cable wire on her soft skin or receive cigarette burns. Children who used to play with make believe guns, now yell of the horrible tortures they've heard.

At some point in 1979, the revolutionary government spawns *Basijis*, a loose volunteer militia, supposedly formed to protect the populace. In reality, they include thug fundamentalists who stop women in the streets and stop cars to confiscate what they like. The group will eventually become an important part of the Revolutionary Guards. As the mullah's version of SAVAK, they are unnamed, unidentifiable and everywhere, charged with identifying those opposed to our new government.

Men have been cautioned that even wrapped in our *chadors,* women are still dangerously seductive. Here are the Supreme Leader's exact words as translated from the Farsi:

Beware that the veil (or the mask) does not suffice to make a woman harmless – on the contrary, if they (the women) put on white chadors, or wear their masks coquettishly, they only heighten the desire and quicken the lust. What's more, they may appear even prettier than they actually are. Hence, it is religiously prohibited and forbidden for women to clad themselves in clean and fashionable chadors. Any woman who does so is sinful, and any man – be it her husband, brother, or father – who lets her do so, shares her sins.

Do not even behold the veil of a woman, because that, too, excites lust. It is imperative to avoid looking at women's clothing, smelling their sweet perfumes, hearing their pleasing voices. It is also incumbent to avoid, at all costs, sending or receiving messages to or from them; passing through passages that they may pass through, even though you may not see them. For wherever there is beauty, there is the seed of lasciviousness and evil thoughts. Beware, that corruption springs from nothing more than sitting in a place or in a gathering where there are women present.

The Supreme Leader has issued orders to ministries, hotels, offices, restaurants, shops, etc., not to serve, accept or deal with a woman not wearing the *chador* or with a woman who is still alluring though wearing one. She will be picked up and carted to jai, "to be educated," typically receiving painful lashes that cut the skin.

One pretty, seventeen-year-old girl was walking home from school when four women jumped out of a car with rifles at their side. They surrounded her, stopping her in her tracks and simultaneously barraged her with questions.

"Where are you going?" "What's your name?"

"My name is Natalia," she answered, "and I'm coming home from school." She held her schoolbooks out for them to see. Nonetheless, though her body and hair were completely covered, and she wore neither makeup nor nail polish, they carted her off to jail where her face was cut up.

The explanation given to her heartbroken mother was simply that she was, "too beautiful," and thus, "the creation of the Devil."

The oppression of women doesn't end with the *chador* and the ban against makeup.

Birth control pills have been banned as an unexplained "imperialistic plot."

Under Shah Pahlavi, the minimum age for a woman to marry was fifteen. It has reverted to thirteen.

The new government's zeal is apparent. We are separated from men everywhere, whenever, wherever and however possible. Women who dare to protest are imprisoned.

Taxi drivers are not permitted to pick up passengers of another sex, so hordes of female cab drivers appear on the roads.

Beaches have separate areas marked for men and women. Yet, despite entire sections of sand designated "for women only," we women still cannot expose our arms or legs – not even in the water.

The oppressive regulations go on and on. If you are a female walking down the street or sitting at a café with a male, he had better be your husband, father, or brother – and you had better be prepared to prove it. Any woman who dares to protest is jailed.

If a female is seen being touched by, touching, or spending needless time with an unrelated member of the opposite sex, she is punished.

Our neighbor's fifteen-year-old daughter and her friend had wandered into a public park, both covered as required. As they sat talking on a bench, two teenaged boys approached them and the four began to talk. Within minutes, all four were arrested and held overnight. The four sets of parents were out of their minds, not knowing what had happened to their children. The following afternoon my neighbor's daughter returned home in great pain, her back bearing gashes from lashes that had cut her young skin.

Men's fashions have also changed. Showing chest hair is taboo and long-sleeved shirts are encouraged as the sight of hairy arms are thought to be too provocative and may excite females. Facial hair is seen as a show of solidarity with our leaders. Neckties and collared shirts are taken as a sign one sympathizes with "The Imperialistic Satan, The United States" and shirts in general are no longer tucked in.

There is a ban on liquor. People are arbitrarily stopped on the streets and in their cars, their breaths smelled to detect alcohol. Homes are searched without warrants, "if alcohol is thought to be on the premises."

There is a ban on dancing, on playing or listening to music … there is absolute zero tolerance. The bans extend to and are reflected in our movies and television shows. Even beloved Iranian singers, like Googoosh, are banned from singing in public. And anyone who dares to protest is incarcerated and tortured.

Whereas historically, we partied in public and prayed in private, we now pray in public and party in private, praying our gatherings will not be crashed by the Guards who might haul us all off to jail for dancing, listening to music, drinking alcohol purchased on the black market, for being in the same room with members of the opposite sex or for removing our *chadors* in the company of unrelated males.

The Islamic Revolution has also caused a rapid deterioration in Iran's relationship with the United States.

America is now, "The Great Satan," and all things Western are shunned.

Streets have been renamed to honor the Prophet Mohammed,

his followers, and important members of the cleric, past and present.

The national anthem has been revised.

Meanwhile, the economy is a mess. Supermarkets are empty, everything is scarce and what is available is exorbitantly expensive.

Schools have been closed so that schoolbooks and courses at all levels of education can be overhauled, ensuring all are anti-shah, anti-Imperialism, adhere to Islam, and say nothing of the Holocaust. Prior publishers have been jailed and publishing companies and newspapers are shut down.

Perhaps the most evil new practice is the rite of gifting plastic rings to young boys affirming their commitment to Islam — to their death if needed — with the promise that if they die in the service of their religion as martyrs, they are assured an afterlife in Paradise with seventy-two virgin maidens.

Maman's cook, Cobra, had a fifteen-year-old nephew who was one of these young boys. Trying to stop an anti-Khomeini demonstration, he attempted to knife the leader of the demonstration, but was easily overtaken and killed with his own knife.

Iranians, educated in the West, had wanted to replace the monarchy with a democracy. This is what their demonstrations have brought us, Khomeini's "government of God."

And I, held hostage in Iran since my return from America and jailed in my miserable marriage, must now wear the portable prison of the *chador*.

I pray for God to help me, for Allah to help us all.

And then there is Rostam.

24

MY ANGEL

Tehran, 1981

This new way of life has again changed the lives of those I care for as well as my own.

Stress fights to strangle us. What keeps me calm is the love I have for my son. I must protect him and to do that, I must remain clear and calm. I also dwell on that magical night at the embassy with Ehsan. Though the years pass, I have never stop thinking of him. I carry him in my heart and replay our night together often.

We have seen one another only once in the intervening years, a night about a year ago when, during one of Ehsan's trips back to Tehran, Rostam surprised me, inviting him to our home again for dinner . The night was a replay of the first. Reza was six by then, yet Ehsan interacted with him as naturally as when my son had been a toddler.

The night was short, but wonderful. As before, we communicated only with our eyes, stolen smiles and simple, seemingly innocuous words. Yet it was reassuring. The only time we touched was when he shook my hand goodnight. He'd held my hand in both of his, and dared prolong it for a blissful second.

He wants me as much as I want him.

I continue to worry about my angel.

I know Ferri can be very stubborn. Nothing will deter her from her continued anti-government involvement. She continued to participate in anti-protests and demonstrations when they'd become violent. Now, she is handing out flyers, trying to organize a women's protest of the mandated *chador*. As always, I am impatient to see her, to know she is still okay.

It is Thursday and The Rat is driving me to the bookstore when he informs me he will be driving to pick somethings up for Rostam while I'm inside and that it might take a while for him to return. I agree to wait outside for him when I am done, delighted to know that I will not be quite so rushed to end my time with Ferri.

I see my angel waiting for me in the rear of the bookstore. With her petite frame covered in the black *chador,* she looks like a large eggplant.

We embrace. "Guess what, *Joonie.*"

"What?" I ask. I notice she is beaming.

"You'll never guess." She is as excited as a kid with a new riddle. "Never in a million years." Her smile is huge, and her hands are fists at her sides, as if she is trying not to jump up and down in her enthusiasm. "Congratulate me."

"Why? What have you done?"

In her haste to give me her news, her words tumble out almost faster than she can form them. "I'm a married woman!" She sticks out her left hand. She's wearing a thin gold band on her ring finger.

"Oh, my god!" People browsing nearby bookshelves turn, attracted by my shout. "You married Hamid!" She nods happily. "*Mobarack!* Congratulations! That's wonderful!" Our *chadors* slip as we reach out to hug, and we hurry to replace them over our hair.

She's bubbling over with happiness. "You know I don't like jewelry. This is both my engagement ring and my wedding ring."

I nod. "I'm so happy for you."

"Hamid won't wear a ring. Muslim men can't wear gold or jewelry of any kind," And she adds, "or silk."

I scoff. "Well, my friend, having been in love with a Muslim man for all these years, I have no doubt you have learned exactly what they can and can't do." She nods.

I've never seen her so happy, so lighthearted. She's married the high school teacher she had been secretly meeting in high school — Hamid, a young man of a different religion and sixteen years her senior.

"We were married five days ago," Ferri says. She's actually giggling like a shy bride. "I know, I know. It was sudden. Right? But not really, *Joonie,* not after all these years! I've been the happiest bride in the world for five days." She holds my arm. I wanted to let you know right away. But there was no way I could."

"What did your parents say?" Ferri's parents had never known the nature of their daughter's relationship with her teacher-lover.

She shrugs. "What *could* they say? They were shocked, of course, but there was nothing they could do about it. It's done. I swore I would never marry anyone else and that I would never set eyes on them again if they didn't welcome Hamid." She pauses, then comes another big smile. "And so, they did." I laugh and shake my head in wonder at this amazingly surprising woman. "They haven't yet been to our apartment, but ... they'll come."

"I'm really happy for you," I say. "But I have to ask, *why*? I mean, you've always been so against marriage." Ferri would always say marriage is an institution that chains women to a home, housework and one man, while allowing the husband free rein to do exactly as he likes.

"Ah, yes, *Joonie*, I was. But if you remember, I was against marriage *Persian style*, like yours to Rostam, your mother's, my mother's, Shireen's, and the rest of them, because the odds of a woman developing herself in a marriage like that – other than domestically – or of ever having a gratifying sex life, are stacked against you." She chuckles. "Trust me, my sex life with Hamid is excellent." I smile. With all that has changed around me, it is heartwarming to know my angel hadn't changed at all.

She's suddenly thoughtful. "But there were other reasons I married, *Joonie*," she says. I wait, already having guessed that, being Ferri, her decision to marry has been based on an array of practicalities.

Her eyes are on me as she speaks. "I always said you ought to have married David. I knew he was your one true love. But you chose not to. I watched you live the difficult results of that choice and it broke my heart." I catch my breath. With Ferri's eyes on me, I refuse to shed even one tear despite her ready compassion. As she takes hold of my hand, her tone becomes light and she scoffs. "How could I not marry Hamid when he asked? I'd be the worst kind of hypocrite."

I dredge up a smile. "I'm proud of you. And I'm happy for both of you."

Her tone becomes stern. "Anyway, in this crazy time, we *had* to marry. It's already illegal to be seen with a man who's not related to you. That's bad enough. Well, *Joonie*, it's still permitted for a Muslim man to marry *a woman of the Book* — you know, a Jew or Christian. But what if these crazy mullahs soon totally prohibit Muslim males from marrying outside their religion? Hamid wanted us to marry before that happens." I nod in understanding.

Ferri's tone changes yet again, and she becomes solemn. "Besides, though I hate to admit it, I want to have a child." I'm not sure why that surprises me, but it does. Ferri must see that surprise reflected on my face. She shrugs. "What can I say? It's a haunting impulse that begs to be satisfied."

Those words, *a haunting impulse that begs to be satisfied* haunt me for some time. I recall how I felt when I tried to find Jasmine, my need to mother her perfectly: *A haunting impulse that begged to be satisfied.* And they are the words I would use to describe my feeling of contentment at being pregnant with Reza then mothering him. That sentence summed it all up: *A haunting impulse that begs to be satisfied.*

"And Hamid will make a wonderful father," Ferri is saying. Having never met Hamid outside the classroom, I have no comment. Yet, if Ferri is sure, that's good enough for me. I nod.

So, Ferri has decided to marry to have a child with the most controversial man possible. Hamid is Muslim and she is Jewish. I refused David's proposal because he was Jewish and I am Muslim. How I envy her ability to think for herself and map her life out as she chose! "Well, my angel, Hamid's got himself the best woman any man could hope for."

"Oh," Ferri says, opening her handbag, "I can't forget. I need to give you my new telephone number and address at the University." She reaches into her handbag and brings out a small scrap of paper with her phone number and address written on it. I notice a brown smudge in the corner of the small piece of paper, a dried drop of coffee. As I am about to remind her that it's futile to give me her address, she tosses her head back. "You never know, *Joonie,*" she says, "Things may change. One day, you just might knock on my door."

My thoughts return to her dangerous anti-government activity. "Ferri, I'm happy for you, but I'm also worried sick about you. You need to be really careful! The mullahs must know that you

153

and Hamid were communists. They're hunting down people like you."

Ferri shakes her head. "It's so ironic. Khomeini says he's anti-communist. But the way he divides the world into the 'oppressed' and the 'oppressors?' That's the same way Marx did. And he calls the United States "The Great Satan" because it tempts excessive material indulgence. Well, that's nothing more than a version of communist anti-capitalist rhetoric."

I look into her large round eyes."Ferri, it doesn't matter," I say, impatiently. "You can't unseat him. It's too late. He's ruthless and he's got Allah behind him."

"I understand." She says and shudders. "But we're definitely no longer part of any political group. Everything is gone, Layla.

"It's all either dust or blood."

The store manager is walking towards us carrying several books.

We both adjust our *chadors*, ensuring that our hair, as well as our body, is completely covered. She passes us, making her way to the bookshelves behind us, and we resume our quiet chat. Ferri continues where she'd left off. "Anyway, that's it, *Joonie*," she says. "Neither Hamid nor I are not part of *any* political group. They're all corruptible.

"We wanted to see Shah gone. He'd made the wealth of Iran his own private piggy bank and never cared for any of his people except for the wealthiest segment, living in Tehran. He tried to westernize us by saturating the country with foreigners when what he should have done was advance the country by educating us. He was like a father who spends oodles on his own whims, generous to everyone but his own family."

She scoffs. "And of course there was SAVAK, with its terrible torture. Fear of retribution always represses ideas. People can't create when they're repressed nor can a country advance when its people are repressed."

I say nothing and look away. But Ferri knows me as well as I know her. "You have to stop worrying about me, *Joonie*," she says, emphatically.

I've never tired of hearing her call me by that affectionate term. Still, I know she is in danger.

She hears my frustration. "Layla, we didn't fight to get rid of Shah to replace him with this illiterate ayatollah and his band of crazy mullahs! They belong in the mosques, not governing our country. You know that."

I add, "I also know that they don't tolerate dissidents."

Ferri remains silent. I try to think creatively, to invoke caution another way. "What if Hamid is caught?"

"It would be terrible," Ferri admits, "but it would be worse if he didn't fight for what he believes in. I wouldn't respect him."

Ferri either doesn't understand the danger, or she does and just doesn't care. Both frightened me. If you won't stop these things you're doing, then please, please, at least be super vigilant." I sigh. "I'd die if anything happened to you. You're my dearest, best friend, the closest person to me and I love you."

"*Joonie*, you know I will be. I love you too. But you've worried about me since we first met. And I've always told you, you don't need to. I'm still telling you. I'll be okay. I promise." A picture of the pitch-black Charlatan, the black cave where she secretly met with Hamid after classes were over comes to mind, and I feel a little calmer.

We hug once more, our *chadors* slipping as we reach out to embrace one another, then say our goodbyes and confirm plans to meet again in two weeks. With one last, "congratulations," I leave the bookstore just as The Rat pulls up.

Seated in the car, I pray Ferri will be at the bookstore for our next meeting.

25

CAMEL RIDES

Late, 1983

$\mathcal{T}$he next time we meet, Iran is under siege.

A wave of repression has been unleashed throughout the country. But it is in the capital city of Tehran that the slaughter is beyond belief.

People are being murdered in their homes, posthumously labeled, "Zionist spies," "spies for the Satan, America," or "Russian spies." SAVAMA, the primary intelligence agency of the Islamic Republic and Khomeini's equivalent of SAVAK, daily round up hordes of people, many young, who are being tried by quasi-military tribunals, found to be "enemies of the Islamic Republic," and executed. Hundreds and hundreds of political dissidents and non-Muslims are killed, their homes, factories and businesses seized, adding to the wealth of the governing Muslim mullahs. The holiest Baha'i site in Tehran is broken into, ransacked and destroyed, their cemetery, desecrated.

Ferri is a mix of anguish and rage. "They're killing everyone!" she says. "Where's the freedom we fought for? The U.S., Israel, Britain and even Pakistan are all helping the bastard Khomeini weed out communists. People are charged with spying and either thrown into dungeons to rot away or they're killed outright."

"Oh, Ferri! I'm so afraid. They're targeting communists and your communist history can be traced. What will you do?"

"Don't worry about me, *Joonie.* I'm tough."

My heart sinks. "Ferri, you're not tough enough to survive a firing squad, a bullet, a knife, torture or a dungeon. And you're Jewish. They're going after Jews as well as communists."

Ferri taps my shoulder and recites a verse from Rumi:

> I hold to no religion or creed,
> Am neither Eastern nor Western, Muslim, Zoroas-
>   trian, Christian, or Jew.
> I come from neither the land nor sea, am not related
>   to those above or below,
> Was not born nearby or far away, do not live either in
>   Paradise or on this Earth,
> Claim descent not from Adam and Eve or the Angels
>   above.
> I transcend body and soul.
> My home is beyond place and name. It is with the
>   beloved, in a space beyond space.
> I embrace all and am part of all.

Hearing the verse, I am transported to that cold, snowy winter day years ago during our high school days.

Ferri and I had been having lunch at our favorite café, Takhte

Jamsheed, and trying to keep warm. We had been discussing the approaching Iranian New Year.

Ferri mentioned that her mother had begun preparations for Passover, which was to follow soon afterwards. Knowing nothing about Jewish religion, I'd asked her the significance of the upcoming Jewish holiday.

She had answered in a dispassionate voice. "Passover celebrates the exodus of the Jewish people out of Egypt to freedom. God supposedly parted the waters of the sea so Moses and the Jews he led could pass, then closed the waters on the entire pursuing Egyptian army and they all drowned."

"What do you mean, *supposedly*? Don't you believe that happened? It was a miracle and you just rattled it off like it was nothing," It sounded fantastic to me, but I wasn't Jewish.

Ferri was looking out the window at the falling snow. She shook her head and shrugged, then turned to face me. "I don't know, *Joonie*. If God parted the waters of the sea to let the Jewish people pass and then drowned their enemies, why couldn't he stop Hitler? The Pharaoh came back again and again."

She shook her head. "Why don't we celebrate the liberation of Hitler's camps? And how about the exodus of Jews out of Europe that led to the creation of the State of Israel? That was the result of blood, lost lives – a lot of tragedy. It didn't happen by a miraculous parting of waters."

Ferri had recently taken to smoking an occasional cigarette, and now she leaned back and lit up a Winston. "Horrible things have happened in the name of religion – because of religious differences. If I had my way, I'd do away with religion."

"Ferri!"

"Relax, *joonie*. I'm not against God – whatever that is. I'm only against the idea of advertising what you name yours and trying to sell your religion to others. You either believe in God or you don't, and if you do, whatever you call God is your business, period. I mean, just be a good person. It seems to me that religion only divides people. This religion doesn't like that one, is better than another one, has a better God than this one, is the enemy of the others, can't marry other ones …"

At the mention of 'marry,' Hamid had come to my mind, and I'd wondered if her love for him was at the crux of her beliefs. "Don't you think of yourself as Jewish?" I asked.

She'd sat a little straighter and took a drag off her cigarette. "I probably should be proud to be Jewish. Jews have survived and even thrived despite intense suffering. They've given the world so many wonderful things. But who's to say that it was due to their Jewishness? And I wonder if the world wouldn't be a nicer place without fighting about religion and killing one another because of it."

"But isn't it human nature to think you're better than everyone else?" I had asked. "That your group is the best? If not your religion, then your race, or school, or family name? Why blame religion?"

"Because that flies in the face of what religion is supposed to do," she'd said, tapping her cigarette ashes into the nearby ashtray. "Or am I wrong? Isn't religion supposed to teach tolerance? *Turn the other cheek? Thou shalt not kill? Love your brother as yourself?*"

The waiter brought us our check then, and Ferri had waited until he left before she went on. "What's really crazy in all this is that the Jews, Christians and Muslims are family. Ishmael and Isaac were half-brothers."

Sadly, I was lost. "Who's Ish- whatever, and who's Isaac?"

She shook her head. "*Joonie,* read the Bible. God commanded Abraham to have children. He was married to Sarah. When she didn't get pregnant, he impregnated her handmaiden Hagar who gave birth to Ishmael. Then Sarah became pregnant and bore a son named Isaac. The Muslims believe Ishmael, Abraham's son born to Sarah's handmaiden Hagar was his rightful heir. The Jews believe Isaac, born to his wife, Sarah, to be his rightful heir. That's it. That's where they parted ways."

How did she know all this?

"So, if Ishmael and Isaac had the same father, they're half-brothers, right? So that makes their descendants – the Jews and Muslims – cousins. Yet, over the centuries, hundreds of thousands, or even millions of these cousins have killed one another and continue to kill one another over Abraham's legacy. Do they even remember why they're fighting in the first place? It's absolutely crazy. Millions murdered because of a family feud carried on through the centuries. So much for religion." She extinguished her cigarette in the ashtray and pushed it away.

I thought it would be a good idea to teach the history of our shared lineage in schools to encourage religious tolerance, and I told Ferri as much.

She'd chuckled. *"Chee meegee?* What are you saying? Do you know that according to Muslim religious law – Shariah – Jews are one of the eleven things considered *haram,* inherently filthy, unclean things, along with – among other things – dog feces, urine and dead animals? Muslims need to avoid sharing our food and stay clear of other things we touch. Our filth is contagious."

My jaw had dropped. I'd waited for Ferri to signal that she was joking; surely, she couldn't have been serious. This couldn't be part of my religion.

To my amazement, she had continued. "Muslims who do come in contact can only rid themselves of the filth by going through a described purification process. Of course, there is no purification process available for a Jew. A Jew can only be saved by converting to Islam."

I was angered at her version of my religion. I stopped walking and turned to her. "Ferri, stop poking fun at my religion!"

She looked at me in surprise. "You think I'm kidding? You've honestly never heard this?"

"No, I haven't. It's simply not true. I may not know a lot about the Quran, but I tell you, no one I know thinks like that."

"*Joonie,* I know that. I'm just telling you that it's part of Shariah law, Islamic law that's supposedly based on the Quran and Al Hadith."

"The Quran and what?"

"Al Hadith. I think that's how you say it. I'm not sure. Maybe Hadith? It's Islamic law that's not written in the Quran. It's based on Mohammad's lifestyle and things he had approved of according to his companions. They have been carried down through the ages and used as the cornerstones of Shariah law."

How could I not know any of this?

To my horror, she'd gone on. "Muslims consider people who aren't Muslim to be infidels who must be converted.

"Layla, I hate to be the one to tell you this, but Islam doesn't view people of other religions as equal. They're not to be tolerated. Though the Quran tells Muslims to revere Jews and Christians as 'People of the Book,' Shariah dictates that Islam is to be the only religion, Allah is to be the only name for God, and Shariah law is to be acknowledged as the supreme universal law. Resistance by the *infidel* is to be overcome *by whatever means needed.*"

I was appalled. "I don't believe anything you said, Ferri.

All she said was, "Hah!"

I'd made a mental note to do some research and continue this conversation and present her with facts that contradicted the strange things she she'd said.

The point in all this is that Ferri has never been religious. Still, I had resented her characterization of my religion as violent and intolerant.

That was before the Ayatollah Khomeini became our country's leader.

Now as we stand in the bookstore, I recall that day.

"Religious persecution is thriving in Iran," I say to her. "We both know that. And I remember your views on religion," I say. "You think organized religion separates people instead of bringing them together. But Ferri, the mullahs are all fervent believers."

She takes hold of my hand. "Listen, *Joonie,* neither Hamid nor I intend to die at the hands of some old religious fanatic. We are leaving this hell-hole."

My heart skips. *I will lose her again!* "You're leaving? You can't leave." Though my initial outcry is emotional – *she just can't leave me!* – my rational mind soon asserted itself.

"How can you leave? It's impossible. You'll be stopped at the airport. When you show them your passport-"

Ferri interrupts. "We're not flying."

"How are you getting out of the country?"

"Over the mountains. On camels. To Afghanistan."

I look at her in utter bewilderment. *Of all her insane ideas!* "Are you crazy?"

She shakes her head. "Others we know have done it and gotten there safely." She could be talking about a brand of toothpaste her friends had tried and liked. As much as I want to dissuade her from this insane idea of riding a camel over mountainous territory across the border to Afghanistan, I know I can't change her mind. I'd never been able to talk her out of anything. Ferri has always done exactly as she wants.

"And when do you plan to begin this expedition?" I ask, not adding "insane," though I'm not at all sure she hasn't lost her mind.

"Soon. Tomorrow or the next day. We'll leave when we finish gathering all our supplies and provisions. So, I have lots to do. I really shouldn't be here, but I couldn't not see you one last time and say goodbye."

She sees the look on my face, the tears that have suddenly gathered. She puts her hand on mine and holds it to reassure me. "*Joonie,* you want me to be safe, don't you? That's why I'm leaving. I promise I'll be fine. I'll let you know when I get there."

I am jerked back to reality. "No, no," I say, "you can't!" I bring out my small address book and grab a flyer from a stack at nearby table that's advertising a new book by a mullah, and quickly copy down Bahman's London address and phone number on the back. "Here. Take this. You can't contact me. But Bahman, Shireen's brother, lives in London. When you get there, contact him. Just tell him …" I try to push my feelings aside and think of a safe code. "Tell him he should call and tell me only, *The package has arrived.* Don't use your name; make one up. Say nothing else, nothing at all. Just say *The package has arrived.* Okay?"

She takes the flyer and holds me close. "I promise. And I promise that the package *will* arrive."

She is so calm.

It is incredible that Ferri can be so calm when she's leaving everything and everyone behind to embark on a perilous journey to a new country — on a camel of all things! — with the Ayatollah's mullahs and the Revolutionary Guards at her back.

"But, *Joonie,*" she says. "You must promise me that you'll be careful, too. You're a mother. Take care of yourself and *Ensha Allah,* God willing, we'll meet again. I want to meet Reza. I love you."

Tears are rolling down my cheeks as I hug her tightly, press against her, burying my head in her curls one last time, trying to get as much of her as I can, enough to last until I see her again, if ever.

The time to leave has come. I grab a mullah's newly published book from the nearby table. "I love you, Ferri. You're my angel forever. Please be careful." I'm wiping away tears now falling like rain.

I leave my angel. With one last look back at the best friend I've ever had, I find my sunglasses and leave the store, still wiping away tears as I approach the waiting car.

Seated in the back seat of the car, I pray my angel will be safe and will add a prayer for her safety to the daily prayer I have been reciting for so many years, praying I will be reunited with my lost daughter.

2 6

CHECKPOINT

1981

*I*t is the last day of October.

After disappearing for a day, Hassan has returned with a fresh gash that starts on his scalp and travels down his forehead, ending millimeters away from his right eye. His arms are studded with purple welts, the skin raw in places. Along with other fervently religious Shi'ite Muslims who publicly mutilate themselves with bloody knives and razor cuts or whip themselves raw in a crazed fete, The Rat engages in this self-butchery every year on the Day of Ashura, the day commemorating the death of the Prophet's martyred grandson.

I avoid him as much as possible that day as well as the following few, unable to look at his wounds without feeling ill. It would have been terrible enough if he'd sustained these injuries at the hands of another. To know that he has inflicted them by his own hand is too much for me to take in. If he can do this to himself, I wonder what violence he can do to others.

The credo of the revolution, "to free the oppressed from their oppressors," has signaled to housemaids, drivers, valets, cooks, gardeners, other household workers and laborers, that they are "no less than" those of the privileged class who are, most likely, sinful. Yet The Rat still serves as Rostam's loyal valet and driver, even though, now that his master's business has disappeared with the ban on music and the hatred of all things American, I surmise he is in danger of receiving a substantial cut in his customary wages soon. His dogged loyalty is proof of the strong bond that has developed between these two men with such different back-grounds.

Many in the upper class have seen their elite status no more than a thing of the past and their wealth decimated, as agents of the revolution confiscate property, businesses, and money from these "oppressors," while ever increasing the mullahs' wealth of the mullahs.

This is the new version of life in our country.

~~~

I am frantic.

The Christian New Year 1981 has come and by the end of January, my world explodes. I've missed my moon for two months and I'm desperate to see my gynecologist. The Rat drives me to her office on what used to be Pahlavi Avenue, then the longest street in the Middle East. Following the Ayatollah's rise to power, it was renamed Mossadegh Street in honor of the former prime minister, so loved by the populace and so feared by the shah, then renamed to Valiser Street in honor of yet another Shi'ite leader.

A division of the Revolutionary Guards, meant to safeguard the Islamic Republic, has stationed men at intersections along the busy thoroughfares where red traffic lights serve as checkpoints, allowing the Guards to peer into cars to ensure passengers are abiding by the law. When The Rat turns onto Valiasr Street and stops at the light, a Guard peers into our car. He cranes his neck and sees me in the back seat, then orders The Rat to pull over. When he instructs us to exit the car, alarms go off in my head. He is carrying a rifle. I pull the top of my *chador* down past my forehead.

"*Barradarr,* brother, I see you have a female in the back seat." Hassan shakes his head. Is she your family? Perhaps your sister? "No. I am her husband's driver."

"So, you are driving an unrelated woman around the city."

My heart flutters and falls to the ground. I am about to be hauled off to jail for traveling with a man that is not a relative. Thankfully, the Guard continues to focus on The Rat who is cowering, his eyes down, as he explains he is taking me to see the doctor.

The Guard sneers. "May Allah bless our honored leader and give him long life. You must know you may not be in the company of an unrelated female."

I have never seen The Rat intimidated and, were I not so afraid for myself, I would have enjoyed the scene.

The Guard slaps The Rat's arm. "*Barradarr,* brother, our days of oppression are over." The Guard goes on with a smile. "She's no better than you with this expensive car that her husband obtained by oppressing the likes of you."

The Rat's nose twitches. He seems at once both starstruck, captivated by this uniformed man with the important job, and afraid, as the man is armed.

"As a woman," he continues, "she's less than you. *Barradarr,* brother, it's a new day! She is a weak, while you are a man, not meant to drive her around like a donkey. She must be driven by one of her own kind." The Rat nods in agreement, and I don't know if he agrees with the Guard, or if he is simply deferring to the man carrying a rifle.

The Guard turns to me. "*Khahar*, sister, do not expect this man to drive you around again." I nod and say I understand. Since the revolution, everyone has been addressing everyone else as either "sister" or "brother," and I understood that it is meant to emphasize the view that we are all part of one big family, children of the Supreme Leader. Yet, when I am addressed as "sister" by a stranger carrying a rifle, it continues to sting.

The Guard notices my shaking hand holding tightly onto the two ends of my *chador,* and the shadow of a smile crosses his face. But his eyes are steely.

"*Khahar*, sister, you will drive with a sister." I will not be arrested. I keep my gaze down, not even daring to nod.

He turns back to The Rat. "*Barradarr,* brother, drive the car back where you got it from, or leave it parked here for its owner to reclaim." He gestures to me. "She will take a taxi to her doctor."

He asks me where I'm going. I try to sound meek and subservient. "My doctor," I echo The Rat in a whisper.

He probes. "What for?"

"A checkup," I say.

The light turns green and he faces the oncoming traffic. He whistles, hails a taxicab while pointing to me, indicating the need for a female cab driver. One stops, and he addresses me again. "*Khahar,* sister, go with her."

I am more than happy to hurry into the back seat of the taxi and close the door, quickly giving the driver the address to my gynecologist's office.

As we drive away, I see Hassan get back into Rostam's car and start the engine.

The next day, Hassan appears at the house wearing a white long-sleeved shirt over a tight-fitting, beige T-shirt, emblazoned with a large drawing of the Ayatollah Khomeini in black ink.

He tells Rostam that he is ending his long service as his employee and to join the Revolutionary Guards.

From then on, he wears his cap and beige chinos with matching shirt, his sleeves a bit rolled up, and a gun in his holster. He will no longer treat my husband as his master. From this day forward, he will be Rostam's equal, his friend, his 'barradarr,' his bother.

Instead of finding Hassan's new attitude cheeky, Rostam is delighted to know he now has a friend in the Revolutionary Guards, a man who knows him well and knows the wealth and power he once had. No doubt, he is thrilled that one who has remained so loyal to him through the years may well be of great benefit to him as a Guard.

The two men begin to insulate themselves in Rostam's room for hours at a time, my husband calling for me to serve them tea if the weather is cold, cucumber and mint water or a yogurt drink when it is hot.

The Rat's eyes mock me as I serve them their drinks. I hear their occasional boisterous laughter, as well as their screams of anger and indignity through the closed door.

Last week, on one of his frequent visits, The Rat stopped on his way to Rostam's room to inform me that he is doing well with the Guards, receiving praise, and is moving up the chain of command with a handful of Guards already under his watch. No doubt, both his ardent following of Muslim traditions and his intolerance of other religions, help him on his upward climb. I know that he's shared the news to taunt me and instill in my a fear of his growing power.

Today, before joining Rostam in his room, The Rat leans against my kitchen counter with folded arms and informs me that the Guards are on the lookout for "that pig Jew girl I hadn't allowed in when she came to our door. Turns out she's a communist and a spy. Her boyfriend, too. Or maybe, you know that."

Of course, he is speaking of Ferri, who had rushed to the house during the ten days Rostam had ordered me under house arrest, anxious to deliver what turned out to be the last letter I would receive from Linda, a warning that she would be taking Jasmine to an adoption agency if I didn't return to Los Angeles immediately. I remain stone-faced as the Rat gives me this news. I am comforted by the knowledge that Ferri and Hamid left Iran two weeks ago and so are either in Afghanistan close to it. I have no idea how long their arduous trip over mountains on camels might take and I haven't yet heard from my angel via Bahman. I can only pray that they are now safe in Afghanistan and beyond reach of the Revolutionary Guards.

The Rat's entry into the Guards gives Rostam a new kind of power and heralds the oncoming doom.

27

BAHAR

1982

*R*ostam has begun having sex with all kinds of women, peppering his female sex partners with an occasional male.

Meanwhile, as intimacy between us has almost ground to a total halt, I no longer take birth control pills.

Still, I am surprised to discover that Rostam has apparently managed to impregnate me, yet again. Tests confirm I am pregnant.

At first, I resent this pregnancy. I so love spending time with Reza, that I want nothing and no one – not even another child – to interfere with our time together. But Reza is getting older – he is seven now – and he's becoming ever more engrossed with his schoolwork and friends, asking to spend more of his free time with his classmates. I eventually make peace with the idea of having another child, realizing how much I enjoy mothering.

Besides, aware as I am of life's unexpected uncertainties, I am comforted knowing that, if his father and I are, for whatever reason no longer available, my son will still have family.

I am carrying low, a sign assumed to mean I am carrying a girl. As the ultrasound shows no penis, my doctor also believes I am carrying girl. Having the chance to raise a daughter thrills me. I decide to name her Bahar, which means spring.

Unlike my pregnancy with Reza, Rostam knows early on that I am again with child. The morning sickness, the weight gain, my swollen belly, and fuller breasts are all soon obvious. And, though everyone else around me is delighted, he treats me as he did during my previous pregnancy, which is to say, like a leper. Our lives become even more separate. He avoids me and spends almost all his time in his separate room.

I am delighted to see that Reza is excited at the prospect of a baby coming into the household. As the months pass, my sweet son takes care of me, insisting that I never overdo any physical work or overly exert myself. He makes sure to curtail our time at the park tossing frisbees, brings a chair to me whenever I am standing, and eventually hovers over my belly to feel the baby's kicks.

Between my son and my husband, I am at once a revered Madonna who can do no wrong and a resented whore, carrying some dreaded contagious disease.

I am my ninth month.

After Reza leaves for school, my water breaks. Rostam goes into a panicked mania. It is as if he's taken a drug. Though my labor pains have not yet begun in earnest and I am still in my slippers and robe, he insists that I hurry into the car without so much as a bag of clothes or a toothbrush. He throws me the *chador* that hangs by our front door, and we start off for the hospital. The Rat is not available so Rostam is driving and driving so fast, one would think the baby's head was presenting.

There are beads of sweat on his face, and, with his jacket off, I see his the wet circles under his arms. He is driving like a crazy man, well over the speed limit.

At first, I try to bite my tongue as he makes random illegal turns and crosses intersections against the light. I must slow him down. I make a simple observation. "You're driving very fast, Rostam. You don't have to go so fast. I'm fine." Then, I dare to raise my voice. "Rostam, you're going too fast. Please! Slow down. There's no rush." His driving is outright reckless. My hand is holding onto my door handle tightly, my body is tense with fear. Finally, I waste no words. I don't try to hide my alarm.

"Rostam, you have to slow down! We'll have an accident! For God's sake, please! Slow down! Slow down, Rostam!" But he doesn't listen. Just blocks away from the hospital, he races through another red light.

The last thing I hear is the sound of crunching metal at my side as a car crashes into me. Just before I pass out, I am aware of intense abdominal pain, a contraction that never ends.

I awake in the hospital in terrible pain to learn that I have suffered substantial bleeding and Bahar has not survived. The doctors explain that the accident had caused my placenta to separate from the uterine wall and was thus no longer able to give my baby what she needed. By the time emergency vehicles came to us and we were taken out of the wreck and transported to the hospital where they realized I was pregnant, it was too late. They called it, "placenta abruption." Had Bahar survived, the resulting lack of oxygen would likely have caused major injury to her brain with untold consequences.

.   .   .

Glass from the smashed car window has left cuts on my arms, chest and swollen face. My right eye is held closed with bandages. I have a fractured collarbone. My right side suffered the direct impact of the crash. My right leg was fractured in two places, and my right arm was broken. The nurses administer blessed morphine, which lessens my physical pain. But these pains are all temporary and will heal. Knowing I've lost Bahar brings far more pain than my injuries. The loss of Bahar cuts a new ache in my heart.

Rostam was discharged from the hospital soon after we had been admitted. Having suffered no more than a broken rib and a gash on his forehead caused by the impact with the steering wheel, he was sent home with his lower ribcage bound in bandages and a hefty supply of pain pills. He will continue to refill those prescription and down the pills several times a day, often with alcohol, long after his injuries have healed.

The accident has been a paradox. The one and only time Rostam tried to do something for me or our baby, he ended up killing our daughter. I begged him to slow down. The hatred that I feel for him is beyond anything I've ever before felt. From this day forward, my hatred of him is insurmountable.

He has killed my child.

～

How confusing my life is!

I'd been eager to have this child. It seems that whatever I want, I can't have, though whatever I either don't want or don't care about, I have plenty of. Condolences, flowers, and kind words appear in my hospital room daily, filling it to capacity, but not my husband. Never once, my husband. I don't expect him to visit me, nor do I expect a word of apology or contrition. I get neither.

After staying in the hospital for more than a month, I am

leaving in a wheelchair today. I have been supplied with crutches, a walker and an order for a hospital bed to be delivered to the house. Rostam has begged off picking me up, saying he had an important meeting, which, of course, is a lie. Babajon picks me up from the hospital and I gladly stay at my parents' house for the first three weeks, taking strong pain pills, my head hardly leaving the pillow.

It is good to be around Reza, who stayed with my parents while I was in the hospital, pampered and spoiled by the grandparents he loves, and he is staying there with me now. Our reunion, holding my young son close and smelling his unique mix of odors, of Ivory soap, egg shampoo with the undernote of his scalp's natural smell, and the aroma of Cobra's vegetable stew recently eaten on his breath, is more comforting than any amount of pain medication.

He sleeps on a cot in Babajon's study, while I sleep in my old bedroom nearby.

I sleep a lot, due in part to the pills I am taking.

When I'm awake, I spend most of my time in my bedroom, my television turned to state-sanctioned programs I don't watch, while Reza does his homework at the desk I used to sit at. When his homework is finished, he reads to me. He hugs me carefully.

"Maman jon, I know you're sad, but I promise I will make up for the baby you lost." Tears come to my eyes. My Reza is nothing like his father. Rostam blames his lack of visits to my parents' home during that time to his, quote, *debilitating ongoing pain.*

When the adjustable hospital bed is finally delivered to my house, I return home to my bedroom at home, now mine alone, bed bound for weeks as my body slowly heals. The cuts and scrapes caused by shards of broken glass healed first and soon the bandages on my eye come off, necessitating eye drops at regular intervals. My plastered leg and arm along with my broken collarbone, take far longer to heal.

Over one month has now passed since the day I came back home, and I am able to stand without help if I move slowly and carefully, and I have learned how to navigate with crutches. When the plaster cast finally comes off my leg, I use the walker. A therapist is sent to the house to supervise leg exercises meant to strengthen my right leg, and when the cast on my arm is removed, she adds some exercises for my arms. I carefully push the walker around the house, but it is difficult to dress. Consequently, I don't leave the house and the chill of autumn makes it difficult to venture into the gardens.

I attribute my steady improvement to what the desire to heal and what positive thoughts I can gather, which are all about daydreaming of the day I will meet Ehsan again. If we are ever able to meet again, surely, I will go to him wherever he may be. I must recover my balance and strengthen my legs. If we are fated to be together, he cannot see me like this. I continue my daily prayers for Jasmine.

This entire time, Rostam has never once so much as hinted at blame nor has he offered a word of comfort. He has simply lived in the largest guest room where he drinks, downs his pain pills, and avoids me as much as possible.

Truly, I am glad he stays out of my way.

Travelling around the house with my walker, I note women coming in and retiring to Rostam's room.

No doubt, they have been ordered there to have sex. The women have most likely agreed to a *sigheh*. Ridiculously, amid so many stringent religious bans restricting the interaction between the sexes, there is the concept of *sigheh*, legitimizing sexual liaisons that would otherwise be immoral and illegal, between Shiite Muslim males, married or not, and what amounts to prostitutes.

Sigheh allow a "temporary marriage" between a man and woman for a limited period of time and with some form of payment to the female.

If a man desires a woman he sees, perhaps on the street, he can, with his wife's consent, enter into a *sigheh*, a legal, temporary marriage that might only last only as long as the duration of intercourse, or up to ninety-nine years and anything in between – as *he* chooses – after which he can end the relationship with no consequences.

The formula is simple. The man merely has to recite something that approximates the following:

With the consent of my first wife, I have married (her name) of my own will, for the period of (the amount of time he desires to be with her, whether an hour, day, week or years), with the gift when we part of (he can give the woman anything from a pen, a piece of paper, a book, a bit of food, a match, money or a piece of gold for her company, as he chooses).

With these words, their liaison is considered religiously and legally blessed. Of course, Rostam has never actually said these words aloud and I've never consented – though, I gladly would. Nonetheless, if the woman he has intercourse with becomes pregnant, a mullah will take his word as a man that he had recited them and that I had consented. On that basis, the mullah will record their union as sanctified by a *sigheh*, allowing the mother to obtain identification papers for her child. Once they separate, Rostam will be under no obligation to support or deal with the child or the mother in any way. There is no limit to the number of *sighehs*, a Muslim man can enjoy at any given time. In short, *sigheh* is a legal loophole that legitimizes prostitution.

I am apathetic to Rostam's parade of women. I have no interest in anything he does. My only wish is for Reza to be insulated from the parade of females. To that end, I have set up a small desk for him in my bedroom, and he has fallen into the habit of doing his homework there rather than at the dining room table as before.

As I convalesce, my parents bring food for the family, all my favorite dishes prepared by Cobra. They visit me in my bedroom. I thank all the gods that they have no interaction with Rostam, who is almost always sequestered in his room, enjoying visits from The Rat and his prostitutes.

Today, for the first time, he barges in while my parents are with me.

Though he is dressed in soiled pajama pants and a t-shirt at three in the afternoon, Initially unaware of their presence, he bellows, "Woman! Where in God's name have you hidden Rostam's wallet?" I am thankful that he doesn't hasn't called me by any of his vile names.

Of course, I haven't seen his wallet and suggest he ask Hassan to find it – The Rat knows where everything he owns is.

Neither of my parents say a word. Maman looks bewildered and Babajon turns red. As he notes the damage done, Rostam smirks more than smiles and says, "hello," before leaving us to ourselves. Babajon looks at me with sad eyes, his mouth hanging open. They are both awaiting some explanation.

When none is forthcoming, Babajon gets up and paces across my bedroom rug, worry beads in hand.

2 8

FOTMEH

1983

otmeh is out of the house and heading for the alley where she will meet Araf.

Her cheeks are flushed, and her heart is bubbling with a new feeling of excitement. She's carrying a brown paper bag, packed a chicken thigh, several stuffed grape leaves and two of those delicious, honeyed pastries Khanom had served last night. She had wanted to include a piece of that delicious cake Khanom had ordered, but it was so soft that she would have had to put it in a small dish, and she was afraid that Cobra, the sort of cook that keeps track of every dish in her realm, would miss any dish she used.

The skies are blue, and the wind has died down, so the sweater and light shawl she wears over her *hijab* are enough to keep her warm.

She is glad The Supreme Leader has ruled that the chador may be exchanged for a *hijab, a* covering for the head that extends down to the neck and stops at the chest. Now the *chador,* the sheet that covers the entire body, the *hijab,* and the *roosaree,* a headscarf tied at the neck, have all been lumped together and spoken of as the mandated *hijab.* She must still be totally covered from her head to her toes, so she's wearing long pants under the pretty blue dress Khanom has given her, and a gray coat, another of Layla's hand-me-downs, that falls just below her knees. When Araf and her are alone, she will unbutton her coat, leaving her pretty dress visible for Afar to see.

She knows she is lucky to be the recipient of all Layla's lovely hand-me-downs. True, she has never come to know the girl well. Layla's last return home from America had caused Zahra Khanom's uproar. She had never heard her mistress yell like that at anyone before and has never heard her yell like that since that day in the kitchen when she had terrorized her daughter.

Khanom had hurled many insults at Layla, insults Fotmeh had never before heard. There were many tears, then the girl had stayed in bed for a few days with pain. She never returned to America. She stayed in Tehran and married the big man with teeth as yellow as her own miserable father's, whom she hasn't seen in years and doesn't miss.

She walks on, her excitement increasing with every step. She has been anticipating this meeting since Araf suggested it. Each time she's thought of it her heartbeat quickened.

Now it is imminent.

Fotmeh often accompanies Cobra to the bazaar to purchase produce.

Three weeks ago, Khanom sent her to the bazaar alone to buy

herbs for Cobra's stew. Fotmeh had approached Araf's father's stall, her eyes darting around, looking for the tall, handsome son she had seen on her prior visits, yet had never dared speak to as that would have been most unseemly for a good Persian girl.

She hadn't spotted him until his father called out. "Araf, come help the lady. Sullie is here and I must speak with him. See what she needs. Give her a good price. Her household is a good customer."

Fotmeh had spotted him then, sitting on the ground, playing with what Fotmeh guessed was a hamster or a mouse. At his father's behest, Araf jumped up, put the small animal in his pocket, walked up to the stall and smiled at her.

To her surprise, he had greeted her by name. "*Salam*, hello and peace to you, Fotmeh Khanom." His manner had been friendly and unabashed. "You look very pretty today."

Fotmeh had blushed, casting her eyes down, demurely. "How do you know my name?" she'd asked.

Araf's eyes had sparkled when he grinned. "I've heard that woman you usually come here with call you."

Fotmeh had been flattered that her name had registered with him. With her eyes still gazing down, she said, coyly, "You must hear many names here."

Araf's grin had broadened. Fotmeh glanced up and noted his teasing eyes. "Not all of them are attached to a pretty face." She was certain her face had reddened deeper.

If another boy had dared make such a forward comment, Fotmeh would have treated him coldly and cut the conversation short. But what would have been brash if said by someone else had been music to her ears when Araf said it.

"I need six bunches of parsley," she'd said.

"Then you shall have the fullest, greenest, freshest six bunches of parsley in Tehran."

He'd rummaged through the parsley bin and selected six

181

bunches that satisfied him, deftly depositing them into a bag, while Fotmeh had studied his hands. They were dirty, but beautiful, the palms plump, the fingers long and perfectly proportioned, the nails uniform.

"Thank you," she'd said. "I also need cilantro, watercress, tarragon, basil, and dill."

"Six bunches of each?" She nodded and he'd set about picking through the various baskets of herbs, choosing only the freshest ones. When he was done, he had put the all the bags in one large one and held it out to her. She took it, careful not to brush against his hand.

For the following two weeks, Cobra had been so busy preparing for Agha Saleh's birthday celebration that Fotmeh, who had been looking forward to seeing Araf again, had happily found herself alone at the bazaar again and delighted when Araf's father, occupied with other shoppers, had again called on his son to assist her.

Araf had smiled at her and asked how she was feeling. She dared to return a quick smile before his father, finished with the other customers, made any further personal conversation impossible. When she was done with her purchases, she'd thanked him and said goodbye. As she walked away, she felt his eyes on her, watching her leave.

Today, she'd been instructed to go to the bazaar alone again.

When she got there, Araf's father had been arranging his produce on the long tables, and Araf was nowhere to be seen. She had dawdled at a distance until she saw a customer approach the stall and speak to Araf's father. She'd hurried to the stall then and was rewarded by hearing the vendor call for help from his son.

Araf had appeared and, while his father was occupied with a sudden string of other customers, she and Araf had spoken.

"How is the pretty Fotmeh Khanom today?" Araf had asked.

"I'm well, praise Allah."

"Tell me, Fotmeh Khanom, do you work for a good family?"

What a question! No one has ever asked her such a thing.

Why, Khanom and Agha Saleh were the most wonderful people in the whole world! They'd given her a fairytale life from the moment she'd experienced her first car ride twenty years earlier, as the three of them drove away from her parents' small, filthy hut at the foot of the Saleh's big beautiful, white summer house in Vallian.

The Salehs brought her into their magnificent home in Tehran filled with beautiful things and even gave her a bedroom all for herself! Because of them, she would never again share that miserable hovel with her parents and four sisters, not to mention the fifth sister and the brother, both born after she left. She would never again share one fly-ridden pot of watered-down soup made with fat and carrots with a scrap of bread and call it dinner. No, Khanom has changed her into a city girl. She now wears shoes and no longer walks around the house wearing a dirty headscarf as she had when she'd met them. Zahra Khanom has also taught her to speak without her village accent.

She is a woman now, stronger, more assertive than before – like Zahra Khanom herself whom Fotmeh so admires.

And, though the new laws make it mandatory that she wear a *chador* when Agha Saleh is home — for Agha is an unrelated male — she's found it impossible to do housework while wearing a *chador*, and Agha Saleh has said that wearing it in the house is strictly her choice so long as they have no guests.

Fotmeh now wears her long raven black hair firmly braided and tied behind her head with a small ribbon, the same shade as her dress. Today the pretty blue dress and matching hair ribbon are hidden, but she is excited at the thought that Araf might notice them.

She had answered Araf's question with a nod. "Yes. They are very good people. May Allah bless them, and may I continue to live in their shade."

He had continued to ask her questions as he'd filled bags with produce. As they spoke, Fotmeh became increasingly comfortable, her shyness, decreasing.

"What about you?" she had asked boldly. "Do you like working with your father?"

He'd shrugged. "I like helping him. I work with him almost every day. We go to the vegetable vendors in the early morning. I help load up the crates, then carry them to our stall here." His lips had stretched into a smile and the twinkle in his eyes had returned. "He is happy I help him, so he's less upset with me for the time I spend sketching."

Fotmeh has never known an artist. She'd asked about his sketches. Araf had told her he enjoys sketching the many beautiful scenes and characters in the bazaar in pencil and charcoal and aspires to paint one day. It had surprised Fotmeh that he found beauty in the bazaar's crowded stalls, but she'd said nothing. She had wanted to ask to see his sketches, but that was impossible.

Araf had volunteered the information that he is thirty-three years old and has a younger brother.

When he'd asked where she lives, Fotmeh was hesitant to give him the Saleh address, so she'd answered, "in the neighborhood."

The boy's eyebrows had lifted as though surprised by the answer. Then he'd nodded, and she had smiled. But her smile had turned into a look of shock when he asked her to meet him outside of the bazaar.

Before she could stop herself, she had agreed.

These few conversations with Araf have changed Fotmeh.

She had never before had a personal conversation with a male. Of course, she answers Agha Saleh when he addresses her, usually asking her questions about where Khanom has gone or when she'll be home. She's spoken with venders. She's also taken care of young boys, children whose parents come to the Saleh home without their nannies. But this was different. Araf is the first boy she'd spoken with who is close to her own age, and she enjoyed his attention. Their conversations in the bazaar have all been completely safe, with his father close by and crowds observing them. He has done no more but help with her purchases.

Fotmeh has begun to wonder if she will ever marry. As grateful as she is to the Salehs, she isn't certain that her loyalty to them should confine her to a life as a spinster. Unsure of her birthdate, she guesses that she is a few years younger than Araf's thirty-three years. Lately, when she watches over the toddlers and young children belonging to her masters' family relations and friends, she finds herself dreaming of the day she will have her own child. She wonders what pregnancy is like and if childbirth is as painful as her mother had sworn it is. She is certain it would be wonderful to hold her own infant at her breast.

But she will first have to marry.

Certainly, Zahra Khanom knows that, expects that. *Doesn't she?*

Will her *khastegar*, her suitor, need Hadi Khan's permission to marry her? Surely, that makes more sense than to ask consent from her own father, the man who abandoned her to the Saleh's home as their servant when she was so very young and has made no effort to contact her since. Fotmeh has not seen her parents since the summer day she left Vallian and traveled to Tehran. In truth, she has never once missed either of her parents, or her sisters, or the small, dark, filthy house that was their home.

And what will happen after she marries? She will likely stay at her husband's home – or more accurately, her mother-in-law's home – and return every morning to the Salehs, like Cobra does.

But she has become accustomed to the luxury she now enjoys, the large room and small bathroom she has all to herself and the privacy it gives her.

But, of course, she will have to give all that up to live with her husband and his parents.

Today, she orchestrated her day, managing her time, getting up early to complete all her chores with enough time left to wash up and dress before meeting Araf.

Leaving the Saleh house, she had run into Abol, the Saleh manservant, doing something with a large plant in the front garden. She felt his eyes linger on her as she made her way down the street, but she will not let that bumbling, old, arrogant servant ruin her day. She will meet Araf at the head of the alley as they have planned, and she will be on time.

She wonders if Araf is already there waiting for her. *Is he impatient? Is he as excited as she is?*

She turns the corner and approaches their designated meeting place. Araf is already there, leaning against the tall stucco wall. As she nears, she can see he holds the small animal in his long hands, stroking it, apparently speaking to it. When he sees Fotmeh, he hurriedly sticks it into his pocket and rushes to meet her.

. . .

Neither of them notices the corpulent man on the corner.

Abol slowly edges toward the two until he can just barely hear their conversation.

2 9

ZAHRA KHANOM'S BREAKFAST

*S*o! Once again, I am correct.

My little servant girl has a boyfriend! According to Abol, he is a lowly boy, probably around her age.

Ahh! How much more can I tolerate?

This is unacceptable!

I will have to deal with her. I will discuss what to do with Hadi. No doubt he will remind me of how reluctant he was to bring her to Tehran in the first place, fearing she might lose her virginity while she was living with us.

"If that happens," he'd said, "her father, uncles, and Allah knows who else, will first kill her for defiling the family name and then kill us for allowing it to happen."

Yet, despite his fears, I had insisted she come to Tehran with us. To allow me to train her to be my perfect maid.

I do find it strange that her father, her uncles, or anyone else would even care at all about her when they haven't once asked about her in all these years. No matter. Hadi will know what to do.

She hasn't yet brought me my morning tea. And, if there is any more of that delicious cake left, I want a slice.

Fotmeh!

Ah! Last night's party celebrating both Hadi's birthday and my beloved grandson's upcoming eighth birthday was perfect.

How long I'd prayed for a grandchild! I'm so very proud of him. Reza is sweet. And already so very smart. When he recited that poem by Hafez, everyone was astounded.

He really is a *shozdeh*, a prince as well as a genius. I think Hadi will continue to bond with him.

My daughter looked so lovely; everyone said so. Like me, childbirth has not damaged her looks. She is obviously happy, yet Hadi continues to wonder. I tell him she must be happy, married to a very wealthy man and has such a wonderful son.

Aye! Where is that girl? Fotmeh!

This is new. She makes me yell for my food!

Yesterday, I sent her to the bazaar to get herbs for Cobra, and instead of being gone for no more than an hour or so, which is as long as it should have taken her, Cobra said she was gone for more than two! She was obviously with this boy. I don't like it at all.

And the impudence of my sister-in-law to tell me how to act with my servants! When Fotmeh finally showed up, and I snapped at her for being late and took away her spending money for the week, Haideh said I was being too harsh. *Imagine!*

Perhaps, I should tell her how to run *her* household, tell her that her flowers are often displayed past their prime, that her dinner plates are gauche, that she serves the same things too often, and that she should see to it that my brother drinks less. It is obvious that my brother's wife is envious of me, and I suppose it's understandable since all her grandchildren are girls.

Where is the girl?

I called for my morning tea hours ago and still it's not here. I don't know what's come over her lately. She's started to dawdle, and I will not stand for it.

Fotmeh! I'm hungry!

My patience is at its end. When she first came here, she was so timid, she ran like a mouse when I gave her so much as a look. Now look at her!

This has to stop!

It's that boy! He has gotten her attention. That's the only explanation for this new dawdling and unacceptable behavior. Whoever he is, he will use her, take her virginity and toss her aside unless I stop this. If she becomes pregnant, *vay beh sarram!* Disaster falls on my head! If her family discovers she has been deflowered, *roozamoon seeyas!* Our future is black!

I must keep her in line, keep a tighter rein on her. She has always had that wild beauty about her, the kind a man would find appealing.

And what does she know of men? She has only known her father, the filthy, illiterate gatekeeper of our summer home, so strapped with all those daughters that he begged us to take one of them home as a servant, and so unable to keep himself off his hag of a wife that he immediately impregnated her again and has since had two more children.

The girl has lived here with us since she was a child and has come to know Hadi, a man who is so gentle, so moral and so good that he would never take advantage of anyone and certainly has no reason to be unfaithful to me. But he is the exception and she is totally innocent, completely naïve, and wholly vulnerable to the ways of the world and men.

We must think what to do. I must see to it that she does nothing to upset the way things are. I am too tired to try to find another maid and train one. I want her to stay.

What is she doing? Where is she?

I want my breakfast!

Fotmeh!

3 0

A CHANGED WORLD

1983

*S*ince the start of the Islamic Revolution, we women have had to be extra careful ... and lucky.

Domestic violence is no longer a punishable offense. The crime of "marital rape" no longer exists. As for rape, unmarried victims rarely report the offense, mindful that they themselves could be charged with "adultery," "indecency" or "immoral behavior."

In any event, it is useless to register a charge because the allegation required two witnesses who were present at the time. (Two female witnesses count as one male).

The issue of rape itself has been transformed. It is a crime to kill a virgin so — too often — the solution has been to first rape the girl, then kill her and pay a few hundred tomans — worth a few U.S. dollars — to her family for their loss.

In this new world, men convicted of killing their daughters, likely "honor killings," receive a maximum of ten years in prison.

That same sentence is given any woman found guilty of encouraging other women to remove their *chador*.

Everyone who can, is leaving Iran.

Visitors are now as rare as Rostam's acts of kindness.

Shireen was stopped by two male Guards as she walked from her car to the dressmaker. One asked if she was a whore or a prostitute. She was dumbfounded.

He took a step closer to her. "Do you want me and my friend to fuck you?" he asked. She drew back, shocked at his daring impudence. She shook her head in disbelief. "If you, classy lady, don't want to be fucked by us, you had better cover yourself." He leered at her. "We may have to kill you then."

By now, we women are allowed to replace the chador with long pants, a long-sleeved coat and a head scarf. Shireen, who wore neither makeup nor nail polish, pulled her scarf forward to make sure all her hair was covered, then followed the Guard's eyes and realized her ankles were in view. Her pants were too short. She quickly apologized to the "brother," turned away, bent down, and pulled her socks up as high as possible.

"That's better," the Guard said. "But I would have liked to fuck you and your big breasts."

Soon after Shireen's confrontation with the Guards, she and Taymoor left for Europe with their children with their nannies accompanying them.

They didn't show up on any list of dissidents. They still own their home in Tehran as well as other properties Taymoor has purchased, including the expensive seaside mansion on the Caspian. Their paper ties to Iran remain and their passports show they take annual trips abroad. So, with all signs indicating that they will return home as they always had, they have no problem flying out of Iran.

My cousin and her husband plan to remain in Europe for the duration of the mullahs' rule. On each of Taymoor's trips abroad, he has funneled what has become a substantial amount of money into several European countries. In addition, of course, Shireen has taken all her jewelry. They also packed as many of the most valuable small objects they could stow in their luggage and shipped many of what was left to Taymoor's two brothers, both already in Europe. One is living a life of leisure in London. The other has started a bourgeoning fashion business in Milan, Italy. No doubt, the brothers will forward these to Taymoor.

Shireen's parents, Haiden Khanom and Mansoor Khan, leave Iran as well, allegedly to be present at the birth of their grandson, Bahman's son. They too, have no plans of returning any time soon.

In short, the revolution continues to upset the lives of those close to home.

But Babajon continues to go to Saleh's laboratories and to preside over Saleh's manufacture of pharmaceutical products.

It seems that with the addition of ingredients imported from Israel the effectiveness and popularity of his products has heightened. The company continues to flourish. Three employees, all division managers, leave Iran early on. Two are Jewish, one is Baha'i.

On a personal level, Babajon grieves the loss of his mother. Nana Joon has suffered a heart attack, her first, at the age of eighty-one. On one of his regular stops at her home to check on her and bring her treats, he found her slumped over on her living room couch.

I loved my Nana Joon and I mourn her loss with him. Growing

up, my Nana Joon took me places that Maman never would. The one time I ever visited a *hammmom amooneh,* the public baths, was with Nana Joon. There was no question that she loved me. I always believed that I had a place in her heart that Jila, her grandchild by Babajon's sister, Elahe, never shared. While I was in Los Angeles attending UCLA, Nana Joon wrote me letters that came straight from her heart. I would put the thin pages to my nose, inhaling her scent. Her words were filled with wisdom and love.

On top of all that, the fact she died of a heart attack increases my concern for my father's heart.

Maman continues to complain. She used to complain about the mandated *chador* every time she wore it. She has now switched to wearing a *hijab.* She wears it with tailored coats and long pants, complaining still.

"Ridiculous!" she says. "To think I have to hide myself because of some old mullahs! I don't pay for manicures to have them naked of color, or have my hair styled to have my head under this ridiculous thing. And why should I have to hide my nice legs and comely figure under coats all the time? Even in the heat! It's ridiculous! Crazy old man! How I miss my shah!"

When her younger sister, Bahia, takes an extended trip to stay with her late husband's sister in Germany, Maman complains. "My brother has gone off to England, and my little sister to Germany. They've left me without a thought. I miss them."

She also complains of a change in Cobra's attitude. "Cobra has become a she-devil. Oppressed? She was never oppressed."

And she is beyond upset with her little Fotmeh. "The girl has forgotten her place. She has found a boy, or a boy has found her, and my life is ruined!"

She is correct. Fotmeh is now a woman in love, sneaking off to see Araf at all hours of the day.

Abol has trailed the boy and has discovered his name and that he works with his father at the bazaar. Of course, Fotmeh has not realized that Maman is aware of her relationship with Araf. Abol, charged with the task of spying on her, has done his job well. Yet there is a limit to what he can uncover.

Though Maman knows about Fotmeh's exploits, she has said nothing to the girl or to Babajon, hoping the relationship would sour. She suspects that Fotmeh may have been sleeping with this boy, but she has kept quiet about her suspicions, hoping the girl won't become pregnant. Apparently, that had been the very thing Babajon had feared would happen if the young girl had come to Tehran.

But then Fotmeh announces she will soon marry Araf and Maman must seek her husband's help.

They are at the dinner table.

Babajon, home from Saleh later than usual, is enjoying the stew of eggplant and okra Cobra has prepared. The dish is one of his favorites.

"Hadi, what will you do?" she asks Babajon. "The girl is determined to marry this boy."

Babajon sighs.

Fotmeh, noticeably absent, left the house early that afternoon and has not yet returned. While she was out, Maman went into the girl's room and had seen three bags and some clothes spread out on the bed. "She is packing. She says she's in love. He proposed to her last night, and she has accepted. She said something about meeting his parents ... today ... or tonight." She shakes her head making her brown curls sway. "Hadi, I don't know what to do. I just don't know."

Babajon wants a second helping of rice and stew, but won't enjoy it with his wife so upset. He places his elbows on either side of his plate atop the shiny mahogany table, where he sees the reflection of the ten small lights on the crystal chandelier above.

His wife goes on lamenting. "I told her that was impossible. But she didn't back down." She looks at her husband and he knows she is bewildered. "She's changed so, she's a different person. She says she loves him. She says so many young men died in the war with Iraq that women her age are racing to find a spouse, and she is lucky to have him."

My father notes that his wife has barely eaten and has taken to playing with her silverware. "What happened to that timid village girl too afraid to look at me?"

He laughs. "She grew up, *azizam,* my dearest. And, she has you to thank for turning her into the strong woman that she is," he says.

His wife waves his compliment away and moans.

"*Roozam see-yah shodeh!* My future is black! What will I do now, Hadi *jon?*"

He reaches out and holds her hand. "You can't blame the girl," he says. "She's in love. Apparently, he is, too." Seeing the look of despair that takes over his wife's face, he adds, "*Aziz,* Precious, it's come to this. It's better they marry than for Fotmeh to become pregnant without a husband."

Maman utters a sigh of desperation, puts her napkin alongside her plate. She sits back in her chair.

"*Azizam,*" he says, "things are no longer as they were." Maman looks at him as if to say she's not stupid and knows that all too well. He continues, "Nothing is the same. You know this country has changed. It has changed the people as well."

She leans forward with a ready response. "But she is our servant!" she says. "I forbade her to see him again. You know what she said? She said, 'I cannot and will not stop seeing him, Khanom.

We are in love, and we will marry. We will not hide.'" She shakes her head. "Imagine, Hadi! What right has she to-"

Babajon interrupts her. "O*mram,* my everything, the days of people like us, people of our class, having influence over people like Fotmeh are over. She feels entitled to do exactly as she likes."

"But what about me?" Maman whines. "Do you know how long it took me to mold her into the perfect maid? My God, Hadi! I plucked her from that hovel in Vallian and brought her to Tehran. She was probably not even twelve! She'd never even worn shoes! I had to teach her everything! And now she goes off, leaves me, and gets married to some boy from the bazaar that we've never even met and don't even know. And I can do nothing?"

"Surely, Abol has done his work," he says, and she realizes he knows Abol has been spying on Fotmeh.

She grimaces. "He's done well, considering. But we don't even know where he lives. All we know is that his name is Araf, and he works at his father's stall in the bazaar, selling produce. That's obviously where they've met. Since the night after your birthday months ago, and likely before that, they've been meeting in alleys and empty garages, like common riffraff. You must do something. Hadi, I cannot lose her."

"Zahra, *azizam,* my Precious, the girl is in love. We can't change her mind. She hasn't asked your permission. She's told you what she's going to do. We must accept that she will marry this boy."

Maman is about to object when Babajon pats her arm to calm her, then says, "If you don't want her to leave, perhaps she doesn't have to."

Maman looks at him, curious, of course she's curious, to hear what he has to say.

"Why not invite both of them to live here? They already have her room, and it will certainly save them money." Babajon can tell his wife is listening, hanging on his words. "And if they were planning to live with his parents, well then, surely, they will be more comfortable here. Fotmeh can continue to work and earn money. He can still work at the bazaar." Maman's eyes haven't moved. She hasn't blinked. He adds, "Maybe he can help a bit around the house as well from time to time."

She thinks about his suggestion. Her shoulders relax and she says, "Yes. I suppose that's a solution." She is her calm again, her controlled self again. She smiles. "Hadi you're brilliant! Yes. I think it can work out."

Babajon returns the smile. He piles more rice on his plate and covers it with the stew, the tomato sauce seeping through the rice, okra and a slice of fried eggplant sitting on top.

The very next day, before he leaves for work, my parents sit down with Fotmeh and share their idea with her, offering up their home to her new husband. Fotmeh is thrilled. She thanks them and praises their kindness.

The two marry three days later. Afterwards, Araf and his entire family are invited to the Salehs' home for dinner. After congratulations are exchanged and dinner is over, his family leaves, kissing their son and embracing their new daughter-in-law. The newlyweds retire to their new quarters.

The arrangement turns out to be beneficial to all parties. Babajon – and Maman as well – find Araf easy to get along with. He is also strong and able-bodied and of substantial help at home when not at the bazaar.

His help is especially appreciated as Abol has aged and rediscovered religion. Lately, he spends most of his time reading the Quran and praying, awakening at dawn to pray before breakfast, then praying after lunch and again as dusk approaches, positioning himself in the direction of Mecca, spreading his prayer rug on the floor and praying.

And Maman keeps Fotmeh.

31
REZA

*a*s my son consumes my days, memories of Jasmine begin to fade until I can no longer clearly envision what she looks like.

My yearning for her remains steadfast and I continue to repeat the prayer Setareh gave me. That red crescent birthmark she inherited from David will be forever etched into my memory. But this beautiful child, my son, must now be my focus.

I adore Reza and vow that he will respect the person I am becoming for I will be the best Layla I can be for him. I will do this mothering thing right.

He was the perfect toddler. Now, at age seven going on eight, he is still perfect – smart, curious, courageous, considerate, kind and good natured.

When school begins, he looks forward to each day with excitement and comes home to share everything he's learned that day, as if he'd gone treasure hunting and is eager to describe the treasures he's unearthed. He reminds me of my own excitement in sharing my schoolwork with Babajon. All his teachers, as well as his classmates, think well of him.

Then as his father begins to descend further into depression, despair and debauchery, Reza's grades begin to drop. He's preoccupied and can't stay focused on his schoolwork.

He has no understanding of the man his father is, this man who walks around the house in his pajamas, slurring his words and saying, "They've targeted Rostam. They've done this to Rostam."

I hate the fact that his father will forever be this horrible man, a terrible role model. When we two are alone, and I assume Reza is reading his assignment but then he looks up to ask what's wrong with his father and I feel like a swarm of cockroaches has landed on me.

All I can answer is, "It's nothing. Sweetheart, our country wasn't like it is now. Neither was your father. Our country had a revolution when you were a little boy and since then, it's been really hard on him, my darling boy. He'll be okay."

"Did he become ill?"

I nod and offer a weak, "Yes."

"Will he get better?" When I nod again, he asks, "When?"

I want to scream out what a bastard his father has always been, but I don't. I just shake my head and shrug, smile and tousle my son's lovely dark curls.

When he's old enough to understand, I will be honest and tell him what I think of his father. Not to hurt either of them, but rather, so that Reza won't be tempted to model himself after the oaf.

I loathe the fact that Rostam will forever be braided into my son's life. I must keep him away from him as much as possible. That thought motivates me to consider separating myself from my only pure delight.

I think to send Reza to London to stay with my cousin Bahman's family and attend school there. I know Bahman will be a worthy guardian for my son. After all, we spent almost every day of our lives together until the day I went into my moon and was forbidden to be alone with any boy, even Cousin Bahman. I'd been the only girl and the youngest in that pack of boys and he'd taken good care of me.

I approach Rostam with the idea.

"Yes! Do that," he says, surprising me. He had wanted a child so much, yet now he is so willing to send his only son away. I don't understand it — until his next sentence. "One less mouth to feed. And I don't need to see you two acting more like lovers than mother and child."

I clear it with Bahman, then quickly set about getting Reza's passport and exit papers together, afraid my husband might change his mind. Rostam signs his exit papers, documenting his permission for Reza to leave the country.

I say nothing to Reza. I will wait until every detail has been taken care of before telling him. I know it will be hard for him to separate from me, both because of our close connection and because his father's increasing instability must frighten him. I assume he won't be happy about leaving me alone with Rostam.

I want to send him away.

I've taken him to the doctor today to ensure he has the necessary shots. I will tell him he will be going to England when we get home. But then we return home to discover that Rostam has changed his mind. He gives no reason.

There *is* no reason. He is simply being mean.

Reza isn't going anywhere.

3 2

ROSTAM, SEX, DRUGS AND
BANNED ROCK 'N ROLL

1983

Imagine living with a man you've known for years, knowing he walks as though he is master of everyone in his path, that he dresses with the care of a king with a closetful of expensive suits, shirts, belts and shoes.

You've watched him light dozens of cigarettes a day with his gold monogrammed Dunhill lighter and heard him lash out at you, his servants and employees, as if we all were no more than a microbe of dirt under his nails.

Then, suddenly, you see him become someone else. Someone who wears the same pair of pants and the same shirt for days on end. A drunk and an addict.

The impossible has happened and you can't believe it. He has managed to become more disgusting than ever.

Slowly, your disbelief, your shock and embarrassment, give way to a feeling of satisfaction, even amusement. You enjoy watching the arrogant bastard stooped to the level of someone who steals what he can wherever he goes and hides from everyone he used to brag to.

Then you look back and realize that it wasn't a sudden change but rather, a gradual fall from grace that began when the Ayatollah's regime introduced government controls on every aspect of life and foreign trade as well, abolishing "unjust economic agreements with imperialistic states," thus outlawing Western music, the very thing that had been Rostam's extremely lucrative business.

Music from America, "The Satan," is considered venom spewed by the satanic snake.

Rostam's hefty income drops like a stone in water.

His once silent partner has been robbed of his crown, exiled from his country, and no longer of any use.

Rostam's business of importing western music to our country dies overnight, his distribution contracts lost along with millions in worthless inventory.

As his assets disappear, his debts begin to accrue. Business calls cease. He can no longer afford the overhead. Before he can close the office, he is evicted.

He is furious.

When the debt collectors first come calling, he laughs at the unpaid bills, saying he will pay the following cycle. But when his creditors will no longer be put off, services are cancelled and withheld. His entire persona begins to crumble. He tries to hold on to his self-esteem, but it has become no more than a light patina that has begun to crack and chip away.

He can no longer afford to have the best of anything. He no longer wears expensive suits. He first exchanges them for casual pants and sport tops.

When his pants no longer fit, they are replaced with inexpensive sweatpants or chinos. At some point, with no one to dress for and nowhere to go, he rarely changes out of his pajamas and shaves sporadically. Not because it is now fashionable for men to have facial hair, but because he has become lazy. He no longer has anyone to impress.

His parents are the first to realize his dire financial situation. They support us for a short time but cannot continue for long. After all, their life has also changed dramatically. His father's business with foreign countries, like his son's, has come to a standstill.

Even Rostam's beloved poker games end abruptly when gambling is declared illegal. His close friend, Tehran's former Chief of Police, has been executed as an appointee of the shah.

And all the while, the man becomes nastier and nastier. "Rostam this," and "Rostam that," and "How dare they do this to Rostam?" and, "Don't they know who Rostam is?" and, "How dare these crazy mullahs? How *dare* they? Kill them all!"

It is as if he believes the entire revolution and the accompanying ban on music has occurred solely to upset his place in the world.

He shakes his head and runs his hand through his oily hair. "Rostam could have told Pahlavi how to deal with these crazy mullahs. Ahh, it's too goddamned late.

"If Rostam ruled the country, we would be in superb condition."

He begins snuffing tobacco.

He used to keep the loose tobacco in a pouch in his pocket, but then he began using a bottle he's pilfered from the home of a friend we'd visited many times. My embarrassment when I realized he's now a thief felt like worms crawling under my skin.

He sticks the tobacco up his nose, then cleans it, or chews some then and spits it into the handkerchief he keeps in his pocket.

If all this has been meant to take the place of chain-smoking cigarettes, it's not working. He still smokes as well, changing to an Iranian brand when the American brand he used to smoke has become scarce and expensive. Both habits are dirty, but the snuff is disgusting as well, hearing him blow his nose and clear his throat before spewing the tobacco into the same handkerchief for days.

He drinks, likely to obliterate his dire reality.

Vodka is his preferred alcohol. The heavy drinking had begun when he was first prescribed pain pills. He begins drinking in the evenings, then the afternoons, then earlier and earlier in the day until ultimately, breakfast for him is coffee, vodka and, occasionally, eggs, eaten without so much as a word to Reza or me. When there is no more vodka to be had, he goes through all the alcohol in the house. For a while, The Rat supplies him with alcohol purchased in the black market. At some point he introduces Rostam to opium, easier for The Rat to obtain and more profitable for him.

As his ex-valet becomes his supplier of both drugs and women available and willing to enter into a *sigheh,* the tables turn and the position of power shifts. As Rostam's place in the world has diminished, The Rat's station as a Revolutionary Guard continues to be rewarded. His standing allows him to procure pills, alcohol, opium, and a supply of sexual partners.

Now Rostam needs Hassan far more than his ex-valet needs his old master.

Rostam steals to pay for his goodies. I first realize it at the home of a friend. I watch him pilfer a small and obviously valuable French silver nut dish, just small enough to deposit into his jacket pocket.

I am not naive enough to believe that dish and his bottle are the only two things he's stolen. The hand-crafted snuff bottle was likely the rare thing stolen for his own use and not for payment to The Rat.

Smoking opium has become a daily habit for my husband — an addiction. His life is all about finding a way to pay The Rat and I continue to notice things in our home missing. He's begun supplement his petty thefts with bartering things from the house.

We two live apart.

My husband no longer desires me.

A male showed up in the stream of women summoned for a *sigheh*, then males became more frequent. I can no longer predict who will be at the door. The men are young and I guess most to be laborers, mechanics, and the like. Once in a while, The Rat ushers in a boy — a minor — and my judgmental mind is disgusted. But I stay out of their way as they pass me on the way to Rostam's room.

Reza isn't blind, of course. Seeing this parade, he asks me who they are. Not meaning to protect Rostam, but rather, dedicated to protecting my son, I tell him some of these people worked for his father, some are cousins, the son of a cousin and distant family, or hired to run errands for his father.

I have heard about Iranian men "doing" children, perhaps young relatives or neighbors … in America, they call it "pedophilia." When sex is forced, they call it "rape." They call sex between two men, "homosexuality." Here, it seems they lump it all together and call it "doing it."

I am vigilant, making sure none of these men address my son. By the time Reza returns home from school, his father has retired to his room, sometimes with The Rat, a new guest or alone, indulging in his current choice of drugs. He stays in the room for the duration of the day and calls for dinner in his room.

I don't care a hair what Rostam does. I only want him to live his life in squalor. He can't interfere with his son's life.

My husband has become a surly, bitter, unhappy addict. I am ultimately stunned by the changes in him and angered by the obvious way he pinches pennies when it comes to Reza's needs yet finds what he needs to pay The Rat for opium and Allah knows what else.

Still, with it all, part of me delights in watching Rostam's entire persona devolve as his ego finds no room for its swollen head.

Then one day the roof falls in.

33
THE BOMB

*I*t is just past noon.

Reza is at school. Rostam is in his room.

I am in the kitchen dreaming of Ehsan and giggling as I recall our conversation years ago about naked caviar. I search in the refrigerator for the new jar of jam when the doorbell rings.

Our servant opens the door to a young man. He looks no older than fifteen or so. I am aghast and thankful that Reza is not home. He heads wordlessly through the house, heading for the large guest room Rostam has moved into. Soon I hear his door slam shut. About two hours later, he leaves as wordlessly as before.

Hassan arrives holding a small bag. With a slight sneer, he too heads for Rostam's room. There is no question that there are drugs in the bag, probably opium with whatever else. I'm mildly curious to know if Rostam mixes drugs. The two remain locked in my husband's room for several hours.

When The Rat finally leaves, it is without the bag.

Honestly? I am glad he has brought a fresh supply of drugs for Rostam. The man is almost impossible to deal with when he isn't under the influence of something, though not much easier to deal with when he is, a condition that has become the norm.

Soon after The Rat leaves, Rostam calls out. "Wife!"

Busy in the kitchen, with my mind on Ehsan, I don't immediately respond. He yells, "Where is my stupid wife?"

I go to his room. He is lying on the bed, the blanket and sheets rumpled with fresh stains. His pajama pants are on the floor by the bed and he's wearing the same dirty pajama top, buttons open exposing his chest, dirty socks on his feet.

"Bring me tea. I have something to tell you."

"What is it?" I ask.

"Get my tea and I'll tell you." His grin is almost maniacal.

I hurry to the kitchen, wondering as I put the kettle on what he wants to tell me. When it's ready, I take the piping hot black tea back to Rostam's room and hand him the cup and saucer. He takes a sip. Then, as though asking for a cookie to accompany the tea, he deadpans, "Give me your money."

My brain immediately sends my heart danger signals. I answer with a forced smile, as though I know he's kidding. "I have no money, Rostam."

His words slur lazily. "Don't lie. Rostam knows you do."

My smile doesn't waver. "I only have money for the market. You know that."

He sighs theatrically and looks up at the ceiling as he exhales in frustration. My eyes follow his and I see a spider there.

His tone is impatient. "You've squirreled it away. Rostam knows. And your parents have given you money." He raises his voice in demand. "Give it."

I must keep my smile intact and stay calm. "Rostam, I really don't have any money. I promise. My parents have not given me any money, and I've used all the money I had for food and Reza's school. It's almost all gone. I don't even know how we'll pay for next term."

"You lying whore!" He sneers, looking like a wild animal about to charge, his face taunt, his eyes filled with venom. He slams his hand down on the bed. "I don't give a damn about Reza's school! Give it now!"

He finds his pipe and takes a moment to fill his lungs. I'm hoping not to further upset him. Reza's school is the priority.

He sets his beady eyes on me. "Do you know why Rostam is broke? Do you know why our country has come to this?" He is speaking as though I am a child.

Unsure of the answer he wants, I say nothing. He grunts. "You don't?" He shakes his head in disgust. "Because of whores like you. Whores that return from America as spies to destroy our country and our religion."

No matter what he says, no matter what he does to me, I will not give up the money for my son's school and certainly not a single piece of the jewelry I have hidden away since our wedding day. He will have to find some other way to pay for his opium.

He scoffs. "You think Rostam can't make you? You are one stupid bitch." The cup and saucer clatter as he tosses them onto his nightstand. He swings his legs off the bed and plants his feet on the floor. His fists are pressed down on the mattress as though he's ready to lunge at me. I take a step back. "Don't you know what Rostam can do?"

Alarms are ringing in my ears. Yes, he is a broken man. But I am still afraid of him. He is dangerous, selfish beyond words and evil. Then he asks, "How is your dear father?"

Babajon? I stare at him with new terror.

He leans towards me. "I asked you a question. How is your father?"

I murmur, "Good. He is well."

He chuckles. But his dark drugged eyes overflow with malice. "Happy to hear that. The Revolutionary Guards will be happy to hear that, too."

Revolutionary Guards?

My heart starts to pound.I have no idea where he is going with this, but wherever it is, I know it's bad. Very, *very* bad. "What?" My voice is barely more than a whisper.

"Aah, yes, my lovely little whore. The Guards will most certainly be interested to learn that your father, the illustrious Agha Hadi Saleh is an Israeli spy. A Zionist spy."

Babajon, a spy?

I almost faint. I stare at Rostam. If there is anything these mullahs despise more than the United States of America, it is Israel. Yes, they hate the U.S. But they are fully committed to the annihilation of the State of Israel and all the Jews within it.

I put together a bad imitation of a careless, carefree laugh, as if we both know he is joking. "Babajon isn't a spy for Israel or anyone else."

"Hah!" He sneers, then booms, "I say he is!"

I cannot remain quiet. Wherever he is going with this, I must abort it, here and now. "You have no proof. It's a lie!"

He smiles, picks up the cup and drinks what tea is left, throws the cup down and turns back to me. "Well," he says, as though he's rehearsed the scene in his head. "All he'll have to do is just prove that to the Islamic courts." His ugly face becomes an exaggerated smile, showing his yellowed teeth. He folds his arms across his chest. "Tell me, how would your father do that?"

His smugness is terrifying. The poker player has seen the cards he holds and is absolutely certain he holds the high hand. "You have to admit, he certainly has a cozy relationship with those Jews, doesn't he." It isn't a question. "Let him prove that he doesn't get the ingredients from their country in exchange for information."

I see the confidence in his dark eyes. He is holding four aces.

I'm mortified. "That's absurd!" I say. "You know that's not true! He's no spy. That's a lie! You know it is!"

It is as if he hasn't heard me. "And, of course, he often boasts about living in the United States while in college." He is a smiling snake. "Like you." He catches one foot on the bed's ledge, bends to grab hold of it, places it on his other thigh and begins to clean between his toes with his fingernail. "He may well be a spy for both the Jews and the Americans," he says.

I think I will die right here and now.

He goes on, speaking calmly and coolly. "Unfortunately, his trial will not be a priority, so he'll have to spend a while in prison before he gets to explain everything." He looks back up at me and shrugs. "It could be years. I'm afraid there's a long line of prisoners, lots of trials will be scheduled before they get to him."

The possibility makes me sick to my stomach. I think of Babajon's heart. My very soul protests. "You wouldn't do that."

He chortles. He smiles, still busy attending to his toes. "And then, of course, there's also the other thing. Most unfortunate." I stare at him. "Don't look at me like that. You know all about it, Layla."

I quickly scan my frozen brain trying to guess what he is talking about and come up with nothing. I stand, staring at this monster, waiting to hear what poison will come out of his mouth next. *Is there no end to his miserable evil?*

He takes his time before continuing. "You will make believe you don't know?" He is mocking me. Then, as though the answer is obvious and I am just too stupid to guess it, he pronounces each word slowly, distinctly. "Stupid whore! I will tell the court he's been making cough medicine containing more alcohol than allowed. You know, above the legal limit." He grimaces. "You very well know." He changes feet, glancing up at me. "After all, Saleh spawned the fortune that sent you, my little whore, to your den of perversions in California you call 'college.'"

213

"That's ridiculous! It's not true! Rostam, you know it's not! None of it is. Rostam, please! Don't do that to my father! He'll die! They'll kill him! You can't."

Needless to say, he doesn't care. Done with his feet, his hand goes to his chin, scratching his beard as though he is musing. "I think I can." He nods. "No, I'm certain I can."

He stands and I instinctively take another step back. "Now, here's the good part," he says.

He turns his back to me and begins to pace back and forth across the room. With his hands clasped behind him, it is as though he believes he's wearing one of his custom-made suits and pacing in his impressive office, dictating to his secretary. I see his nakedness, the sallow skin under his open pajama top almost totally covered in black hair and the deflated penis below. He repulses me.

"After I turn him in, I will humbly ask for a modest *bakshish*, a token, for having turned in the name of my own father-in-law, a spy who works tirelessly for our enemies under the guise of *business relations* and has been doing so for years."

He pivots. "Oh, I will tell them Agha Saleh is shrewd. I will tell them that in addition to his treason, the man dares call himself a Muslim despite the fact that he has committed not only the worst possible crime against our country, spying for those bastard-Jews. For many years, Hadi Khan has also had the gall to commit what is perhaps the most blatant sin against the Quran as well as against our people, performing an abomination on hordes of our unsuspecting and devout brothers and sisters who buy his products. Observant Muslims throughout the country – probably even the most holy and revered members of the clergy, the government and the court — as well as ourselves, our wives and our daughters."

He flops back onto the bed to retrieve his pipe and takes another hit. "I will tell them that Hadi Saleh has been violating the regulations on alcohol in his products as though they are a joke."

This from the pig swimming in illegal drugs obtained through a renegade Guard.

Having fired off his bullets, he moves onto his side and faces me with his head resting on his bent arm. "How much do you think such information would be worth to them, Layla?"

He smiles as he puts his stupid head against a pillow, his dirty hands — only he and Allah know where they've been — behind his head. He is looking up at the spider again. Both spin webs. He goes on. "I think they'll be amazed at my courage and grateful for the information." He looks at me. "Don't you agree?"

This degree of pure hatred is astounding, both his apparent hatred of my family and mine of him.

"It's a shame, though. He may or may not be tortured in prison. If he survives that, he'll have a trial – you know, where the robed mullahs preside as judges.

"I imagine you will testify at his trial. Too bad Taymoor won't be able to. He's wealthy, and he's made large donations to their mosques, so they would have put some weight on his testimony, and it might have helped your beloved Babajon. Certainly more weight than they'll put on yours."

He nonchalantly scratches his testicles and smells his fingers. "Then they'll execute him." He picks up a sock laying on the bedsheet alongside him and tosses it onto the floor.

I understand: *Me and my family are under his thumb and he will use us all, me and Babajon. And my father's death would be of no more significant to him than his life is*

My hands go to my stomach, and I swallow bile.

He shrugs. "There's really no other way. You can see that. Right? He will stand accused both of treason for being a traitorous spy *and*" he stresses that word, "for breaking Sharia law with his unlawful alcohol fiasco."

I am mute. This is all too much for me to process. Then he adds, "Of course, they might well wonder if your mother, the elegant Zahra Khanom – and even you – knew what he was doing and are involved as well."

My head is reeling. I put my hand out and hold onto the nightstand. "Why would you do that, Rostam? What has my father ever done to you? He's a good man."

"Shut up, idiot bitch, whore! You give your father a message from Rostam. You tell him Rostam has said that if he pays me," he looks around the room before setting those devil eyes back on me, "say half a million U.S. dollars, I will forget his transgressions."

No! I'm shaking my head. "A half a mill – he doesn't have that kind of money."

Rostam laughs, a hearty laugh. "You stupid fool. Of course, he does. He's hidden a fortune in Jewland alone. Rostam is not stupid, Layla. He obviously travels there to deposit money in those Jew banks, like that worm Taymoor hid a pile of money in Europe."

He begins to clean his fingernails with the tool he uses to clean his pipe. "Perhaps your Babajon has bought some valuable property in Israel as well. I'll bet he has." He shrugs. "Sure he has." He shrugs again. "No matter," he says, waving his hand as if he is an important man and this entire conversation is beneath him.

"I'll tell you what I'll do. Only because the man is my father-in-law. I will give your wonderful *Babajon'* – the bastard says 'Babajon' so that it reeks with sarcasm – "two weeks from today to get me the money. He can sell his house, sell his goddamned company, do whatever the hell in Allah's name he has to do to get me the money." He nods, pleased with his clever master plan. "He has two weeks from today to get it to me. If he doesn't, you may as well throw him a goodbye party because you won't be seeing much of him any longer. And make sure to invite Rostam's dear friend, the very promising and esteemed Revolutionary Guard, Hassan. You know, he has made some powerful friends."

I stand frozen. Once again, my husband has a friend on the inside like his poker buddy, the former Chief of Police. In fact, I realize it was likely The Rat who came up with this plan. Rostam dismisses me. "Go. Get out. Leave. I want to relax and meditate on my good fortune. Go tell your father to get his money together."

It takes me a moment to get my body moving. As I leave the room, silent and shaking, Rostam picks up his pipe.

My world is about to cave in. I leave the room with my head reeling and my heart hammering. I find my room and sit on my bed.

<hr />

What just happened?

Of all the miserable turns life has taken, this is by far the most terrible. The sky is really falling and it's filled with exploding bombs.

What can I do? I have no answer.

Did he really just threaten to turn my father into the Guards with a pack of lies? The miserable bastard has just done exactly that.

What chance would Babajon have if Rostam carries out his stupid threats? Testimony from The Rat would be damning.

Babajon only wants to help people, his employees, the public … It is so ironc that Rostam is threatening him because of the very ties Saleh has with Israel that makes his products better. Once again, Israel plays a major role in my life.

I must think!

Saleh Pharmaceuticals has had ties with Israel businesses ever since contracts were signed years ago that grant Salah Pharmaceuticals ingredients indigenous to the area. But those contracts were with *private companies*, not with the Israeli government, not the State of Israel.

As far as I know, my father has not traveled to Israel since the Revolution. *How does he continue to obtain those ingredients? Are they sent? Are they still in Saleh's products?* I must find out.

Babajon has always had Jewish employees in executive positions at Saleh. *What would that mean to a Muslim mullah-judge if he went to trial?*

Though everyone connected with Saleh thinks the world of Babajon, none would likely be able to testify for him. I picture the judges with those turbans and robes and immediately visualize a horrific image: Babajon rotting away in some prison, tortured in horrible ways by the Revolutionary prison guards, all because of false, intolerable, untruthful allegations made by my husband and his his cohort.

I must think!

The accusation about the illegal level of alcohol in Saleh's products won't be a problem as the levels in his medications can easily be measured. No, that shouldn't be a problem.

But what if Rostam alleges that Babajon sells alcohol allotted to him on the black market for profit? In this time of insanity and mindless fanaticism, so many have been executed for purported indiscretions, "for crimes against Allah."

Who will believe that Babajon is innocent of the brute's accusations? And how can I chance it? What if they execute him just to show that no one is indispensable?

How can I possibly expose him to these risks?

Nothing will change Rostam's mind. I know that. He needs money desperately. He has none and is asking for a lot. I have seen him steal, and I know he will do whatever it takes for a lot of cash – and half a million U.S. dollars is a lot.

My good, innocent, kind, wonderful father is in very grave danger. I have to save him. It is up to me to save him.

But how?

I must warn him.

I know that it will be at the cost of finally telling him who Rostam really is, something I've been guarding against since the day I married. I only hope I won't be forced to admit *why* I married the horrible, ego-driven son of a bitch.

Yet come what may, the priority is to make Babajon understand how critical his situation is. Then we can think of a solution. He has two weeks.

I look at my watch. I need to get to my parents as soon as possible. If I leave immediately, I'll have a little more than two and a half hours with them before Reza comes home. I call my parents to confirm they will both be home, saying it is urgent that I speak with them as soon as possible. Babajon is working in his study and Maman says she had no place to go and no one to see. Curious, she asks questions, but I tell her she will soon know everything. I hang up and leave the house.

Ferri had once said that when she thought of me living with Rostam, she pictured me sitting on top of a barbed wire fence.

That fence has just been electrified.

34

BREAKING HEARTS

I wish that I was blind, so I couldn't see it, I wish that I was deaf, so I couldn't hear it, and I wish that I was mute, so I don't have to be the one to tell you.

— ~ *UNKNOWN*

*J*t is a deceptively beautiful day, the sun shining in a blue sky, mocking the darkness that has taken hold of my life.

When the taxi stops in front of my parents' gate, I am still in shock, my mind a fog with no idea what I will say.

I must make Babajon understand that my husband will happily throw him to the dogs if he fails to comply with his outrageous demand. *How can I face him and tell him that? Will he even believe me? How am I supposed to tell Babajon the truth about Rostam?*

How on Earth can I save him?

How has this happened?

Before we even sit at the dining room table, I am sobbing.

Babajon closes the door and asks Maman to tell the others in the house that we are not to be disturbed. I wipe my eyes and take the seat I have always sat in.

With a shaking voice, I begin finally to tell my parents the truth about the man I married and my life with him. I feed it to them piece by piece, giving them only as much as it takes to make them believe that Rostam is a bad person, both desperate and terribly, terribly serious.

They must understand that Babajon is facing the real threat of arrest, prison, torture and probable death.

Maman refuses to believe me.

"What have you done to him, Layla?" she says. "He must have a reason. You must have done something to him or said something that made him this angry."

My mouth falls open. I am bewildered at Maman's reaction. But my father immediately knows I've spoken the truth. I can see things falling into place for him as he listens. His face has reddened and paled. Before I can respond to Maman, he speaks. "Zahra, she's telling the truth. It's not her fault. I've always known our daughter has been very unhappily married."

"You're telling me you both believe Rostam would do that?" Maman asks.

"Yes," says Babajon. He goes on. "And knowing our daughter, she's only giving us the tip of the iceberg. I have no doubt that he is worse than what she's saying. May Allah cut off his two hands. *Ensha Allah*, Allah willing, I know he has hurt her."

Maman looks at him with dancing eyebrows as he passes his palm across his forehead and then down a side of his face. Her eyes fall on me, waiting for me to go on.

But Babajon hasn't finished. "Layla, you have lived with this ...

this monster for so many years but never complained. *Why?* How have you done it all this time? I don't understand. How could you live like that and not tell me? Don't you know I would have protected you?" He doesn't wait for an answer. "If not me, why didn't you ever say something to your mother? I don't understand. Don't you know we both only want the best for you? We would have done something. We'd have made certain he never saw you again."

When he stops, I answer quietly, tears dropping on clasped hands that rest on my lap. "He vowed never to divorce me and promised that if you did anything to separate us, he would make sure to drag your names through the mud."

Maman winces. Babajon wrings his hands. He is angrier than I've ever seen him. "That motherless, fatherless son of a bitch!" I've never heard him speak like this. "I want to know what he thinks calling me a spy and throwing me to the Revolutionary Guards does to our name?" He gets up from his chair so fast, it almost topples. "You've never said a word to us yet he still wants to destroy us!"

He reaches into his pocket and brings out his worry beads then begins to pace around the room, worry beads in hand.

I am worried for my father. I worry for his heart. Placing this stress on him is like shooting him with a gun. It is far too much for him, and for Maman.

"I want to kill him," I say looking down, feeling guilty and miserable. Babajon looks as though he's processing the possibility of acting on my statement for a second before waving it away.

Still weeping, I finished the whole sad story. "I'm so sorry, Babajon. I'm so sorry." I catch my breath. "You have to do something."

Maman is stonefaced now, having realized in minutes that everything she has convinced herself to be true about her son-in-law and her daughter's life for all these years has likely been no more than a fantasy. She looks at Babajon, wide-eyed. "What are we supposed to do?"

He inhales deeply, closes his eyes, exhales, then says, "I have some cash, but not that much. I won't give him the company's money. Saleh's account is separate from mine. Even if I could gather that kind of money in two weeks, who's to say that would satisfy him? He could always demand more. He could also act on his threat, even with the money."

I am filled with shame. "I am sorry, Babajon, but you're right. It's true. He is ruthless, a narcissist and broke. He needs money, and he'll do anything he can to have it." Babajon nods sadly in understanding.

I go on. "He won't stop! He thinks you have a fortune in Israel. He'll just want more and more. I would have done anything to prevent him from hurting you, but I didn't see it coming. I think Hassan, his old valet, now a Revolutionary Guard, may have thought of this. He's become indispensable to Rostam's drug addiction. He provides the drugs to Rostam and also wants money.

And then I lamely repeat, "I'm sorry. You don't deserve this, Babajon. Not you."

He shrugs, his shoulders falling. In the ensuing moment of silence, I remind myself that I must be home before Reza. I notice the Dresden clock on the credenza reads fifteen minutes past ten and register that it has stopped.

"I need to leave the country for a while," Babajon says, shocking me back to the moment and realizing that this is what we've come to: Babajon, leaving. But if this is our solution, so be it. Rostam cannot win.

"Babajon, you need to be away for as long as we have this mullah-led government. Who knows how long that will be?"

Maman says, "I'm leaving with you."

"No," Babajon answers. "You stay here, Zahra. Act normal."

Maman lifts off her chair and pounds the table with her fist, one of the most surprising things I've ever seen her do, and the first time I've seen her oppose her husband so strongly. "You will not leave the country and leave me here, Hadi. If you leave, I go with you."

"She's right, Babajon. If you leave, he'll go to the Guards, and they'll arrest Maman to force you your return."

Maman repeats, "You are not going anywhere without me."

Babajon scratches his chin. "Well, I can't see a solution other than leaving Iran." He looks first at Maman. "Can you?" Then, "Layla?" I shake my head.

I cannot believe my parents are actually talking about leaving their country. Their home. And it is my fault. My ridiculous stupidity.

Babajon continues. "Okay but we must leave quietly. If he realizes that we're leaving, he'll go to the Guards, and I'll be arrested before we can escape. We need to be fast, prepare quietly and quickly. No one can know. No one." He watches Maman for her reaction. She sits, as if in a trance.

I want to die. *What have I done to my beloved Babajon? And Maman?*

"What can you do in two weeks?" I ask.

He shakes his head. "Liquidate as many assets as possible. Pack, see to our passports and leave."

"Sell my house?" The very idea of losing her beloved home is almost impossible for Maman to accept and I don't blame her. It isn't only a house, it is the wonderful house that her husband built as a monument of his love for her, and the home she has furnished with love. "Where will we live?" She waves her arm. "What will we do with our furniture?" Her eyes linger on what she can see around her: the table and chairs, the chandelier, the hand carved sideboard and the valuable pieces that sit on it.

"We take nothing, Zahra. Zero. Only one suitcase for the two of us. That's it. We must be smart. We need to move light and to move fast. And quietly. The house and the furniture will stay."

She flinches and he hurries to add, "For now. It is impossible to sell the house quietly and not in two weeks. Once we're safe, I'll contact my attorneys to take care of the sale. In any case, we'll suffer a loss. No one is buying houses now and our money that was seven tomans to the dollar is now what? Over eight hundred tomans to the dollar. But we'll be okay. For now, we'll pack and leave. I will gather our important papers."

"My house!" It is a cross between a plea, a question and a wail.

"*Azizam,* my dear one, Fotmeh and Araf can stay and house-sit until we sell it. That way you can relax, knowing everything will stay as it is."

He walks around the table, fingering his worry beads, and stands by my chair and speaks tenderly.

"Layla *jon*, once we're gone and he realized I've outsmarted him, you'll never have peace. He'll make your life far worse."

I think of Reza. *Would Rostam dare hurt my son in a fit of rage, realizing Babajon has escaped? How will it affect him to witnesses his father constantly lashing out at me when he realizes his plan has failed?*

The obvious solution – the only option – hangs in the air, waiting to be given voice. "I will leave with you," I say. "Me and Reza."

Both parents stare at me. The sudden silence is filled with their wordless surprise. I watch their faces pass through shock to their acceptance of the truth. I too, like my father, have no choice. I must escape with them.

Ever practical, Babajon says, "Your exit papers need his signature."

"I'll figure it out," I say, wishing I could feel more confident.

"How? What will you do? What will you say?" Maman asks. I realize how frightened Maman is and that, too, makes me sad.

I am beside myself with guilt for catapulting my parents into such a heightened degree of stress, hating myself, hating Rostam. Yet even now, Babajon takes charge so naturally, making life-changing decision after decision. Though Maman wanted to deny the truth I unveiled, my father immediately understood that catastrophe looms, and accordingly, has made the most momentous decision of their lives.

This is probably the way he has made so many decisions about his life and his business, with neither fanfare nor sentimentality. Meanwhile, not in my right mind, I don't realize how close to hysteria Maman is. This is all too much for her to take in. It is her complete trust in her husband that allows her to lean on him, knowing he will take charge, make the right decision, and do what is best for us all.

Babajon eyes me, concern for me now overriding concern for himself and Maman. "Layla, how can he allow you and Reza to leave Iran?"

"Let me find a way," I say, dredging up what little confidence I have. "You start packing." I look from one to the other. This is unbelievable.

Khodayah! God! *What has the bastard done?*

"This is a nightmare," I say. "And it's my fault." A new wave of tears floods my eyes and I become smaller in my chair. "He's so evil. I'm so sorry." Tears form rivers along my cheeks and down my neck.

Babajon continues pace."This is Rostam's fault, Layla, not yours," he says. He's no doubt thinking while fingering his worry beads. "Perhaps, I'll pay him a small amount now, so he'll trust that he'll get the rest at the end of the two weeks." He addresses me. "Layla, tell him I'm putting the money together."

I nod. "Babajon, what will happen to Saleh?"

My father's pharmaceutical company has become the major pharmaceutical company in the country, employing many people and creating all sorts of home remedies.

"They'll know exactly what to do without me," he answers. "I have always delegated duties and tried to make the company a well-run machine. They all own a part of it, and they'll take good care of it. Once we're safe, I'll have my attorneys deal with some things and, who knows? Maybe one day I'll return."

He brings the subject back to the immediate priorities. "Layla, take no more than one suitcase for yourself and Reza." He looks at his wife. "And you will take no more than one for the two of us. Remember: We move light, fast and quietly."

Before leaving their house, I take a minute to visit my old bedroom.

Seeing the open window that I had looked out of so many times through my earlier years, I put my head out for what might well be the last time. I feel like I'm in a dream. The air is fresh, and though it is not yet warm enough for the sweet fragrant night-blooming jasmine to blossom on the vines, I recall their sweet scent. I see the lace-like branches of the mulberry trees that seem to fragment the sky like so many pieces of mosaic.

Turning back to the room, I remember the day I came into my moon and stood before this mirror inspecting my body for changes. I recall lying on this bed, counting the days before I would be leaving for California. And I can never forget lying in this same bed writhing in discomfort realizing my mother had ordered my hymen sewn back. I look in my closet, drawers and scope the room but see nothing I want to pack.

So much has happened to me, to my country and to the people I love since then. Too much to say, enough to write a book.

But who would believe it?

35

THE AGREEMENT

*L*ast night, Babajon told me he wanted assurances from Rostam that he would not ask for more once he's paid.

Today I type a note for him to sign saying just that. I fold it, put it in my pocket along with a pen, and take it to his room along with his lunch.

The room has the musky smell of opium mixed with body odors. He is either sleeping or in a dope-induced slump. Either way, I'm relieved not to have to hear his voice. I place his tray on the table alongside his bed, set there for this purpose and quietly leave, closing the door behind me.

At some point in the late the afternoon, a woman arrives. Like the others before her, she heads wordlessly to his room. She leaves as Reza and I are about to sit down for dinner.

When Reza and I are done with dinner and Reza is occupied with his books, I return to Rostam's room. He is lying in bed, filling his opium pipe. I cannot look at him. I want him dead.

He is obviously high. He asks if I've passed his message to my father. I nod. "And?" I would kill him if I could. He pulls himself up and leans against the headboard. "Tell me, is he scared?" He is hanging on to my every word.

Yes, you crazy bastard. Yes! He was scared! Of course he was scared. Running scared! If I had a gun, I would shoot him. Multiple times. Blow his head off. My hatred of this man locks my throat and I have to push the words out. "At first, he didn't believe me."

Rostam's excited impatience is evident in his raised voice. "But then, he did?" He's gloating. The smug bastard believes he has set the perfect trap.

I want to grab the knife alongside his plate and lunge at him, stabbing him countless times. I nod. "He will get you the money."

He laughs lazily and wriggles on his dirty bed. His arms fly up as though his team had just made the winning run. "Excellent! Excellent!"

"But that's all he has," I say. I bring out the agreement I have typed up. "He wants to know what assurance he'll have that you won't want more or take his money then turn him in anyway."

"He has Rostam's word," he bellows, as though his word has more weight than two overcooked peas in rice.

I return the agreement to my pocket and nod. "I told him so." I will tell Babajon that my husband has just confirmed our need to escape.

What day is this?" he asks. He no longer keeps track. Every day is the same.

"Monday."

"Stupid woman! What's the date?" I realize he wants to calculate the date he'll receive the money from Babajon.

I tell him the date is March 5th. Reza's birthday is on March 17th. Rostam expects his money on the 19th. Norooz is on the 20th. He is pleased with his shrewd trick, believing he will have half a U.S. million dollars by the new year.

I long to strangle the bastard. I could suffocate him with the semen-spotted pillow. Instead, I tell him what Babajon has instructed me. "He says he'll pay you a small amount soon, as a show of good faith."

Rostam's smile broadens. He is so happy with himself. I pray he will be so overjoyed that he will have a coronary. I yearn to throw myself on top of the bastard and rip his eyes out. I pray he will smoke all his hashish and opium, swallow all his pain pills along with any alcohol he may have stashed away in his room, overdose and die before the end of the day.

I curse the Islamic Revolution. I loathe the impact that our new government and its theology has had on the lives of those I love. The Ayatollah's rule has changed my world, making my life with Rostam completely and utterly intolerable. It has made our judicial system one that allows my husband to create these lies and actually believe he can benefit from them, one in which the mullahs can allow this kind of outrageous blackmail to be rewarded. Under this regime, my husband has reached a new level of abuse.

The idea of escaping Rostam is, of course, as old as our marriage. After failing in my escape on that first day as his wife, I had given up all hope of leaving him. Rostam can abuse me and terrorize me. But he may not hurt Reza and not Babajon, whose life he has put at risk. I must get my father out of the country, beyond the reach of Rostam and the Revolutionary Guards, and I am forced to leave with him. This time, failure is not an option. I leave the pig in his stinky room. There is much to do.

I do not allow Reza to see my tears nor sense my anxiety. He cannot yet know he will be leaving his home, his father, his school and his friends behind. Not until everything is done and we were ready to leave. A single word to anyone could completely foil our fragile plan.

For my father's sake and for my love of Reza, I pray we four will be able to get out of Iran to safety.

I filled with questions about our future.

What lies are too impossible to tell?

What trust is too precious to break?

How can fate deny me and my loved ones this chance to save ourselves, to survive?

Will our attempt to escape be the key to our survival or cause our demise?

⸻

I need my passport.

Rostam has locked it in the safe in his study, along with the bulk of my jewelry. He has not been in the room for months.

In the middle of the night I call a locksmith to come break the lock. It must be done so very quietly. The locksmith is a young, swaggering man who seems rather full of himself, asks a lot of questions, and flirts with me. As soon as the safe is open, I pay him and bid him farewell. I don't want him to see what is inside. I rush back to the safe and remove my passport and all the jewelry inside, then close the safe.

I hug my passport to my heart. *How long I'd wanted this!*

The first thing Maman did when I returned home years ago was to hide my passport from me to ensure I would not be able to return to America. Then, after my failed attempt at escaping him, Rostam locked it away. Twenty-four years later, I hug my passport to my chest.

I tackle the next problem. If I am to leave Iran, I must have my husband's signature confirming his consent for me to travel out of the country.

What will I do now?

I bring out the consent letter he'd signed for Reza to leave Iran, still with the pamphlets of London schools, one of which Reza might have attended. I study Rostam's signature. It is the signature of a successful businessman, scrawled and almost indecipherable. The only choice I have is to forge his signature onto my consent letter. I practice duplicating it, over and over, trying to mimic his writing, his large, interlocked, stylized initials. Each attempt fails, and another letter finds its way into the garbage can. Hours and dozens of tries later, with fingers gripping the pen, eyes peeled to the task, fingers moving slowly, I try again. I compare the two signatures. I'm finally convinced that this forgery is the best I can do.

I put our two consent letters with our two passports and identity cards. This mandated bundle will be needed to escape Rostam.

Through the next days, while Reza is at school, I discretely pack a suitcase for the two of us. We will be flying to London. My heart skips realizing how close we will be to France. Maybe we'll go to Paris, and I can see Ehsan. That wonderful thought is liberating.

Nine days later, we are ready to leave.

Will Rostam be able to find us?

36

PREPARATIONS

March 15, 1984

*M*inutes after Reza returns home from school, we two quietly leave the house.

We are taking only one suitcase and the large Hermes tote bag packed with some toiletries, our IDs, exit papers, passports and my jewelry. Reza's navy blue backpack holds his portable game device, the book he was reading, his school books and his newest book of puzzles.

In the cab on the way to my parents' house, while eating a snack, he wriggles around in his seat, filled with questions. From the time we've left our house, he has asked where we're going. I still haven't decided what to tell him, how to phrase our escape, and how to tell him that, if things go well, he will never return to the only home he's ever known, or to his father, his friends, his school, teachers, and classmates.

"Maman *Jon*, why have you brought a suitcase?"

"You'll see. It's a surprise."

"Maman *Jon*, why are you speaking English? Speak Farsi."

"I'm speaking English because you must learn to understand English perfectly and speak it even better than Farsi."

"But why, Maman *Jon*?"

"I've told you my love, it's a surprise."

When the cab pulls up in front of my parents' house, my parents are already outside. Maman looks flustered, on edge, shifting from foot to foot, her lower lip curled in, hidden in her anxiety. And, though I can imagine how Babajon feels, he appears calm, as though, for him, this is just another day. We add my suitcase to their suitcase and Babajon's briefcase, already in the trunk. The four of us pile into his car and head to Mehrabad International Airport.

Reza, all curiosity, repeats his question."Where are we going?"

Babajon answers. "You are going on the greatest adventure of your life, Little One," Babajon tells him, calling him by the name he has used from the time Reza was in diapers.

Hearing this, Reza becomes more excited and more curious. His questions are now directed to his grandfather. He sits forward in his seat. "Babajon, tell me, where? My friends will be so envious. I can't wait to tell Alex and Pedram when I see them tomorrow."

I decide that this is as good a time as any to tell him. "Reza *jon*, you're not going to school tomorrow."

This is a total surprise. "I'm not? But Maman *jon*, I'm not sick. The teacher won't like that."

Once again, Babajon takes over. "Because, Little One, while your friends are in school, you will be on a giant airplane."

Reza's eyes open wide, and he turns to me. He is silent for a moment while again, I wonder how all this will affect my son. He has recently turned nine and is filled with curiosity. The next wave of questions come. "*A plane?* Is he right, Maman jon? Really? Is Babajon telling the truth?"

I confirm with a nod and a smile. "Babajon always tells the truth. But you must speak in English, my love."

"Where is the plane taking us?" I hesitate and he repeats himself, attempting English. "Maman jon, where the plane is taking us, please?"

I reach out and give his shoulder a quick rub. "You'll see," I say.

I have become secretive. Reza doesn't appreciate my evasiveness. He has resumed wriggling and asks again, his tone more urgent.

Babajon answers. "We're going to see your cousin Bahman and his family in London."

"London *kohjas?*"

"You must speak English," I say.

He asks, "London is where?"

I don't correct him. I'm looking ahead at the heavy traffic headed to the airport. It has been like this the entire way, as Maman has reminded us several times. Now it is at a standstill. There has apparently been an accident up ahead. The car behind us honks, as if there is something Babajon can do to speed things up. The impatient driver honks again. Maman leans over and holds down our horn for a few seconds.

"London is in a country named England," Babajon says.

Reza appears to be thinking, digesting the information. Then he looks at me. "Is Papa coming?"

I let him ask in Farsi and shake my head. "Not right away."

He sits back in his seat, looks up at the car's roof, then asks, in a soft voice, "When is Papa coming?"

"I'm not sure," I say. I'm unsure if my son wants his father to join us or would prefer him to stay put in Tehran. "It depends," I say. "He may not want to come."

He is quiet then. I pull him close to me and wrap my arm

around him. I take in the scent of his hair, more delicious than the most expensive perfume. *Will I ever tire of his scent?*

Traffic starts to move again, and I wonder, even as every minute takes us further from home, if I am doing what is best for Reza. I have no real knowledge of how children are affected by these things, but I know that stability is important for a child, and Reza's stability is being shaken with his home, school, friends and his father falling off like so many leaves off a tree, quite possibly never to be seen again.

"Do you want to play with your game?"

He shakes his head, happy to just sit. He moves closer and nestles in my arm.

And so, time passes as we make our way to the airport.

When we arrive, Babajon parks his car, and we all get out. My father's briefcase and our two suitcases come out of the trunk. Babajon locks the doors and starts to put the car key into his pocket. He stops, looks at Maman, shrugs, opens the car door, puts his key on the driver's seat then closes the door.

That says it all.

37

THREE STRANDS

*I*nside the terminal, we three wait on the check-in line while Maman sits on a nearby bench.

While Babajon confirms our tickets, I am flooded with memories of that first morning as Rostam's wife when I waited on this same line to exchange two round-trip tickets to Italy for a one-way ticket to Los Angeles. The anxiety I am experiencing today mixes with memories of the fear I'd felt that day and I take several deep breaths.

We check our two suitcases. We will take my tote, Babajon's briefcase, and Reza's backpack on board.

We make our way to the control desk, our major hurdle. We are quiet. I have instructed Reza not to say a word no matter what.

I had passed through this area twenty-four years ago as I was making my failed attempt at an escape from Rostam. Here I am again, to escape from him again, this time with my nine-year old son and my parents. I pray we will not have any problems.

Will I be successful this time?

A young man sits behind the table, wearing the uniform of the Revolutionary Guards.

He is posted here to stop those of us who are not able to leave, those blacklisted and those trying to escape the Ayatollah. This Guard is broad-shouldered and rather handsome, despite the unshaven look men have these days.

At the Guard's request, Babajon takes his passport of his brief-case and hands it to him. The Guard reviews Babajon's passport, checking his name against the list of those people the government is looking for. If your name appears on that list, you'll be arrested on the spot.

Assured that his name does not appear on the list, he asks my father why he is leaving the country and where he is headed.

Babajon smiles. "I'm taking my lovely wife, my daughter and my grandson to London for a family reunion. My nephew is there with his Iranian wife, and they've had a baby."

"How long will you be gone?"

"Oh," my father's hand moves as though to wave away a distasteful smell. He frowns. "Not as long as I'd like. It's been decades since I've had a vacation. My business needs me."

"Do you have ties to Iran?"

Babajon is prepared for this question and digs into his brief-case. "You mean besides my company, Saleh Pharmaceuticals, the building that houses it and managing my employees? Yes. I own my home and a rental home." He withdraws a file from his brief-case containing papers evidencing all this.

Impressed by the fact that the man standing before him is *that* Saleh, the man smiles and relaxed. "And this is your wife?"

Babajon nods. "I'm a lucky man," he says. "And this is my daughter and her son."

"*Barradarr,* brother, please step away so I can address Khanom."

Maman has opted to wear a full *chador* today in the hope that she will have an easier time if she appears to be a conservative and observant Muslim woman. She gazes down, tightens the holds on her *chador* and jerks it down over her hairline until it almost covers her eyes.

"She's very shy," Babajon says. He hands the man Maman's passport, identity card, and exit paper signed by him and again, the agent scans the list of names he's been given. He does not see her name listed there.

"*Merci, khaharr,* thank you, sister." I see Maman bristle slightly and I know it is in reaction to being called this man's sister. Yet, to the agent, her reaction probably seems normal for a very shy woman spoken to by an unrelated male.

He turns to me. "*Khaharr?* Sister?" I hand him Reza's passport and papers first. "This is your son?" I nod, putting my two hands possessively on Reza's shoulders. He checks Reza's birthdate to make certain he is younger than thirteen as boys older than that are required to remain in the country, available for conscription into the armed forces – possibly as suicide bombers. Next, he confirms that I am his mother as stated on his identity card.

"I need to see your identity card," he says to me. I hand it to him along with my passport and letter of consent bearing Rostam's forged signature and hold my breath. After eying my identity card, he checks my name against his list of those wanted by the Islamic Republic to verify that I am not on the "no fly" list. Then he leafs through my passport and returns both to me. He next looks at the letter of consent and I am relieved to see him nod. He is about to return everything to me. Then, as he picks up Reza's consent letter, he suddenly re-opens mine. I immediately feel faint. Babajon realizes the crucial nature of the next few seconds and tries to distract the man.

He looks at his watch. "*Barradarr,* your job is important for the security of our esteemed leader and for the country. We appreciate what you do." Then he looks at Maman, Reza and me. "Come on," he says, "let's get to the gate. It's time."

But the Guard is still holding the two exit letters, his eyes on the two signatures, examining them, comparing them. Finally, he looks up. "Why are these two signatures different?" His steely eyes seem to go through me. I am certain I am about to be arrested. I will not be able to leave. Once again, my escape will be foiled, and Rostam will be the victor. At least, Babajon and Maman will escape. I will send Reza with them. I adjust my *chador*. "*Barradarr*, the signature is my husband's, my son's father. He did not sign the two letters at the same time. He signed my son's letter earlier. He was … ill … quite ill when he signed mine." He will probably call Rostam now to confirm what I just said.

He looks up at me before turning his attention back to the two signatures, comparing them. "I will be back. Please wait here." As he pushes his chair back, he takes a sort of walkie-talkie off his belt and speaks into it. "I need to be relieved. I'm going to our superior."

This is exactly what I have dreaded. My forgery has not succeeded in fooling him.

What will happen to me now? And what will happen to Reza?

My son may be allowed to leave with his grandparents, but it would be too much for him to lose everything he has known as well as both of his parents all in one day.

I must leave!

Babajon speaks. He is smiling, his ingratiating smile, stretched across his face, teeth showing. "*Barradarreh aziz*, dear brother, we truly admire your diligence in protecting us all from harm." He reaches into his wallet and brings out a thick wad of money. "Please, accept this as a token of our esteem. Please understand. We really need to get to our gate."

The agent looks at the money and then at my father. "Agha, I am surprised that you would think your money will distract me."

At this point, I have absolutely nothing to lose. I reach into the bottom compartment of my tote bag and grab the first thing I can get my hands around. It is the necklace that Rostam had designed for the Coronation, the three strings, one of rubies, one of emeralds and one of diamonds.

I pull it out and offer it to the Guard. *"Barradarr,* please, accept this. It was designed for the late shah's undeserving wife. I would be humbly honored to present this to you as an agent of our Islamic Republic and our Supreme Leader."

The agent's curiosity propels him to take the unusual necklace from my hands and study it, as if he knows anything about precious stones. As he does, I see the look on Maman's face. Her mouth hangs open, her eyes widen. She is incredulous that I would part with something so very valuable.

"Notice the workmanship," I say. The regularity in the sizes, and the clarity of the stones. Those are real emeralds, real rubies and genuine diamonds."

"It is very pretty. How many carats?" he asks.

I cannot help but chuckle. The man is holding what is easily the most valuable piece of jewelry I have, and surely, the most precious thing he will ever hold, yet he is asking about the number of carats as though deciding if it is a gift worthy of being accepted. I've no ties to it and won't miss it in the least for I have never really believed it to be mine. Rostam designed it and had kept it locked in his safe. I had only worn it at the events we attended that evening as part of the coronation festivities. In any event, even if it were my most prized possession, I'd be more than happy to part with it in exchange for passage. As for the number of carats? I'd never thought to ask Rostam.

"I don't know," I say, "But I assure you, it's a lot. It's an extremely valuable piece. It can make you a very rich man." In fact, there's a good chance he would be the wealthiest Revolutionary Guard in the Islamic Republic.

He holds the necklace up by its ends. Even in the airport light, the jewels gleam. "The three strands can be taken apart," I add. "If you ever decide to separate the strands, you should know that each one is worth a fabulous amount. It was designed by Van Clef and Arpel and was designed for Farah Diba, and her love for excess." I assume this man has no idea who Van Clef and Arpel is, but I add the information because I want it said that the designer was European, not American.

As I'm speaking, he continues to hold the necklace, moving it this way and that, enjoying the sparkle. "*Barradar*, brother, I'm sure your wife – if you're married – will appreciate it."

At this point, every second counts. We have to make our flight. My parents and I are holding our breaths as we await our fate.

The Guard turns the necklace around, examines the back, then holds it up again to look at it in the light. He looks around. There is no one nearby.

"Okay," he says, nodding, "I accept."

He slips the necklace into his pocket and holds out the two passports and accompanying paperwork. I resume breathing normally.

"Enjoy your vacation," he says, with what I would describe as an endearing smile. "*Khaharreh azizam*, my dear sister, I advise you to have your husband sign another consent letter when he's feeling better."

"Yes. I understand. Thank you."

We lose no time gathering our things as the agent speaks into his walkie talkie again. "Forget it, *barradarr*," he says. "I'm staying at my station. You do not need to relieve me."

A Revolutionary Guard stands about thirty feet away, holding the receiver to his ear. He turns and walks away. A young woman wearing a *hijab* and holding a toddler has turned a corner and is approaching the control desk with a man, unshaven and dressed like hundreds of other Iranian men in a loose, collarless shirt and pants. As soon as we walk away, these three arrive at the young man's table. Now far wealthier than he can know, the Guard asks for their passports.

I shudder to think what would have happened if these people had arrived moments earlier.

We arrive at the gate as the boarding is almost over. The replay of my time here twenty-four years ago continues and I recall that I had made it to the gate, about to board, when I was nabbed by airport security and returned to Rostam. As I board the plane with Reza and my parents, my legs wobble . I am enveloped in a surreal feeling.

This is really happening!

3 8

MESSAGES

March, 1984

O ur estimated arrival in London is two o'clock in the morning.

As we board and find our seats, I notice that most of the passengers are Iranian, and the majority of Iranian women have removed their *chadors* and *hijabs*.

My seat is in the aisle and Reza sits beside me. Babajon sits across the aisle with Maman at his side. As soon we are seated, Maman removes her *chador* and arranges her hair, then brings out a mirror, examines her face and applies lipstick and blush. I remove my *hijab.*

Reza passes the time with his books and game until dinner is served. It's been an eventful day for him and having eaten, he falls asleep and sleeps the rest of the way. Maman hardly touches her dinner, complaining that it is too salty and far too fatty.

Babajon and I quietly share our relief at having passed the control desk. I think about our situation and pray our luck will continue. I am comforted knowing there is more jewelry in my bag.

We land at Heathrow Airport at eleven London time.

We disembarked and find our luggage. Reza resists being awakened and falls back asleep in the cab on the way to Bahman's house.

We arrive to a darkened house. Only Bahman is awake, awaiting our arrival. He greets us all. Lifting Reza up into his arms he plants a huge, wet kiss on his cheek.

"Finally, I meet the love of Layla's life." Reza's head rests on his shoulder. Too tired to respond, Reza rubs his closed eyes.

Bedding accommodations have already been made for us all. Traveling has made us weary, but the emotional rollercoaster that began with Rostam's threat has exhausted us. Finally feeling safe, I sleep soundly for the first time in what feels like forever.

And I am exquisitely aware that London is not far from Paris and Ehsan.

The next morning, we meet Bahman's wife.

Mahnaz is stunning with a perfect figure. She has lovely green eyes and long, light brown hair and full lips in a round face that makes her look even younger than her twenty-eight years.

She has prepared breakfast for all of us, bread along with scones, cereal for Reza, scrambled eggs and halvah, a favorite treat of mine, made with a hardened mixture of wheat flour, sugar, butter and cardamom and other aromatic spices.

Today is Reza's ninth birthday. His excitement is evident. At the end of the meal, we sing "Happy Birthday" to him, in both the

Farsi and English versions. Babajon tells him that part of his birthday gift was flying in the airplane and another part is being here in London.

I'm glad to see Bahman conversing with my son, asking him questions about school and his friends. Then he says, "Your mother always enjoyed the company of young boys. Did you know that she played with me and my friends when she was your age, and younger? She was the only girl, and younger than all of us, but she kept up with us." Reza is captivated.

Bahman's toddler, with the proper British name of Jeremy is adorable, and when breakfast is over and the singing ends, Reza decides he will teach Jeremy the names of three fruits he lays on the rug between them, an apple, a pear and a banana. I hear him reciting their Farsi names and I take the opportunity to teach him the English words for each. He is anxious to learn the language that Bahman, Mahnaz, Babajon and I continue to lapse into while Maman sits wordlessly, no doubt feeling excluded.

With breakfast finished, we all leave Bahman's house. Outside it is drizzling and skies are gray. We take a short walk before the drizzle becomes a heavy rain, forcing us to return to Bahman's house where we continue to chat, exchanging news, reacquainting ourselves with Bahman and getting to know his wife.

Maman's brother, Mansoor Khan and his wife Aunt Haideh are in London too with Shireen and Taymoor. Shireen leaves her children with their nannies and the four of them join us. The sound of the rain makes our circle cozy, and Mahnaz served lots of hot tea and refreshments. This partial family reunion is a wonderful relief for Maman, and it is good to see her come alive again and conversing in Farsi. We laugh at our shared anecdotes and compare our experiences and emotions on leaving Iran. The others are impressed at how I gained passage with the price of a necklace.

Babajon, Maman and I bring the others up to date about the news and goings-on in Tehran, all of us bemoaning the situation in our homeland, complaining that our lives have been snatched away from us. I describe Ferri's escape with Hamid, riding camels over the mountains to Afghanistan, a dangerous trip, both because of the topography and because we imagine that the mullahs have taken precautions to prevent anyone crazy enough to attempt the trip by posting Guards along the borders. Now that my own situation has calmed down, my anxiety attaches to her. I ask Bahman if he has received a phone call saying, "The package has arrived." He has not.

Thoughts of Ehsan pull at me. I have thought of him far more than I should, dwelling on him even as I prepared our escape.

Seven long, lonely years have passed since the magical night we met. Knowing I'm so close to him now in London, my heart jumps. I can call him. I have no doubt he would be happy — and surprised! — to hear from me. Once we've settled in London, I can fly to Paris to see him and he can visit me here. Seven years, and still the thought of seeing him puts a smile on my face.

In the afternoon, with Reza occupied with Jeremy and the adults chatting, I am ready to telephone the Iranian Embassy in Paris. In these seven years, the world has changed so. As an emissary of Iran, Ehsan has been in the head of the political storm and I realize now, so filled with the immediacy of dealing with crisis after crisis, he may well not remember me other than as that silly woman who'd worn red to a black and white ball.

He may not even be an ambassador any longer. Since the revolution, many of Iran's embassies have closed. The one in Paris continues to function, but there is no guarantee that Ehsan is still the Iranian ambassador to France. After all, our government and its leaders have changed …

My God! I realize that, like so many others who were aligned with or chosen by the exiled monarch, he may have been executed by the present regime! I must know his fate. I take a seat in the chair by the hallway phone and call the embassy in France.

A woman answers. I ask for Ehsan Bakhti, praying that he's alive, still at the embassy, that he can be reached at this number, and that he's available. Praying he is my destiny.

"Who's calling, please?"

My throat closes. "It's personal."

The woman is the slightest bit impatient now. "I understand, but I must have a name."

I'm not sure if I should volunteer my name. If he was targeted by the mullahs and they discover that I am associated with him our problems will increase.

"Please tell him it's the woman that prefers her caviar naked."

She hesitates, probably wondering if she should again ask my name. "One moment, please."

She sounds impatient and judgmental. I should have thought of a less controversial message. I continue to hold the line and wonder where she has gone. A minute passes, then another, and another, and I wonder who she's given my message to. I wonder if they can trace this call, perhaps, know where to find us. But then she comes back on the line. "One moment, please. I am connecting you now."

The next voice I hear is his. "Layla, is that you? How wonderful to hear from you."

My world opens and my heart is happy. I am no longer anxious. He's alive and speaking to me. He remembers me and sounds thrilled to hear from me. It is as if we'd spoken that morning. Happiness fills my heart. He *is* my destiny! He is mine.

"Yes, it's me, Ehsan. You remember me."

He chuckles. When he speaks, his voice is filled with smiles. "How could I forget you? Never."

"Well, I'm in London and I'm wondering if you might know of a place where I can get naked caviar."

He laughs, then becomes immediately serious. "Tell me, are you in London with Rostam?"

It's my turn to chuckle. "No, I'm in London without him. I've left him and I'm here with Reza and my parents. We won't go back."

I hear the slightest pause as he takes in what I said. "You've left Rostam?"

"Actually, we *escaped* Rostam. He threatened to turn my father and possibly Maman and me into the Revolutionary Guards on bogus charges unless my father paid him a small fortune with no assurance that he wouldn't want more and wouldn't turn him in anyway."

"He did that? To Agha Saleh?"

"Well, he's not the same man you knew, Ehsan. He's changed. He's become a drug addict. And he's broke so he's become a petty thief. He needs money, and he's – well, he's evil."

"Actually, my dear," Ehsan says, "he sounds exactly like the Rostam I knew. I understand. He has lost his lucrative business. But many have seen their fate tumble and are still responsible husbands and fathers."

"I'm sure that's true, but not Rostam." I'm done speaking of the oaf. "How are you, Ehsan?" I recall his daughter's name. "How is Lisette?"

"We're fine. I hear your voice and I have no complaints. I've never stopped thinking – dreaming – of you, Layla."

There's a pause before he says, "Hold a minute, please." I hear a man speaking in the background and Ehsan responses, "Not now. Put it down and leave." Then, "Please see that I'm not disturbed."

I am thrilled beyond words. Ehsan remembers me! He's said he's missed me and that he dreams of me.

Then he says, "As I was saying, I have never coveted another man's wife. But I have wanted you from the moment I saw you. It seems like it was last night. I remember the entire evening from the moment you walked in the door. My only wish has been to spend time with you alone, Layla, and to know more about you. I want to know you completely. But, of course, that hasn't been possible. You are a married woman."

I scoff. "I intend to divorce Rostam as soon possible. Can you come to London?"

"Are you kidding? Absolutely! Let me look at my calendar." A momentary pause. "I can be there on Friday and stay through Sunday night."

"That's wonderful! How I've dreamed of seeing you again, Ehsan."

He laughs that wonderful, confident laugh. "Miss Saleh, if I may speak truthfully, I have dreamed of not only seeing you but seeing the whole of you, unhampered by red silk, no matter how lovely the dress. I call it 'naked Layla.'"

"Why Ambassador!" I say in mock indignation. "I just might report that language to our Supreme Leader."

"If you must," he says.

"We're staying at my cousin's house. Where will you stay?" I ask.

"Give me your phone number and I'll let you know the particulars."

I hesitate. "I'll probably be out a lot. I'll be meeting with lawyers with Babajon, and looking for a place. My cousin has an answering machine so if you call and we're out, I'll call you back."

Just then, I hear Babajon call out to someone, probably Maman, as he enters the hallway. "I'll call my doctor now," he says, "It won't be a problem."

After briefly agreeing that our reconnection is a marvelous thing, promising to talk again before we meet, we hang up, still smiling. We will be together within forty-eight hours.

Babajon takes his small address book out of his pocket, sits on the chair I have just vacated, and calls his doctor in Tehran for a refill of his heart medication to be sent to a pharmacy close to Bahman's house.

When he's told that the pharmacy is out of stock, he asks if there is a pharmacy nearby that has a supply. The pharmacist makes a phone call, then regretfully says there is not. He will need two days to fill it and will call the house when it's ready.

Fortunately, jetlag is minimal. So, despite the continued rain, we decide to do some sight-seeing with Bahman in the lead. Mahnaz decides to stay home with her son and is happy to have Reza, who is enjoying his time with Jeremy, stay in as well.

We visit Taymoor and Shireen's London home. It is far more modest than their home in Tehran, yet lovely, a two-story brick house boasting front and back yards and a huge terrace on the second floor filled with greenery.

While enjoying a round of cocktails, Taymoor confirms they will be leaving for Switzerland the following day. Aunt Haideh and Mansoor Khan will be staying on in London with Bahman for a while.

On the way back to Bahman's home, Babajon insists on buying Reza a birthday gift. The stores are closing, but he finds a large set of Legos I know my son will love and Taymoor buys him a young scientist's kit. Still raining and turning colder and darker, we return to Bahman's house, umbrella's left outside along with wet shoes.

Reza loves his gifts and I am still walking on air. I have reconnected with Ehsan and we will be meeting soon again. I will soon be in his arms.

We freshen up and sit down to the wonderful dinner Mahnaz has prepared, English prime rib with vegetables and Persian rice.

As we eat, she asks about our afternoon, then turns to her husband. "Bahman," she says, "I was in the shower and missed two phone calls. The answering machine picked up, but I've been busy with Jeremy and preparing dinner, so I haven't listened to them. They're probably from Abe, asking if you'll be at the seminar next week in Cambridge."

"Ah, yes! He's been after me to go with him," Bahman says. "I'll get back to him after dinner."

When dinner is done, he excuses himself and leaves the room to listen to the messages on his answering machine. Within minutes, he reappears, a strange look on his face.

"Layla, I think you should listen to these messages." The grim expression on my cousin's face signals that the message is from Rostam.

I pull myself up out of my chair.

I don't want to hear the message. I don't want to ever hear Rostam's voice again.

Babajon has seen the look of dread on my face. He silently follows Bahman and me. We three leave the dining room and return to the hallway. The answering machine sits on top of a narrow wooden table, covered with a paisley fabric, indisputably Iranian.

My cousin rewinds the machine, passes over several beeps and hits "Play." It is Rostam's voice. He is laughing, his speech, slurred. The three of us are listening.

"You stupid whore." I feel my heart drop. Bahman and Babajon hear him call me that vile name and, though I have become accustomed to it, I can see that my father and my cousin are shocked. "You, stupid, stupid whore. Do you really think Rostam doesn't know where you've gone? Stupid fool!" He laughs again and ends up coughing, then clears his throat, the sound of phlegm obvious. He spits, and continues. "I know you've run to London to your cousin's house. Do you really think Rostam will let you get away? You and your rich Jew-loving father and my Shozdeh?" I am surprised he's noticed that his son is gone. The man has spent so little time or energy on Reza that I would ever have guessed he would miss him so soon. We hear him slurp as he takes a swig of a drink and then a leisurely drag on a cigarette or pipe. Babajon has his worry beads out and is looking at me, watching me, ascertaining my reaction. "You forget, my lovely whore, the Guards are everywhere, and Rostam has connections with a certain well-ranked Guard and his friends.

"Do you think Rostam will let go of you, or Shozdeh, or your spy father and his money? Don't you know Rostam better by now?" He laughs yet again, a guffaw, and I want to take that answering machine and throw it, shatter it and destroy his words.

"So, my little whore-wife, this is what you will do. Today. You will return to Rostam with Shozdeh and convince your father to return with you. If you do that, I will not turn you or your arrogant mother in to the Guards. But if you do not, Rostam will direct the Guards to either assassinate your father, the stupid man who tries to gyp Rostam out of money that is mine," *His money?* "or perhaps, shoot him in the leg and bring him back to face his future here." *Future? What future?* The click signals the end of the message, a one-minute message that has completely ruined what has been a pleasant time in London and the belief that we were free of Rostam. We had believed we'd outsmarted the oaf bastard. But once again, he has proven that he is difficult to get rid of.

Before any of us utter a word, the next message begins. It is also in Farsi. "Hello? Hello? I know you hearing this. I am Hassan Amirzadeh of the Intelligence Division of the Revolutionary

Guards of the blessed Islamic Republic of Iran, appointed by our Supreme Leader to defend against enemies of the Islamic Republic of Iran. This is for Layla Saleh-Shamshiri, Zahrah Saleh and Hadi Saleh. You three are hereby commanded to return to Tehran at once under the authority of our Supreme Leader, Ayatollah Khomeini. You are all fugitives from the law. The fact of your attempted escaped is a certain sign of guilt and you will be dealt with harshly. I warn you. If you do not return immediately, Guards will be dispatched to your location and summarily bring all of you forcefully back. Return now!" There is a click as he hangs up and another as the machine signals the end of the message and shuts off. I stand, gazing down at the machine's worn buttons. I don't know what to say. I feel I need to apologize to Bahman and Mahnaz for having corrupted their machine with such evil.

Babajon runs his palm across his forehead, then reaches for my hand. "Layla, I promise you. He will never find us. We will leave London immediately and go where he will never be able to find us."

I scoff. *Did such a place exist? Could he be thinking of France?* "Where Babajon?"

"America. We shall leave tomorrow."

I lay in bed that night filled with fear for Babajon, Maman, Reza and myself. If Rostam finds us, there will be no hope for us. Along with it all, he has pulverized my hopes to meet with Ehsan as soon as Friday. And, with my heart securely tied to Ehsan, the knowledge that I will be returning to America after twenty-four years barely soothes my heart.

Early the next morning, while everyone is still asleep, except for Mahnaz who is feeding Jeremy, I call Ehsan again, glad that I now have his personal phone number. I tell him that Rostam has located us and that we are leaving England and heading for America. He sounds as disappointed as I feel. With relations between The Islamic Republic of Iran and the United States as torn as they are, he is not sure when he can travel to America. I promise to let him know where we are so he can join if and when possible.

39

ASYLUM

*A*fter a quick breakfast of tea and scones topped with butter and jam, my father and I leave for a meeting with a London-based attorney specializing in U.S. immigration.

Babajon takes his briefcase, loaded with documents. It is freezing out and the wind bites, but I'm glad to see the rain has stopped.

At Attorney Langer's office, we learn there are two ways people in our situation can enter the U.S.

One is to file at the American Consulate here in London for refugee status and wait here until our paperwork is done, then enter. It is impossible to say how long that will take. We cannot do that. While we wait, we would be sitting ducks for Rostam and Hassan.

The second and faster way is for us to enter is as tourists, either for pleasure, with a letter from someone there inviting us to visit, or for business purposes. Since we don't know anyone in America that will vouch for our visit, entering for business is our answer.

Babajon applies for a temporary business visa to locate ingredients for his products. The immigration status of Maman, Reza and I will follow under the umbrella of his visa.

Once in the U.S., we'll file for asylum based on the fact that if we were to return to Iran we will be killed. The evidence for our claim will be our joint testimony and recorded threats on Bahman's answering machine — both Rostam's and The Rat's promise to find us and kill us or force us back to Iran. We can only hope that Rostam will lose our trail.

Our next stop is the American Consulate. The Consulate is in the center of the Mayfair district of London by Grosvenor Square and boasts a lovely park across the street. As we pass the Lycée Française, the building comes into view. Though preoccupied with my thoughts, I don't miss the presence of high security in the area, likely due to threats from the IRA.

The building that houses both the American Consulate and the American Embassy is imposing. Bahman, himself now an architect of some success, notes that it was designed by an American architect. Inside, we are directed to a woman who sits at a desk with a black metal strip that announces her name is Jan Weiss, Deputy Consul. She is likely in her mid-40s with light brown hair in a pixie cut. Babajon and I sit in chairs set in front of her standard issue desk. She interlocks her fingers, leans forward, and smiles a smile meant to put strangers at ease. "Hello there. How may I help you?"

Babajon explains that he needs visas for himself, his wife, his daughter, and his grandson to enter America on business, specifically, to scope private businesses there in search of ingedients to be imported to Iran for his pharmaceutical business. He shows her evidence of his ownership of Saleh Pharmaceuticals and our Iranian passports. The clerk nods and calls for a Farsi to English translator to verify the contents of the written documents. A heavyset man, obviously Iranian, joins us almost immediately and I assume they have a full lineup of various translators ready to be summoned as needed.

She asks if Babajon intends to remain in the States permanently. He chuckles. "My good woman, how can I? I own the largest pharmaceutical company in Iran with hundreds of employees and many commitments awaiting me. I also own a million-dollar home I painstakingly built for my wife, filled with furniture that she's hand-picked from around the world." He chuckles. "You don't know my wife, but believe me, the woman would kill me if I dared to even suggest that we leave them." He also brings out papers evidencing his ownership of both their house and the second house they have rented out. All these are ample evidence of ties my parent have to Tehran and proof they will return to Iran if given visas to the U.S.

The agent turns to me. "What about you?"

I'm somewhat startled. "Me?"

"Do you intend to remain in the United States?"

"Oh, no! My husband is in Tehran and expects me back." When she continues to look at me, apparently wanting more, I add, "I attended UCLA when I was younger, but stayed only one year. I was too homesick to stay. I love Iran. I want my son to grow up there." The translator informs her of the contents of my documents. She nods, apparently satisfied. This time, the forged signature has gone unnoticed.

All four passports are stamped with B-1 visas, signifying temporary entry into the States for business.

We book our flight to America that same night and make sure to take the tape from Bahman's answering service with us.

40

BACK IN LA

March, 1984

We leave for the States the next morning.

I feel on edge. The bastard has made it impossible for us to stay in London. I've lost the chance of seeing Ehsan this weekend. I won't be living just a short distance away from him. But the pain I feel is soothed, knowing I'll be returning to Los Angeles and Jasmine.

Maman's whining continues. "I don't see why we have to go to that Godforsaken country!" and "How am I supposed to live in that disgusting sex-infested place?" According to her, the United States is filled with an immoral population and indiscriminate sex is the norm.

I know her views on the country all too well. I've known them from the time I was preparing to leave for UCLA. She had not wanted me to go to college. She believed that education is unbecoming a female.

In her view, I ought to have forgotten all about microbiology. More, she hated America. She had intended me to stay in Tehran, marry, and supply her with grandchildren as soon as possible. No doubt Maman is stuck on the silent fact that we will be living in the city where I lost my virginity.

But today her complaints seem inane, for we are bound by necessity more than choice. Yet she goes on. "How long before we can go back home?" and "I finally had someone to talk to in London and you took me away!"

Her objections are endless. I can't imagine how my father tolerates all her whining. He has never displayed the least bit of impatience; he never would. Yet it must annoy him as it would annoy anyone who is trying to make plans for survival amid such negativity.

When we land in New York, we set our watches back eight hours as we wait on the line for immigration officials to attach a piece of paper to our passports, stating we are lawfully in the country for a stay not to exceed six months.

As tired as we all are, we do not leave the airport. The first day of Spring is almost here, yet the city is having snow flurries with temperatures hovering in the high forties.

We have a terrible dinner as we wait for our connecting flight to Los Angeles.

We're sitting at the gate. Maman continues to protest until we board. "California! I would never dream you would take me to that hellhole, Hadi. You are determined to take me to the most morally decrepit city in this God forsaken country? What about our grandson? You want him to grow up amid the filth of these people?"

Babajon takes reaches over and strokes her back. "*Azizam,* my precious," he says, "it is far too cold for us in New York. It's like London, overcast and cold. It rains and snows a lot. Summers are very humid. The weather in Los Angeles is like Tehran. It's really a very lovely place." She shakes her head, and he continues. "I've always wanted you to see it. It has the beaches, the mild Pacific Ocean, mountains ... and everywhere you look, there are flowers and trees and green–"

"And immoral people filling their days with drugs, fighting, and sex, and ... she struggles to find the word ... hippies!" she finishes. She casts me a sour look. I am silent.

Babajon repeats himself. "*Aziz*, my cherished, did you enjoy the cold, overcast weather of London? That's the climate here. Los Angeles is warm and dry."

He's selling the weather to her.

Two hours later, we board the plane that will take us to Los Angeles and again set our watches, this time three hours further back.

My mother moans. "I never thought I would live to see this day," she huffs. She continues finding fault with LA. "I don't understand. You know how I feel about this dirty country and *especially* your Los Angeles."

In truth, I cannot help but feel bad for her, knowing how she detests America. But this is one time she will not have her way. It is as if poetic justice has manifested itself. The world has turned and turned again, forcing her to either fry in the pan she has so oiled, or, hopefully realize that her complaints are unjustified and be grateful that America is saving her, her husband and their family from mortal danger.

It is obvious that my father is stressed, his health taxed.

He looks pale and thinner in the few days since we have left Iran. He has done so much, borne the responsibility for staying on the move, keeping us all safe from the son-of-a-bitch. He's been under a huge amount of pressure. He must be tired.

I am worried and I worry that he was not been able to refill his medication in London as planned because of our unscheduled departure. Again due to the piece of garbage that is my husband.

We spend our first night in Los Angles at a nice enough hotel in the mid-Wilshire area. The next morning, Babajon calls his doctor in Tehran, but his office is closed because of the time difference and he can only leave a message that he will call again.

Then we set out to find an apartment. We stop at a newsstand and are surprised to see a Farsi newspaper. Apparently, there are now enough Iranians in the city to merit it.

Over breakfast, we scope the classified section, searching "Apartments for Rent." We circle several we want to see, most in Westwood, the neighborhood I had lived in while a student at UCLA. The area is so populated with Iranians that it is now known as "Little Tehran."

As we walk the area, street names sound vaguely familiar to me. When I glimpse the two movie theaters on opposite corners in Westwood Village, my heart rate quickens. I had spent so much time in this area with David. We had seen "Exodus" in one of these theaters, the movie that had started David thinking about Israel.

David!

We nix two apartments in the Fairfax area, not too far from our hotel.

"We need a car," Babajon says. "We can't keep taking taxis." And so, our next stop is a dealership. Babajon has always been partial to Buicks and now he buys a year-old blue Buick Skylark, the first time he has opted not to buy a new car.

Reza is tired and hungry. The child has not had the chance to catch up with himself. He wriggles in the back seat. "Maman, when will we get there?"

I assume by 'there' he means *home*. This sudden departure from London has probably confused him. He enjoyed his time with Jeremy, Bahman and Mahnaz and liked seeing Shireen and her family again, Our present homelessness may be making him anxious.

I gesture him to come sit closer to me. He snuggles up against me and I hold him against my breast and run my fingers through his hair. "Soon, my love," I say, "soon."

When he says he's hungry, Babajon stops at a market and goes in as we three wait in the car. If there is nothing else in this city that my mother would like, the size of the market impresses her. A few minutes later, Babajon reappears with water bottles and some fruit. He hands Reza a bottle and an apple.

Within two hours of driving off the lot with our new used car, we rent a furnished, two-bedroom apartment one street away from Westwood Boulevard, a street lined with shops and markets, many with Farsi signs. That's a good thing, as Maman neither reads nor speaks English. I'm sure Babajon shares my hope that Maman can be comfortable in this neighborhood, function in Farsi and hopefully make friends. Perhaps her complaints will end. Perhaps, they'll be fewer.

We return to the hotel to pick up our suitcases and drive to our new apartment.

The following day is Norooz.

We are celebrating in a new land, with a new apartment, a new car and hope for the future.

The immediate priority is to deal with Babajon's medication. It is almost finished.

Our first day in the apartment our phone line is installed and he thinks to call the London pharmacy, asking that they transfer the prescription to a local pharmacy here. The London pharmacy is closed.

He calls his Iranian doctor to request that a new prescription be sent to Los Angeles and is told that it can take up to six business days to arrive in the mail and cannot be faxed to the neighborhood Save-On.

He decides it will be faster to meet with a new cardiologist at nearby UCLA. That way, he will be have a local cardiologist and an expedited prescription. He provides the doctor's office with his medical history. When he complains of chest pains, he is given an appointment the very next day. He has not mentioned any pain to us and now he insists it is nothing serious.

For the first time ever, he is dead wrong.

41

HEARTBREAK

I'm awakened this morning by Maman's screams.

I race to my parents' bedroom. My dear, dear father, my Babajon, is in bed on his back, partially hanging off his side of the mattress. His open eyes are staring at some ill-defined spot on the ceiling.

Maman has apparently awakened to his lifeless body.

"No, no!" she wails, "Don't you dare, Hadi! You can't leave me! Not now. Not here," she screams. "*Ayy!* You can't leave me alone here!" She sits up, leans back against the headboard and begins to punch her head with her two fists. "What will I do without you? Hadi! How can you die and leave me alone?"

Babajon's right arm is flung out over the mattress, his palm open. I see a pill on the floor by the bed. It is sitting in a small puddle of water that has apparently spilled from the overturned glass inches away. It appears my father died while reaching for that glass of water to take with this pill, his last — the pill that would have saved him.

I sit on the bed beside Babajon and tenderly close those brown eyes that will never again shine, will never again look at me with endless love. I can never again look into his eyes and know I am loved and safe. I embrace his body and kiss his forehead for the last time.

Maman continues screaming. "Is he gone?" She asks, knowing he is. I nod. She covers her face with her hands and weeps. "How can this happen to me? What will I do now? How can I go on without him?"

My heart breaks for her, even forgiving the fact that she sees herself as the victim here and not her recently departed husband. I try to soothe her. "You'll be okay, Maman *jon*. I'll take care of you."

She draws back as if from a snake. "You?" she says. Is it hostility or sarcasm that pours out of the word?

"*You? You?* You're the reason he is dead! You're the reason we're in this God-forsaken country, in this cheap, tasteless apartment. You're the reason I had to leave my beautiful home and everything I loved. You're to blame for all the worry and stress that killed my Hadi. It's your fault we had to leave everything behind and run like fugitives." She turns away. "*Ayy!* What will happen to me?"

I keep my mouth shut. I know she will never forgive me. I wouldn't be surprised if she still believes Rostam's threats were because of something I did to him. I sit on the floor by the bed alongside Babajon and cry. For my lost father, my poor distraught mother and my young son who has just lost his grandfather, his sole role model and a man who adored him; lost him so soon after leaving everything and everyone he's known behind, including his own father.

Maman is right to blame me for all this. It was my stupidity that led me to marry the very worst man in Iran and for the most naïve of reasons.

Reza appears at the threshold of the room rubbing his eyes. "Maman jon, what's wrong? Why is Maman Bozorg crying?"

I get up, dry my tears, swoop up the glass and the pill then go to him and lead him into our bedroom. The poor child has been through so much chaos and change in the last week. "Darling, your dear grandfather died during the night in his sleep."

He looks up at me and gasps. "Why? What's happened to him?"

"It was his heart. It stopped working while he was asleep. But he died without pain."

"Why?"

"He had a weak heart, my sweet. He took a pill very day to keep his heart healthy, but then they finished. He was supposed to go to the doctor today and get more." Hearing myself, I am overcome with grief. It is frustrating to know that the last pill had dropped from his hand before his heart stopped. I break down and weep.

He brings me tissues. "I'm sorry, Maman jon." He's empathizing with *my* loss. After a moment, he asks, "Maman jon, Do you have a weak heart?"

I wipe me eyes and smile at him. "No, my love." I hold him close. "My heart and your heart are both very, very strong."

"Does Papa have a strong heart?" When I don't answer right away, he asks, "Is that why he's like that?"

My answer is, at best, noncommittal. "I don't know if his heart is weak," I say. I hug him tighter, wrapping my arms around him tightly, protectively, amazed at the fact that that my Babajon is dead on the run from my own husband, a mean addict who's threatened to take his very life with lies. It is too much. I pray Rostam has the weakest heart in all the world. "It might be," I say.

I kiss Reza's head.

Babajon's death devastes me.

I feel like my skin has been ripped off. I can't imagine a world without my father. He had been my world for the years before I left for California and even that was thanks to him.

It was those young years spent at Saleh Laboratories that

created my love for the sciences. Throughout my school years, I would come home eager to share all I'd learned at the dinner table with Babajon. The talk of germs annoyed Maman terribly, but her disapproval never stopped Babajon from asking more questions about my science classes. He proudly displayed every award and certificate of high commendation I received in his office at Saleh. After high school graduation, when Maman fought to have me remain in Iran and marry, my father surprised me with the gift of UCLA at a time the university had newly initiated a program devoted to microbiology.

He loved me and was always – Always! – in my corner, wanting to arrange things so that I could have what I wanted out of life. So different than Maman. His love was shown not only in words, forever calling me his "Golden Girl," but in his actions, as well.

I will forever honor his memory. We have lost him at too young an age. He deserved to live a long, healthy life, comforted by the fruits of his labor. And Reza deserves to have his grandfather with him for many years to come, to learn from him and be guided by his example.

I call Ehsan, give him the sad news and cry to him. He is as comforting as he can be and frustrated that he cannot be with me at this sad time. Today's news here is that the U.S. has put Iran on the list of nations that have "repeatedly provided support for acts of international terrorism." Ehsan feels trapped. He wants nothing to do with the Islamic Republic and is counting the days until his term ends.

He tells me that Iranian boys between the ages of twelve and seventeen are being selected by local clergy and designated as divine martyrs by Allah and Khomeini in Iran's war against Iraq. They are sent weaponless into battle against full-blown Iraqi armor to locate bombs and land mines. Before being deployed, they're gifted headbands to wear and keys to hold. With these they will enter heaven in the event they are killed.

Ehsan is sick to his stomach.

"They're bound together in groups to prevent desertion. They test the enemy's minefields and even throw themselves on barbed wire so Iran's tanks will have a clear path." I am equally disgusted.

"The back of their shirts," he says, "reads, *I have the Imam's special permission to enter heaven.*" I hear his inhale then a sharp exhale.

"I cannot do this much longer," he says. "I'm representing these mullahs, and meanwhile, you need a man there with you. I don't want you to have all that on your shoulders." For as long as Ehsan is the ambassador from Iran, he will not be welcomed in America.

Yet, we tell each other that we'll be together soon.

Maman is useless, locked away in her grief, so I must set about dealing with the funeral arrangements. I buy today's Farsi newspaper and find a mortuary.

Arrangements are made, Iranian style.

4 2

ADULTING

March, 1984

*I*t's Noruz.

Shops on Westwood Boulevard have been plastered with signs wishing all a Happy New Year.

We will not celebrate this year.

Babajon is buried in a small cemetery near the Westwood library, close enough to the apartment for Maman to walk to. The name of the mortuary translates in English to "Eternal Blessings." We sprinkle rose water on his grave and cry.

Maman is lost in grief, self-pity, and an overall depression. She is mostly silent, moving around the apartment crying. Used tissues are balled up and tossed everywhere. Most days, she eats no more than tea and bread and won't venture out, other than to visit Baba-jon's gravesite. She is no longer interested in shopping. A large part of the Zahra Khanom that I've known my whole life has died with her husband. I try to interest her in the latest news in Iran, but it is mostly useless and she insists the West is making up the worst of it for political reasons. Of course, she has zero interest in learning English.

We visit Babajon's gravesite daily to sprinkle more rosewater on his grave. Sometimes, like today, Maman just cries. Sometimes, she admonishes him, angry for daring to die without even a warning. Sometimes, she jumps from one complaint to the next — many having to do with how inattentive I am to her needs— hopscotching through the list of injustices she endures.

Her depression affects Reza. I hate seeing him curl into himself in her presence. We are both walking on eggshells in the small apartment, so I make a point of taking him out as much as possible. He goes everywhere with me and soon comes to know the people who work at the markets we favor, quickly grasping the names and location of streets and shops in our area.

He is to start school in the fall, and I am aware of how important it is for his English to continue to improve. I am always on the lookout for books and anything else that can help him better his English. At home, he dwells on my mother's depressed state, so I plant him in front of the television and find shows made for children.

Whereas in Iran his television time was limited – in reality, he had little interest in the state-sponsored shows – in my eagerness for my son to learn English, it is now on almost all the time. As time passes, I see results. He shyly asks for something he's seen advertised on TV. I bargain with him then, agreeing to buy it for him provided he can tell me about it and why he wants it – in English. He's learning fast.

I sit beside him on the floor. He is so young, so sweet, so innocent and has already been through so much.

I love being close to my child.

Once again, the lectures of Rene Dubos, my favorite professor at UCLA, come to mind.

Professor Dubos theorized that one's longevity is not determined by the number of difficulties one faces in life, but rather by how well one faces those difficulties and survives them with resiliency.

The events that have shaped my life have been challenging, and I have — so far — survived them all. Fair to say, I have remained resilient.

I am now living what is probably my greatest challenge. I am in a country I knew as a young, college student more than two decades ago. While mourning the death of my beloved father, I must put my emotions aside and piece together the puzzle that he has left me to decipher. I must stand in his shoes and protect my son, my mother and myself from Rostam.

I must be resilient.

I must find us a means of support. I have no doubt that Babajon has arranged for us to receive income while in America. *But how? From where? When will it come? How much?* I have no idea. He had said he would contact his attorney in Iran to deal with my parents' home, their other assets and Salah. *Who is that attorney and how do I contact him?*

I must also deal with our immigration status. It is of paramount importance. It's up to me to make sure we can permanently remain in this country after our six-month visas expire. The three of us had piggy-backed on my father's B-1 visa. *What happens to us now that he's died?*

These questions buzz around my head with so many others:

Will my Reza be happy here?

Jasmine – *where do I begin to look for her?*

Will Maman ever acclimate?

Ehsan – *when will I see him again?*

And Ferri — *did she make it to Afghanistan?*

My immediate challenge is to make sense of Babajon's plans to provide funds for our future.

Everything available to me to work out the puzzle is in Babajon's briefcase.

Opening his briefcase, I am flooded with his energy. As I set about organizing its contents, his handwriting soothes me. I spent so much time at his office that I am as familiar with it as I was with our house in Tehran.

I feel his presence as I picture him at his desk, completing these forms and creating these notes. I will have to examine every document. I know each one has gone into his briefcase because it is significant. Leave it to Babajon to compile all his important documents to carry with him to destinations unknown. I must decipher the significance of each and how they all fit together. Hopefully, I will find answers. I purchase a set of manilla folders, and begin to tag each sheet of paper as I sort through them.

I create three groups of documents. The first consists of personal papers. Babajon has brought Maman's health records and his own. I have brought my own health records and Reza's. I put these on the first pile along with Babajon's school transcripts dated a little over four decades ago from UC Berkeley along with my own school records, a few of his most beloved photos of Maman and me, which I later thumb through with Reza, and other miscellaneous personal attachments.

The second group consists of all the documents relating to our immigration status, our passports that contain our B-1 visas and I-90s as well as the documents we needed to leave Iran and to obtain our visas.

The third, a substantial pile, is made up of documents concerning Babajon's financial life. I try to group them by subject.

There are deeds and papers confirming insurance on his properties, including the land Saleh Pharmaceutical sits on – the buildings, the laboratories and offices – and the vast acreage he owned on Karaj, the road leading to Salah Pharmaceuticals. Saleh Labs as well as his two homes – the one he built and the one lower down in the hills of Shimran that we used to live in, now rented out.

There is information about the business, showing the profits for each year of its existence, his employees' profit-sharing plan, as well as various bank statements. As I create this pile, I am stunned by the realization of just how successful my father — a self-made man — was, and how organized these papers are.

I sigh. I miss him *so* much! My heart overflows with love and pain.

He has included two business cards among these papers. One is in Farsi and provides the information for his Iranian attorney, Massoud Bouria. The other is from John Kroft, Atttorney at Law. Under Kroft's name it says, "Business and International Tax." He is located in Beverly Hills, California. I wonder at this.

When had Babajon retained an attorney in California?

I call the number on John Kroft's card and introduce myself then say I'm in Los Angeles with my mother and son and that Babajon passed soon after our arrival. I say I have found his card among my father's files and would like to meet to consult with him.

Attorney Kroft conveys his condolences on Babajon's passing. He informs me that he had been retained by Babajon and had spoken with Babajon several times, somewhat regularly during the last year and then several times in the last two weeks. He suggests we meet as soon as possible.

As his calendar is full for the next several days, he suggests we meet over lunch the tomorrow at one o'clock.

We meet at the coffee shop inside his Beverly Hills building.

I arrive first and take a seat at a booth facing the door to the lobby. Minutes later, he enters through that door and makes a gesture of acknowledgment to me and I smile as he makes his way to the table, his stride long. He appears to be about sixty years old. He is tall, his limbs long and lanky. One of his shoulders sits higher than the other.

His camel colored jacket is almost the same color as his short, curly hair. He approaches, and I note his green eyes behind the wire framed glasses. He slides onto the red leather seat. "Salaam." I appreciate his attempt to make me feel comfortable with the Farsi greeting. I return the same to him.

His eyes circle our unassuming surroundings, and he says, "Sorry this is all I have to offer."

"Well," I say and chuckle. "It *is* Beverly Hills,"

He scoffs. "Right."

We look at one another across the Formica tabletop. I have set Babajon's briefcase beside me on my side of the red leather booth.

"I really appreciate accommodating me."

"It's my pleasure. Miss Saleh, I'm so sorry for your loss. From what I knew of your father, he was truly a wonderful man. Enlightened. I would have enjoyed knowing him better. It's a very sad loss. I know it must be difficult for you. How is your mother taking it?"

"Not well." I say.

"I'm sorry," he says. "Please extend my condolences to her."

"Thank you," I say. "It's been hard for us all."

"I see you're wearing a wedding ring. Is your husband here with you?"

It's the first time I realize I'm wearing Rostam's wedding ring. I will have to decide on what to do with it. It must be worth good money.

My thoughts are interrupted by the waitress who comes by to

276

take our orders. I order iced tea and a tuna sandwich on wheat bread. Attorney Kroft also orders tuna but asks for white bread and coffee.

The waitress leaves. "No," I answer. "My husband is in Iran. I'm here with my nine-year-old son, Reza." I adjust myself in my seat. "He needs to learn English and I want him to get used to being around American children. I'm going to arrange for him to start school in September."

"I see. Are you divorced?"

I squirm a bit and decide that I have to be honest, give the attorney all the information I can about us.

"Mr. Kroft, my parents, me, and my son, left Iran to escape my husband who was blackmailing us. He was going to report my father to the Revolutionary Guards with made-up allegations that were total lies and probably add that my mother and I had helped him. If we hadn't escaped, my father would have spent his life in jail and been badly tortured or, most likely, been executed by the mullahs, and God knows what would have happened to my mother and me."

Attorney Kroft looks somber as he notes that our unexpected escape was necessary to save our lives. "I can't even imagine what your family has been through. Your father told me he would be leaving Iran in a hurry but never explained why." He's shaking his head. "Terrible. Absolutely terrifying."

I nod. "Yes. We had to leave quietly and within two weeks, without my husband's knowledge, or even his slightest suspicions." I pause to take a breath and my attention is drawn to a young couple sitting at the next table, their voices raised, possibly arguing. I'm somewhat surprised that the well-dressed, middle-aged woman facing me, has smudged her dark lipstick and is apparently unaware she is flawed.

I turn back to Attorney Kroft. "So, now we're here – my son, my mother, and me. I don't know what will happen to our immigration process or how we'll be able to manage. We need money." I sit back, embarrassed. "I'm sorry, I don't mean to complain. But, well, there's rent, food, bills to pay … lawyers to pay … and my son will be starting school. He needs things." I start to tear as I identify the root causes for all this stress. I catch myself and take a deep breath. This is not the time or place for tears.

"Okay, Ms. Saleh-"

"Layla. You must call me Layla. I hope you can help us. I think you know about my father's business – his finances and how we can get some money here." I see that he's nodding vigorously and my relief is major.

"Okay," he says, "I'm well aware of your father's financial profile. We've spoke and he's sent over documents. I'll need a few days for our office to complete sorting things out, complete a profile of your father's finances with all the information he's given my office — and it's a lot."

"When did you speak to him? He didn't know we were coming here."

He waves an arm.. "Oh, he's been feeding me information from Iran through the mail and fax – and of course, we've spoken on the phone as well." He smiles. "As I said, I'm well aware of his financial profile. I can help. "

"Okay." I reach into my handbag. "I have documents here that he brought with him from Iran. There may be some things here that you don't already have." I hand him the file. "These are my only copies. If it's possible, I'd like them back."

He takes the file and assures me that his office will make copies and return these originals to me.

"I also have his Iranian attorney's card."

"No need. I have his name and number upstairs and probably have all or most of these documents as well, but I'll make sure." Then he changes his mind and puts his hand out. "Come to think of it, this may be another attorney. So, yes, give me that number." I give him Massoud Bouria's card.

"Look for my call in two or three days at the most. I'll have what you need by the end of this week. Try not to worry. I'm sure we can arrange to send monthly income to you for your needs."

To say I am relieved is a huge understatement. My chest is no longer tight. I can breathe freely again. I take a long, deep, delicious breath and relax in my seat. Money is coming. After a pause, I ask, "How long do you think it would take? I mean to actually receive the money."

The attorney leans across the table. "Well, once I arrive at the figure that I know is assured, my firm can immediately loan you the money you need for, say, the next month or so. When you receive it from Iran, you can reimburse my firm along with my fees."

"That would be wonderful! And so kind. Thank you."

"No problem."

We are finishing our sandwiches. I am taking the last sip of my tea. "Mr. Kroft, I hate to impose on your kindness, but the three of us need to straighten out our immigration position. I have to see to that as well. We can't return to Iran."

"Yes, I see that. My office doesn't do immigration law. But I can look into it and refer you to a knowledgeable specialist."

"I can't ask for more that, and I thank you so much for all you're doing."

"I'm glad to help," he says. "I'll do what I can for Hadi's family." I'm not surprised to see that what little this man knows of my father has made him a fan.

The check arrives. "Please, allow me to pay, Mr. Kroft. It's not a lot, and I'd like to thank you for taking your lunch time to talk to me about my problems." I hurry to add, "Of course, I expect to be charged for your time today as well."

Before I can reach for the check, Attorney Kroft takes it and brings out his green American Express credit card. I wonder if I will ever have one.

"No, Layla. My pleasure. Your father was a special man and it's a pleasure to know his daughter. I apologize for the venue." He gestures, taking in the coffee shop. "This was the only time I could meet you, so it's no problem at all."

"Thank you."

We leave the table and go into the building's lobby where we will say goodbye and go our separate ways.

"Thanks again," I say. "I guess I'll be hearing from you."

"Absolutely. And again, Layla, your family has my deepest condolences." He shakes his head. "You're a strong woman and your son is lucky to have you as a mother." I smile, wondering if he would think I'm strong if he knew my history.

He returns upstairs to his office, and I go home to wait for his call.

43

SANDS OF TIME

Since Babajon's passing, the mood in our apartment has been bleak.

The three of us mourn our loss in our own way.

I lay awake thinking about the father I have lost, feeling the hole his death has left in my life, and hoping he would be proud of how I will carry on in his place.

Maman is inconsolable. She is angry, as though he'd planned to rid her of the home she loved, bring her to America and then die and leave her.

"I don't understand," she says, as though there's something more to understand. "How could he?" She incessantly speaks of returning to Iran. "Hadi is gone, dead. Rostam can do nothing now. I want to go back home. I miss my house. I will die of loneliness. Layla, please. Arrange for me to fly back."

But I am far from certain that it is safe for any of us to return to Tehran. I also wish I were more confident that Rostam can't somehow locate us here with his contacts. I fear a physical confrontation and the possibility that he can take Reza away from me.

In one of Maman's desolate complaints, she interjects a memory of how the couple met. Babajon had recently graduated from college and returned from America. One of his college friends was marrying one of Maman's girlfriends, and Babajon began courting Maman. At the time, he was developing plans for his pharmaceutical company. According to her, she was very much sought after and had dozens of *khostegars*, many even wealthier than her own substantially well-off father. Babajon's family did not have money. His college education in the U.S. had been the result of scholarships.

She chuckles, recalling. "My father said I'm crazy to have any interest in him. His suits were not tailored, and his home was modest, his family name was unknown, and his sister – his sister was an ugly, overweight pig, engaged to a man who had 'failure' written all over him." She takes a fresh tissue and wipes her tears. "But Hadi had great plans. He said he would create a business like none other in Tehran and he would do it all for me. And he did. He did it for me."

Reza hovers quietly like a mother bird. He wants to know what he can do for Maman and me, constantly asking if we're all right.

I know he is in pain, of course he is, and I try to comfort him as much as I can, holding him, staying close to him, and reassuring him that though we're all sad, we'll be okay. Babajon still loves us and is watching and over us and I am here to make certain we will be fine. I coax him to play, but even then, he is often as quiet as a mouse.

When he plays in front of the television, he keeps the volume low so as not to intrude on Maman's emotional crisis.

I worry about Reza.

My son has had to mature rapidly since leaving home so

suddenly. He makes no trouble and asks no questions. He has not once mentioned his father or anything else he's left behind, not his school nor his friends. I know it is impossible for him not to be experiencing some anxiety, some confusion with all that has happened, yet he sits calmly, playing with the Rubik Cube I bought him.

"How's my boy?" I ruffle his hair. He smiles in answer. "Are you hungry?"

"Yes, Maman, I want cereal, please." He loves American cereals and could happily have one or another for breakfast, lunch, and dinner. In the kitchen, I pour some Lucky Charms into a bowl, add milk, and set it on the table for him. Then I make myself a cup of instant coffee. He sits, swaying his legs back and forth as he does when he likes what he's eating. I watch this wonderful child before me and realize he needs to know that there are still things to be enjoyed beyond cereal. I have not given him much caring attention lately; he has been caring for me.

God only knows what awaits us in the future. Yet, somehow, I have expected this child to react to his changing, challenging world like an adult. But he is a child. My child. And I love him. He needs a break. There is so much that I must take care of that my head is swimming. We both need a break.

I'm grateful that the meeting with Attorney Kroft went as well as it did and I am hopeful that we can flourish here.

"How would you like to go somewhere today that's really fun?"

He looks up. He is holding a spoonful of cereal and his mouth is wide open. "Can we go to Disneyland, Maman jon?"

"That's a great idea, Reza. Yes, we can. Let's do that another day. It's too hot today for Disneyland. How about the beach?"

Tehran is not close to an ocean. The only body of water Reza has seen is the Caspian Sea and only once. About a year before leaving Iran, the two of us accompanied Babajon and Maman when they were invited to the beachside home of a wealthy factory owner. His servants had laid a Persian rug on the sand with an urn of *chai*, cups, saucers, pastries, nuts and a large bowl of fruit.

That sort of luxurious life for the wealthy has become rare, and the number of very wealthy has declined, while the mullahs wealth has sky rocketed.

Each of our host's two teenaged sons drove their own pink dune buggy back and forth on the beach, and Reza had loved riding with them. As Maman and I sat in the sun all covered up, Babajon took Reza into the water. When they were about twenty feet out, I saw our host's man servant go into the sea heading out to them with his shoes off, pants rolled up, a wide smile on his swarthy face, holding a large brass bowl filled with fruit for them. They each opted for a cluster of grapes, which I suspect killed the taste of salt.

Reza loves the idea of going to the beach. In his excitement, he jumps up in his chair causing milk and cereal to spill onto the table with a *clunk*. He claps his hands. "Oh, Maman *jon*, yes. Let's go to the beach, please."

I am delighted to see him so happy. It has been too long since he's been excited about anything. "Okay, how about this? I'll pack a lunch of peanut butter and jam sandwiches and some fruit. We'll get some bottles of water, too. Then we'll stop and buy us some cool bathing suits and we'll go to the beach."

He looks as if he will burst with excitement. He wipes milk off the table, takes his bowl and spoon and deposits them in the sink, all in his happy-march.

"You're the best mother in the whole world," he says.

Buying swim trunks for Reza makes it obvious that he is growing and I no longer feel the need to pinch pennies.

So, along with the trunks, I buy him a pair of casual jeans, chinos, two pairs of shorts, some T-shirts, and a pair of dressier pants, two shirts and lightweight sweater. Searching for a swimsuit for myself, I am amazed at the amazing number of styles available to choose from. The idea that I will be showing my legs, my arms, and my cleavage all at one time is a welcome shock. Iran's bathing suits are anything but attractive, made solely to cover as much as possible of the female body. I buy myself a conservative but pretty, one-piece suit, black with colorful flowers, and a simple cover-up. As a last-minute thought, I also buy a pail and shovel for Reza. I change in the Ladies' Room after making the purchases. Reza changes in the car.

I take Olympic Boulevard all the way down to the beach and park in the lot. We carry our sheet, towels, food, and Reza's bag of toys to the sand where we set ourselves up close to the shoreline.

Reza immediately runs for the water, and I run with him. He has not learned how to swim, so I am very careful, making sure I see his excited face after every wave. We play, splashing one another and laughing. We eventually return to our sheet and dry ourselves off.

The water has awakened our appetites. While we're eating our sandwiches, Reza notices the ferris wheel about a mile away from us and points, excitedly. Of course, he wants to ride on it. I am hesitant. I'd have to put all this back in the car and get some cash because we'd likely need to pay for entry to the pier as well as for the rides, then we'd walk the distance to the pier. The thought of all that is off putting, the logistics too much to deal with today. I make us both a promise to ride that Ferris wheel before long. Reza nods his acceptance and pulls my arm. He wants us to go back to the water.

"Reza *jon*, we've just eaten. Our food needs to first digest. I'm going to lie down in the sun for a few minutes. You can rest, too, or play with your pail and shovel." He goes for the pail and shovel.

"Maybe you want to make something in the wet sand, like a

palace? Or, you can dig with your shovel and see what you find. Stay nearby. Don't stray. And don't go in the water."

He nods and goes a few feet closer to the water. Other children of varying ages are lined up along the shoreline, digging and he joins them.

I stretch out on the sheet. The hot sun feels good, and lying on the thin sheet, feeling the heat of the sand coming through the thin sheet, feels wonderful. I realize how tense my body is as the muscles of my back, shoulders and legs begin to relax. Coming to the beach was a good idea for us both.

My mind drifts to memories I have of time spent on this same beach decades ago. Adam first brought me here after I dared to get into the car with him. Then, almost every weekend he'd drive us to various beaches up and down the coast. He showed me Hollywood, Beverly Hills and downtown Los Angeles. He took me to movies, the finest restaurants and we even took the ferry to Santa Catalina Island.

It had been a perfect day. We'd biked around the island and visited the bird sanctuary. As the time to board the ferry neared, we walked along the narrow beach. It was wonderful to be there with Adam. I trusted him completely by that point. I felt so close to him, He was like the brother I'd always wanted.

We boarded the return ride on the ferry. I was feeling relaxed after that wonderful day. The scene was beautiful — the ocean, the blue sky ... the breeze against my face ... Adam's hand finding mine. Then suddenly, he turned me around and kissed me. For that momentary second, with his lips on mine, I was in heaven. Then I pulled apart and began to beat him up.

It was the end of our relationship.

I believed that the kiss had marked me as unmarriagable — I was certain any man could see I'd been kissed. I was damaged goods. I felt betrayed by Adam, the boy I'd trusted, and I was disgusted with myself for having spent time alone with him.

Maman had so often warned me, *they will do anything to win your trust and then have their way with you.*

Then Jila's 'wakeup call' so long overdue, destroyed all the old myths I'd been brainwashed to believe about sex and men.

Meanwhile, Adam's kiss had sparked my sexuality.So, being the scientist that I was, I conducted an experiment to test the truth of Cousin Jila's radical theory – that a man can't tell if you've been kissed. I'd come to this beach with Brad, a boy in my lab class. We kissed. I told him that had been my first and he believed me. When he couldn't tell I'd been kissed by Adam, my experiment proved Jila correct.

I was so sorry for what I'd done to Adam. I had beaten him up and ended our friendship because he'd kissed me! So stupid! So ignorant! So naive! I'd thought I'd lost my virginity with that kiss! The thought is so ridiculous that even now, I cringe.

I missed my friend terribly and ached to contact him. I would have put my pride aside, apologized and continued as we were. But I knew it would never be the same, never as wonderfully spontaneous, and I doubted he would ever feel the same towards me.

With my new outlook on men and sex, based on my newly acquired knowledge, I went searching for a kiss equal to Adam's. I yearned to experience the delicious sensations it had evoked.

I'd quickly learned that all kisses are not equal. Brad's kiss hadn't compared to Adam's. My dating life began in earnest and I enjoyed discovering my sensuality. And then that night with Anthony deCordova made me realize how vulnerable I was, how easily I could be assaulted and raped and I put an end to it all — no more dating.

Until David.

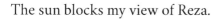

The sun blocks my view of Reza.

I sit up and find him digging furiously and depositing sand crabs into his red plastic pail. It's good to see him play. I think how wonderful it would be to find him a way of passing these summer days with children his age.

Now that I'm sitting up in parental mode, the list of things I must do immediately fills my mind and I again think of Babajon and how much I miss him. I know that I must attend to our financial situation and our immigration problem before continuing my pursuit of Jasmine. I will have to figure out a way to contact Linda and Adam. But I push all my thoughts away. That's all for tomorrow. This is time for Reza to enjoy our day at the beach.

He runs over to me. "Maman *jon*, look! Look what I have!" He puts his pail down on the sheet in front of me. There must be at least fifteen sand crabs in there.

"Bravo! Good work, Reza."

"Maman jon, let's go in the water, please?"

Together we run back into the water, edging in until we can feel the crash of the waves. I can see he is enjoying himself tremendously. That makes me feel good and again I confirm how much we both needed this time to frolic.

After we dry off, I spend a few minutes writing the letters of the alphabet in the sand. Reza needs to learn how to read and write English as well as speaking the language. I don't go from A to Z, but rather, simply make the point that there are letters that stand up, like I, P, R, D, and K and letters that lay back, like C, G, O, and Q. That's enough for his first lesson.

Eventually, we pack up and return home. Fortunately, neither of us are sunburned, but we are nicely tanned. Today made it clear that Reza spends far too little time being carefree and no time at all with children his age.

That must change.

I shower and begin searching for a camp.

There is one that opens in Mid-May. The hours are from nine a.m. to four p.m. and it meets at Rancho Park on Pico Boulevard, close to the apartment. It is perfect and it is affordable. Unfortunately, like the other camps, it begins when school is out for summer vacation, a couple of months away. I enroll him in it.

I decide to pay a visit to the school I will likely register him in for the fall. I meet with the principle, Mrs. Berg, a well-groomed woman who looks like she's in her fifties and shops at Saks. I give her a brief sketch of our history and our present situation, Reza's need for both a stable routine and to be with other children. She responds with the appropriate compassion.

I tell her that Reza is an excellent student and I would like to register him for the fall. Because of his lack of proficiency in reading, writing and speaking English, he will start the year off in third grade and either stay there or be moved, either back or forward.

I ask if he could possibly join in classes immediately, not as a full student, but as an onlooker. I'd like him to begin to socialize with American children his age and to acclimate to the school, the schedule and an environment where only English is spoken. To my delight, she agrees and informs me that there are also after-school activities that he might also like to join in. I know his social interaction with other children will be good for him and bolster both his confidence and his fluency in English.

Monday will be his first day at school. Reza is excited.

4 4

CALLING BAHMAN

*T*aking a walk down Westwood Boulevard this morning, I pass an antique store with an ivory statue of two camels.

I immediately think of Ferri and Hamid riding their camels to Afghanistan.

She was to leave a message with Bahman when she found safety, but I realize that Bahman can't call us because he doesn't have our new telephone number. What's more, none of the family members have been told of Babajon's death. It is strange that Maman has not shared the news of her husband's death with her sister Khaleh Bahia or with her brother, Dayee Mansoor and his family.

They have to know. As soon as I arrive home, I call Bahman. Aware of the eight-hour time difference between Los Angeles and London, I hope I'm not interrupting his dinner. He sounds relieved to hear from me. "Thank God you're in safe."

"Yes. We're here in Los Angeles. In fact, we're in the same neighborhood I used to live in as a student."

Bahman isn't in the mood for light conversation. "There was no way of letting you know. Layla, you don't know, you don't know. On Allah's soul, the man is crazy!"

The son of a bitch must have contacted him again! "What's happened, Bahman? Has Rostam called again? Did he threaten you?"

"No, no. He didn't call, Layla. It wasn't him. A man came to the house! A Revolutionary Guard, walking around London dressed in his khaki uniform!"

"Oh, my God! What did he do? What did he say?"

"He came looking for you. Well, no, he asked for your father, Hadi Khan. I only thank Allah that I was home when he came. To think Mahnaz could have been alone with the baby! And thank Allah you had all left. Anything could have happened."

I understand his fear. The Guards hold a lot of power and that power is intimidating. A flush of guilt sweeps over me, covering me mercilessly. Rostam's evil has extended to Bahman, bullying and hurting us all. I am to blame. I speak softly, trying to calm my fear.

Bahman continues. "He said he knew you were all here and that if you were found here, I would be arrested along with you, for harboring an enemy of the Islamic Republic."

Oh, my God! With an even voice, I ask my cousin what he looked like.

"I'll never forget," Bahman says. "He was short and muscular ... his face looked like his features had somehow been squeezed together .... and he had an ugly scar running down his face."

May Rostam die a terrible death and may The Rat's dead body fall on top of him! He has just described The Rat!

So, Hassan was definitely involved in piecing together Rostam's devious plot. I'm not surprised. I'd figured it was his idea to blackmail Babajon with that pack of lies. Rostam couldn't have come up with a scheme like that by himself. His brain is too muddled by all the drugs. He can't think clearly enough.

"Did he try to come in?" I ask.

"No. I said you weren't here. That you'd all left. He asked where you went and I said I didn't know. That I woke up and you were all gone."

"And he believed you?"

"Well, no, he wanted to come in then, but I asked to see a warrant of some kind. That shut him up. I wouldn't have let him in, even with one. I'd have fought him. I would have protected my family. He just got angrier and said that if I was lying, I would be sorry."

"Bahman," I say, "that's Rostam's friend. He used to be his valet, now he's a Revolutionary Guard. But I'm one hundred percent sure he was acting purely on his own when he came to your place. He has no power to disturb you." I took a deep breath. "Besides, Bahman, his threats against Babajon are worthless. He's gone. He passed away."

"What? What are you saying, Layla?"

"My father. Babajon, your uncle. He had another heart attack. He died in his sleep."

"Oh, Layla! Oh, my God! Oh, my Uncle Hadi!"

"You have to forgive me for not calling sooner to tell you. He died last week. Things have been crazy here. There's been a lot to take care of."

"Of course. Oh, Layla, I'm so terribly sorry for your loss. How sad. Your father was a great man. He was different from other Persians of his generation. He was so progressive. He was – he was a wonderful man." And then, "How is your sweet mother doing?"

"As you can imagine. And she's in a strange country that she doesn't like. We three were the only people at his funeral. Babajon didn't deserve that. He deserved so much more."

I ask him to relieve me of the burden of giving the sad news to his parents and his sister and we speak a bit longer. "Again, Bahman, I'm really so sorry you had to go through that."

Just as I am about to hang up, I remember to ask about Ferri and the package, but before I can ask if he's heard, Bahman says, "Oh, Layla! Don't hang up. I need your phone number. And you have a message." My heart rate speeds up. "It was a woman. I don't know what she was talking about, but she said some package had arrived in America?"

"America? Are you sure she said, 'in America'?"

"I'm sure, Layla. That's what she said."

But there's no way that Ferri would know I'm in America. She must have meant that *she's* in America. *Ferri's in America?*

"Did she leave a phone number?" I ask.

"Yes. I have it here. Let me get it. She said you might want it."

I grab a pen. Bahman is back before I find paper so I write the number he gives me on my palm. "Thanks so much, Bahman. Give my love to Mahnaz. Kiss Jeremy. I love you!"

"And you please send my condolences to Ammeh Zahra. It is a great, great loss."

With that, we say goodbye.

45

THE PACKAGE ARRIVES

Ferri is safe in America!

The thought gives me a warm feeling. I have lost my father, and have found back my best friend. She's actually *here*! Could she possibly be in California, too? Oh, I so badly need good news.

Before dialing her number, I call the operator. "Can you please tell me where area code 413 is?"

She answers, "Massachusetts. The Springfield area."

I know Massachusetts is northwest of California, much closer to New York than to the west coast. *Why Massachusetts?*

It is time for me to pick Reza up from school. On the way home, I make a quick stop at the library adjacent to the graveyard Babajon lies is. I drop my son off at the children's section. He's thumbing through a book he's taken off the shelf. As I walk away, I see a girl around his age approach him. I have seen her outside the school building when I dropped Reza off and remembered her because of her long, red, curly hair and her red Wonder Woman backpack.

I tell him I'll be right back and go to the section marked

"Research." I pull out a book about Massachusetts and flip through the pages. The small state is marked on a map of the U.S. I scan the first paragraphs, reading some random sentences and fragments of others. It's an old state, a very cold state, and the home of the Kennedys. Nothing I read sheds light on why Ferri is there.

When we arrive home, Maman is again lying down in her bedroom. I enter her room and she mumbles something about a headache. I close her bedroom door and return with hot *chai* and a headache pill I leave on her nightstand. Then I prepare a snack for Reza and when he's done, I ask him to play in our bedroom while I make a long-distance phone call.

Alone, I dial Ferri's number. She picks up. Before I've had the chance to tell her who I am, she recognizes my voice.

Her excitement is obvious.

~~~

"Layla? It's you. Layla *jon!*"

I'm equally excited. "Yes. It's me, Ferri. Thank God you're safe."

"Well, I'm here."

Her answer strikes me as odd, and I wonder if she is implying that perhaps, she's *not* safe. "What happened? What are you doing in Massachusetts? How did you get here? And don't tell me you rode there on a camel."

Ferri doesn't appreciate the humor. She takes a deep breath in before she begins, surprising me with a warning. "I'm telling you, Layla, it's a terrible story."

I find a chair close to the phone and sit down. I'm alarmed. This is Ferri. Calm, strong, daring Ferri. *What could be so terrible if she is safe in Massachusetts?*

"Did you get to Afghanistan?"

"Yeah, we got to Afghanistan. It took forever and I wish we never had. I wish the camels had collapsed before we got there, but we did. It was a hard trip, but we got there. We were tired and hungry. We had to pay off guards along the way and by the time we got there we were completely broke."

She stops. I sense that it's difficult for her to go on. I am a mix of curiosity and mounting fear. The silence is broken by her deep sigh. And then she says, "It was late. We were both exhausted. The camels were tired and we needed shelter.

"Eventually, we saw a small inn-type place and smelled food. We hadn't eaten for over a day. We were starving! So, we knocked on the first door we saw to ask for any kind of food and permission to sleep under their roof. A man opened the door holding a large knife — you know, the kind with that big square blade, a cleaver. We'd walked into a large kitchen, and I figured he was the owner. We asked for some food.

"Layla, it turns out that we'd ended up in some God forsaken area where the Afghans didn't understand Farsi. Whoever this man was, may he be buried under the earth and rot in Hell forever and may they spit on his grave, I sensed he was dangerous. He was big and filthy and smelled so terrible. He was oily looking, you know? With hard cold black eyes. He'd been cutting up some kind of animal with a cleaver. But we had to eat."

"Uhuh."

"So ...." she drifts off, then starts again. "I'll just make a long story short. He went for me. Tried to rape me. The last thing we'd expected. We were exhausted, filthy and starving. Parched. He knocked me down and I was suddenly on the floor. From out of nowhere! Hamid grabbed a big pan and hit him over the head with it but the horrid man never even felt it. I wish he'd picked up the cleaver and killed the bastard with that."

She stops. My ears feel tight, like the ears of a dog that's intent on not missing a sound, Ferri has my total attention. She goes on. "Instead, the bastard grabbed the cleaver and attacked Hamid, slashing his face, his arm, his stomach – he wouldn't stop!"

As I gasp, Ferri begins to sob. I'm speechless, picturing this unbelievably horrible scene.

She calms down enough to continue. "Hamid was screaming and bleeding, and – oh! He was so bloody! I yelled and yelled, but the man … he wouldn't stop. I tried to pull him away from Hamid, but … he was too big. He just kept slashing at him. My poor Hamid. He was on the floor, blood pouring out … it was terrible, Layla! I ran to him where he lay and put his head on my lap. In seconds, I was covered with his blood. He was bleeding every-where, his neck, chest, face … blood was pouring out everywhere!"

"Oh, my God, Ferri!" I take a breath in momentary silence, afraid I might gag. "How's is he now?"

"He died." It is barely a whisper.

"What?"

"Yeah. He died. I can't forget the way the blood was every-where, Layla."

"My God, Ferri! That's horrible! I- I- I can't believe it. I'm so so sorry!"

"Yeah. Me too. My poor Hamid." I hear her start to cry again.

"Then the man came after me again. He didn't care that my Hamid lay dead alongside us. While he was tearing my riding pants off, I got hold of the cleaver, lunged at his face and hit his eyes with it. Oh, did he scream. Blood gush out. And then, I guess I lost control. I didn't know what I was doing. It just felt so good to slash at him while he was busy screaming and holding his eyes. I just kept cutting, holding the cleaver in both hands. He was so big, I couldn't miss. He tripped over Hamid's body and collapsed by his side, screaming out in pain. I stood above him until he got quiet. I was pretty sure I'd killed him. I pushed him off of Hamid.

"I could still see my lover's lifeless body and his eyes staring up at nothing. My empty stomach wretched. I was so weak. I didn't know what to do. I sat on the floor and just held Hamid and sobbed, not wanting to believe he was dead, not wanting to leave him there, not knowing if there was anyone else in the house. My Hamid … He can't be dead. He can't be dead. He-" she drops off and I can hear her sobs.

My poor Ferri. She has cried so hard for so long. She's had a most terrible, highly traumatic experience, worse than any I had ever feared for her.

"I couldn't leave him there. But then I though I heard a noise from the rooms above. That's when I realized I had to get out of there. I hastily looked for something — anything to eat. I found some bread on the counter. I took it ran out the door and kept running, not knowing where I was or where I was going." She takes another deep inhale, probably trying to calm herself.

This vengefulness is a side of Ferri that is new to me. But how can I blame her? I'm crying with her. "Ferri *jon*, I can't believe what you've gone through! And to lose Hamid! Poor Hamid! I'm so sorry."

Ferri speaks haltingly through her tears, stopping every now and then to blow her nose or catch her breath. "There was no way I could let him touch me, Layla. Hamid was the only man that had ever done that." Hearing her quiet sobs breaks my heart.

"I ran out of there and just kept running, turning in those back alleys whenever I could … I was petrified that someone would see what I'd done to him and come looking for me. I left Hamid lying on that filthy floor. God knows what they did with his body. God knows what they would have done to me if I'd been caught. They could even have thought I killed them both. I just kept running, just kept going, turning left and right. It was pitch black. It wasn't even a village. There were just these small houses built in the dirt. I was running, praying no one would catch me."

I listen to my best friend's story of fear and sudden loss with a pounding heart. I simply cannot imagine what she's gone through. This is my angel. Hamid was her one true love. Their love had lasted years despite all its challenges and they had finally married and escaped Iran less then a month after being actively pursued by the Ayatollah. After all that, after their arduous trek and all they'd been through, Hamid had been killed almost immediately after they'd arrived in Afghanistan and murdered so horribly, just when they thought they'd finally reached safety.

I wipe my tears and ask, "There was no one who could have helped you?" I know the answer. There was no one.

"No one. I couldn't let any of them see me. And I couldn't speak the language so I couldn't explain what had happened. Like I said, they could have said I'd killed both men with the blood on my clothes and the state I was in and running away from the scene. I'd have been arrested for sure, and worse. I thought about it later. I don't know what the hell their laws are. How could I have defended myself? Maybe rape isn't a crime according to their laws.

"Anyway, leaving Hamid there was almost impossible. At some point, I pictured his lifeless body and fell down on the dirt sobbing. I flipped out. I had no idea where I was or where I was trying to get to." Her voice starts to fade away as she continues. "No idea. I couldn't run anymore. I had no food in me and my mouth was completely dry. But a voice in my head told me I had to keep running for my life. I don't know how I did it. I wanted to lay down next to Hamid, and hold him, bring him back to life or die right there with him. He didn't deserve that. He died protecting me and I left him."

"No! You did what Hamid would have wanted you to do. You know that. He'd want you to save yourself."

How did she get from Afghanistan and that horror to Massachusettes?
"What happened?" I ask.

Ferri takes another deep breath and sniffles. Her tears may have finally subsided. "Suddenly, I was on a road. Just like that, out of nowhere. I saw a few cars drive by, but they didn't stop, and it was just as well. I was afraid that if they did, they'd rape me, or kill me.

"But I just couldn't go on. I couldn't take another step. I had no more energy, and it was all too much. I dropped where I was by the side of the road and passed out until the sound of a passing truck brought me to. After some time, a car finally stopped and the driver, a young man, got out to see what was wrong with me. And, Layla, by a miracle, he spoke English! Not even Farsi! But English. Imagine! In the middle of that God forsaken place – in the middle of nowhere! In between dirt hovels, the man that picked me up spoke English!

"Absolutely. I get it. Thank God. What happened?"

"He saw how weak and tired I was and saw the blood on me. He just about carried me to his car. First thing he asked was if I was alone or if I was with anyone and I started sobbing. He asked me what had happened, but I had zero energy and couldn't tell him."

I am on the edge of my chair. "And?"

"He was an angel. I truly believe my Hamid sent him to me. An absolute angel. He stopped at a roadside café and insisted that I eat and drink some hot *chai*. I hadn't eaten for days and not much before that, so I was in no condition to *tarroff*, politely decline. And I ate." She pauses, and her tone becomes desolate. "I felt so guilty that I had eaten and my poor Hamid had died hungry."

The sobbing resumes. "Layla, it's my fault he died. He was trying to save my honor!"

I can't stand to hear Ferri cry. She's the strongest person I know. To hear her say she feels guilty for what happened is intolerable. "Ferri, It's a horrible story and Hamid died a tragic death. But don't you dare feel guilty. Hamid saved your honor because he wanted to. He was your husband. He loved you. And he was a good man.

"He may have saved your life. You don't know what that man would have done to you after he'd raped you." I hear her sniffles. "You have nothing to feel guilty about. It was that bastard's fault.

All of it. May he rot in Hell for evermore and his soul never know peace." In the momentary silence, I assume she's digesting what I've said. Hopefully, it's helped soothe her.

After another breath, she says, "Maybe," then goes on. "Anyway, it was a long drive and I eventually, told him everything. I broke down hearing myself. I couldn't believe what I was saying. It was like I was talking about a movie I'd seen or a story someone else told me."

I say all there is to say. "I'm so sorry, Ferri." It's not enough,

"Yeah. I know," she says. "I told him our story. When he heard we had escaped Iran because of our politics and that we could have been killed by Khomeini, he said I should go straight to the U.S. embassy and apply for refugee status so I could enter the United States. He even gave me some money. I took his information so I could pay him back. Anyway, to make a long story short, I did. And now I'm here."

"That's a terrible story. I'm so, so, sorry for what you've gone through. It was a nightmare." My curiosity eggs me on. "But Ferri *jon*, why Massachusetts?"

"I hate it," she says. "It's always freezing here. Like ice. I haven't been warm since I got here."

"Why did you go there?"

"Because I didn't know that. Hamid's cousin lives here. They were close friends when he was in Iran and when he left, they stayed in touch. He was easy to find, so I'm here."

I haven't recovered from her story. "I just can't believe what you've been through."

"Yeah. I called his family and told them he'd died. It was really hard." We are both quiet for a moment. I sit, gazing at my hand with her number written there in blue ink.

"So, Layla, how are you? Where are you? And how come you're able to call me?"

"Me?" I'm jolted back to the realization that Ferri knows

nothing of the events that have taken place in my life. "I'm not with Rostam. I'm in California with Reza and my mother."

"Are you telling me that you actually, finally, escaped the ass?"

"Yes. He threatened Babajon, so we had to escape. We went to Bahman's house in London – the cousin that you gave that message to – but Rostam found us, so we came to California. Babajon had a heart attack soon after we got here and passed away."

"My God, Layla. I'm so sorry! I know how close the two of you were. You loved your father so much and he adored you. He was a special man."

"Yes, I miss him terribly. Right now, we're under his six-month visa. I'll be asking for asylum, too, so we can stay here. I need to find an attorney. It's a long story. We haven't been here long."

I recall the last meeting I had with my angel, standing in the bookstore. I told her I'd never again try to escape Rostam and she told me she was going to Afghanistan and I shouldn't worry about her safety. Our stories played out differently.

"That son of a bitch Rostam," she says. Then, "You'll look for Jasmine?"

"Of course." I say. I just haven't yet figured out how. "Ferri jon, why don't you think about coming to California? You can stay in our apartment.

"No, no. No. Thanks but I'm going to stay here for now. I've been given permission to work and Moez — that's Hamid's cousin I'm staying with — has found a job for me translating for the courts and I like it. No more politics for me. It's interesting work and easy."

"But it's so cold there. And you don't know anyone other than him."

"It's cold but it will warm up. And I'm meeting his friends. He lives alone in this big house, so I'm okay here. I'll come visit you when I can. And I know you'll find an attorney."

Then before I can insist, she says, "Listen, it's wonderful to hear your voice and talk to you. I could talk forever, but I have to go." I want to tell her about Ehsan, share Maman's constant complaints, and tell her about Reza, but she adds, "By the way, I'm pregnant!"

"Oh, my goodness! Congratulations! How pregnant are you?"

"Almost eight months. So much for that 'haunting impulse.' This baby is Hamid's gift to me. Look, I really have to go. Let me take down your number. I have paper and pencil. Okay, what's your phone number?" I give her our number, savoring the freedom I have to speak with my angel from my own house whenever I want. A residual perk of deleting Rostam from my life.

"Okay. I really have to go. We'll talk. But Layla-"

"Yes. What?"

"You once told me you'd realized that you're Muslim and were in love with a Jewish man and I'm Jewish and loved a Muslim man. Do you realize that both of our two loves, died and we both carried their child? Okay, got to go. Bye, *Joonie.*"

I sit with the receiver in my hand, trying to picture myself going through what Ferri has endured. The long, hard trip over treacherous terrain on a camel for God knows how many days, constantly on the lookout for anyone who could hurt or arrest me and send me back to Iran and prison, only to see the only man I'd ever loved murdered in front of my eyes, then stabbing the man who killed him, then running, without a clue where I was or where I was going, hungry, exhausted and scared.

I've survived my challenges so far, yet I am not at all sure I could have survived what Ferri has gone through.

46

LOOKING FOR ANSWERS

*I*t has been twenty-four years since I last held my baby girl.

Anything can happen, a life can be gone in a heartbeat.

Speaking with Ferri has again brought me to the reality of life's unpredictability. That kicks my search for Jasmine back to the top of my priorities.

I've recited the prayer Setareh had given me at least once daily for twenty-four years. Yet, I am by no means certain that I will reunite with my daughter. Then I remind myself of life's many surprises.

I'd long ago given up any hope of returning to America, yet here I am back in Los Angeles, the city where I'd lost her.

My starting point is obvious.

I start up the Buick and as I wait to pull into traffic, I again note that traffic in the area has increased multi-fold. Parking meters are now everywhere.

I head for the Dunn house, the home of Margaret and Ralph Dunn, Linda and Adam's parents. I'm able to locate it with little difficulty.

Initially delighted that I've found the house, my mood deflates like a popped balloon when I see the "For Sale" sign on the property. I park, go to the front door and ring the doorbell. When the door opens my hopes rise up again. But it isn't the Dunns who greet me. It is a man in a trendy blue suit and tie, holding a leather folder with the clean measured look of a young man determined to walk the path of a successful salesman.

"Welcome," he says, with an open smile. "Please come in. You're looking at a home with four-bedroom plus a maid's quarters, with four-and-a-half renovated baths, a large family room, a living room, dining room, remodeled kitchen with an island, and a lovely pool and jacuzzi in, what you'll see, is a spacious backyard." He hands me a sheet of paper with a photo of the house and detailed information about it.

I'm stunned! The Dunns no longer live here!

I loved visiting them. There were two places I felt totally safe and comfortable in during my secret pregnancy. Once was Linda and Adam's apartment and the other was here — their parents' home. I had such warm affection for Ralph, such a kind man. He had gone out of his way to get a large, personalized, signed photograph of Elizabeth Taylor for his children's friend. And Margaret Dunn — "Maggie" to me — was more like one of us kids than a mother.

"Oh, no, thank you." I know I look preoccupied, still processing this unexpected turn of events. "I don't want to buy the house. Actually, I'm looking for Mr. or Mrs. Dunn."

I feel like I've slammed against a wall. Like I've hit a dead end. The Dunns are the only lead I can think of to their children, and only Linda and/or Adam can tell me where they took Jasmine.

Once I know the name of the adoption agency, I can find my daughter.

"Dunn?" he says.

"Yes. The sellers?" My fingers are crossed.

He hesitates. "Oh." he refers to a sheet of paper in his portfolio. "Yes, Ralph Dunn is the seller."

"Do you know why they're selling the house?" I ask.

"Yes. They've outgrown it," he says. He smirks. "You know, the adult children leave the nest … His wife's in a facility, so he doesn't need a big house. I sold him a little house in Palm Springs." This time, it's less of a smile and more of a self-satisfied smirk. Then he continues in his professional tone. "As I said, his wife is incapacitated, so he was the sole signatory on our papers."

What happened to Maggie?

"Do you have a contact number for him?"

The agent frowns, reminding me of the salesman's frown when he assured Babajon he couldn't lower the price on the Buick. "I'm sorry, I can't give out that personal information."

"Look, I understand but it's not about buying the house. I'm a very close family friend and I've just traveled miles to get here from Iran and I need to speak to him. I just want to ask him or Margaret – where their children are. It's really vital, a question of life and death. Please. Just give me any information you can so I can try to contact them."

The agent hems and haws but ends up cooperating. I whip out the small notepad I've begun carrying around with me and take down the information he shares. He gives me Ralph Dunn's number and has even found the phone number for Margaret Dunn among his papers. She is living at the Beverly Hills Garden Home.

Back in the car, I pray I will be able to contact Ralph or Maggie and find out how to contact their children.

Driving home, I remember that David's parents live — or lived — in this same area. I suppose it's possible that they, too, have sold their house. They, too, may have outgrown the large house with their only child buried and now in the sunset of their years. There is nothing either of David's parents can tell me that would be of any use to me now. They certainly have no knowledge of Adam or Linda.

They don't even know they have a granddaughter.

As much as David loved me, his Jewish mother hated me for being Muslim, and I was determined that she would never be in a positions to harm Jasmine or to make her feel unloved.

Now I wonder if I had made the biggest mistake of my life by keeping them away and denying my daughter her family.

I push away memories of time in that house with David. Right now, my priority is finding the Dunns.

Returning home, I go directly to the telephone, intending to call Ralph and then Maggie Dunn. I put the phone down. Maman is home and can't let her overhear my conversations. Though she doesn't understand English, she might still ask unwanted questions. I will wait until she leaves the apartment.

I sit down feeling edgy. I have several hours before picking Reza up from school. I need to calm down. I need to digest what's happened today.

The unexpectedness of finding the Dunn house up for sale today makes me realize the reality that twenty-four years can bring a lot of changes. Life isn't static. The Dunns no longer live in the one house I'd seen them in. Suddenly, a chuckle escapes me as I realize all the things that have changed in my own life through these twenty-four years.

Hah! Amazing!

The ringing phone startles me. I reach for it.

Attorney Kroft is calling to tell me that things are moving slower than he'd hoped. Our Iranian attorney has told him that the Revolution has slowed down all bureaucratic processes requiring a sign-off from governmental agencies and banks to a crawl. It's impossible to say how long it will take, but Attorney Kroft assures me he is doing all he can to expedite matters and will call as soon as there's a change.

More unexpected bad news. I hang up feeling lost. I'm depressed. A gray cloud covers everything. I'd thought we'd be receiving an influx of cash soon that would end our troubles. Now, again, I must be patient.

The news triggers my impatience, which only add to my anxiety, impatience and frustration. After decades of waiting and praying, I'm finally, actually back in Los Angeles, and I'm still questioning whether my prayers will be answered.

I cannot stand the uncertainty around finding Jasmine. It wasn't as simple as a trip to the Dunn house.

I need a break.

47
THE DAM BREAKS

The unexpected news about the Dunns has put me in a foul mood, and Attorney Kroft's phone call has only added to my despair.

Everything has suddenly become a problem and the problems have piled up. I don't only *miss* Babajon, I *need* him to take care of us. The stress I'm under has accumulated. The list of things I need to do is constantly tumbling around in my mind and nothing seems to get done.

I'm angry at my fate. I'm angry that Babajon died and left me with Maman, his lesser half, without money, and with this huge feeling of responsibility that doesn't let me pursue my own agenda, namely only caring for Reza and looking for Jasmine.

My nerves are tender. Exceedingly tender.

Maman has left her room to make a cup of tea for herself.

She sees me sitting by the telephone, but says nothing. She does not ask if I want a cup.

"Hello, Maman," I say. She just nods.

I decide to ask her if she plans to go out this afternoon. If she does, I'll stay home and make those phone calls. If she's staying home, maybe I'll visit Maggie.

"Maman, will you be home this afternoon? I'll pick Reza up and bring him home, but after that, I'd like to go out for a couple of hours. Will you be here? Can I leave him with you?"

She's standing in the dining room, facing me, holding the cup of tea in one hand and the saucer in the other.

She looks at me as though I've asked her to cut off her arm and then she strikes out at me and it's one time too many.

"*Heh!* You leave me in this strange country and go out for a good time, while I'm stuck here babysitting for you. You're meeting your friends? Looking for *that boy?* Did you find *that boy* back yet? God only knows what disgusting things you're doing while you leave me here alone babysitting for you."

She accuses me?

It's too much.

Babysitting? For God's sake, she's his grandmother! And I don't even know when the last time was that she 'babysat.' And he's not a baby. She doesn't spend any time with him. I just want to know he won't be home alone. She complains incessantly and I am tired of it!

I cannot bear Maman's complaints and accusations in my state. I can barely tolerate her voice.

Babajon spent a lifetime listening to his wife's complaints and doting on her. But Babajon had made a lifetime commitment to her. I didn't and I don't have to tolerate her narcissistic complaints.

In minutes, decades of silence breaks, and every terrible thing she has done to me — the frustration, resentment, hostility, the lies and blame — it all comes rushing to the surface and pours out of my mouth.

I sit fuming and breathe, but I can't shut up. Not anymore. Her ignorance, her abuse and her narcissism are all too much. She has gone way too far with her comments about *that boy.*

How dare she?

I can't hold back any longer and don't even want to. I'm done. Totally and completely, done. She ruined my chances for happiness at every step. My long-seated resentment for what she's done to me is eating me alive. I have to vent it. Now.

I lost Jasmine because of her. I had a stupid hymenoplasty because of her. I married a horrible, evil, self indulgent and abusive man just to get away from her. If it had been up to her, I would never have gone to UCLA. My God! I didn't dare marry David because of *her! And she blames me!*

I'm simply done.

I turn to her.

"The boy, Maman? *The boy?* Did I find *the boy* back? No, Maman. No. I didn't find *the boy* back. I didn't go looking for *the boy,* Maman. There *is* no boy. *The boy* is dead. *The boy's* name was David. David Kline. And for your information, I loved that boy. Not that you care."

She will not tower over me. I stand and face her with folded arms.

"I'm sick and tired of your ignorant ranting and your constant complaints. I'm sick and tired of *you.* Yes, Maman, I'm sick of you! From the second we we'd decided we had to leave Iran you have done nothing but complain and whine. You hen-pecked Babajon non-stop about America. As if you didn't care that coming to America was the only way to save him from prison, torture … death! America is saving us! But you, you don't care about anything but yourself and your complaints."

She stands frozen with the cup and saucer still in her hands.

"Because of you, you spoiled girl," she screams. "Your father spoiled you all your life and you thought your husband owed that to you too, to spoil you. And when instead, he expected you to be a wife and a mother, you did something so bad, that hurt and angered him so much, that he had no choice but to strike back! Only Allah knows what you did that made him so angry that he struck out at all of us and the person he knew you love most, your Babajon."

She's apparently ready to let out some of the animosity and resentment she's been feeling about me, and she goes on, her face fierce, her look, piercing.

"Hadi wouldn't believe anything was your fault. Of course he didn't. Nothing was ever your fault. He never really knew the truth about you or what you were capable of. He never knew what you did and how you carried on in your beloved Los Angeles. I shielded you from that. But now I see I it was my mistake. You couldn't keep your husband happy."

"*Hah!* My *husband*? Do you know why I married Rostam?"

"You wanted to."

I laugh at the thought. "No, apparently, you don't. Let me enlighten you. You think I didn't know he was an arrogant fool, talking about 'Rostam this' and 'Rostam that'? I knew. I just didn't care. I married him for one reason and one reason only: to get me away from you, give me back the travel documents you hid from me and take me back to Los Angeles.

"That's right, we were supposed to come here on our honeymoon. I'd made him promise that we'd come here for our honeymoon before I said yes to him. And if he had brought me here, I would have lost him in a second and found my daughter!"

The look on her face has changed from anger at the fact that I dare to speak to her in this tone, to pure astonishment at the mention of a daughter.

She freezes.

312

I don't give a damn. I'm glad she finally knows. I care nothing about her. For once, I don't give a damn about her feelings and don't pretend to. She never bothered with mine. I give her the same lack of respect she's always shown me.

If I were more in control, perhaps I be kinder. But I am out of control, and Maman is my focus. I may be sorry for hurting her later, but right now I feel vindicated. I will finally let it all out and tell her everything I've kept silent about for all these years. I'm tired of shielding her from the truth of who I am, who I was, and the horrible effect she's had on my life.

"Yes! I said, *my daughter!*" I take a step closer to her, nodding vigorously.

"That's right, Maman. I give birth to a child here. Her name is Jasmine. Her father – *that boy* – is Doctor David Kline, and I was as completely and totally in love with him as he was with me. He was an amazing man and a fine doctor! He loved me, Maman. He wanted to marry me. But you wouldn't know about that. You never knew anything about him, just like you've never known anything about me, about who I am or what I've wanted in my life. You never did. You never wanted to. You've only wanted what *you* wanted for me.

"You have no idea how you've ruined my life! I lost my child because of your total conceit and your controlling manipulation. It was always all about you. I was supposed to return for her that summer, but you kidnapped me and hi-jacked my life! You jailed me! And when I didn't go back for her they gave my daughter away! They took her to an adoption agency and gave her to strangers. *Strangers! My child!*"

I don't even try to calm myself down. She stands, spellbound, the cup of tea rattling in her hands.

"That's right, Maman. When you took me to that backroom doctor who sewed me back up, he could tell I'd just given birth and didn't tell you. He must have known since it had barely been a

313

month since I'd delivered." I chortle. "The truth is, the wonderful Zahra Khanom's daughter lost her virginity and got pregnant all in the same night."

I take a step closer to her, my arms, folded. "And you know what? I seduced David. Yes! I seduced *that boy!* That's right! He would never have tried to seduced me. He knew all about keeping my virginity for my husband and agreed to respect that because he loved me that much. But I wanted him, Maman. I loved him and I wanted to give myself to him."

She barely sets the rattling cup and saucer down on the dining room table and falls onto a chair. She is as pale as fog. *Good!*

"*Hah!* You wouldn't know about love or sacrifice, would you, Maman? You've never had to sacrifice anything. I don't think you've ever really loved anyone. Not *really.* Even your love for Babajon was not real love, but some sort of dependence. You loved what he gave you, the beautiful house, the status of being married to a kind, powerful man who gave you everything you had ever wanted." I almost spit it out. "You're disgraceful."

A part of me is enjoying this. "So, yes, I married that monster. He was my ticket back to my daughter." I let out a laugh. "But you know what, Maman? The joke was on me. Rostam lied, too. He never intended to come to California. No, he had other plans, with tickets to Italy, but I was desperate to get back to my child."

I'm standing on the other side of the table and she is staring at the wall behind me. She hasn't moved a muscle.

"You want to know how desperate I was to get back to my child? First, I married the oaf, and when that didn't work, the morning after our wedding night – which proved your barbaric surgery a success – I tried to run away. That's right, Maman. I ran out of the house to the airport and was about to board the plane to Los Angeles. Alone."

Now her eyes travel to me and her eyes momentarily open wide before she looks away. The news has shaken her up.

"Yes, Maman. When I married him, I finally had possession of everything you'd hidden from me – my identity card, my passport and the consent to travel." I'm nodding vigorously. "That's right. I was ready to leave Rostam and was about to board the plane to come here when I was grabbed by airport police — Rostam was good friends with the Chief of Tehran's police." I take a breath recalling the sting I felt all those years ago, seeing Rostam enter the airport to take me home to my hell. "They sent me back to Rostam."

Maman is a statue, sitting still and mute. "After that day my life has been a nightmare, an absolute nightmare. I never told you. Not because I had any illusion that you would care, but because I knew Babajon would have been outraged at the things Rostam did to me and I didn't want to hurt him. He loved me. You never did. You don't know how to love anyone. I could never tell Babajon that his son-in-law was a mean, abusive bastard. But he found out, didn't he? You think I don't know that in the end, Rostam cost Babajon his life, anyway? Now that he's gone, I truly don't give a damn. I have nothing to hide."

My anger is coming out unfiltered and I am not about to stop. Not yet. I welcome getting all this out, to face her and unburden all the hatred and anger I've held inside me for so very, very long. It feels good. Cleansing.

"You want to know where I was today? I didn't go looking for *that boy!* I went looking for my *child,* for your *granddaughter,* Maman. For Jasmine, your granddaughter. I slept with David, and I bore his child. And believe me, Maman, I loved that child more than you could know. Certainly, more than you ever loved me.

"And, *that boy?* He died in Israel. My David died trying to save the lives of others.Not that you care. He wanted to marry me, and take me to Israel with him but I refused. You know why?"

Of course she doesn't answer. She's mute. She just stares at me. I couldn't stop now if I'd wanted to.

315

I stand over her and lean down. I want to look into her face as I speak. "I asked you if you know why! Not because I didn't want to marry him. Not because I didn't love him. David was the love of my life. No. I didn't marry him because I could tell *you*, The Great Zahra Khanom, that I was marrying a Jewish doctor. I lost him because of you! I lost the man I loved because of you and your ridiculous ideas of what I should and shouldn't do with my life, Maman. And I lost my child because of you, too, my beautiful, innocent baby."

I take a breath. The worst has been said. I take a moment to wipe some tears from my face and run my hands down my dress. I sniffle and feel a tinge calmer. But my chest is still tight with anger. I'm not done. I take another deep breath. Years of being mistreated by her won't dissolve with a few harsh words. Now that I'd begun, I am vomiting up years of hurt and resentment.

Of course she is completely shocked beyond comprehension and sits, staring at me. She would never have dreamed in a million years that I would dare confront her, and she certainly could never have guessed the truth. But I don't care. I've had more than enough of her manipulation, her complaints, her complete lack of care for me or anyone else. The hatred for what she's done to me is coming out, oozing out like pus from a wound.

She has said nothing since I've begun my tirade. Not a word.She's looking at me questioningly, as if she's never seen me before. In truth, she hasn't.

I go on. "And you can forget about going back to your beloved Iran. *That's* the Hellhole, not America. Going back means Rostam could still throw me – and you – to the Guards. Even with Babajon gone, they could still hold us as his accomplices. And under no circumstance will I allow Reza to live with that man."

My arms are still folded. I walk around the table and stop when

I'm directly across from her. "I'm staying right here with my son. After twenty-four years of torture, I'm not going back. I'm going to stay right here and look for Jasmine. If I'm lucky, I'll find her. And when I do, I'll never lose her again.

"I'll never again give up anything for you and for your warped ideas of what love is — of how to live."

There is nothing more to say.

I take myself into the living room and sit in the club chair, worn and soft. I take deep breaths. I need to leave in the next few minutes to pick Reza up from school. I sigh, grateful that he wasn't there to hear me.

I am not sorry for a word I've said to Maman. It's all been true.

It felt good and it's been a long time coming.

Maman gets up, goes to her bedroom and slams the door.

48

THE BEVERLY HILLS
GARDEN HOME

*J*ust before I leave to pick up my son I call Ralph Dunn, uncaring that Maman is in the apartment.

His phone rings several times before the answering machine picks up. His recorded message says he will be out of town for ten days. I'm disappointed and hang up without leaving a message. I will try calling him again if I can't get a hold of Maggie.

Next I call the number I've been given for his wife.

"Good afternoon. Beverly Hills Garden Home, this is Ariel. How may I assist you?"

"Hello. I'm looking for Margaret Dunn."

"One moment please." A pause. "Are you a relative?"

"No, a friend." There's a pause and I assume she's checking the list of residents for the name.

"Yes, Mrs. Dunn is a resident here in our assisted living quarters."

I am thrilled to hear that she's, in fact, there. "Great. Um … can you please connect me to her room?"

"I'm sorry, but Mrs. Dunn does not talk on the phone."

That's strange!

"Can I visit her?"

"Yes. Visiting hours are Monday through Friday from nine to five, before dinner is served. Saturday and Sundays from noon to six."

"Okay, that's great. Thank you."

I hand up and realize I wouldn't have much time with her if I go there today after I pick Reza up. I decide to visit her tomorrow, a Saturday, a day there's no school. I will take Reza with me so Maman doesn't have to 'babysit' her grandson. I will introduce Maggie to my son.

Surely, she can either tell me where Linda sent my baby; or if not, then she can tell me where to find her children.

I find my handbag and leave to get my son.

It's Saturday.

Reza is home and has noticed the chill between me and Maman this morning.

His eyes keep darting between us as he has breakfast, but he says nothing until I'm in the kitchen washing the dishes and Maman has retired to her bedroom once again. She has been in her room almost exclusively since yesterday. She's probably reading one of the books she's bought from the Persian bookstore, either the biography of the late Shah Pahlavi, or a series of short stories by famous Iranian writers. Or perhaps, she's just feeling sorry for herself.

He finally asks. "Maman *jon*, are you all right?"

"Yes, Reza. I'm fine. Why do you ask?" He shrugs.

"Are you worried about your grandmother?" I ask.

He hesitates, then nods.

"She's okay," I say. I'm not at all sure that she is, but I can't have

Reza worry about her. "We had an argument. Nothing important. She'll be fine. There's nothing for you to worry about. She'll get over it." He trusts me and nods, and I'm certain she will soon come out of her room to whine.

"I'd like to take you to meet an old friend today," I say. "She lives in a place like a hotel. I don't know their policy about having children visit, so bring a book and something to keep you busy just in case. We'll leave soon. "

I'm in the living room waiting for Reza to gather what he wants to take with him when Maman appears. I stifle a chuckle. Just as I thought, she's back to herself. She's reappeared to complain about something.

But no, she's silent. And then I notice that she's wearing lipstick and her green dress with walking heels. And she's carrying her handbag.

She heads for the front door and wordlessly leaves the apartment, slamming the door behind her.

It is just past eleven o'clock in the morning as I start the car and head to the Beverly Hills Garden Home.

We arrive less than ten minutes later. It's on Wilshire Boulevard on the other side of the San Diego Freeway in a picturesque setting, set back behind expansive grounds. Even I know this area isn't Beverly Hills. I assume the name gives it the panache it needs to charge residents high rates.

The valet takes my car, and we enter a lobby that's comparable to that of any stylish hotel with a doorman, a concierge, and elegant décor, including crystal chandeliers.

A neatly dressed woman in black approaches. "May I help you find someone?"

"Yes. I'm looking for Margaret Dunn."

"All right. Let's see if I can help you. Please step this way and sign in."

Reza and I follow. There is a sign-in sheet atop a long desk. It asks for our names, the name of the resident we will be seeing, our relationship to her and the current time. I note it also requires a sign-out time. I stealthily turn to the prior page to see if Adam or Linda have recently been here to see their mother. Neither name appears.

I complete the form for Reza and myself, using the last name Saleh. Under the column asking for our relationship to the resident, I write "friends."

The woman scans what I'd written and smiles. "Very good. Let me see," She leafs through her book and looks back up at me. "Mrs. Dunn is in Room 317." I thank her and take Reza's hand.

Apparently, young visitors are not excluded. I will take Reza to her room with me. As we are walking away, making our way toward the elevators, the woman calls out. "Excuse me, Miss Saleh?"

"Yes?"

"Have you visited us before? I mean, Mrs. Dunn."

"No."

"Well," she smiles. Her eyes never leave mine. "I'm sorry. I don't mean to intrude on your privacy, but, well, Mrs. Dunn in on the Assisted Living floor."

"Thank you."

"Yes, of course. I only mention that because it's your first time here."

"Thank you."

"You're welcome. I might add that the residents on that floor are incapacitated to a great extent."

"Oh!" I say. I'm shocked.

My memories of Maggie Dunn are those of a young woman who was even younger at heart. An avid tennis player who usually wore tennis outfits or shorts, tied her hair in a ponytail and danced with Linda, Adam and me to the hottest hits of the day. A woman with a big heart who was extremely kind to me. Her home had been the only place – outside of her children's apartment where I lived – where I'd always felt comfortable and accepted, despite my pregnant belly. I always felt welcomed at her home and at her family's table.

"I see," I instinctively hold Reza's hand tighter. It's hard to believe she has changed.

"Residents usually meet their guests in the lounge if they like, but residents on that floor spend most of their time in their room. Unless they're taken out for fresh air." She smiles again. "Enjoy your visit. I hope she's having a good day."

"Yes. Thank you."

The gilded mirrored elevator takes us to the third floor. Having heard the news about Maggie, I'm experiencing anxiety, not knowing what I'll find. We find Room 317 and knock. A young woman wearing a white uniform opens the door.

"Hello," I say. I'm holding Reza's hand and smiling. "I was told this is Margaret Dunn's room?"

"Yes, that's right. Please come in. Is she expecting you?"

"No. My name is Layla, and this is my son, Reza. I'm an old friend of the Dunns and just returned to Los Angeles. I'm eager to see her."

She nods. "My name is Lucia. I'm her afternoon nurse."

"Hello, Lucia."

"Don't be surprised if she doesn't remember you," she says as we pass through the small entry area.

Gripping Reza's hand, we go inside. A Margaret Dunn look-alike sits on a chair parked in front of the television. She wears a lavender silk robe that would have looked lovely on the woman I remembered, but on the woman sitting here, it just hangs, as if on a skeleton. The volume on her face is gone, leaving it gaunt, sagging and wrinkled, the jowls hanging. And the eyes – the eyes that once shown are hollow, the rims, red, the expression, empty.

I stand at her side, careful not to block her view of the TV. "Maggie?"

There is no response. I repeat her name again. "Hi, Maggie. It's Layla." She makes no sign that she's heard me. My heart sinks.

Her nurse walks around Maggie's chair and stands directly in front of her. She bends over a bit, until their eyes are at the same level. Maggie doesn't react. It is as if she is looking right through Lucia to the television.

Lucia moves out of Maggie's way. Her eyes are still fixed on the television, but I now understand that she is not aware of what she's watching. Her vacant stare just happens to be fixed in that direction.

"Mrs. Dunn? Margaret? Someone is here for you," Lucia says. Still no reaction. Lucia looks at me and slowly shakes her head. "Sorry. Guess she's having a bad day."

I feel my heart twist in my chest. This is too sad. "Do you think – I mean, if I come back tomorrow – do you think she'll remember more?"

Lucia shrugs. "There's no way of knowing."

Reza looks up at me questioningly. He's understandably uncomfortable.

I tap his head. "We're going, my love."

We retrace our steps out of the unit, thanking Lucia at the door.

Before we exit, I think to ask if Maggie's children visit her often. Lucia shrugs. "I've just been assigned to Mrs. Dunn. This is only my second day, so I don't know. No one visited her yesterday or today. You're the first."

"Well, thanks for taking good care of her," I say. "She's a wonderful woman."

In the lobby, I sign us out and we leave, with my heart broken for the Dunns.

Back in our car, Reza asks what was wrong with *that woman*.

I try to explain as honestly as I can without causing him anxiety. I say that her mind has aged faster than her body, so it's not always working well.

"Will that happen to you Maman *jon?*"

My son's life has been so greatly shaken up. In addition to moving to moving to a new country and all he's been through since we left Iran, he's recently seen his grandfather die of a heart attack and has now seen dementia up close. Whether he actually wants Rostam with us or not, I know he cannot understand why his father is *not* with us. It's a lot for a nine-year old boy who has been taken away from his friends and classmates, his school, his home and his country. I must do all I can to ease his anxiety.

I chuckle, making the very possibility sound absurd. "No, my love. That will never ever happen to me."

Seeing that I am in an answering mood, he presses on, concerned now about his grandmother. "Is *Maman Bozorg,* Grandmother okay?"

"She'll be fine," I say.

"Why are you angry at her Maman?"

I sigh. *What can I tell him?* "It's a long story, darling. But she really hurt me. If I ever hurt you, I want you to tell me. She hurt me and I told her."

He nods as if he understands, but I doubt he does. I take my eyes off the road to look at my little man. My love for him is deeper than I can express. "I love you," I say.

"I love you, too, Maman *jon.*"

I turn on the radio looking for something upbeat and find

Michael Jackson's "Beat It." We both love his music and his fancy footwork. For Reza, who was born into a country where music is banned, the choice of radio stations offering up innumerable songs is a tremendous source of pleasure.

Before the song is finished, we are back on Westwood Boulevard, heading south.

49

ON THE STREET

Sirens are blaring.

I pull over and stop to let the ambulance can pass. It stops just beyond the next corner. As I slowly drive by, I can see a crowd has formed in front of a market. I slow to a crawl, curious to see what I can of what is likely a critical situation.

The crowd parts to let the paramedics through with the gurney and I catch sight of a green dress. It's Maman's dress! And there are her beige shoes! She is lying on the sidewalk. I slam on the brakes.

"Maman, is that Mamanjon Bozorg?"

I don't answer. "Stay here," I say and jump out of the car. I run into the crowd and wheedle my way to the three paramedics taking her vital signs.

"That's my mother," I say. "Please. I'm her daughter. What happened?"

"Step aside, Miss. Give us room."

I take a step to the side and repeat my question. Maman looks deathly pale. But what alarms me is her complete stillness. Her eyes are closed and she doesn't move at all.

"Maman, are you all right?" No response. "Maman, what happened?" No response.

I speak to the blond-haired paramedic. "What's wrong with her?" No response. "What's wrong with my mother?" No response.

I ask a second paramedic. "Can you please tell me what's happened to my mother?"

He speaks way too slowly. "Sorry, Miss. I can't tell you that. We were told a woman had collapsed on the street. We're taking her vitals. She's non-responsive. We'll be taking her to the hospital."

"Which hospital?"

"UCLA."

"I'll follow you," I say.

They put Maman on the gurney and into the ambulance as I hurry back to my car.

Reza's head is stretched out his car window. As soon as I'm back in the car, he asks, "Maman *jon*, that was *Mamanjon Bozorg!*" I nod, dizzy with a new fear.

"What happened to her?" he asks.

I know he is catastrophizing, believing the worst. He has been losing everyone in his world. He's either left them behind in Tehran and then London, or, they've died. And he's just seen his grandmother lying on the street … If he were at the fair shooting ducks in a row, he'd win the grand prize.

"They don't know yet, sweetheart.We're following them to the hospital so we can find out."

I try to answer as calmly as I can.

We follow the ambulance to the Emergency Room parking lot at UCLA's hospital and hurry inside.

After dealing with the registration desk and nurses, plying them with questions, I am able to get a bit of information about

Maman, namely, that there is nothing anyone can tell me about her condition. No diagnosis. No prognosis.

After all, she's barely arrived.

Reza and I sit and wait. Hours pass. We take a quick break for lunch in the coffee shop and return to sit waiting. Finally a doctor finds us.

"We'll need to take further tests," he says. "We're admitting her overnight."

"You have no idea what's happened to her?"

"At this point, it appears she's had a stroke."

I'm stunned. *Maman has had a stroke?*

"A stroke?" I know nothing about strokes. "Is that serious?"

"It's too soon to say. We'll know more after tomorrow's tests." He sees Reza and his face takes on a tired smile. "I suggest you go home. Get a good night's rest and come back tomorrow. We should know more then."

"Can I see her?"

He nods. "But be prepared. She hasn't yet opened her eyes or moved at all yet."

I almost fall over. This is serious.

The doctor sees my reaction and adds, "For now. These things do sometimes improve." I say nothing. *What is there to say?* "Have a seat," he continues. "I'll have someone escort you to her room." Remembering the protocol, he tells me I will need to fill out standard paperwork before I leave.

I look for a name tag but there is none. "Doctor, can I know your name?"

"Dr. Drake. You won't likely see me after tonight. I'm in the ER."

I nod dumbly to signal my understanding and return to my seat. Reza sits, mindlessly turning his Rubik's Cube around. He is curious about my conversation with the doctor and asks after his grandmother. I say that nothing is yet known for sure. They will be taking more tests. I tell him she is resting comfortably.

I opt to complete the paperwork before going to her room. A form asks for the usual information about Maman and any health insurance she may have (none). Under 'emergency contact,' I fill in my name, address, phone number and relationship to her as her. I return the pages to the lady at the desk and tell Reza that I'll take a quick look at his grandmother and be back soon.

I am escorted to her room.

Maman is lying flat on her back. She's hooked up to an IV and has several wires and tubes connected to her from various machines with green, yellow and white lights lit up, some showing waves and lines, others displaying numbers. Her eyes are closed.

I approach. I am not trying to be quiet. I am not afraid I might make noise. No, quite the contrary, I shake the metal rails at the side of her bed and speak loudly. I am hoping she will startle, move an arm, a hand, a finger, a leg, her foot, her head, her eyes … anything!

I stand at her side and speak, not knowing if she can hear me. "Maman," I say, "I'm so sorry this has happened. If it happened because of what I said, I'm sorry. I know I hurt you and I'm extremely, sincerely sorry. I'm beyond sorry. I– I– I hope you get better. Soon. I love you. Reza sends his love, too."

Not a move. Not the slightest jerk of a finger, not the movement of her eyelids. Nothing.

I start to cry. I look around the room, so bare except for machines. I will bring flowers tomorrow to cheer her up. I stand looking down at her for a few minutes. I've lost my beloved Babajon just weeks ago and now my mother lies here, unable to move.

. . .

I just left the heartbreak of Maggie and now my own mother lies helpless, unable to even sit up or fix a blank stare at anything.

Reza stands to meet me in the waiting room. "Maman *jon*, How's Maman Bozorg?"

I cannot allow my son to know the full truth. Not now. Not yet. Not until I know more. I wrap my arms around him and hold him close to my bosom. "She's not very well right now, Reza *jon*. She'll be staying here for more tests."

This isn't what he wants to hear and his face takes on the expression I've seen on his face far too often lately.

I smile and speak with as much vigor as possible, daring to sound light-hearted. "Let's get some food to take home for dinner," I say taking his hand.

I am overwhelmed. I need someone to understand what I am dealing with, someone I care about, who cares about me. When Reza is in bed, I call Ehsan and relay the news about Maman. Ehsan is shocked. He says he wishes he could be with me, hold me, and ease my burden. His compassion brings back the tears. For now, Reza and I will be alone and I will pray for Maman.

I hang up still feeling an uneasy anxiety. Despite Ehsan's compassion, my fear is there.

I must do everything possible to ensure that Maman has the best care possible.

Another unexpected event has occurred that might change my life dramatically.

50

DOCTOR SUNG

I anticipate what today will bring.

I try not to drown in my anxiety about Maman. I imagine the news will be positive. Maybe the doctors will tell me she's herself again by now, moving and speaking today like nothing had happened. Maybe the doctors will want her to stay at the hospital for just a few days, only to make certain she's okay.

I would welcome hearing her stream of complaints.

I call to find out how Maman is doing, praying my wildest wishes have come true and she's better.

The nurse on the phone is unable to provide any information, but assures me that I will soon be hearing from her doctors.

Reza has his usual cereal for breakfast. I'm too nervous to have anything more than a cup of tea. I drive Reza to school, make a quick stop at the market and return home. I'm putting away my purchases, and will call the hospital again when I'm done.

The phone rings.

"I'm calling from the UCLA Ronald Reagan Hospital. Is this Layla Saleh?"

"Yes."

"Your mother is Zahra Saleh?"

My heart is pounding. "Yes. That's right. What's happened?"

"The doctor would like to meet with you to discuss your mother's condition."

"Has something changed?"

"I really can't say. But if you can come in and meet with her-"

I look at my watch. It is almost eleven thirty. "When does she want to see me? I can come now."

"Unfortunately, the doctor is not available today. Can you come in tomorrow morning at eight thirty?"

"Yes, I'll be there. Thank you. What is the doctor's name?"

"You'll meet with Dr. Sung. She'll meet you in the waiting room on the fourth floor."

"I'll be there. Thank you."

I assume that if the doctor can put off meeting with me today, if isn't crucial, if it can wait, Maman's condition hasn't worsened. It seems the doctor will meet to tell me what happened to her and tell me when they'll be discharging her.

They might also want her to start some physical therapy.

I drop Reza off with a bag of lunch, some snacks and a kiss.

At eight fifteen I am on the fourth floor of the hospital. I take a seat and wait. Promptly at eight thirty a woman wearing a blue and white uniform calls my name. I follow her past the reception area and through a maze of long hallways with roo on either side.

I meet Dr. Sung in a small office in the corner of one hallway. She is sitting at her desk, shuffling files, but stands to greet me.

"Good morning, Ms. Saleh. I'm Doctor Sung. Thanks for coming in. Please, have a seat."

Dr. Sung is a petite and relatively young Asian with a pretty face. She picks up a file on her desk and opens it. "Zahra Saleh.

Yes." The muscles of her face tighten, and for a second, her lips disappear. I'm afraid.

"How is my mother, Doctor?"

She scans the file, stopping now and then, probably to examine certain notes more closely. Then she closes the file and crosses her arms on the desktop.

"Well, Ms. Saleh, from the tests we've taken," she says, "it appears that your mother has suffered a stroke."

"Yes, I know. I was told last night. How is she?"

She nods but doesn't answer my question. Instead she says, "It was a serious stroke that may have substantial effects."

"Serious? How serious?" I ask.

Dr. Sung looks past me at the window before her eyes return to me and she answers. "We don't know that yet. But let me say, in cases like this, conditions often improve in time with rigorous therapy."

So. Maman has not improved. "When you say, *in cases like this,* what do you mean?" And I repeat, "How serious is it?"

"Well, it appears she's suffered a massive stroke."

Massive stroke? *Massive?*

I need answers. I have so many questions. It takes a second to find my voice. "What does that mean? How is she? Does she know?"

Dr. Sung shakes her head, her short, dark hair slapping the sides of her face and I dimly notice her name tag hanging on some kind of string around her neck: *Dr. A. Sung, Neurology.* "She hasn't regained consciousness," she says.

Oh, my God!

"She's never had a problem before," I say, as if I've been called in to school by the teacher to speak about a child whose misbehaved.

"Unfortunately, this most often happens without warning," Dr. Sung says.

Massive.

"How serious is it?"

"Yes. Well," She gets up and goes to a large rectangular poster that hangs on her wall depicting the brain. "This is a bit simplistic but it gives you an idea." She points.

"The brain is divided into lobes and each has certain functions. Your mother's stroke was caused by very large blood clots. And, unfortunately, they occurred in both the right and left temporal lobes." She's pointing to two areas in the brain, marked 'Right' and 'Left' and continues. "Now, the left lobe governs the right side of the body, and the right lobe controls the left side of the body. Unfortunately, in your mother's case, both sides were affected."

"What does that mean?"

"It means that at this point, since both sides of her brain are affected, she is presently immobile."

This is horrible!

I just look at the doctor as she goes on with more horrible news. "The left frontal lobe is usually the dominant temporal lobe. It allows us to understand language, to learn and remember verbal information."

I'm afraid to ask, but I plod ahead. "And the right side?"

"That controls non-verbal abilities."

"So, Maman can't move, can't speak or understand language and can't form ideas?"

The doctor nods. "Like I said, Ms. Saleh, that's an oversimplification. Her medical records would help us but, unfortunately, we have none." With that, she returns to her seat.

I can't dwell on the horror of it now. I need to respond to the doctor. I open Babajon's briefcase. "I've brought you a copy of her medical records right here, Doctor." I hand her the file I'd found among Babajon's paperwork. Dr. Sung glances at it and lays it down on her desk.

"This isn't English. Is it Arabic?"

"Persian ... Farsi." I feel foolish. These records are of no use. "Sorry."

She smiles for the first time. "It's not a problem. We have Persian neurologists and neurosurgeons here," Dr. Sung says. "I will get this to them. In fact, I presume your mother — and you — would be more comfortable in your own language, so we'll assign her case to Dr. Morady, an excellent doctor." She scribbles a note and attaches it to the papers I've given her.

"Well," she says, "for now, let me ask you some questions."

"Of course." I'm still trying to understand what Dr. Sung has said about my mother's present condition, but the priority is what I'm here for: I need to focus on answering any questions she has.

"Tell me, has anyone in your family or your mother's family suffered a stroke?"

I say I know nothing about her father, but that Khanom Bozorg, my mother's mother hadn't had a stroke, nor had her sister, Bahia, or her brother, Uncle Mansoor.

"I see," she says.

"Why do you ask, doctor? Could it be hereditary?"

Dr. Sung shakes her head. "Not really. Just that we sometimes find strokes run through generations." She pauses and runs her fingers through her straight black hair and it falls right back in place. "Was she depressed?"

I nod. "She was. We've recently left Iran. Actually, we were forced to escape with very little warning. She wouldn't have left if it wasn't vital, but our lives were in danger. Then, days after we arrived here, my father died of a heart attack."

I stop, bite my lip, and push on. She has to know. "The day that she had the stroke, I had an argument with her. Well, not really an argument so much as – well, I got tired of her constant complaining and I said some things to her that," I stop again and sigh, "that I'm sure she didn't want to hear." Tears are sliding down my cheeks. I hasten to add, "True, but hurtful."

Dr. Sung looks at me as though she's trying to figure something out as she leans forward to hand me the box of Kleenex.

"Doctor, do you think that caused her stroke? I certainly didn't mean for that to happen!"

"No, no. Ms. Saleh. Please don't blame yourself. One conversation does not trigger a stroke."

"Well, what does?"

"Depression raises the risk of a stroke, though we don't know why. Same with stress. Was she a smoker?"

"Barely. Not really. She smokes, but very rarely."

"High blood pressure?"

"Not that I know of. No."

"Has she had any arterial disease?"

"No."

"This was her first stroke?"

"Yes."

"Her blood tests show she doesn't have diabetes," she says.

"No. That's right."

"And her cholesterol levels are fine. Do you know if she was taking hormones?"

"I doubt it very much. My mother doesn't believe in them."

"Did she exercise regularly?"

"No. She's exercised very little."

Following his heart attack, Babajon's instructions had been to take daily walks. *Why hadn't Maman ever joined him?*

Later, I will be warmed by the thought that Rostam never exercises and smokes incessantly.

"Doctor Sung how bad is she?"

"Well," she wrings her hands, still resting on her desk. "Let me explain. Your mother suffered blood clots that caused a sudden stop of blood flowing to her brain and that loss creates damage to neurological function, sometimes resulting in physical, cognitive and mental disabilities.

"In your mother's case, there were clots in both the left and right lobes as I've already said, which means, unfortunately, that both sides of her body were affected. The longer that stoppage of blood flow, the longer the brain will be deprived of oxygen and other nutrients. In your mother's case, we don't know how long it took for the paramedics to be called and then for them to get her here. Brain cells are affected — damaged and can even die."

I understand this is what has happened to Maman. "Can't the brain cells regenerate?" I hang on her answer.

"Generally, not."

I'm feeling woozy. "What about rehabilitation? Physical therapy?"

"If the functionality is still there, we can improve it. Generally, therapy is most effective if done in the first months. But, Ms. Saleh, the functionality must be there. That means, the brain cells haven't died."

I'm walking through a minefield in the dark. Dr. Sung's answers to my next questions may blow up our lives, but I have to keep going, despite the explosions.

"We're still testing. However, I must say that the fact she is still unresponsive is not a good sign. That leads to the possibility that your mother had a brainstem stroke."

My God! A massive brainstem stroke?

"What's that?"

I can see that it's hard for the doctor to continue giving me this news, emotionally trying for her to explain the horror of what's happened to my mother, and to explain it in terms I can understand.

"They tend to leave the patient in a coma."

She watches me then, and I know *this* is the reason I've been called in. She looks away and begins to play with her ballpoint pen, the top clicking as it goes up and down against the desktop. Then she says, "A brainstem stroke leaves the person unable to speak and paralyzed, other than the ability to perhaps move the eyes up and down."

I am stunned!

"Is that what's happened to her? Will she stay in a coma?" I'm praying to God she says, No. I'm praying she will tell me not to be silly, that that would never happen.

She shrugs. "We're still testing, retesting, confirming. But I thought you should know so you're prepared." I nod dumbly while wiping my tears with another Kleenex.

"In the event she might need intensive care, our people here will assist you in placing her."

I look up at her. "She can't stay here?"

"Well, unfortunately, we don't provide long term boarding and care. She will need to be in a facility."

My stomach falls. "Of course. I see."

"A social worker has been assigned to your mother's case. She will reach out to you and help you in any way she can." She pauses

"Do you have any questions?"

I have so many questions. I have hundreds of questions. But she will tell me that it's too early have the answers, so I tell her I have none.

She gets up and walks around her desk.

"Thank you for coming in, Ms. Saleh. I know this is difficult. But we're all hoping our tests give us the best results for your mother." She comes around her desk and leads me to the door. The meeting is over. She's done what she set out to do.

"Thank you, Doctor. I hope you will keep me informed of any news, any news at all."

"Yes, of course. You'll also be hearing from Dr. Morady with any news." She nods. Perhaps she thinks these reassurances will ease all my anxiety.

"Any news at all, Dr. Sung," I repeat. "Please let me know if she opens her eyes."

"Ms Saleh, your information is listed as her emergency contact. That means you'll be contacted with any news, any news at all." She opens the door. "Thank you for coming in. Good luck with your mother."

That's it. She's told me what I was called in for.

I leave her office, shaking as I take the elevator, push the button for the ground floor and find the exit.

God help Maman!

5 1

THE KEY

April, 1984

The morning sun momentarily blinds me as I pass out of the glass doors of UCLA's hospital and walk out into another sunny, beautiful Los Angeles day.

My heart pulls for Maman. It's so very sad.

She can't enjoy this beauty. She can't even walk. She can't leave her bed ... she can't move at all ... she can't even open her eyes. With the thought that she might not be able to do more than possibly roll her eyeballs up and down behind her closed lids, my empty stomach heaves. I swallow back tea and bile.

Despite the heat, I feel chilled. Maman's prognosis is not good. Not good at all. Her future is so bleak, the thought of it scares me. And I am helpless to help her.

I head home, not really paying attention to the road. I'm replaying what Dr. Sung said, taking deep breaths trying to ward off this terrible feeling of loss and panic. Maman might never again hear me when I speak to her! She might never again speak!

How horribly ironic to realize she will never again be able to complain when she finally has so very much to complain about.

At least I know that, as her emergency contact, I will definitely be contacted if there is any change. They have all my information. That soothes me just a bit and at first I imagine that's the reason those two words, *emergency contact*, go 'round and 'round in my head repeatng themselves.

Her emergency contact.

They have all my information because I'm *listed as her emergency contact. Emergency contact, emergency contact. Emergency contact …*

The words have pulled my thoughts away from Maman's situation and hang suspended in my mind. *Emergency contact. Emergency contact …* Suddenly, it clicks.

Emergency contact! That's my answer!

It's the key to finding Adam and Linda! They must be listed as Margaret Dunn's emergency contacts!

They're likely to still be living in Los Angeles, probably still on the Westside, close to their mother. Even if they have her husband's contact information on file, they most probably also have her children's information on file. Ralph Dunn is living in Palm Springs, at least two hours away and unable to get to the hospital quickly if an emergency were to arise. So, The Beverly Hills Garden Home must also have her children's contact information. They're Maggie Dunn's emergency contacts!

When I enter the apartment, I immediately call Ehsan at his home, without even thinking of the time difference. He picks up. I relate the latest news about Maman. He listens to my fears. I try to be strong. I will myself not to cry while I'm speak to him. Yet, I'm sniffling constantly.

"I'm so sorry, Layla *jon,* " he says. "This is terrible news. This is all too much for you. You have far too much on your lovely shoulders. It kills me that these mullahs are keeping me away from you when you need me and I want to be with you more than anything."

With Babajon gone, Ehsan is now the only one who can soothe me.

"Layla *jon,* do whatever needs to be done for your mother. Money is no object. I will take care of her as well as you and Reza. Let me know what you need, how much and I will send it immediately. I can wire it to your bank. Do you want me to come there now? I can get away for a couple of days."

"No, Ehsan. Don't come now. We still don't know the results of the tests. Stay and take care of whatever needs to be done so you can stay when you get here."

When we hang up, I resume crying and soon, I'm bawling. I'm as good as an orphan.

By the time I pick Reza up from school, I'm all cried out. It's just as well. I can't let Reza see me crying. I can't let him know – not until I have to.

He gets into the car with two books, books that the other children in the class are using. Grateful for the teacher's kindness, I promise myself to make time every day to help him read these books in English. We begin today. It is a worthy distraction from my morose thoughts.

When we get home, I call the hospital again. I give them my name and Maman's name and ask for Dr. Morady. When I'm connected to his office, he comes on the line and tells me he has Maman's health records, but has not yet been able to read through the file and will contact me as soon as he has more information. All I can do is thank him.

I hang up and sit there, my mind jammed with thoughts of Maman and all that will need to get done. I sit on the sofa, then lay on my bed. I begin to pace.

The list of "to dos" is long, but I'm in no frame of mind to do anything on the list.

I've just dropped Reza off at school and returned to the Beverly Hills Garden Home.

I park and enter the lobby. The same woman that signed me in last time, signs me in again. This time I ask for directions to the office. When she asks why, I say it's about paperwork concerning Margaret Dunn. When she asks for details, I answer assertively, "It's personal." I can tell from the way her shoulders move back and down that she isn't happy with my answer, yet she shows me the way and leaves me standing in the hall, outside the partially open office door.

I peek in and see a middle-aged woman sitting at a small table, speaking on the phone. I wait until she hangs up, then knock softly, say a prayer to Allah in Farsi, then follow with a prayer in English and enter. It's crucial that I have every bit of help I can get.

My first impression of her? She's messy, messy in the way depressed people often are. The uneaten half of some sort of meat sandwich still in its wrapping sits on her tabletop, alongside a can of Diet Coke and a pile of papers that look like invoices. Chocolate crumbs decorate her otherwise nondescript grey blouse and have fallen onto the papers as well.

She's overweight and out of shape. Her skin is pale, and her mouse-brown hair has escaped the two pink panda berets she wears. She takes her narrow-framed glasses off and turns her head up to acknowledge me. She's not smiling.

"Yes?" She's looking at me as though I am an uninvited problem. The truth is, I most likely am. I'll need to charm her. Either way, a smile can't hurt. I smile as radiantly as I can.

"Hello. I'm Layla Saleh. I'm a good friend of Margaret Dunn." She looks blank. "She's a resident here. She has memory problems."

She props her eyeglasses onto her nose, rolls her chair over to a blue metal cabinet, opens a drawer and locates a thick, red-covered book. She opens it, scans several pages, then puts her finger on what must be Margaret Dunn's name.

"Yes, she's on our Memory Assist floor."

"That's right." I take a breath and refresh my smile. "I'm a friend of the family. I've recently returned to California and I'm trying to locate her children, Adam and Linda Dunn. We very close friends – we were roommates in fact – and it's imperative that I find them. I know they're listed as their mother's emergency contacts, and if you could give me their number, I'd appr-"

She's been scanning the opened page. She slaps the book closed and wheels back to her table, leaving the book atop the cabinet, and shakes her head. "I'm sorry, Miss. That's not possible. We can't give out that information." She turns her attention to the paper-work on her desk. She's dismissed me.

"Yes, of course," I say. "I understand your position," I say. "But this really is an exception. I'm sure they'd want you to give it to me."

I pause. She looks unaffected, so I add, "I asked Margaret for their numbers, but, of course her memory is gone." She's still shaking her head. "Please," I say. She ignores me and picks up her pen. "I promise it's okay," I say, still trying to keep the smile on my face. "They'd want me to have it." She's resolutely shaking her head. "If anything happens, tell them it's my fault. I'll tell them I made you give it to me."

She tosses her pen down and folds her arms against her chest. "Please leave. I can't give you that information, and I won't. Now, please. I have work to do."

I'm no longer smiling. "You don't understand! I *have to talk to them!*" The first tears fall, and I wipe them away with my hands. "It's life and death! I need their number! Please! I *must* talk to them."

She's no longer shaking her head, but her frown is even more pronounced. "Okay, look. You need to get hold of yourself and stop carrying on. It won't change my mind."

She leans back in her chair, reaches somewhere behind her, and hands me a box of Kleenex. I can't stop crying. This is my last chance to connect with the Dunns.

"I need their number!" Hot tears are falling. "I *need* to talk to them. I *have* to call them. They're her *emergency contacts*! This is an *emergency*!"

She's holding the key to my future in her hands. The answer I so desperately need is on that paper that lists Maggie's emergency contacts. She *can't* deny me. She simply cannot.

"Now stop it."

I don't know if it is because of my persistence, my tears or the word *emergency,* but she's holding a clipboard out to me with a piece of lined paper on it and hands me a pen. "Look, write your name and number here."

I'm suddenly hopeful. I wipe my eyes again and write my name and number down and hand it to her. My tears subside but not my sniffling. "I'm sorry. I got-"

She interrupts. "Now, look. You need to leave. I'll contact her emergency contact and tell them you were here and give them your number. They'll call you if they want to. Okay? Now please leave. I have work to do."

I feel enormous relief. "When will you call?"

"As soon as I finish what I'm doing here, so, the sooner you leave, the sooner I'll get done and call them. Hopefully, it will be this afternoon."

I can't believe it! My shoulders relax and I let out an enormous sigh of relief. My hands join and my fingers intertwine as though thanking the heavens for my luck. "Oh, thank you! Thank you so much! Thank you! Please, please call them. Please! Don't forget. It's really, really important."

"I will. I told you, I will. I'll tell them. Now leave."

"Thank you." I start to walk away. "What's your name?"

"Tammy. But you don't need it."

"I nod. I just want to thank you, Tammy. Thank you so, so much! Really. You don't know what this means. It's so important. If they'd rather I call them, then please, just let me know. That's no problem."

"Okay. You'll be hearing from me – or them."

"Today," I add.

She sighs, sounding resigned. "Today," she repeats.

There is nothing more for me to say. I leave her office and sign out of the Garden Home to wait for the call that will change my life.

That afternoon Tammy calls as Reza, home from school, is sitting down to a glass of milk.

"I'm calling from the Beverly Hills Garden. Is this Layla?"

"Yes. My heart, my brain and all my cells are all alert. Tammy?"

"Yes. I spoke to her daughter, Linda Gates. She said it's okay to give you her contact information. Do you have a pen ready? I don't have a lot of time. This has already set me behind in my work."

I want to kiss this woman with the stringy hair. "Yes. Please. I'm ready."

She rattles off a number. "Did you get that?" I repeat it. "That's right," she says. "And the address we have for her is 107 Perugia Way." I repeat the address. "That's right. Goodbye now. I hope you won't disturb me any further."

"I won't. Thank you, Tammy, thank you so, so much! You can't know how grateful I am. Thank you."

She's hung up.

Linda! I've found Linda!

For twenty-four years, I have prayed that I will one day find

Linda and Adam, the links to finding my Jasmine, and now, twenty-four years later, Linda's phone number and address are in my hand. I am just a step away from reuniting with my old friends and then, my daughter.

Linda Gates.

So, she married. I wonder when and to whom. And Adam? Where's Adam? Wherever he is, I'll bet he's not far from Linda. I'll get his address from Linda if they're not together. I wonder if my old friends have children.

Almost the second I hang up from Tammy — or Tammy hangs up on me — the phone rings. It's Ehsan. He's asking after Maman, bringing me back to her terrible situation. I update him, then share that I've found Linda, an old UCLA friend, and will be seeing her soon. He says he's glad.

I haven't told Ehsan about Jasmine. I will. But not yet. Hopefully, soon.

I start to call Linda, make plans to meet. But my hands are shaking uncontrollably. I drop the receiver back in the cradle. I am far too nervous, my thoughts too jumbled, my heart too anxious. The culmination of all my hopes and memories and all the trauma I experienced around Jasmine are rushing at me.

I breath deeply several times. I go into the kitchen and make myself a cup of *chai* sweetened with *nabot* to ease my nerves. As always, the hot jasmine tea mixed with pieces of rock candy soothes me some and I am back at the telephone, Linda's phone number in my hand.

What can I say after we've spent twenty-four silent years apart? I can't start off with, *Where's Jasmine?*

God only knows how angry Linda and Adam are with me for never having returned to LA and my baby. I was supposed to have been back in LA from Iran in four weeks, not more than twenty-four years later.

Do I start out with apologies and explanations? How can I explain

347

that Maman and then Rostam kidnapped me and tied me to Tehran? Would they believe me?

The more I think about it, the less appealing the idea of a cold call becomes. And, if Linda's not home, I definitely won't leave a message about all this on her machine.

And, if she's home, she might hang up on me.

I should speak to her in person, apologize face to face. Yes, that seems like the right thing to do.

Tammy's given me Linda's address so, I assume she's open to the possibility I might visit her at her home. The initial moment might be a little awkward, but then we'll be fine.

Yes. That's what I'll do. I'll drive to her house and take the chance that she'll be home.

Tomorrow. I'll see her tomorrow.

5 2

OLD FRIENDS

I hurriedly dress.

I look in the mirror and see myself as Adam and Linda will see me today, transformed from the young college student they'd known to this forty-two year-old woman.

I wonder how they look. I wonder what they've gone through since we said goodbye and if either has gone through anything like what I have. I wonder if they are happy beyond the sadness around their mother's dementia.

All the way to school this morning, Reza talks about his newest friend. I'm delighted that he's looking forward to another day with children his age speaking English. He is excited about the story his class has been reading and discussing, about a sister and brother who find themselves on ship going to China. His English had improved enormously, but his reading ability has been slower. I drop him off with his lunch and a kiss, aware that he has not asked about his grandmother today, a first.

Then, directions in hand from my Thomas Guide, I head to 107 Perugia Way.

Driving on Sunset Boulevard toward the Bel Aire enclave, I

pass streets lined with the beautiful homes and manicured grounds I've gotten used to seeing on the Westside. I follow a black Rolls Royce into the entrance of Bel Aire. Behind me is a red Maserati. Up ahead is a black car that looks like an overgrown Jeep with wheels ridiculously oversized. These cars are all a far cry from Adam's red and white '56 Chevy convertible I grew to love, sitting in the front with the top down, feeling the breeze on my face and laughing at another of Adam's silly jokes. My heart races, knowing I will soon see him again.

In these intervening years, my feelings about my friends have merged with my feelings of losing Jasmine. At first, losing track of my daughter had angered me. I hated the unfairness of it all. But I never blamed them for finally taking my baby to the adoption agency. There was nothing else they could do. I hadn't returned long after I was expected back.

It is unrealistic and unfair to think they had a choice. I can't have expected them to continue caring for her while I kept putting off my return. They were both college kids. Linda was only nineteen then and Adam was eighteen. They waited for me far longer than I had any right to expect of them. They gave me every chance to return to my baby. In fact, had they waited for my return, they would have ended up raising Jasmine, now a young woman of twenty-four.

Well, I'm back!

I step on the gas. I will go to the adoption agency and track my daughter down. I will find her. I'll explain. I'll tell her everything that happened. *Maybe* she will forgive me … And then maybe, just maybe, I can forgive myself.

I make the right turn onto Perugia Way, a winding street, off Bellagio Drive. Linda's house is tucked away on a cul de sac. I park, and, as I walk down the path amid the expansive front lawn to the brick English-style house, I peek a view that stretches from the UCLA campus east to Century City.

I'm at the front door. This is it. I am about to learn where Jasmine was taken.

I take a deep breath and ring the doorbell.

The door is opened by a petite woman, immaculately groomed, with perfect posture, and the authority of one who has been long-employed.

She asks my name, then disappears, leaving me at the threshold. I assume this means that Linda is home. A moment later, Linda appears. Her look of disbelief says it all. We stare at one another.

"Layla?"

"Linda! Yes, it's me."

There's that moment of awkwardness and, as I wait for her next reaction, I notice the many lines framing her eyes and the deep smile lines. She is no longer the lithe young woman she was. She looks like what she is: a middle-aged woman.

She throws her arms around me, and I return her embrace. She's crying, which surprises me. I would never have expected such an emotional welcome.

"Layla!" she says, "I can't believe it's you!" She's speaking through her tears. With her arms wrapped around me, she speaks into my hair. "You knew!" she says. "Who told you?" Her voice is muffled in my embrace.

I'm lost.

Is she talking about Maggie's situation?

Then I realize she's wearing black. That heavy black that speaks of funerals.

"Told me what?"

She pulls away and eyes me questioningly. "You didn't know?" She rubs her red-rimmed eyes with the worn wad of tissues she holds and repeats, "You didn't know?" I wait. She sees my expression. "You didn't, did you." It's not a question. Then she says, "Adam died," and my head drops.

I'm almost certain I've heard wrong. I feel faint, awash in pure shock. She can't have said *Adam died.* She'd never say her brother died so calmly. I look at her. She nods, sobbing. "He died three days ago. AIDS."

My heart sinks. "Oh, no, Linda! No!" I start sobbing.

She nods again, wiping her eyes. "Poor baby. He was sick for so many months."

I'm completely blown off balance. This is the furthest, most insane thing I could have every guessed!

"Oh, Linda! Don't … I can't … I don't …" I feel woozy. "I can't believe it. Not Adam! Oh, my God! Not Adam!"

I need to sit down. But Linda starts to walk away, nodding, and I have no choice but to follow, hanging on her every word, wiping my tears away with my hands. We pass through a large living room and behind her, I see her tight curls bounce.

"He was living in Ojai with his boyfriend. They were so good together. Adam got sick and went to the doctor. Then he got sicker and sicker. Had lesions everywhere …"

This is too awful!

Listening to her, picturing Adam like that, I feel nauseous. That robust boy, so full of life! A picture comes to mind of what of what he might have looked like as AIDS gnawed at his body and I push it away, feeling nauseous.

No, no!

"Oh, it was a nightmare!" As she continues walking through the house, she turns back to look at me. "And now, Levi – that's his darling boyfriend – now he's dying." Her hands are two fists at her sides. "Oh, it's so awful! All their friends are getting sick and dying or they're already dead."

I take Linda into my arms and hold her there. This is the

woman who had comforted me during those long painful months of my secret pregnancy. I was Adam's friend, yet, though his sister didn't know me, she'd opened her apartment and her heart to me and had supported me in every way. I want to comfort her in this terrible time of sadness, of such great loss. I know better than most how close she was to Adam. He was more than a brother — he was the closest person to her and, for some time, he was the closest person to me.

I want to comfort her as Adam had comforted me when he found me sitting on that bench outside of the UCLA Medical Center the day I'd learned I was pregnant, certain my life was over. Realizing my situation, he had taken me – no, he'd practically *dragged* me – to the apartment the two of them shared.

When I'd wanted to die, brother and sister had cared for me. When I had no one to turn to, no one I could tell of my shame, they had both cared for me like a sister.

Then days before Jasmine was born, Adam had begged me to marry him! Just to legitimize my baby! I refused, of course. And when, just two weeks after Jasmine's birth, I had to return home to Iran to live my lie for what was supposed to be a month, they had both taken over the care of my newborn baby.

Now my knight in shining armor is gone, dead from this impersonal, horrendous epidemic that is eating men alive, and all I can do is cry with Linda and hold her in my arms and comfort her as she tries to cope with the untimely, cruel death of her beloved brother.

"He can rest now," I say. "He doesn't have to be brave anymore."

She stays in my arms until there is a break in her tears. She sniffles and nods. "Let's get some coffee."

We pass through the dining room with the ornate table and chairs and enter the kitchen. It's large, easily the size of the living room in my apartment. It is an immaculate space, pristine white with splashes of turquoise and has a center island, the first I've seen.

The aroma of brewed coffee permeates the air. The same woman who had opened the door for me is at the dishwasher, emptying dishes. When she sees us enter, she moves towards the coffee pot, but Linda tells her that she will help herself. The housekeeper leaves the kitchen, mumbling something about the laundry.

Linda deposits her wad of used tissues into the garbage can. When she takes out a fresh Kleenex from the box, I take two for myself and dry my newest tears.

She sets two turquoise mugs of coffee on a tray made of mother of pearl and adds creamer, sugar, and a plate of cookies. She reaches for another Kleenex and wipes her eyes, then blows her nose with another and tosses both into the waste basket.

I notice that the kitchen has access to a lovely side garden where a small round table stands under a dark green rollout awning. It's white and its legs are painted with green and gold leaves.

I follow Linda out the side door of the kitchen and to the table where we sit, the tray between us. Colorful flowers edge the grass beyond. The soft breeze at my back feels good. Birds sing in the majestic eucalyptus and pine trees I see beyond the glistening pool. Beyond, the view expands west. It's too lovely a day to be mourning the death of someone we both loved.

"So," Linda says, "if you didn't know that Adam died, why are you here after all this time? The woman who took my number said you were hysterical." Her curiosity has momentarily outmaneuvered her grief.

"I'm looking for Jasmine." I lean towards her. She reaches for a mug, and I take a gentle hold of her outstretched arm. "I went to your family's house, Linda. I know it's for sale and that your dad is in Palm Springs-"

"He moved there recently." She sighs as her eyes look up toward the tall trees. "Mom is-"

"I know. I've visited Maggie."

Linda's expression registers surprise that quickly turns into sadness.

"I'm so sorry about Maggie, Linda. I'll always remember your mother as an amazing woman and a great mother. She was so kind to me. So was Ralph. You all were. I couldn't have made it without you and Adam. You kept me alive."

I pause and decide not to share my own story right now, replete with my own challenges and heartbreaks. Right now, it is thoughts of Adam that fill my mind. "I know it's a bad time for you, Linda, I really do. This is obviously terrible news. I loved Adam deeply. He was sweet and fun, kind and generous. I was looking forward to seeing him, too."

Linda moves her hand away from my hold and lifts a mug to me. "Have some coffee." I take the mug and set it down. I have no interest in coffee or cookies. She clasps her hands together and scans the garden as though trying to arrange her thoughts.

"Where is the gravesite?" I ask. "I'd like to go and say my goodbyes."

She's continues scanning her yard, shaking her head ever so slightly. "He wanted to be cremated." She sniffles, and new tears start running down her face. "There was a service for him in Ojai yesterday and – well, afterwards, those who were nearest stayed. His ashes were cast over the Ojai Valley. John and I arranged for a dinner last night, and here we are." Her eyes find me. "And life is supposed to go on."

"Mom." It is a young male voice, calling from inside the house.

"Out here, honey," Linda responds. She addresses me. "That's Nathan. My son."

Nathan appears at the door to the garden. I guess him to be about eighteen. I'm a bit jarred when I see him because he resembles Adam who'd been that same age when we met. Linda introduces me as a college friend and roommate.

"I thought Adam was your roommate," Nathan says.

I realize that Linda has shared part of her past with her son. I admire their relationship. I have not yet shared anything of my past with Reza. Of course, he is still a young boy, but I wonder at what age I might even begin.

"Layla lived with us for almost a year," she says.

"Hello, Nathan," I say. "Your mother and your uncle Adam were both extremely kind to me. I will never forget how wonderful they were. And your grandparents, as well."

"Yeah," Nathan acknowledges. They're good people. I was pretty close to Adam." His smile is bittersweet.

His tone changes then. "Mom, I'm taking off. Going to Danny's house and then a party downtown. Don't know when I'll be home. Okay?"

"Who's driving?" His mother asks.

"I am. I'll be careful. Promise. Are you okay?"

"I'm okay," she says.

"Sure?" Linda nods. "Okay, Mom," he says. "Call me if you need me. Nice to meet you, Layla. Bye." He's gone.

"He's wonderful," I say. "He's your only child?"

Linda nods, but fidgets in her chair as if the question has made her uncomfortable. I wonder why. Several moments pass without an answer from her. But I can't go there right now. I need to charge ahead. I've waited too long for answers.

I change the subject to the reason I'm here. I introduce the subject cautiously. "Linda. I've came back to California less than a month ago. It's the first time I'm back since I left that summer."

She is genuinely surprised. "You're kidding! I figured you came back a long time ago and just hadn't gotten in touch with us or hadn't come back because you didn't want to. You know, a husband, a new life in Iran ..."

I shake my head. "No. I desperately wanted to get back right away. With all my heart. But I couldn't. It was impossible. I couldn't even get in touch with you. I tried. Oh, how I tried! But I wasn't able to do that either. First, my mother took my passport and things and wouldn't let me return. So, I got married. Just so I could come back here on my honeymoon. I was going to lose my husband as soon as we landed and come to you for Jasmine. But that didn't work out either. Then I tried to escape, but I was caught. I've been stuck there until now."

"Jesus, Layla! How did you finally get out?"

"It's a long story. Things were a lot worse after the Islamic Revolution." I shrug. "Eventually, I got somewhat used to things as we all did … but then I couldn't anymore. I had to escape with my parents and my son or, most likely, be killed."

"You didn't mention your husband. Didn't he come with you?"

"No. He's the reason we had to flee." I really don't want to go there, not even to explain the comment so I continue before she can stop me with another question.

"Anyway, when I got that last letter you sent me saying you were moving, I called you, but by then you'd already moved, and your phone was disconnected. I know you thought I got married and wanted to forget all about Jasmine, but Linda the opposite was true. I went to Iran and realized that I wanted her more than anything in the world. I would have done anything to get back here. I wanted desperately to raise her. I didn't want to send her away. I was devastated that I had lost touch with her – because I lost contact with you. But I need to know where you sent my baby."

Linda's elbows are on the table, and she leans her head on her hands. Her face mirrors confusion and surprise. "I had no way of knowing," she says. "How could I have known any of that? You said you'd be back in just *weeks*! Three or four *weeks*! You were gone for *months and months*!" She's defending what she did, describing the situation from her point of view, counting with her fingers. "I had school. I had to go to classes. I couldn't stay home and watch a baby anymore. Adam had moved out to live with some boy he'd fallen in love with for the first time-"

"Linda, I don't blame you at all. Really, not at all. Not one bit. You did everything you could do and so very much more. I've always been so grateful to you and Adam for all you did. But now I'm here. I only want to know what you did with her. Tell me where you sent her so I can find her. Which adoption agency did you take her to?"

Linda has begun shaking her head before I've finished the question and she's still shaking it when I'd done. Something is not right.

"What is it?" I ask. "What's wrong?"

"I have no idea, Layla. *I* didn't take Jasmine anywhere."

"What do you mean? Adam took her?"

"No. My mother did."

"Maggie?"

She nods. "She had a girlfriend who'd divorced and moved to Texas, opened some sort of place where babies were adopted. Lots of rich people went there to adopt."

This is something I had not expected. "Where in Texas? Dallas? Houston?"

"I don't know. I have no idea."

"Linda, Maggie can't tell me anything. You have to think. Please! Try to remember. Where did she take her? What was her friend's name?"

"Layla, I know how important this is to you. I'm a mother. I know all about Jasmine. I'm not stupid. It's hard for me to think right now about anything. Let me think." She's speaking to herself. "Was it in Dallas? Houston? Austin?" She shakes her head again, shrugs and frowns. "I honestly don't know. It could have been in one of those cities." She throws her arms up. "I don't think she ever even told me."

"Think about her friend's name."

"Well, it was something like Joan? Jean? Jane? or Jeanette? … Judy?" she nods. "I think it was Joan, but I'm not at all sure."

I lean across the table and grasp Linda's hand. "Joan what?"

Linda shrugs and frowns again.

"I need to find my daughter, Linda. Please! Imagine it was *your* child. What if it was Nathan you were looking for and I kept saying, I don't remember?"

She's suddenly defensive. She adjusts herself in her chair and smirks. "Yeah, but it's *not* Nathan. And I'm sorry, but I don't remember. *I* didn't leave Nathan and go off for twenty-four years and then come back, show up and expect people who thought they would never even see me again remember things that happened twenty-four years ago because suddenly, I'm back."

"I'm sorry, Linda," I say. "I don't mean to be insensitive. But let me ask you if you think Ralph would know." I'm fully focussed on my need.

She shrugs. "I don't know. Maybe Mom told him. Maybe not."

There is nothing more I can do here. I suddenly hate the flowers around us, hate the turquoise mugs and this house. Hate that I know that Adam is no longer in this world.

It is pointless to vent my frustration on Linda. It serves no purpose. She's not to blame. All I can do is to hope the information will pop into her mind.

My God! What do I expect?

Adam has just died! She's mourning her brother. The last thing she needs is my harping about a daughter I left behind so many years ago. I must sound heartless when the truth is that I'm devastated by his passing as well.

"Linda, I'm sorry. I know this is a terrible time for you and I don't mean to be selfish. It's good to see you. I'll give you my telephone number," I say. "You can call me when you remember something. Is that okay?"

When she nods, I take my pen out of my purse and write down my telephone number down on the small spiral notepad I carry with me. I don't need to ask for her father's number. I have it and have already called him. I will call Ralph again to offer my condolences and maybe ask what he knows about what happened to Jasmine.

"I am so very sorry that Adam is gone." I say. "He was so very, very sweet and I loved him like the brother I never had." Then I add, softly, "He was the first boy I ever kissed."

"Adam kissed you?"

I nod. I'm surprised and warmed by the thought that Adam never shared this information with his sister, despite their closeness. "And I made him miserable because of it," I say.

I don't tell her that a week before I gave birth, Adam begged me to marry him.

"Well, poor Adam," Linda says. She picks up her napkin and dabs her eyes with it. "He won't be kissing anyone." She sniffles. After a moment she says, "I know he cared deeply for you."

"And I cared deeply for him."

I stand up, ready to head inside. "I'm going to leave now." But then I add, "By the way, my father passed away almost as soon as we got here, and my mother's just had a massive stroke. I'm going to go see her. She'll most likely need full time care."

"Oh, Layla, what a shame! Mom's been in a home now for three years."

"I know. I was shocked to find out. Maggie was always so active and youthful."

"At least she doesn't know about Adam." Linda says and gets up, too.

"I know how close you and Adam were. I'm so sorry," I say. "He really was a wonderful person. I was looking forward to seeing him again. Please give my love to Ralph. How is he?"

She sighs. "Dad? Between Mom and now Adam, he's a compete wreck. He's living in Palm Springs. Comes in to see her, though I don't know why. She has no idea who he is."

I dare to ask. "Do you think Ralph would know where your mother took Jasmine?"

"Probably not. But I'll ask him and let you know."

"Thanks, Linda. Really. I appreciate it. You can't imagine how desperate I am to find her. And please convey my condolences to your father. I have wonderful memories of my time with you all."

"My family loved you, too, Layla."

I gather my handbag. "I'd like to stay in touch with you now that I'm living here. Is that okay? Maybe Reza — that's my son — and I can take you and Nathan to dinner?" There's not enough I can do to repay her kindness. "I would like to rekindle our friendship."

"Sure. That would be fine."

"Okay, count on it."

After hugging Linda goodbye, and making certain my phone number is in a safe place, I follow her inside the house and we retrace our steps to the front door. Once there, we embrace once more before I leave.

Back in the car, I just sit there, stunned. It's so hard to believe Adam is gone! And such a terrible death, so harsh and untimely. Wealth has not kept sadness away from this wonderful family. And I've lost one more person, one more person who was important to me, one more person I cared about.

I take a deep breath and start the car. I am no closer to finding my daughter than I was yesterday or twenty-four years ago when I called Linda's Los Angeles apartment from Ferri's house in Tehran to find the line disconnected and Jasmine gone.

I head back down the hill filled with disappointment,

53

GRIEVING

*T*he deflation I feel after leaving Linda's house is indescribable.

The news of Adam's passing has left me understandably depressed. I loved him in a special way. For those two years that I knew him, he was the brother I'd always wanted. He was so generous with his friendship, loyalty and caring. Before I'd met David, Adam had been my best friend in Los Angeles and we'd had barrels of fun together.

He'd been the first boy I'd befriended since the beloved pack of friends I'd played with as a child. I'd been yanked away from them the day I came into my moon. Boys were taboo. Then I was in Los Angeles and with no one in Tehran watching and I broke that barrier with Adam. I spent so many wonderful hours with him — until that kiss.

He'd written a letter to me while I was in Tehran, telling me that he'd recently realized he preferred the company of men in bed but had not yet told Linda or his parents. He wanted to wait until he was certain. It said it was easy for him to tell me because he felt I would understand. He apologized again for kissing me that day on the ferry. He had a deep affection for me and believed that if a relationship with a girl would work, that girl would be me.

I loved him and I mourn his passing.

In addition to hearing the terrible news of Adam's terrible death, seeing Linda had proven to be fruitless.

The visit led to another blind alley, another dead end, and for the first time since I'd lost Jasmine and the psychic Setareh gave me that prayer promising I'd find my daughter, I am devoid of hope. I feel the pain of deflated hope.

Had I come to terms early on with the fact that I would never again see my daughter, perhaps some of the pain of losing her would have diminished by now. Instead, the constant hope kept the possibility of finding my daughter afloat and now I crash.

I don't know what to do with myself.

Visiting Maman at the hospital is pointless. There again, I feel only dead hope. She has not moved an iota since she collapsed in the street. She will probably never regain any movement, likely never again open her eyes or speak. I visit her room, silent except for the sound of machines and barren. I never even brought flowers.

I have called Dr. Morady, her Iranian neurologist at the UCLA hospital, so often that I am surprised he continues to return my calls. Dozens of MRIs EKGs, and other tests have been taken and retaken. The news is always the same: nothing good.

Whatever else, she is and whatever she has done to me, she is still my mother. My compassion flows to her.

The call I've been dreading comes from the hospital's social worker to let me know that she's there to help in the next step for my mother – placing her in a facility that will care for her around the clock. The hospital will be discharging her soon.

We must find her a place where they will provide her with all the treatments available so she has the best chance of recovering as much as possible. Yet, I wonder if she isn't better off remaining in a coma, completely unaware of how grave her situation is. What if she responds to treatment just enough to register how disabled she has become?

For Babajon — and to unburden my own sense of guilt for having contributed to her stroke, despite what the doctors say — I must place her in a top-of-the-line facility with cutting edge treatments.

I wasn't able to participate in placing Jasmine in a loving home, but I can place Maman where they have the best equipment and tools available, with employees and staff that care about their patients. Of course, it has to be spotless as well.

God forbid, she might one day open her eyes and see something dirty.

Maybe it is strange, but I'm hoping for my mother's best possible outcome.

After all is said and done, I don't understand the woman. I don't even like what I know of her. Yet, I love her; she's my mother. I want only the best for her. It must be some primitive instinctual thing.

The last time we spoke, I hurled insults at her and told her she'd ruined my life. Not that it all wasn't true. She *had* ruined my life and I finally unloaded on her, emptied a two-barrel shotgun at her, firing all the angst I'd built up through my life at once.

When she discovered I'd lost my virginity, her orchestration of a hymenoplasty was the work of an obsessed and overly controlling mother. I recall the look of shock on her pale face when I told her that I'd happily lost my virginity to David, that in fact, I was not his victim, but his seductress.

And when she heard the news about Jasmine! That was the shot that got her right between the eyes. That Zahra Khanom's unmarried, young daughter had gotten pregnant and given birth in a strange land – the very thing she had so dreaded when I'd first left for school in Los Angeles — that was the last straw. Of course she was devastated!

How could I expect her to take all that in her stride?

I don't care what those fine UCLA doctors say. I know what caused her stroke. On top of hating her life here, and losing her husband, there was my tirade, which was an unexpected, unfathomable horror to her. The shock of all that I'd told her, was the final straw on top of all her unhappiness, her trauma, her anxiety around our escape, her grieving and depression at Babajon's passing, her loneliness here and it was the sum total of all that misery that caused her systems to shut down. With no interest in living her new reality, she simply shut off in the same way she used to shut off whenever I spoke about microbiology.

The truth is, it's understandable that she would want to return to Tehran where she was comfortable, where she was privileged, and where everyone around her knew it. It was traumatic enough to awake to find her husband of forty-five years lying dead beside her. That alone would be enough to send her into a depression. On top of that, her day-to-day life in this small, unpleasant apartment in the corner of a hallway has been understandably difficult for her after having lived her life in gracious and spacious surroundings.

Life changed for Maman the day the she was forced to hide under a *chador*.

She could not depend on a cook like Cobra or servants like Fotmeh and Abol who had been with her for so long. The recent ever-increasing number of band aids on her fingers are testimony to her attempts at cooking.

She was lonely and is lonelier now. The Revolution had separated her from both her siblings and the many friends who'd fled the country. She had to leave her beloved home and all the furnishings she'd so carefully collected through the years with impeccable taste and had to abandon her closet full of beautiful clothes and furs.

She never stopped letting us know just how hard it had been, both practically and emotionally, for her to leave the only country she'd known and to leave in such a hurry, only to end up in the one country she'd always detested, and in the city she deplored.

Yes, she complained day and night. In retrospect, I'm not all that sure that I blame her. I still wonder if I was wrong to finally confront her. It was largely uncontrollable on my part, a sudden flooding of emotions that had been pent up for years and years. Yet, had Babajon been alive, I would never have given way to that outburst.

She is no longer a young woman and has lost so much in a short time. Flung out of the only life she'd ever known and forced to live here, was like being flung out of a twenty-story building. And her husband wasn't there to catch her or ease her fall or comfort her. Then I dealt her that devastating blow, leaving her knocked out and literally down, like a boxer down for the count.

On top of all that, her day-to-day life here was a challenge she wasn't up to. She refused to try making new friends. The Iranian women she passed on the street and in the markets were *dressed worse than villagers,* and *an insult to all Iranian women.* The butcher *spoke an illiterate Farsi*, and it went on and on.

She had zero interest in learning the language of this country. She had learned to say, *How much?* when shopping, *Peleeze, Tanks,* and *no English.* I couldn't imagine what it would have been like for me if I had arrived in Los Angeles with as little knowledge of English as she had.

Without a doubt, Maman has never been *resilient.*

Yet, though all that is true, I am still convinced that I am the reason Maman is in this horribly pathetic state. My feelings of love and compassion join my feeling of guilt, and I weep.

I weep for Maman's lost life, cut unexpectedly short, though she continues to breathe. I weep for her inability to enjoy life in any way or to even take the most basic care of herself. I know how embarrassed Zahra Khanom would be to know she cannot even wash herself.

There is so much to grieve!

I cannot stop weeping.

I weep for my own wasted years spent wed to a man like Rostam. I weep for the lies, his and my own, the wicked scheme to trick him into believing he'd married a virgin with no agenda other than to spend her life with him.

I weep for the loss of my beloved father who died too soon and who had to leave behind the successful life he had built, a success he was not able to enjoy. I weep for him because he always did so much for me and for so many others, yet he died alone in the night, without any warning and with only the three of us to bid him farewell. He deserved so much better.

I weep for my son who cannot respect his father. I weep for the many losses he's endured, so young. He has been carted around from country to country, without explanation and has lost the love and support of both grandparents as well as the father he never really had. He has only me.

I weep for the loss of Bahar, my unborn daughter killed in the accident, and for the loss of Jasmine, the child that was the result of a blissful night spent with the man I so loved. I must accept the fact that I lost her out of my own foolishness for having believed I had no choice but to hide her, as if she were unworthy.

I weep for my daughter, now in her twenties with no knowledge of her natural parents and without a clue of how sorry I am for having abandoned her or for how sorry I am. What I've done to find her. How I've prayed we would be reunited.

I weep for my lost life with David and Jasmine as a family.

I weep for David, who didn't know he had a child and died alone on a foreign battlefield, murdered by an enemy.

I weep for my longing to be with Ehsan, to be his in every way.

I weep for Ferri, who lost the love of her life when Hamid was murdered in front of her eyes.

I weep for the unknown future.

Knowing the pain of deflated hope, I have come to fear it.

As I realize that this is the first time in twenty-four years I have not ordered a cake with pink frosting on Jasmine's birthday, the phone rings, jarring me from my thoughts.

The hospital's billing office is calling regarding arrangements for payment.

I imagine that by now the figure is in the hundreds of thousands of dollars. Thinking it would be best to speak to them in person, I make an appointment to go in. We set our meeting for tomorrow.

"Ask for Leticia," the woman on the phone says.

I find Leticia's office and I'm led to her desk.

She is a large woman, probably in her early forties. She's dark-skinned with a round face and large eyes. She's wearing a navy skirt and matching jacket with a white shirt. Her professional attire matches her attitude.

I sit at her desk and watch as she brings up Maman's file. Her eyes scan and re-scan the list of hospital costs to date then summarizes my mother's current debt to the hospital. The figure is staggering. All I can do is explain that I am unable to pay. I explain my immigration situation and my family's recent journey. I'm getting weary of repeating our sad tale.

"I see," Leticia said. "Well, you've all had quite hard time. Let's not worry about payment now."

Did she just say, *Let's not worry about payment now?*

She sees me squint. "You have your work cut out for you as the sole person overlooking your mother's medical care. It's not easy. I've seen similar situations before. Likely not the same, but similar."

I don't know why the thought that others have had anything that compares to my situation surprises me.

She continues. "There are organizations that underwrite cases like this."

I notice she stayed clear of using the word "charitable" to describe these organizations. But my eyes widen at the possibility that someone who has never even met Maman might be willing to pay any part of her astronomical bill. I note the name of the organization. When money regularly begins to arrive from Iran, I will repay the money. Meanwhile, the news of this incredible generosity is extremely welcome.

"Are you aware of my mother's prognosis?" I ask Leticia.

"This office is not contacted by the doctors regarding their cases. We basically do paperwork here." She hands me a folded brochure, *When You Need Help with Hospital Bills.* "But this bill reflects a serious situation and I am sorry for your family."

I like Leticia. She is friendly and helpful. "Okay," I say, as our meeting ends. "Thank you for all this information. The help is really welcome. I'm going to try to contact her doctor for information about how she's doing today."

Leticia smiles and wishes me and my mother good luck.

I leave her office and find my way to Maman's room. I enter. She looks the same as she did that first day. She is still lying flat on her back in bed, eyes closed, not moving, all those tubes connected to machines. I kiss her forehead and stand by her, focusing on my love for her, trying to heal the wounds I've caused.

I let out a sigh.

I must accept that her life – and mine – will never be the same.

Eventually, I leave without a goodbye.

54

WHAT I AM LEFT WITH

I need money.

The hospital bills are taken care of, but I still need to find a facility for Maman and I doubt that any charity will foot that bill.

Maybe it's more accurate to say that if there is a charity that pays for it, it's the wrong facility, for I know it will be among the least expensive and not what I want for Maman.

Meanwhile, Attorney Kroft has yet to call with news that I'll be receiving money from Iran and I can barely pay next month's rent on the apartment.

Attorney Kroft called this morning as though he's heard my desperation.

"Ms Saleh, I have some news for you. I think you'll be happy to hear it. I have gathered all the information your father had sent me. By our calculations, he had a handsome income. His monthly income came from the rental of his house as well as Saleh Pharmaceuticals, fair interest on some loans he'd made and distributions from investments. Also, pursuant to the advice I had given him, we constructed a contract by which Saleh Pharmaceuticals pays him for renting the land it occupies, which, of course, he owned. With all that along with some other minor income, and other assets, I think you will be receiving between twenty-five and thirty-five thousand dollars a month." I gasp.

"I apologize for that wide an estimate. It's only an initial figure, but I wanted to get that to you as fast as possible. I hope that eases your financial concerns. There's also an annual payment from Saleh Pharmaceuticals to your father as CEO and President of the company that has yet to be added to that figure."

"Surely," I say, "that will stop since he's deceased."

"Actually, Ms. Saleh-"

"Please. Call me Layla."

"Okay. Thank you. Actually, Layla, according to documents in place, including his will and trust, that amount is paid in perpetuity and is to be paid to his wife upon his death."

"My father wrote a will in English?"

"Well, not exactly. He gave us a copy of his original Farsi. We had it translated and he signed it. It is in keeping with what I have told you."

I wonder why a copy of my father's will not was among his papers, but say nothing.

"In essence, you and Reza are the beneficiaries, with a life estate preserved for your mother. That means your mother has access to all the assets only during her life and then it passes to you and Reza."

"I see." The wave of relief I feel is incredible. "Attorney Kroft, my mother will likely remain like this indefinitely. She may recover somewhat, but the doctors tell me she will never … well, the degree of permanent damage is still not known, but it's probably extremely serious. At this point, she still has no movement at all. I have no idea how much her treatment will cost, but surely, good round-the-clock care will be costly. Now that I know I can pay for one, I can find a facility for her."

"Yes, well I really hope that your mother recovers. I truly do. But, if she remains incapacitated, you can find care for her with the available assets."

I am filled with even more gratitude and love for Babajon. I feel a huge weight come off my shoulders. Going forward, Maman will enjoy the fruits of her husband's labor as she lies motionless in a quality facility.

"Mr. Kroft, I'd like you to direct Attorney Bouria in Tehran to begin liquidating our home in Tehran and the furnishings in it. They won't be returning there. There's no rush, so we can wait for prices to go back up. And there is so much valuable furniture in the house. Things, that are priceless. Thanks to the news you've given me, I'm in no rush for the cash right now, but we will need to buy a permanent home once our immigration status is taken care of. So, please ask that he takes some time and get top dollar for it all."

"If home prices are down," Attorney Kroft says, "maybe you should consider renting the house out for a while. That would add to your monthly income."

"Yes, possibly. I hadn't thought of that. Thank you. Could you confer with Attorney Bouria to see if he thinks that's a good idea and, if so, request that he make it happen?"

"Okay. I'll discuss it when we talk next. We have another phone call already scheduled."

"That's wonderful. Thank you so much for all this. You can't know how much you've helped us. I appreciate all you've done, and I will expect your bill. But what happens now? I mean, when will I get it? I could really use some of that money now."

"Layla, drop by the office and I'll have a check made out to you. That way you'll have an advance, so you can start paying off some of your bills. At some point in the future, we'll simply wire the money directly to your bank account here. You have one?"

"Yes. I opened a small account based on my passport along with my visa and my driver's license."

"Okay, my office will call you to get the information."

"Thank you," I say.

There's a hesitation before Attorney Kroft says, "Of course. I'm not able to tell you exactly when you'll get the first payment. It will take some legal work, a coordination between my office and your father's Iranian attorney, Mr. Bouria. I believe your father gave him a Power of Attorney. But once the first payment is received, the rest will follow on a monthly basis."

"Thank you so much. This really is good news."

"My pleasure. There will be a check in your name at the front desk for twenty thousand dollars, if that will do. You can repay my office in a few months, after you've received some money."

"Yes, that would be appreciated. Thank you so much." This news is better than anything I had expected. Far better! Soon money will not be a problem.

"Fine. Well, I'm happy to give you the news. Of course, I will also be sending you copies of all the income streams and amounts. I can mail that to you and you'll receive it in a few days. I'll need your address."

"That's fine. Please mail it." I give him our address. "But I can also pick it up when I pick up the check. I assume I can deposit it in my account?"

"Well, see what the bank says. If you have that account, it should be no problem."

"Okay. That's great."

"Listen, if there's a problem with the deposit, let me or my assistant, Sheri, know, and I'll take the check back and pay you cash."

"That's so very kind. Thank you."

"It's no problem. Glad to help."

"It's a big help!" After a heartbeat, I add, "I wonder if you can help me with the other problem." I know I'm asking a lot from him, but I have to ask.

"Mr. Kroft, I need an immigration attorney. My mother's situation makes it impossible for her to leave the States, and my son needs to begin school in the fall. We were all under my father's B-1 business visa. Now that he's passed and we need to stay here, I need help with our immigration."

"Okay. You need an immigration attorney. I know some excellent ones, though there aren't too many of them around. The fact that your English is excellent leaves you with more options."

My fear of losing Reza trumps even our immigration situation. I have been deathly afraid that Rostam might find a way to locate us and take my son away from me. I couldn't survive that. I can't lose another child. If I'm eventually deported, I need to be deported with Reza at my side. If I stay in this country, I need him with me.

"Thank you. Would they be able to help me with Reza? That's extremely important. I mean, according to Iranian law, the father has custody, and I'm considered a kidnapper. I want to divorce him but keep custody of my son. His father is an opium addict and a blackmailer who was ready to file false charges against his own wife and in-laws if he didn't get half a million dollars in cash within two weeks. If we go back, we'll be killed."

"Well! He certainly sounds like an unfit father. I'm sorry for that but you can discuss your available avenues with an expert. As for your son, perhaps the immigration attorney might be able to help you with your rights. I image many immigrants have similar stories. If not, let me know and I'll put you in touch with an expert in family law."

I thank him yet again and we end the call.

I have not heard from Rostam since we've arrived in Los Angeles and I have no reason to believe that he knows where we are, or that he knows Babajon has passed.

Still, I dare not assume anything when it comes to my husband and his friend, the Revolutionary Guard I call, The Rat.

I'm about to leave the apartment to pick up the check from Attorney Kroft's office when the telephone rings.

It is Ehsan. I am happy to hear his warm voice. It automatically soothes me as it always does. But today he is so excited that I can't understand what he's saying. He couldn't have just said what I think he said.

"Calm down, Ehsan. You're too excited. Now, what did you say?" I need to make sure I hear every word correctly.

"I'm coming to Los Angeles," he repeats.

I drop my handbag on the floor and sit down on the chair by the phone, still not completely certain that I've heard him correctly. I'm afraid to believe he's just said what I think I heard.

"You're coming here?" The possibility that I will have what I so crave makes my heart quiver along with my voice.

He sounds confident. "My term as ambassador is finally up, Layla *jon!*"

His voice is strong and when I hear him attach that term of endearment to my name, I feel reborn.

"I need to wind things down here," he says, "pass the information to the incoming ambassador and close up shop. I should be in Los Angeles in about a month."

I am speechless. The universe is sending me money *and* love!

He continues, "I'm coming for you, Layla. Make no mistake. I've never wanted a woman as much as I want you. I've told you that. I must have you. And now, I'm going to show you. It's been my dream for years and it's still my dream, more than ever. I must have you in my arms."

My ears have become two strings tied to my heart, determined to bring me joy. *Ehsan is coming!*

"And I expect you to be there for me, since," he chuckles, "I'm coming for you. I'm making arrangements for Lisette to follow, if that's what she decides to do when her school is up."

I can't find words. I don't need any. I have nothing to say and no questions. He has answered them all.

I hang up to a new world. Ehsan is coming to be with me! I will be with Ehsan!

Riding on today's roll of luck, I decide to call Ralph one more time.

But no, once again he doesn't answer and the call goes to his message machine. Though it's been more than ten days since I first called him, his answering machine still has the same message, saying that he's out of town for the next ten days. I hang up without leaving a message. I've already left him one. I end the call.

I float out of the apartment and drive to Attorney Kroft's office and pick up the check. Next stop is the bank where I deposit the large check. I am no longer broke, and I will no longer be alone. Once again, my life has changed in minutes. Perhaps, I'm approaching the top rung in that ladder of challenges.

When I leave the bank, it's still early. I decide to celebrate my sudden good fortune. I leave my car parked on Roxbury Drive in Beverly Hills and find a coffee shop on the corner where I treat myself to a nice lunch. I pay the bill, leave a generous tip, then take a walk down Wilshire Boulevard past the department stores.

May has arrived and both stores are showing summer clothing, displaying summer dresses, shorts and swimsuits. One window has a backdrop of a beach umbrella in real sand.

Ehsan will be here this summer.

I'm looking forward to go shopping again.

I love California!

55

GREAT SCOTT

*L*inda hasn't called me.

I'm not sure she will. I've come close to calling her to ask if she's had a chance to speak with Ralph about the adoption agency, but I suspect they're both focussed on the loss of Adam and I respect that.

I call Ralph. I his answering machine picks up. I leave a message extending my sympathy. I'll let him know I've just recently return to the city and would love to see him when he's available.

Then I go back to waiting.

~

The phone rings this morning.

"Hello, Ms. Saleh? I hope I'm pronouncing the name right. This is Sabrina calling from Attorney Kroft's office. "

"Hello. Yes, this is Layla."

"Good morning, Ms. Saleh. I'm Mr. Kroft's secretary. He's

asked me to call you. You'd asked that he refer you to an immigration attorney."

My heart leaps. "Yes, Sabrina."

"Great. Do you have pen and paper?"

"Yes. I'm ready."

"Okay. His name is Nathan Scott. Our office has already alerted him that you'll be calling." I write the number down as she dictates it.

"Thank you. Please thank Mr. Kroft for me. I'll call Mr. Scott right away."

"All right. I'll do that. Bye now, Ms. Saleh. Have a nice day."

I hang up and call the number I'd just jotted down. I make an appointment with Attorney Scott for this Thursday at two o'clock, three days away. A few minutes later, his office calls back. They've just had a cancellation and when they ask if I can make it today at one o'clock, I eagerly agree.

His office is in downtown Los Angeles, and I'm unfamiliar with the area, so I allow myself an hour to get there.

I meet with Nathan Scott in his large, bright office on the fifteenth floor looking out over freeways and hotels.

We share some kind words about Attorney Kroft. Then he begins taking a notes as I place our four passports and his desk and summarize our history.

The attorney pushes his golden hair off his forehead. I guess him to be in his late thirties or early forties. In any case, he can't be any older than me. He pushes his chair way back and crosses his long legs. I can see his shoes. They're obviously made of fine leather.

He smiles and I take that as a positive sign. He leans forward and says, "First, Ms. Saleh — or may I call you Layla? That's a lovely name."

"Yes, please do."

"Okay. First, Layla, Attorney Kroft has shared the news of Mr. Saleh's passing with me. You have my condolences. And I empathize with what you're going through with your mother. He also told gave my a brief summary of her situation. No question, you've had a difficult time."

I nod. "Yes, it's been hard. Thank you."

"Well, you were lucky to get out of Iran."

Lucky!

Lucky? Staying would have meant the death of Babajon and possible arrest of Maman and me. As it's turned out, Babajon died as soon as we got here and I'm pretty sure that Maman's present confinement is worse than what she would experience in any jail.

Once again, I pray Rostam will pay for his sins.

"I understand you're hoping to file for asylum. Are you Jewish?"

I shake my head.

"Baha'i?"

I shake my head. "Moslem. But we've never been religious. Our religion is not why we need asylum."

"On what grounds do you propose to qualify for asylum?"

Attorney Scott uncrosses his legs and grips his desk, scooting his chair back behind it. He picks up his pen and starts scribbling notes as I speak.

I summarize our history from the time of Rostam's threat to our aborted stay in London when he discovered we were there and the two messages left on Bahman's answering machine. (I tell him I have them but he does not want to hear then now. When I tell him, he says, "Great!" And instructs me to leave the tape with him so he can listen to it later.)

I tell him that Hassan Amirzadeh, now an officer in the Revolutionary Guards, until recently, Rostam's valet and now his best friend, procurer, and accomplice who made an unexpected visit to my cousin's home in London looking for us and that made it impossible for us to stay in London.

"As you can see, our futures — my own, my, mother's and my son's who is nine and will start school here in the fall — all require planning. So I need to know, now that my father has passed, what happens to us?"

Attorney Scott is smiling! May God forever hold in his hand and guard him against all evil!

"You've had quite a time of it." He shakes his head. "Again, deepest condolences and I hope that your mother's present situation will improve.

"The good news is that it sounds like the three of you qualify for asylum. Of course, your mother can also apply for medical need, but I don't think that's necessary. Her asylum application should be fine."

"Exactly what do we need to prove?"

"Well," he says, "We need to show that you would be prosecuted and possibly killed if you were to return to Iran.

"I've heard some horrible tales from your countrymen and women who have had to flee Iran for different reasons, sometimes, because they were just too rich. Factories, multi-million-dollar businesses abandoned, family members tortured or held as ransom by the government, hung as spies for the U.S. or Israel … awful things. You are a strong people."

"But how can we prove that?"

"He gestures to the tape on his desk. "That for one."

"Yes."

"I'll make sure it's safe. We can show you've already tried to stay in England, and couldn't. You were found and threatened there as well. So much for the possibility that there would be another country you would be safe in. And you entered the U.S. legally with visas obtained by the American Consulate in London."

He takes a quick look at his watch. "Of course, the immigration department can argue that a fraud was committed by you — or your father — in your visa application because you applied for a temporary visa though you intended to stay permanently.

"But your case for asylum is strong. Added to that, it's rare for someone seeking asylum to have the financial resources Attorney Kroft has told me you will have available. That's also a plus as you won't be seen as a possible drain on our economy. Make sure you file your taxes. "

I nod and close my eyes, grateful that I have found an expert who sounds like he knows this area well and is ready to help us. And he thinks there will be no problem.

"Let's do this, Layla. Let's move you into a conference room where Sarah, my paralegal, can take down the information we'll need about you and your family. How old is Reza?"

"He's nine."

"Okay, so he'll be joined to your application." He reaches for his intercom, pushes a button and speaks into it. "Have Sara meet Ms. Saleh in Conference Room B."

I move out of my chair. "So, we'll be granted asylum before our visas expire?"

He walks around his desk and as we two walk to the door, he says, "Probably not. But not to worry. It won't matter. Once we file your applications, you'll just hold on to the receipt. It will cover you until your case is heard. You'll all be safe, legally here until your asylum case is heard.

We walk down the hall a bit to a conference room. Attorney Scott tells me I'll be hearing from him and takes his leave. "Pleasure meeting you, Layla. I'll pray for your mother. We'll be talking. You'll hear from me or Sara. We'll keep you informed."

I thank him and enter the conference room.

It's a cozy room with a round table that seats four people.

I've barely sat down when the door opens and an attractive woman enters, carrying two folders and a legal pad. She's roughly my age with red hair, cut short, green eyes and freckles. Sara introduces herself with a firm handshake, then takes a seat across from me.

Our meeting takes quite a while as she notes down all the pertinent information required to file asylum applications for the three of us. Copies are being made of our four passports and they'll be returned to me before I leave.

I first give her some background information about my father – who he'd been, the importance of Saleh Pharmaceuticals, a little about the products they make and their arrangement to import ingredients from Israel.

Then I repeat the information about Rostam. I understand that she needs to know all this – any judge needs to know this – as well as his relationship with Hassan, The Rat, to fully understand both the desperate nature of Rostam's threat and the real danger he has exposed us to.

"As Attorney Scott will confirm, we already have material from prior cases, evidencing that music was banned in Iran. That will go towards showing your husband's desperate financial situation — his state of mind. The tape will be excellent, but we'll need affidavits from you and your cousin in London stating that you both heard the taped messages. Your cousin will also state that this man came to his door and what transpired. We can also request affidavits from anyone else who was aware of the threats he made or who has first-hand knowledge of the situation. Your son is considered too young to testify, but your affidavit and your cousin's sworn affidavit should be enough. And the other facts of your case are also beneficial, or Attorney Scott would not have had me take down the specifics. I think, you have an excellent chance of being granted asylum."

I nod in understanding. "Sara, what about Rostam's rights to our son? I mean, if he were to find us here and try to take Reza away, could he do that as his father?"

"Well," she draws the word out. "I'm afraid that's not something I could help you with. I just don't know about that."

"I see. I'll ask Mr. Scott," I say.

"No." Again the word is dragged out as though she's thinking as she's speaking, trying to decide where or who can answer that question, other than Attorney Scott.

After a few seconds, she says, "I doubt that he knows. He specializes in immigration." I wait. "Though, maybe," she says, "I should put the question to him." She's apparently had a change of heart. "He just might know the answer."

She rolls her seat away and stands. "Can I ask you to stay here for a minute or two while I ask Mr. Scott how we can help you with that?"

I nod. "Okay."

She's about to walk out. "Would you care for some tea or coffee?"

"No, thank you. I'm fine."

"Okay, I'll be just a minute."

And she's gone.

56
JOLIE

*A*lone in the conference room, I get up and walk around the small room, tastefully designed to send a message of success.

There is only one window in the room. It has black lacquered French shutters that are folded open. I assume they're useful for blocking sunlight when needed. I study the view. It's not nearly as panoramic as the view from Attorney Scott's office.

I turn away and continue my stroll around the glass table. The walls are covered in a cushioned silk fabric in a shade of bronze that shimmers slightly even in this amount of sunlight.

There's a black lacquered sideboard against one wall with four glasses, a pitcher of water, an ice bucket (empty) and a half dozen small bottles of plain water. There's also a lucite tray holding four sets of black cups and saucers, sugar, with and cream at the ready.

As I return to my chair, Sara returns. "Sorry to keep you waiting, Ms. Saleh. It will be just a few more minutes." I nod. "Are you sure there's nothing I can get you?"

"I'm fine." I gesture to the tray. "I'll just have a bottle of water."

She hands me bottle with a napkin, smiles and nods. "I'm happy to say, our family law specialist is available for you."

"You mean now?"

She nods.

———

The door opens again, and another young woman enters the room as Sara leaves, telling me I'll be hearing from her.

This second woman turns to face me and I am immediately struck by her face. She has sandy blonde hair and beach blue eyes.

"Hello, Ms. Saleh," she says, extending her hand. "I'm Jolie Gold. Nice to meet you." When she parts her lips to speak, I see a perfect copy of David's gap between her top front teeth. Her resemblance to David is so remarkable that I gasp. Only her skin tone isn't David's. It's darker. Dusky. Like mine.

"Hello, Jolie." My voice sounds strange to myself. My eyes are riveted on her. She could easily be David's family, but her name isn't Kline, it's Gold.

She sits down and turns to a fresh page on her yellow legal pad. She writes my name and today's date at the top of the page. She looks up and smiles. Her smile is lovely. The gap is endearing.

"And you are Layla Saleh. Correct?" She spells out both my names.

"Yes, that's right. Saleh is my maiden name, which is what I go by now." My eyes never leave her. "My married name is Shamshiri." I spell that out for her.

"It's very nice to meet you," she says. She smiles again and I'm staring at the gap between her two front top teeth. "I'm going to take some notes if you don't mind. Some of it may be what you've already gone over with Sara, but they're necessary so, I apologize for the repetition." I nod. "Okay. What is your birthdate, Ms. Saleh?"

I am silent, staring at her. She can't be David's niece. *David was an only child!*

"Ms. Saleh?"

I hurtle back to the present. "Yes. Please. You must call me Layla. My birthday? Yes, it's January 22, 1942." I peer at her. I chuckle and ask, "May I ask, when is *your* birthdate, Jolie?"

As I wait for her to say her birthday is May 16, 1961, I am so anxious, I rip a fingernail under the table. But she doesn't say what I'd hoped. Instead, she answers, "August 27, 1961."

The year is right, but not the month or day. She's about three months younger than my Jasmine. She's not my daughter. How absurd to think this random person is my daughter! As reality sets in, I tell myself I'm a fool.

"And where were you born, Ms. Saleh?" she asks.

"Layla, please. Call me Layla. Tehran, Iran." When she's written that down, I ask, playfully, "Where were *you* born Jolie?"

She looks up at me and laughs. It is a lilting laugh, the laugh of a coquette, the laugh of a woman who knows she's pretty. "I feel like I'm being interviewed here," she says.

I smile in return and say, "I'm sorry. I don't mean to be rude."

She shakes her pretty head, and then her eyebrows go up, just so, reminiscent of David and her lips curve into a smile, exposing that lovely gap. "No, I don't mind at all. I was born in Dallas. Texas."

Okay, so she is not my daughter. But Linda had mentioned Dallas as a possible place Maggie had gone to place Jasmine with an adoption agency and I wonder at the coincidence.

Of course, it's just a coincidence, nothing more.

"So," she continues. She's facing me again, and, as she speaks, I'm studying her face closely. Very closely. I examine her hairline, forehead, eyebrows, bone structure … every inch of her face, every pore, down to her chin and neck.

Her skin color is similar to mine, just a tad lighter, and my skin color is not common. It's probably an unusual skin tone for someone born in Dallas, Texas.

She's put her pen down. "Let me first explain, Ms. Saleh. I'm not an attorney. I'm a paralegal. I work with Attorney Solomon who heads up our family law division. I'm here to take down your information, but I can't advise you. Okay?"

I nod my understanding as she retrieves her pen and continues. "Now, I understand that you're applying for asylum, and you're afraid your husband may exercise some rights he may have over your son. Is that right?"

"Yes."

"You're still legally married?" I nod, absolutely amazed by her resemblance to my David. "How old is your son?"

"Nine. But in Iran, the child stays with the father so, according to Iranian law, I've kidnapped my son."

"Do you plan to divorce your husband?"

I nod. "Oh, yes. As soon as possible. "Definitely. I'd very much like to do that if I can without returning to Iran. I can't go back." I'm still nodding, preoccupied with the girl who's asking questions.

As she's adding to her notes, I study her profile. Her nose is similar to mine, her eyes, the same hazel. I notice she's wearing a ring crowned with with a sapphire. "That's a lovely ring. May I ask, are you married, Jolie?"

She looks down at her hand reflexively. "Soon to be, I hope."

"Congratulations! When is the wedding? Do you mind my asking?"

She puts her pen down and turns to face me. "We're aiming for the autumn. Right now my priority is studying for the Bar exam so I can be an attorney before I devote the time needed to organize a wedding." She sighs.

"Wonderful. That's all so wonderful."

"Thanks." She's back to business.

"Well, about your son. Legal custody becomes an issue to be

resolved if and when you divorce. Of course, the fact is that he's also *your* son and with *you* now. You know, *Possession is nine tenths of the law,* and all that. But, of course, Attorney Solomon is the expert."

"Could I possibly get custody of him? I worry because the law in Iran is, for the most part, so ironclad and in favor of men. You divorce, the children stay with their father."

"Well, we're not in Iran. And I just got a thirty-second summary from Sara. I believe you're not able to return to Iran because you're afraid your husband will have you and your mother killed? Is that right?"

"Yes. That's right"

"Well, in this country, there are no special rules that govern who has custody of the children in divorce, though generally, young children will be placed in the custody of their mother unless she is proven to be unfit. Attorney Solomon could arrange for a child custody hearing. I can say that any U.S. judge who hears of your husband's threats would never grant him custody. "

The weight I'd been carrying for what seems like a lifetime, starts to peel away. Most of my problems have either been solved or will be. I have money, I have a way we can apply for a green card and permanent U.S. residency. My Ehsan will be joining me soon and it's possible or even likely that I won't lose Reza. Only Maman's situation is dire. Though it breaks my heart, money will not be an issue in finding her a new home.

But meeting this girl has upset my equilibrium.

She smiles at me again and that gap between her teeth almost makes me swoon. It is David's gap inside David's lips. I move my gaze away from her mouth and back to David's ocean-blue eyes and hair color, reminiscent of the color of sand in a summer's late afternoon.

This girl is Jasmine!

But no, it's not. It is. It's not. It could be.

Too ridiculous! Things like this don't happen in life. I've been searching for her without any luck, and I'm supposed to believe that she just appears before me in my lawyer's office? Ridiculous! Besides, Jolie's personal information is at odds with Jasmine's. The birthdate is wrong. Her place of birth is wrong. Everything is wrong.

But why does she look just like David? And why, Dallas?

Though I know it can't be her, I become aware of David's presence. He's in the room. I'm dizzy.

She sees me sitting with my eyes closed, my head resting on my palms and asks, "Are you okay? Ms. Saleh?"

"Yes. Yes, I'm fine." I sit up straighter and smile. "I'm just so relieved. It will be a blessing when Rostam is forever out of our lives," I say, then shake my head. "I can't imagine him gone from my life forever. Finally! The misery he's caused me. I've always been afraid of him, even before his threats of killing us. He was abusive." Then I tell Jolie, "He stopped me from finding the daughter I had to leave behind in California when I had to return home. I've begun searching for her now that I'm back." I bring out a tissue from my purse. Jolie brings me a bottle of water from the credenza and I thank her.

"Anyway," I say, "I worry about my son, far more than myself. As it was, I did all I could to keep him away from his father and shield him from the truth of who the man is. I hope and pray that Reza will never have to suffer his father again."

Jolie nods, then puts her pen down again. "Trust me," she says, "I know how you feel."

I push it. "You do?" I ask. "Are you divorced? Were you unhappily married?" I don't care if I'm being nosy. She's offered the information and I want to know more. I want to know as much as I can about this lovely young woman. And if her husband or her ex-husband was abusive, I will knock down his door and beat him up. Even though she's *not* Jasmine.

"Well, no, I've haven't been married. But I had a father that used to beat me."

"I'm so sorry! That's terrible" I want to tell her the man is a bully and completely worthless. I want to kill the son of a bitch for laying a hand on her. Without thinking, I reach for her hand and feel a wave of familiarity.

"Yeah. Well, that's over," she says. It's apparent that she didn't feel what I felt when we touched.

"A father!" I say in genuine anger. "He should have been arrested!" She's dropped her pen and looks at me in wonder; I've overreacted. "I'm sorry," I say, "but no parent should ever hurt their child. My own father was so gentle. I can't even imagine him ever even coming close to hitting me."

"Well," Jolie says, "He was your real father. My father wasn't. I was adopted."

She says that, almost as if it was barely worth mentioning. The statement erases all doubt.

She was adopted! In Dallas! This is Jasmine!

In one split second, I'm ecstatic. I've found Jasmine! Then I'm heartbroken, realizing that my daughter didn't have the home I'd hoped for. I'm to blame for her shameful home life. I want to find the man who hurt my child and hurt him. Badly.

Oh, how I've failed her!

How could she forgive me? Why would she?

What can I say? How do I tell her? Where do I begin?

Why could she believe that I've prayed every day since I lost her that I'd find her again?

How ironic that I would find her in the law office I've come to for help putting my new life together. She has no idea who she's sitting with.

How can I hope she can understand?

"Jolie, do you mind my asking if you've tried to find your real parents?"

She looks as if I've hit a nerve and I pray that I haven't upset her. Maybe she feels bad for not having searched for them. I'm about to apologize when she speaks.

"Yes. As a matter of fact, I have. I've searched, but wasn't able to find them. She leans into me as if to share a confidence, "That's how I met Attorney Solomon. He was helping me look for them."

My heart falls. "So he found them?"

She sighs. "I wish! No. I've done everything I possibly could. I even went to Texas to the place where I was adopted, but it was gone and there was nothing left but dead ends." She can see I'm interested. In fact, I'm spellbound.

"You were adopted in Dallas so you assume you were born there. Right?"

She nods. "How do you know that?" she asks.

I smile.

The phone on the conference room table rings and we both jump. Jasmine-Jolie pushes a flashing button and answers. She listens, then says, "Okay, I'll be right there."

"I'm so sorry," she says, "I just need to show my boss where I put something. I'll be right back."She gets up and heads for the door.

As she walks away, my eyes follow her. With her back to me, I see the red crescent birthmark on the back of her calf.

She reenters and takes her seat.

"Sorry for that," she says. "I promise we'll have no more interruptions."

I smile. I put my hand on hers. "Do you have the time to hear my story, Ja — Jolie?"

"Of course," she says. "That's why we're here."

I chuckle. She has no idea how right she is. It's *exactly* why we're here. "It will take some time," I say. It could take the rest of my life to help her understand why a mother would do the unthinkable.

"No problem. We're here for as long as it takes." I have her attention.

I take a sip of water and begin.

The End

*Read Layla's Story in Book One, **Persian Moon** and Jolie's Story, in Book Two, **Moon Child**, both in the Moon trilogy.*

DISCUSSION

In Part 1 of *Moonlight*, we revisit Layla in Tehran where we left her in Book 1, *Persian Moon - Layla's Story* and take her through the Islamic Revolution of 1979.

1. Was there material about the subject that was new to you? Discuss.
2. If Rostam had been psychologically tested in the U.S., what do you think his diagnosis would be?
3. Shah's Coronation was a spectacle during which he crowned himself. Do you believe his reasoning was valid?
4. Do you relate to Layla's feelings of conflict between the two cultures she was exposed to? Are you bicultural? What have been some of your challenges as a bicultural person?
5. Before the Revolution, Layla is enmeshed in her clan, in regular contact with family members. That ended post-Revolution, when many left Iran. Discuss.
6. Can you justify Zahra's actions taken in regard to Layla?

7. At various points in the story, Layla feels she must lie to her father. Do you agree with her decision?

8. 8. Once Layla and Ferri meet again in the bookstore, they continue meeting. If you were Layla, would you have figured out you could have met her friend sooner?

9. Discuss the extravagance of the festivities surrounding the 2500 anniversary of the Persian Empire in Persepolis.

10. When Layla first catches a glimpse of the "Phantasy Man," she is affected. Have you ever been affected by a glance?

11. Do you believe that you can meet someone and keep them in your heart after spending one evening together, like Layla and Ehsan did when they met at the Embassy Ball?

12. In Part 2 of Moonlight begins after the success of the Islamic Revolution.

13. What if you wear mandated to chador because you were a women?

14. Do you believe it was poetic justice for Laela to have bribed her escape with the extremely valuable choker of three strands Rostam had designed for her?

15. How would you describe the dynamic between Rostam and Hassan, The Rat, before and after the Revolution?

16. Does it surprise you that Fotmeh in love was determined to marry, regardless of whether or not the Salehs approved?

17. How did David's death affect you as a reader?

18. Discuss Rostam's threats and Layla's reaction to them.

19. Do you think Ferri and Hamid would have been better off had they stayed in Iran?

20. Layla had a series of misfortunes on arriving in Los Angeles as well as dead ends. Discuss. Was she brave or a victim of circumstance?
21. How did you react in the final chapter on discovering that Jolie was Jasmine?
22. Do you think Jasmine will forgive her mother for abandoning her?
23. Do you blame the Saleh's misfortunes on Layla? Discuss.
24. Do you believe Layla was a victim? If so, was she a victim of her time? Culture? Religion? Mother? Rostam? Her father's love that sent her to UCLA and changed her outlook? Discuss.

I sincerely hope you enjoyed Moonlight. Thank you. Guitta

BOOKS BY GUITTA KARUBIAN

Moon Trilogy: The Saga
Persian Moon: Layla's Story - Book One
Moon Child: Joie's Story - Book Two
Moonlight - Book Three

Target - Homage to the Underdog
You, Me and I - Poetry Collection - Book One